PRACTICALLY FAMILY

SURFSIDE BEACH SERIES

Practically FAMILY

KELLY CAPRIOTTI BURTON

First Printing, 2023

This is a work of fiction. Names, characters, organizations, places, events, and incidents are either products of the author's imagination or are used fictitiously.

Published by Kell of a Story
Cover design by Sarah Sweeney, Rod Burton, & Jade Alexa Guttman
Author photo by Amy Jane Photography

ISBN: 978-1-7361174-9-1

kellofastory.com
Surfside Beach, South Carolina

DEDICATION

To Mike & Carla Hopkins,
for making me believe when you see the best,
making me laugh as we fix the worst,
and for being practically family.

PROLOGUE

"I can't believe you made me leave! You let Sam and Kayla and David do whatever they want."

Fifteen-year-old Brittney was fuming in the front seat of Daddy's truck, twirling and pulling at a lock of almost-no-longer-blonde hair around her finger and craning her neck to look at Mikayla behind her. Randall, used to the protests, did not slow down.

"You had no business being at a college party, Brit. You're fifteen years old."

"But it was *Sam's* friend—"

Randall held up one hand to the desired effect of Brittney closing her mouth. "It doesn't matter. Sam wasn't even there. Sam is at home with his wife and child, by the way. He would tell you the same thing."

Brittney was glad her dad couldn't see her rolling her eyes. He was right about one thing, and that annoyed her to no end. She'd heard Sam and his friend Josh talking about the party when she was at Sam and Abby's house the other day. Sam told her to stay away. He *was* just like Daddy.

"It was fine. I was just *having a conversation.*"

"Brit, I know how your conversations go. You could sell water to a drowning person, and that guy was looking at you like a steak dinner. Not like a lovely young lady. Is that really what you want?"

"It was fine," she murmured again. She thought about the way Austin stared into her eyes when she told him about her newspaper deadline and the story she was writing about the ridiculous, archaic, chauvinistic dress code. He agreed with everything she said. And then when she showed him a picture of her pushing her three-year-old nephew, Travis, on the swings, he told her "they" were adorable. She was certain that being an aunt made her seem a little older than she was. Most college guys wouldn't have given a tenth-grader the time of day, but he kept talking to her. He was about to get her a drink when he looked over her shoulder and said, "Hey, um, do you know that guy?"

That guy had been Daddy, of course. "You could have at least sent Mikayla in to get me," she said, glaring at her sister in the back seat. "This was so embarrassing."

"You'll probably never see those people again," Mikayla answered in her reasonable tone that sounded too much like their Mama and made Brittney see red.

"Shut up, Kayla! You don't know what I'm going to do!" Brittney snapped.

She thought Daddy would yell at her to stop being a brat, but he had gotten pretty adept at tuning her out when she was fired up. She could admit that was a lot of the time. All she wanted to do was talk to some different people, not the same boring ones that went to high school with her. Not the duds Mikayla hung around with. And at least Mikayla could drive now. Brittney was at her mercy, or that of their parents, if she didn't want to be stuck at home with their little brother, playing Pokémon or some nonsense.

"No one knows what you're going to do, Firecracker," Randall said evenly. "We just want to keep you safe, so you can grow up enough to do it."

Brittney stewed at his use of her nickname. She only liked it when she was happy, and that was definitely not now. How could she be a firecracker if she got yelled at or grounded every time she approached a flame? Firecrackers weren't meant to sit inside a box. They were meant to explode.

NINE YEARS LATER

Fake conversation was her biggest pet peeve, so Brittney was questioning her career choice for the millionth time that month, setting up another Business After Hours at the Hard Rock Café, Myrtle Beach, in the good old days when it still looked like the most bizarrely placed pyramid on earth.

The Chamber of Commerce position was new and vague, one that her former boss Woody had basically scored for her when he and his partner Lee had decided to retire, shuttering the oldest advertising firm on the Grand Strand and ending Brittney's first career job when it was just getting started.

At the Chamber, she wasn't really doing marketing and wasn't exactly an administrative assistant, so she basically drifted around the office like a puppy hunting for something to do. But she had a specific duty on every third Thursday, being on location to set up sign in sheets, name tags, and raffle prizes for whoever attended the monthly happy hours. She wasn't the hostess; that might have actually had some meaning. She was like the faceless, behind-the-scenes flunky to the hostess.

Why, why, why couldn't Lee and Woody have waited a few more years?

After setting up her tabletops, she had gone to the bar and ordered a club soda with a twist. The bartender ostentatiously read her name tag out loud, "Brittney Oakley, Assistant Marketing Coordinator." "You can get a real drink, you know," he added. His bright blue eyes stood out and twinkled in contrast to his dark hair, dark beard, dark hat. He pointed to the plastic pinned to her shirt. "A bigwig like you at one of these events always gets the first one or two on the house."

"Haha. Whatever you say. No. I'm still the new girl in the office, so I better play it safe. Thanks, though." She looked down at the Formica bar top, feeling her face burn.

"I'll take her free drink."

Brittney jumped in her seat a little and turned toward the voice. It belonged to a man seemingly her age, his sandy brown hair cut short and precise, his hazel eyes playful and eager. He was wearing the typical uniform of the young Myrtle Beach business guy, Bonobos khakis and an athletic-cut white dress shirt that said two things: he was investing in his professional image, and he worked out, probably a lot.

"Sorry, dude." The bartender, who was quite the opposite in his top-to-bottom black and tattooed sleeves, dismissed the intruder out of hand and turned around to do something else, probably plot Bonobos' demise. Brittney stifled a giggle into her glass. The mild flirtation of two polar but attractive opposites had already made her day.

"He'll probably still let you *order* a drink," Brittney said in consolation.

"Probably spit in it," the stranger said, taking two steps closer. "I interrupted his moment with a beautiful woman, and I kinda don't blame him for being resentful. Do you mind if I make it count and sit here?"

She shrugged, trying to look cool and like she belonged. He was immediately in the seat next to her.

"So, you're here for the Chamber event?"

Brittney sighed as quietly as she could. She also hated networking, which was an unfortunate obstacle to her success in marketing. She liked sincerely talking about the good qualities of their town and what it offered tourists and residents; she liked glossy campaigns and awesome website upgrades and successful interviews and viral word-of-mouth. But this part? *Ugh.*

"I am," she finally answered, feeling a little flush.

"Me too," he said. "Student loans up to my pecs, and I'm the advertising manager for an *HVAC* company. Livin' the dream."

Pecs? Good grief, what a douchebag. His voice had a New England lilt that she couldn't place, but it was the implied disdain for his industry that gave him away.

"Where did you live before you went to Coastal?" she asked. *Ugh.* She had shot for a charming lilt to her voice and landed instead on *flirtatious.*

"Columbia. Maryland, not South Carolina."

"You don't say."

"How did you know?" His eyes twinkled, and she noticed the emerald flecks in them.

"HVAC is one of the safest bets around here," she said. After a swallow that emptied her glass, she added, "Everyone needs their A/C from April to November, so they will love your service forever, or at least, need it. And your other options are construction, big box health care, or, of course, hospitality. You gotta pick the least of the evils. Or move."

"Let me guess." He was sizing her up. She was wearing her own version of the Young Coastal Leaders uniform, a periwinkle and cream striped pencil skirt, a cream-colored camisole with just enough substance to be considered a real shirt, big earrings that were wicker and coral and highlighted by her curated messy bun, and buff-colored wedges. The skirt had a little slit, and she was always tan. His gaze had started at her pedicure and finished back up at her eyes. "You have one of those 'Native' stickers on your turquoise Wrangler?"

She shook her head, smiling. "I definitely don't have a Jeep. But my sticker is actually 'Respect the Locals.' Much more subtle." That sticker campaign referred to leaving nesting sea turtles alone, but the *natives* knew it had multiple meanings.

"If you say so." He shrugged. "I've been in this town for seven years, and that whole southern welcome wagon is a myth."

"Is it a welcome wagon? I thought it was hospitality, and we have plenty of it, as long as you don't come here and want to make everything the way it is up north."

"Eh. Not everything, but at least the traffic flow."

"Please. How's the rush hour in Baltimore this time of year?"

"Touché."

She wished his eyes would stop their twinkling and the constant looking-over of her.

"Is this how you usually kill time before events start?" he asked. "Educating the non-natives?"

"I don't come from natives," she said, tucking a stray tendril behind her ear. The bartender had caught her eye and rolled his. "My family moved here a few years before I was born. So I take kindly to all unless you give me reason not to."

The bartender turned, stifling a giggle. Brittney was torn over which guy to give her attention to. But the one in the barstool next to her stuck his hand out at that point and warmly told her, "I'm Bradley. And any friend of air conditioning is a friend of mine."

She laughed. "I'm Brittney. We probably have time for one more before the less eager attendees start to arrive."

The bartender started their next round with a barely masked sigh.

And years later, Brittney could still remember the sound of his exhale. She should have chosen him.

She and Bradley had been happy. For two years, starting with that silly start at the Hard Rock, they spent every Thursday night together, usually going someplace meant for tourists just for the kitschy fun of it. They'd spent a lot of other nights together, too, and by the third week of play dates and past-midnight phone conversations, it seemed to be official. Bradley brought her to a happy hour with his work friends, and she brought him to Sunday supper with her big, chaotic family. Her mama, sister, and sister-in-law seemed cautiously optimistic. Her brothers did not like him. Her daddy, surprisingly, did.

Bradley had two older brothers and a younger sister up in Maryland. His parents were still married; his father was a judge, and his mother was a realtor. All the pictures Brittney saw of them intimidated her some with their formality, but Bradley wasn't like that. He was fun-loving, always wanting to do something, see people, go places. He took Brittney fishing off the Garden City pier, something she'd never done despite living practically next to it. They went tent-camping right in Huntington State Park. They jet-skied in the Intercoastal, attended concerts at Brookgreen Gardens and House of Blues, took day trips to Charleston for the ghost tours or just to shop the city market, spent weekends in Savannah and one in Atlanta. They booked a cruise for New Year's during their second holiday season together, but Bradley's grandfather was in the hospital and the family called him to come home. Thankfully, his grandfather had recovered.

When he returned from that trip, some of his light-heartedness had melted away. He skipped out on their Thursday date night, a murder mystery show, citing an emergency at work. She knew it was a lie. He knew she knew. But she didn't see him again until Sunday supper, and there, he played basketball with her nephew Travis and helped her mama serve cake, so she pretended like everything was fine.

And then, after he left – they'd come separately because he was going to some office team-building thing – her older brother Sam confronted her.

"Brit, I knew this guy wasn't on the up and up. Travis said he was checking his phone every time his hands weren't on the ball. What is so important? Who's he texting? And why haven't you met his family in all this time? You already scheduled time off work; you could have gone to be with him."

Brittney had, of course, flown off the handle at Sam, telling him he was full of crap, he was spying on her and overstepping every boundary, that he resented her happiness, and probably stuff that was even more ridiculous than that. True to his nature, her big brother didn't take the bait. He shrugged and told her to be careful. But she knew he'd probably be Googling private detectives the rest of the night.

She played an amateur one as soon as she left Mama's. She drove to the bowling alley where Bradley said he would be, and his car wasn't anywhere to be found. She drove past his apartment building; it wasn't there either. By that point, she'd been on the brink of hyperventilating. She turned Avril up loud and drove to his office. No sign of him.

Maybe they'd taken the party somewhere else. Maybe she misheard what he said. Maybe he hadn't been distant since his trip up north, and she was just imagining things. Maybe Sam was wrong, but damn him. He rarely said anything unless he was pretty sure.

She pulled into the Turtle Market, went inside to grab a Cheerwine with extra ice, took a deep breath and a long drink, then texted him.

WHAT TIME WILL YOU BE DONE? I WOULD LOVE TO COME OVER AND CATCH UP. OR YOU COULD COME BY ME. EITHER WAY.

The telltale three dots stayed on the screen for way too long. Then they disappeared. She cursed and swiped the tears falling down her face.

WE JUST STARTED THE LAST GAME. I PROBABLY JUST WANT TO CRASH AFTER THIS.

Her heart pounded.

IS THE NEW BOWLING ALLEY NICE? I NEED A FEW IDEAS FOR BUSINESS AFTER HOURS THIS SUMMER.

Immediate answer,

YEAH. IT'S GREAT.

She shook her head, barely able to type.

GREAT. HAVE FUN, BRADLEY.

That will show him. She never called him by his name. He was always "Babe" to her, or just B. Bradley sounded strange and formal, which was how she felt.

Her hand was shaking a little as she scrolled to a new playlist. She turned Pink up even louder, shouting words as she drove down Highway 17 with no particular destination. It wasn't dark yet; the sky was just a crummy January gray. She finally turned in at Huntington State Park, which was not where she normally chose to go to the beach. Maybe a change of scenery would distract her.

She walked along the shore for a few minutes, convincing herself everything was fine as she braced against the cool January wind. All of it was normal. Lots of millennials had non-traditional dating relationships. So what if she never met his parents? So what if his brother who lived in Atlanta was out of town when they visited? So what if they still weren't Facebook official; he barely used his social media anyway, said it was only for business networking purposes, and it was nobody's business who he was dating.

Apparently, it's not even my *business. There has to be someone else, you idiot.* She left the beach, calmed herself with a little Tom Petty, and decided she wouldn't be a drama queen or a big baby. She would ask him. Confront him. Show up for herself and deal with the consequences.

It had all seemed smart until she was back in his parking lot, waiting to see his Grand Cherokee pull in. But then it did, and he walked to the passenger side, opened the door, and out came a pair of long, female legs, clad in leather leggings and unnecessary Uggs. They were attached to a woman with a thin, porcelain face, bee-stung lips, impossibly long mahogany tresses that were blow-out perfect, and a sparkly laughter Brittney could hear across the parking lot and through the window.

And Bradley was holding her hand. *He was holding her hand.*

Before she could think any clear thoughts, Brittney was out of the car and scrambling toward them. "B!" she called. He didn't turn, so she raised her voice. "Beeeeeeeeeee!"

Mahogany turned around before he did. She looked at Brittney, whose hair was in an unraveling side braid and whose face was mostly make-up free, and then looked at Bradley.

"I think your number is up," she said. "Can I have your key?"

He reached in his pocket and handed it to Mahogany. She sauntered away without a second glance, and Brittney felt her breath catch.

"How is this happening?" she finally said. "Who the hell is that?"

"Oh Brit…"

"Do better," she seethed.

He stuck his hands in his pockets and looked at his stupid, ugly Nikes with the orthopedic looking soles. When he looked up at her, his expression held no remorse. He almost looked amused.

"We always knew this wasn't going to last forever."

"What?" She tilted her head as if she could clear her focus. "I mean, what?"

"Us, Brit. We have fun, but… I need to start thinking about the future."

"Are you *kidding* me? I *have* been thinking about the future. I thought about it when I introduced you to my *grandmother*. I thought about it when I bought you that watch, when we took *family* pictures for Christmas. I thought about it when we booked a cruise together and you changed everything at the last minute and didn't take me with you."

"Did you ask yourself why, Brit? Why didn't I take you?"

"Why didn't you?" She felt her face flush.

"My family won't accept you, Brittney. Come on. My dad is a political figure. My mom is old money. I can't bring home some random girl from the beach whose family could have been on *Teen Mom.* I thought you would have figured that out by now. You gotta get out of here and see some of the rest of the world, you know. Most families aren't like yours."

Her stomach was churning. She wasn't sure what felt most like a gut-punch: His vitriol and judgment, her own stupidity, or the phrase "some random girl."

"You always had good reasons for everything," she finally said, cursing her own naivete.

"I wanted you," he said, and for a moment, he was *her* Bradley again. "I knew from the start it wouldn't be for the long haul, but we had so much fun. And Brit..." He finally walked closer to her. She stiffened, but he pretended not to notice and put his hands on the sides of her face. "I still want you."

She felt her ears burn and her insides twist. She still wanted him. His deceit was only minutes old to her. She still *loved* him.

"I don't even know you," she finally said, as evenly as she could, placing her hands on his wrists and pushing his touch away from her.

"Oh, Baby. Come on. This doesn't have to change *us...* just the expectations going forward."

"Are you actually insane?" she cried. She'd used up all of her stoicism in just a few words. "We can't go forward. We aren't *us.* You lied to me today. You would still be lying if I hadn't come here like an idiot. You probably lied to me about New Year's and your poor grandpa. And I'll never know how many other times. There is *no* us!"

"Don't be ridiculous," he said, and this time, his hands went on her shoulders, his face an inch from hers. "You knew all along what this was. And you're still mine." He planted a soft kiss on the left side of her mouth. "And I'm as much yours—" He placed another on the right side. "—as I've ever been."

Part of Brittney melted in the closeness of him. He smelled like his signature Burberry Hero. His stubble was at its perfect, sexy, scratchy length. He knew exactly where to touch her and how to kiss her.

And it was all fake.

Her anger at him was only trumped by her disgust of herself. Where was the firecracker in her? Where was the flame? She was just going to let him do this to her?

"You've *never* been," she said, evenly once more. And then she took a step backward before slamming her fist into the side of his jaw.

She jumped back, her hand stinging, her adrenaline screaming a small sense of satisfaction, but there was no girl-power anthem playing. She was not in a movie. He grabbed her by the wrists, his hazel eyes narrowed, his voice hard.

"You don't *tell* me," he said. "I know what we have. I know who we are. You don't get to erase everything because *you* misunderstood."

"How can you say—"

"Ssssshh." He stepped closer to her, keeping his left hand locked around her right wrist, but moving his right index finger to her lips. The touch made her tremble, but not in the way it had for the last two years. "There's nothing wrong with having fun, Brittney. You never seemed like a girl who was looking for a ring. Don't whine about it now because you think someone else is getting one. Emma is just a glorified friend. Our mothers went to Tufts together. I don't know what's going to come of it, but I need to see it through. I owe my parents that."

"I don't care." She was surprised by the coolness in her voice, thankful she wasn't betraying her own emotions.

"My jaw would say otherwise."

"Just…" She yanked her wrist from his grasp. "I'm leaving."

"Brit." His eyes took on a softer look again, one that was pleading, one that almost convinced her to pause. "Don't. If you walk away like this, it really is over."

"Like that's a question. *I* am telling *you*: it is *over!*"

He came toward her again. No, he lunged, a lurch, like an angry dog on a leash when an unsuspecting runner passed by. Except there was no leash. He backed her up against the Ford Explorer right behind her in the lot, mashing his body against hers, his hands pressing on her shoulders, his mouth wide open and hungrily covering hers.

She tried to tell him to stop, but his lips were pressed so hard against hers she couldn't get the words out, and his body was pressed so tightly against hers that she couldn't wriggle from his grasp. Hating her own weakness, she darted her tongue inside his mouth, made the most turned-on little noise she could muster, and waited, silently pleading for him to believe her. He made his own sound, and she felt the melting begin. He moved a hand off her shoulder and down toward the elastic waistband of her joggers. It would only take him a moment to maneuver his hand inside, so she had no time to hesitate. With all the force and fearlessness she could muster, she thrust her knee up hard, straight into his crotch.

At first, it seemed to backfire. He gripped her so hard

she would have finger-shaped bruises on her shoulder and hip for days. But his adrenaline was quickly eclipsed by his pain, and he let go as he dropped to the ground, clutching himself.

He was yelling at her, calling her awful things. She yelled right back as she scurried away. "Don't ever touch me again. I will ruin you!" She screamed curses even after she closed and locked her car door.

She had sounded much braver than she felt. How could she not have known? How? With her shoulder and hand throbbing, her lips tingling, and her breath coming out in hyper convulsions, she sped away from him, or so it seemed. The real imprints he left were going to follow her for years.

Jessie

"WHICH ONE IS IT THIS TIME?"

I stopped mid-way through the inevitable toss of my phone onto the kitchen table. I was disgusted, but my husband's knowing, charming grin never failed to disarm me.

"I'll give you three guesses." My coffee was cold, and I started getting up to put it in the microwave. Paul took my mug out of my hands and did it for me.

Over the hum, he said, "David?"

My youngest son, the youngest child of our blended brood, was finishing up his studies at University of Tennessee, and while he was The Baby (intentional capitals) he was not usually one to call before noon.

I shook my head. "Try again."

He raised an eyebrow. "Katy?"

That was actually a better guess. Paul's youngest, born a few minutes after her twin sister Julie, knew who was the softer touch between her daddy and me. I wasn't her mama, but I was her ally, and that was not a secret.

"No," I said with a smirk. "But the day is young. One more try."

"Must be the other non-blonde. But please don't sing it."

Paul smirked at me, and I managed a small smile back. Dolly, the corgi that Julie, of all people, had given to us, was curled up and snoring by my feet.

"Brittney lost her lease. She has to move out at the end of the month."

Unphased, he answered, "Well, with property values doing what they're doing, she had to kind of expect that."

His penchant for reason was steady, endearing, infuriating. "Expect it? Maybe. Plan for it? Are you kidding?"

"So is she moving in the thirtieth or the first?" He nodded toward the hall off the kitchen, which led to one of the jewels of our *whimsical* beach cottage, a tiny, private suite, which had already been inhabited by three of our offspring for various seasons.

I sighed. He could be as reasonable as he wanted as long as he kept being so lovably unflappable. I was the opposite. As soon as Brittney had finished saying, "I have to move," every nerve ending in my stomach exploded into scorpions. I'd surpassed butterflies long ago.

"She said, and I quote, 'I would rather pay weekly rent on a shared single wide at Myrtle Manor than move back in with my mama in my thirties. I'll figure it out.' So the answer is…" I didn't even know how to finish.

"The thirtieth of *next* month?" he quipped.

I swatted at his hand playfully, but as usual, he saw through me.

"It's okay, Jess."

I went with it. "What's okay?"

"It's okay for your thirty-one-year-old daughter not to

want to move in with you, especially since this wasn't her childhood home, and you don't share it with her daddy. And it's okay to be offended about that because your home is the coziest place on earth, and you're the most loving, gracious mother that ever lived. And it's okay that you're also relieved because you like drinking your coffee with no pants on whenever you feel like it. And you like it when I do, too."

I walked over to him and planted my pantless self on his lap, expecting and accepting his arms around my waist and all the reassurance they brought.

"It's a private suite," I said.

"You and your children have very fluid boundaries," he replied.

"Shhh," I answered, and to ensure he listened, I covered his mouth with mine and tried to forget about my grown daughter's dilemma.

Brittney

"THERE IS NOTHING - LITERALLY NOTHING — more annoying than having to find a new roommate. *Nothing!* I am thirty-one years old. I shouldn't even *need* a roommate. I have a college degree in something *real*. I work for the fastest growing place to live in the United States. Why do I need roommates?"

Brittney threw her phone on to the passenger seat and waited for a telltale "cha-loop" notification from Mikayla on their Marco Polo video chat. She probably wouldn't answer right away, because Josie, The Blessed Child, would either be nursing (don't want to interrupt the flow), napping ("Never wake a baby! And this is my *me* time!") or doing something so adorable that Mikayla would have to snap 100 photos, share them on the family iCloud album, and make them into a reel set to an instrumental lullaby version of a T. Swift song.

If anyone else did that stuff, Brittney would hate her.

But Mikayla was her just-a-little-older sister and basically a saint, so she tolerated the absurd because she loved having that much good accessible to her. She wasn't really aggravated with Mikayla anyway. No. Her rage was for Cristina, her boss at Boardwalk Square – *the* entertainment district in Myrtle Beach, who had ducked out of the office early three times the past week for supposed *meetings* but told Brittney she couldn't come in thirty minutes late for a dentist appointment; she'd have to take a half day of PTO. "The other employees see *you* getting away with it and will follow suit."

"Follow *this*," she grumbled. Mikayla's video message chimed in. "Brit, that sucks. You know you can stay in our extra room until you figure it out. I mean, I know you don't want to, but you can. Come over after work. Altan is finishing a job tonight, and Josie hasn't made it to Thai food. I'll make coconut curry if you save me a trip to the store and bring something chocolate."

Damn her. Brittney was supposed to meet El at Fishwalk Tavern for a happy hour and figure-out-the-world session. Hmmm…

"Can El come?" was her only response.

Her sister's voice (she couldn't see her face when she was being a responsible driver and leaving the phone on the passenger seat) answered immediately. "Only if he promises to read Josie *The Very Hungry Caterpillar* because he has set an impossible performance standard for the rest of us."

How did this become about Josie's bedtime story?

She waited and weighed her choices. Her sister would inevitably calm her down and help her explore decent options, and her coconut curry was really, really good. On the other hand, her best friend El would probably buy the drinks, and even if he couldn't solve her housing problem, he would run into six different people while they were out, and one of them would know someone whose neighbor's girlfriend's mama was renting something out in Conway, which would not be ideal but would still be less humiliating than crashing with any of the members of her family who would be generous and selfless enough to offer.

You're the only selfish one, Brit.

Well, maybe David is a little, too.

"Hey. Change of plans. Meet me at Kayla's. I have to pick up dessert, so let me know what you want to drink. Two brains are better than one."

El's reply was immediate.

"Three brains, Brit. That would make three brains. If Kayla's cooking, let's have wine like grown-ups. And tell her I'll put Josie to bed."

"What did I do to deserve you? Also, I feel pretty brainless at this point, so I'll be happy with the two of yours."

"Stop it. Let me know what time." He never let her get away with claiming she was dumb, incompetent, or desperate. But at the moment, she felt certain she was all of them.

"It's clearly the answer," Mikayla said, dipping her madeleine into her coffee. "El has the room now, and he's offering. I don't know why you didn't do it years ago."

"Um, Daddy," Brittney deadpanned while El, wide-eyed said, "Oh my God, your father."

"You really think he would have cared that much?"

"Are you eating that cookie or making out with it?"

"Gross, Brittney!"

"Well, good Lord. Calm down. You're like… sucking the chocolate off."

"Do I need to run out for more?" El asked. "Or do we need to just leave you alone with the ones that are left?"

Mikayla shut her eyes and chewed slowly, but Brittney could see the smirk breaking out in the corners of her closed lips. She liked chocolate-dipped madeleines. She also loved the attention from someone not wearing a diaper.

"You always think Daddy was so hard," she finally added. "How much were you really in trouble? He let you talk him into a whole lot of things that I never could."

"Only because you never tried."

"Oooh, burn." El followed his own cookie with a long swallow of wine, waiting for a signal that the sisters had crossed from banter into resentment.

Mikayla cleared her throat. Brittney took the signal.

"*Anyway*, El," she said. "*You* need to take a day and sleep on it. Fixing my homeless situation would be a big change for you and your loner situation."

"Umph." There was an unintelligible grunt from behind El's wine glass. Brittney hadn't been to his house more than a dozen times through the years. He'd moved in after breaking up with his only live-in girlfriend, and since, they always hung out at Brittney's place, Fishwalk, Neal and Pam's, somewhere *else*. She sensed it was because it was a family beach house, not his, and El was forever weird about his family. But her situation wasn't much better. She'd been renting a mobile home from a guitarist in El's band for years. But she *loved* it. "You're not a situation," El insisted. "And you wouldn't *have* a situation if it wasn't for Geno's stupid breakup."

Brittney shrugged, while her sister smiled in the knowing way that annoyed her to no end. Mikayla always believed Brittney and El should just get over their platonic soul-mates thing and be in love and get married and have six children who attend Carolina Forest schools. It was Mikayla's be-all, end-all, so she thought it was everyone's.

Truthfully, Brittney and El had made out three times, once when they went to the tenth grade Homecoming dance together, once on New Year's Eve when they were both home during their first year of college, and the last time when they'd both moved back after graduation, utterly defeated that they hadn't scored dream jobs in some exotic *other* place. That time had been on Brittney's parents' old front porch, one that faced the beach and usually felt magical. That night it had only felt like a little relief from boredom and anxiety and embarrassment, and also served as the concluding proof that they were, in fact, purely *platonic* soul mates. But they hadn't stopped before Brittney's dad walked outside and saw them, and that was the end of El being able to crash at their place because Daddy never fully believed her when she said that they were just friends.

He never fully believed anything she said.

Brittney thought about the six months she'd crashed at Mama and Daddy's almost-empty nest house, with her younger, boundaryless teenage brother just feet away from her in the bigger extra bedroom, with her mama constantly telling her who was hiring and which of their friends', the Jamesons, cute little apartments were available for rent.

That was the best time she'd ever had with her dad. Instead of her defaulting to feeling like she was a total disappointment to him, she started getting up every day so they could have breakfast together, and he never asked her how the job search was going. She was working at Ocean Lakes Campground, paying them some rent, and applying everywhere from Charlotte to Charleston to Atlanta, and because he wasn't asking, she was happy to update her dad on the *lack* of opportunities coming her way. And even though she wasn't asking, he was always giving her pep talks and twenty-dollar bills when he thought she needed them.

It was the last time she'd lived with a male of any kind, the last time she'd lived with family. At the end of those six months, she got her first job at one of the oldest marketing firms in Myrtle Beach, found a situation with two other twenty-somethings just getting started, and never looked back. And the day she moved out, after driving the truck and setting up her bed, Daddy had pressed an envelope into her hand that was the cash equivalent of all the rent she'd been paying.

Maybe Mikayla was right about him.

But Brittney hadn't talked him *into* any of that. It was when she stopped trying that Daddy had usually shown up like a champ for her.

She wished she could ask him what to do this time, but she couldn't imagine him supporting her decision to move in with El. Even though he'd married Brittney's mom, Jessie, when she was barely out of her teens *and* the single mom of baby Sam, and even though Sam had almost repeated history when he got Abby pregnant with their oldest, Travis, before they were married, Daddy remained pretty conservative. He declared himself open-minded and full of grace, sure; but he wanted traditional, *normal* lives for his kids.

Living with El would probably be more like the plot of an '80s or '90s sitcom, but it would be fun.

"Think about it," Brittney insisted, refilling her own wine glass. Then she grinned at the only man left she trusted. "But say yes."

Jessie 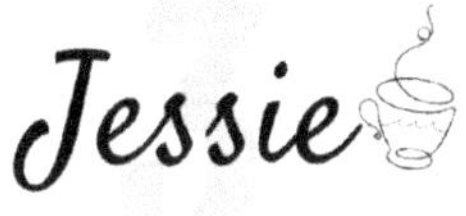

FLUID BOUNDARIES. PAUL WAS NOT AT THE tearoom with us, but his voice was booming in my head as I grabbed two plates of Abby's quiche of the day (Farmer's Market Quiche, which meant anything goes) and brought them to a table where Brittney and a large pot of rooibos tea were waiting.

I smiled at the table and poured my cup wordlessly. Brittney was my hardest child, perhaps my hardest relationship, to navigate. She was fierce in all things – her loyalty, her protection, her love, her point of view, her need to be right, *and* her independence. So if I ever wanted to actually guide her, I had to wait until she opened herself to it. Otherwise, our interactions turned *mutually* fierce, and then some.

"Mama, you can say what you want to me. I know you don't love the idea."

Could I, though? We would see.

"Brit, you're, in your own terms, a grown-ass woman. You've been living on your own for almost ten years, and you don't need me to advise you in this. You pay your own bills."

She took a bite of her quiche and shook her head. "Did Mikayla tell you to say that?"

"Believe it or not, Brit, I come up with some stuff on my own." I shoved a bite into my own mouth. We were already on the precipice of fierce turning into fiery, whether she realized it or not. Did these kids think I suddenly turned stupid when I turned sixty?

"I just know you have something to say, Mama. No offense, but you always do."

I dropped my fork with an intentional clang. "Do you *want* me to have something to say?"

She stiffened and took a pause, which was a good sign from her. "I actually do want to know what you think. I know I'm acting like it's no big deal, but it feels like maybe it is."

Any show of her vulnerability was my cue to dial all the way in. "Okay, Brit. This might surprise you, but I don't actually think it's that big of a deal. El is your oldest, closest friend. You've already navigated past the whole *men and women can't be friends* B.S. He has a house with room. And everything is temporary."

"God," Brittney exhaled. "That's not the kind of thing you used to say."

An immediate image of Randall popped into my head. He spent the first few years—okay, maybe the first two decades—of our marriage convincing me that some things were built to last. He convinced me that we were forever. And we were. We are. Even though he went ahead and died way in advance of when I thought he would, even though I was married to Paul, Randall was not temporary.

His presence in our lives was lasting. But his absence from our lives changed me to my core. I was mostly happy, but *forever* had turned into a pretty fluid concept for me.

"I'm not the same person."

We waited out the beat of that. I didn't mean for the conversation to get heavy, but I was weary of convincing my kids that I was different from the anxious, micromanaging, approval-seeking woman who'd raised them. They'd just have to keep seeing for themselves.

"So… you think it will be fine? Or should I wait until I can find my own place again?"

"Well, babe, the market is awful right now…"

She nodded. "I talked to Sam about my… you know… inheritance money." Sam was the de facto business manager for all his siblings. "He said a down payment is a great investment, but…"

"The market is awful right now."

"Exactly."

"Brit." I allowed myself to reach over and cover her hand with mine, briefly. "Stay with El for a while. It's fine."

"I just thought— I thought by now I would be…"

"You're not behind," I affirmed.

"I *feel* behind."

"Why?

She looked around the tearoom, which I had purchased six months prior with Abby, Sam's wife and basically another daughter to me. There were two tables occupied. One of them held what looked to be a mom, her grown daughters, and two little granddaughters, one in a stroller and one pre-school aged. Her gaze stayed there for more than a moment.

"You don't have to be doing what everyone else is doing. Or on their timeline."

"I know."

"I know you know. But you've hit a pothole, so now you're doubting. Brit, you're successful. You have a great job. You're close to your family. You have fulfilling friendships. It's okay to want more. But you're... fine."

"Everything's fine," she muttered.

We both laughed at that. It was a trendy saying *and* a family saying. Bleeding out your eyeballs? Car on fire? Husband dead, boyfriend left you, and your dog died? (Ahem, literally my life less than two years before...) *It's fine. I'm fine. Everything is fine.*

"He hardly wants to charge me any rent, Mama. I'm just not sure that's right. I don't want to risk hurting our friendship when it's one of the most important things to me."

I thought of my own tentative beginnings with Paul, one of my closest friends when Randall and Paul's wife died in a car accident. I remember weighing the risks and swallowing my fears. This was different. I pictured Elliot... El... the boy-turned-man who'd been coming around since Brittney's freshman year of high school. El was a little bit of a clown, not much focused on school, and didn't seem to have much supervision. I never even met his mom until their graduation. But having been a pregnant, unwed teen myself, I had a specific list of priorities for the boys my daughters found interesting, and El never seemed to pose a risk. He was respectful of Brittney; he always included the much-quieter Mikayla and the pesky baby brother David; and Brittney dated a string of other guys throughout high school, which confirmed my belief that she and El just didn't see each other *that* way.

Admittedly, in the last few years, I'd wondered why not. As my own weird and surprising second marriage was proving, best friends could make the best partners.

"Brit. I truly believe you're not at risk. There are a few

things you can count on in your life, and El is one of them. And you know, if it all goes to crap for some unforeseen reason, your mama is another."

She accepted that in silence, focusing on her meal and daring to take a sip of tea. Brit loved the tearoom but barely tolerated the beverage of choice. There was usually a small stash of Dr. Pepper or one of his cousins somewhere in the fridge for her *and* Sam *and* Paul. Maybe we should have bought a 7-11 instead.

"Okay," she finally said. "I'll try it. I mean, I guess, what's the worst that could happen?"

Brittney

BRITTNEY SAT ON TOP OF A BIG BLUE TOTE that held some combination of books, candles, coasters, her Christmas stocking, a few niece and nephew toys, and whatever other randomness had been shoved in her living room's sole end table. Her hair was scooped into a messy bun and soaked with sweat, but every last thing she owned was packed.

Altan, her stalwart brother-in-law, had gone to pick up the U-Haul and, likely, breakfast, since there wasn't a crumb to be found in the little mobile home she'd rented for the past eight years. True to their friendship, with El repeatedly rescuing her, he had alerted Brittney to its availability when his bandmate Geno's mom had passed away, leaving a fairly cute single-wide a mile from the beach available at a rent she could afford by herself. She'd snatched it up and lived in complete contentment there. She barely had room to turn around, but she didn't cook, and she never had to worry about her younger brother crashing there for more than a night or two. And her parents, who were *conventional* if not a little snobbish, couldn't even argue with her when she called it minimalist. Mikayla called it shabby chic. Whatever. It was cheap, clean, functional, near the beach, and decorated just how she wanted, mostly white with pops of pink and all her band posters. There was Aerosmith, Tom Petty, and Pearl Jam, because her mama's influence could not be resisted. Prince and Reba McEntire, because musical taste was the one thing about her daddy that made no sense. Taylor Swift, Imagine Dragons, and 5 Seconds of Summer, because she acted her age. And most recently, The Doobie Brothers, because her stepdad played them on repeat during a Taco Tuesday, and she found that she'd previously underappreciated one of the best bands ever.

She rolled each one carefully and stuck them in a green, zippered bag meant for wrapping paper that her mama had gotten her at The Container Store. She'd made fun of it at first, but it was actually perfect. Posters would be transported across town in her Kona, along with her coffee mugs (only four of them, but actual ceramic ones that she, Mikayla, and their cousins had made together at one of those pottery-and-wine places), the vinyl collection she'd inherited from her grandparents, and all her work stuff. Everything else would be shoved in the truck and would probably take less than a regular workday to load and unload.

She didn't have that much stuff. Minimalist.

Or depressing. Directionless. Non-committal.

Ssshhh, she told that voice. She could almost see Daddy shaking his head a bit, questioning her choices without saying a word. She spent so much time worrying about his reaction to her choices, and now that he was gone, she tried to spend the same energy remembering the times he'd shown up big for her.

FIVE YEARS EARLIER

She'd been wrapped in her fuzzy blanket covered with pink and turquoise pumpkins, skipping the commercial break on her DVR'd episode of *Dancing with the Stars*. The knock on the door caught her by surprise. El had his band rehearsal that night, and Mikayla, newlywedded, was rarely heard from after dark. Brittney's heart started to race, but it had been weeks since she heard from Douchebag Bradley. She was probably safe.

Her exhale came in relief *and* surprise when she saw her dad standing there.

"Daddy?" she opened the door and stepped onto the porch, into his hug.

"Hey, Firecracker." There was something in his voice that made her wonder what he knew, even more so than his unannounced visit at 9:30 on a Thursday night. She didn't end the embrace as quickly as she normally did.

"You smell like air travel," she finally said, breaking away from the scent of pink industrial soap and Altoids. "How was your trip?"

He followed her into the house and smiled. There was a bag of tortilla chips and a bowl holding remnants of guacamole on her coffee table, and Len Goodman saying something hilariously British and snotty on the TV.

"Not as good as your evening." He sat on the sofa. "The meetings were efficient, my flights were on time, and I ate a steak in Omaha. That's pretty much the best I can ask for. Your mama is out with Aunt Maggie tonight, and David is just fine, so…"

"I'm glad you came! I'm just surprised. Do you want anything? Did you eat?"

"Airport –"

"Steak and Shake," she answered. It was the only one left on the whole Grand Strand, and Daddy loved his Frisco Melt and Double Chocolate Fudge milkshakes.

"I'm all set for the night," he said, patting his modest Dad-belly.

"Well." She sat next to him, wadding the blanket into her lap and trying to assume a put-together, grown-up posture while wearing tiny Captain America shorts and a Florence + the Machine hoodie with the sleeves cut off. "It's good to see you."

"I'm not here to talk to you about your report card grades, Brit."

She faked a giggle. "Can't help it. This is pretty uncharacteristic of us."

He studied her face, which did not in any way result in her relaxing in his presence.

"What's up, Brit?"

She scrunched up her whole face. "What's up, Daddy?"

"Firecracker. Come on. Your mama noticed it right away, and as usual, I'm slow on the uptake. You've missed Sunday supper a whole bunch. You're quiet. And Mama thinks you're avoiding being alone with her."

Brittney pulled the blanket tightly over her lap. She thought about pulling the hood over her head, too, but she generally tried to stop short of ridiculous.

"And Bradley hasn't been around since he got back from his urgent trip."

She yanked at the drawstring so hard that the other end disappeared.

"Brit."

"We broke up," she said. *Stay calm. Stay calm. Do not*

cry. Do not picture his face. Do not picture how…

"Aw, Honey, I'm sorry."

She shrugged.

"We all thought the cruise was going to be when he would finally ask…" He let himself trail off, and her tear ducts betrayed her. "Well crap. That was exactly the wrong thing to say."

He pulled a trusty blue and white plaid handkerchief from his pocket and handed it to her, which made her cry harder. Daddy was a relic, a hero from a distant time, who had saved her mama and Sam from a life of dismal prospects and long winters and inadvertently gave his daughters, at least this one, an unattainable standard for what a husband should be. Mikayla seemed to have done pretty okay; Brittney was certain her sister had used all the good luck.

Even so, he was struggling to rebound while he watched her fall apart. "You dumped him, I hope?"

She gave a small laugh through her tears. "I guess you can say that."

Does it count if it was never real?

"Brit? You want to talk about it?"

She shook her head as she started crying harder.

"Oh, Baby." Daddy scooted to her and wrapped her up again. For the first time in three weeks and four days, her grief was unbottled in front of another person.

When his shirt was all but soaked and she could breathe again, she offered the only information she would allow herself to give.

"It was all a lie. He was never going to marry me or stay with me. He thought I was decorated trailer trash." *And maybe I am.*

"Brit, come on." Daddy pulled far enough away to look at her, but he still had his hands on her elbows, and she felt safe. "Why would you say that?"

"Because he told me! He said it was all just for fun. I thought we were heading toward, you know, a future, and it was never even real! He told me I was stupid and he couldn't believe I thought..." She couldn't even finish.

"Brittney Abigail!"

"Sir," she mumbled.

"The only name you ever need to answer to is the one God gave us to give to you."

"Yes, sir."

"You are 'your father's joy.' And anyone who would treat you like less than the *joy* you bring and the joy you *are* is *actually* trash. Do I need to remind him? Do I need to put him there?"

It was tempting. If she told him the whole story, he wouldn't ask permission. Bradley would have to run for his life.

"No, sir. I just want to forget about him. Forget we ever happened."

He patted her hand. "Sure Brit. But... it did. And you can't forget. You won't. But you have to learn from it, so it doesn't ever happen again."

She nodded. *No current plans to ever let anyone get close enough to try.*

"I know, Daddy. Just, for now, can you do me a favor?"

"I'll try."

She smiled at the handkerchief squeezed in her hands and handed it back to him as she said, "Don't tell Mama."

He grasped the cloth and looked close to tears himself. "Firecracker, your mama is going to know. She's already mentioned a half dozen times that you missed Sundays. Your absence is duly noted."

"I know I have to tell her we broke up, but I... you know how she is about bad guys." The story of Sam's biological dad was part of Mama's "birds and the bees" talk to her and Mikayla, which was repeated through the years when they started dating, or asked to go out with friends, or had a crush on a celebrity. "If she knows he was a douchebag that whole time and I never saw…"

"She will feel terrible and guilty that *she* didn't see. And she will plot his slow death with her and Maggie as the executioners."

They smiled at each other, and for the first time since her face-off with Bradley in the parking lot, she had felt safe again.

"Oh, these beach houses," Altan said, plopping on Brittney's couch, which fit right in front of the windows in her new bedroom.

"I know," she told her brother-in-law. "Thanks for being willing to store the kitchen table for me."

It was, in fact, the only piece of furniture she had that wouldn't fit in the bedroom. El's house was a vacation house, with big rooms and hardly any hallways, which meant she was in between a bathroom off the short corridor and another bedroom that was empty except for a sad futon relic and whatever music equipment El had thrown in there at any given time. They already agreed that she would hang a Pirate's Voyage flag on her door in the odd instance she might have a visitor when El had a sudden urge to enter the makeshift studio and strum "Interstate Love Song" on his acoustic.

The house also sat about half a mile from the beach in Surfside, two miles from where Brittney had been living, less than that from her Mama's new house with Paul, and Mama would certainly be here soon. (And it wasn't really a *new* home for them anymore, Brittney had to remind herself. Daddy had been gone for two years. Mama and Paul had been together almost that long, and well… best not to go down that road. They all had lives to lead, and Brittney certainly didn't want anyone telling her how to live *hers*).

"It's nothing," Altan said. "Besides, this way Mikayla will feel like she's helping you, since she's been wringing her hands about it for two weeks."

"Sorry, man," Brittney said, grateful that he totally got the vibe between her and her sister.

"You have shelves to hang?" he continued, looking around at the pale blue walls. "I will get them done before *Anne* gets here with the food."

Altan always called Jessie the Turkish word for *Mama*. "She cooked?" Brittney said, starting to feel a little excited.

Altan shrugged. "She did not expressly tell me that, but it's one in the afternoon, and you don't cook. I'll make the educated guess."

Brittney couldn't even pretend to be insulted. She "cooked" frozen appetizers in the air fryer Mama had gotten her, and when she really felt daring, she made scrambled eggs with Daddy's secret ingredient: cream cheese.

"Let's hope so. I'm starving, and all El knows how to make is salsa. So after today, it's huevos rancheros for the rest of our lives."

"I am sure *Anne* would teach you to cook other things."

Brittney picked up a random throw pillow sitting on top of three crates and tossed it at his face.

"I don't want to cook like her anyway," she said. "Too much pressure."

She was smiling, but Altan was not.

"Pressure? To make meals for her family? Is that what you think?"

She began unloading the box of towels and setting them in piles on the bed, focusing way too hard for such a simple task.

"You're avoiding my question?"

"You're asking a lot of questions," she muttered.

"I don't think *Anne* feels that way. Is it you who feels that way?"

"Altan—" Brittney stood with her shoulders back and finally turned to him. "Mama is *good* at what she does. Probably as close to perfect as you can be. She can host and cook and hug and be quippy at the same time. She does it so well she owns a restaurant now. Why would I try to duplicate that?"

He studied her quizzically. "Duplicate? No, little sister. Just learn. Pass on. That's what we do with family, yes?"

She shrugged.

"We let Mikayla make us yogis. We surf with David. We even let Julie sign us up for 5Ks. Why can't your mama teach you cooking?"

Brittney stared, first into blank space so that a highlight reel could play in her mind: a lifetime of birthday cupcakes, celebratory dinners, late night milkshakes or nachos, standing Sunday suppers. Her mama was the common thread in all of it. Even after Daddy died and nothing felt right, much less the same, Mama kept the door open and the coffee ready and the kitchen smelling inviting. She did it even when she was grieving over Daddy, even when she was embarrassed over Paul, even when she didn't think any of them would show up.

But they always did, even when they were sad about Daddy, or mad about Paul, or disgusted with each other over something. Mama always made them want to come home.

Brittney turned her eyes to Altan, who lived so far from his home, he was probably projecting his wistfulness on her.

"I love what Mama does," she said. "I just don't know

if that's in me."

He tossed the pillow back at Brittney's head. "She's in you, crazy girl."

Jessie

"Mags, I'll call you later. Let me know about Moni, though. She's probably the only kind of roommate Brit would tolerate."

"Except for the singer in a band who isn't gay and she ain't shaggin'?"

"F-F-S, Maggie." I sighed and turned the A/C up as I parked in my daughter's new driveway. I tried to stay pleasing to Jesus, so I could only drop an actual F-bomb so many times a day. "He's a marketing executive, not some dude who panhandles between gigs. And he is *not* gay!"

"Well, glory. I still cannot understand why they're still not together."

I almost quoted Nora Ephron and Billy Crystal, but it would fall on deaf ears. When my bestie was on a roll, she might as well have been talking to herself. And she was fired up over her own daughter possibly moving back to the beach from Greenville, where Maggie and her new husband and step kids all lived, with her other daughter and grandson not far, and *goodness, aren't we all just a circus?*

"I am *sure* Brittney would *love* to explain it to you. It's one of her favorite things to do. Really." I really wanted to get inside and help my kid, and Maggie's rant had already gone on too long.

"Meh. Whatever. She gotta do what she gotta do, and so does Brittney, and so do I. Maybe I'll just take my Sheldon and go back to sweet home Chicago."

I grimaced, partially under the weight of the huge tote bag filled with food containers, partially because –

"That might actually be the dumbest thing you have ever said, sister. Now shush. I'll text you later."

She was drawing breath for her next diatribe when I tapped the "end" button. I didn't know why she was more volatile than usual, but I didn't have time for Hurricane Maggie when the eye of Hurricane Brittney could have possibly been waiting inside.

I lugged everything up the stairs, feeling momentarily wistful for my own beach house, one Randall and I had moved to when David was the sole kid left in the house. It was second row with an unobstructed view and basically perfect, and sometimes I had no idea why I sold it, other than my whole life had turned into a hurricane two years before and I'd been trying to control whatever aspects of it I could.

I loved the house Paul and I lived in, one he'd picked out to surprise me, one that was full of magical touches and plenty of space. But living across the street from the beach was a hard kind of magic to beat. Hopefully, Brittney would appreciate it for however long she had it.

I was prepared to set down my load and knock, but the bright pink door (a perfect beach contrast against the house's turquoise siding) was wide open. The Black Crowes' "Remedy" was shaking the walls. Neither Brit nor Altan was in view, but the back of a head I assumed was El's stuck out from the refrigerator. I noisily dropped my tote on the counter; he still didn't hear me.

Noise didn't bother me, and since Brit grew up in my house, it probably was fine with her, too. I'd never been at El's before, but I assumed the role of Everyone's Mom and started unpacking.

"Food!" I looked up expecting to see El's familiar face. Instead, it was a redheaded, pink-cheeked man around El's age, impossibly skinny with most of his youthful face hidden behind a full beard, just across the counter from me. Based on his attire (ripped jeans, Violent Femmes t-shirt), I assumed he was one of El's band buddies. Whoever he was, he walked straight up and hugged me, all the while leering at the Pyrex containers.

"Um, hi," I said, always unfazed by hungry humans. "There's crustless quiche, and there's also tortellini soup. It's Brittney's favorite. Maybe a few other things." I wasn't going to offer up her special request cranberry-orange scones or her childhood favorite, meatloaf muffins. Those would be gone in seconds to these manly vultures. "I'm her mom, Jessie, by the way."

"Mama!" Another voice called from across the room in an exaggerated accent, and only then did El remove himself from the depths of the fridge and notice anything was going on around him.

This did not cause confidence in my daughter's level of protection in the house, but as the pair of arms attached to the fake Italian accent wrapped me up, I had a typical Jessie gut response that she would be, well, loved.

"I knew there would be food!" the voice said. I giggled nervously and broke the hug, beholding a middle-aged man barely taller than me, his head covered with dark brown curls and a smile reaching both of his ample cheeks. I might have been mistaken, but he smelled like flour.

"I'm Geno!" he said, now vigorously shaking my hand. "Came over to help Brittney get settled. Least I can do since I had to reclaim my old trailer."

Ah. So this was the guitarist ruining Brit's life. He seemed nice enough. I smiled at him.

"Oh, Mama Jess. Hey!" That's when I noted the white buds in El's ears. These two guys did seem a bit boisterous for his mellow personality. I accepted a third hug and began to wonder if Brit was actually there. "You brought food? Awesome. I figured eating might be better with Brit as a roommate."

"Don't count on delivery service as a regular thing," I said, approximately half-joking. We all knew if one of my kids requested food from me, the least I would do was drop off burgers from Bruiser's, and the most I would do was roast a quick chicken with veggies. It was the *A-B-Cs of me, Baby.* "And definitely don't count on Brittney cooking anything besides eggs any time soon."

"Maybe she'll surprise us," he answered, sweet-naturedly, and I started to feel more at ease. El was the best friend my daughter could have asked for, and unconventional living arrangements were the new conventional. I was frankly surprised it hadn't happened years ago, but Brittney *liked* living by herself.

"For real, you're talking about me already?" And there she was, her dyed, ash-blonde hair piled on top of her head, her unironic Beach Boys t-shirt cut to a crop, just barely showing off her tanned, taut belly above her cut off jean shorts. She still looked fifteen to me. She still wore the same expression of perpetual indignation as she let me put one arm around her slight (but strong) shoulders and tentatively squeeze.

"Just talking about food," I reassured, and with that, she jumped into action, pouring over every container, side-eyeing the guys, now immersed in their own side conversation about the legit harmonies of Brian Wilson, et al.

"Thanks Mama!" she whisper-exclaimed, and took off to parts unknown with the scones under her shirt. I was taken back to the pinnacle of motherhood for me, when they all lived at home, our grandson Travis and a revolving door of friends were around all the time, and Brittney and Mikayla were constantly hiding snack food so it would last more than a day. Had my child gotten herself into a ridiculously immature and boundary-less living situation, or was she happily reclaiming the chaos of her childhood?

Randall's voice in my head told me *You are overthinking at an alarming rate.* I shook my head and waited, and there was Paul's voice, chiming in with a simple, *Calm down, Jess.* Some days, he saved himself the trouble and wrote it on my arm with a Sharpie. Some days, I did. Every day, the voices of my late husband and my new one swirled all together in one of the strangest, most comforting concoctions of my current reality.

"Mama!" Oh. Apparently, I was supposed to follow her. Was I supposed to bring all the food? The guys were still distracted by each other. I covered everything with the tote bag and followed her voice.

"Is it safe to leave meatloaf near all those men? Oh!"

Her room was already cozy. Had she been there for two hours or two weeks? The walls were painted a perfect Robin's egg blue, and even though there were boxes stacked neatly against one wall, her bed was set up and made with the patchwork quilt we'd worked on together across her middle school years (and had finally been finished by the *ladies at church* when we decided maybe we weren't those kind of people after all), and her framed picture of her and Randall was on the rattan nightstand.

"I know. But don't open the closet. I just wanted as much of it out of my sight as possible for now. Scone?"

She had flung herself on the sturdy sofa against the window while I took a scone from the stash and sat on the bed, facing her.

"Thanks, Baby. So. What can I help you with? Do you want me to work on… whatever is in the closet?"

Brittney scrunched up her face. "Don't make it sound so eeky. No. It's mostly clothes and my records. Altan ran to get some better anchors for my shelves, and that's where those will go. That's it. I'm not going to go too crazy…"

"Unpacking isn't crazy. Do you need a dresser or something? You have room for one…" I wondered if she was going to unpack her clothes at all, or if she would just bide her time until a better solution presented itself.

Brittney shrugged. "I'm good. Should we make coffee? These are kinda dry without them."

"Whatever!" Ungrateful brat. She was right, though. "Actually, yes. But before we go back out there…"

"Mama—"

"Just wait," I said, emphasizing by making a stop-in-the-name-of-love hand sign at her. "What's the vibe here? Do those guys hang around a lot? And are you comfortable with that?"

She shrugged. "They're fine. They were here when we pulled up, and we had the truck unloaded in about seventeen seconds. They're both in El's band—"

"You don't say?"

Eyeroll. "—and they are playing at Zach's tonight, so they're trickling in over here before they go set up." Zach's was actually Neal and Pam's, owned by Zach Baker, and one of the busiest bars in Surfside. Incidentally, it has also been the site of Paul's and my wedding reception. We loved going there, but I didn't know if she'd appreciate us hanging around when her crowd was present.

"They're just very… huggy…" I said.

She rolled her eyes again. "Not all the time. Anyway, Geno is a baker. Like an actual one. So you have a few things in common. They're all… harmless, even though that idiot let his wife kick him out and had to take my home back from me."

I knew she wasn't going to get over that any time soon. As strange to me as it was, how much she loved that little trailer, it had been the first home that was all hers, and never having been in her shoes, I could just accept it as something I couldn't understand – and didn't need to.

It took me years of complicated *Momming* to reach that particular flex.

"What else do we have in common?" I asked cautiously.

"Oh. Well. He adores me." My shoulders stiffened immediately. "*Not* like that!" she added. "Ew."

The dynamic was sure going to be interesting. I could already see that.

A few hours later, Altan had shelves *and* pictures hung, empty boxes broken down and carted away, and a belly full of my soup and Geno's baguettes. Brittney had allowed me to hang her clothes while she organized the bedroom and arranged the rest of her somewhat meager additions to the kitchen. She even acted excited when I presented her with a Happy Planner recipe book, which had the recipes for everything I'd brought that day written inside, and the promise of at least one more addition per week.

"I *will* try," she protested to Altan's shaking head. "Give me like one week. Mmmm, well, wait. Let me get past the launch of that tacky magic show, so two weeks. Two weeks from Saturday, y'all come for breakfast. Brunch. We'll have quiche and soup. It can't be that freaking hard."

Altan laughed while I said, "That's what I've been trying to tell you…. For like twenty years, by the way." Mikayla was experimenting with homemade pasta the summer before high school. Brit spent high school bribing her for late night grilled cheese sandwiches.

"It's a deal," El said, coming up behind us. "Hey, we gotta go, but the guys wanted me to tell you that they'll help paint the living room if you hate it, and also, Mama Jess, y'all should come hear us tonight. We just added 'Vaseline' to the set."

"Sweet Baby Jesus!" I had no cool, absolutely none, when it came to Stone Temple Pilots, and El's band, The Salty Lips, specialized in moody '90s and some 2000s alt-rock, my jam. "Brit, are you going?"

She scowled first at El, then at me. "Why would they paint the living room for me? It's gray. It's *fine*. And no, Mama. I mean, if I go, it will be later. Look at me. *Smell me*. I just moved."

"Is she always this cranky?" El asked, looking at Altan. Brit did not like her people joining forces against her. She threw her spoon in their general direction.

"Time to leave!" she half-yelled, only I knew she wasn't kidding. There'd been a lot of random togetherness for one day. We weren't used to having Altan around without Mikayla, and we weren't used to not having Sam and Abby around for such endeavors.

"Hear that, Anne?" Altan asked me. "We have outlived our usefulness."

"Shut up," Brit told him, punching his shoulder. "I really do have to get some copy written. *Thank you*, thank you, thank you." She kissed Altan's cheek and then hugged me quite tightly. "Now, get out."

In a fit of cuss words and giggles, we gathered Altan's tools and several empty food containers and packed to leave. Brit hugged us both again at the top of the stairs, holding on a little longer, reminding me that the fierce, slender sprite who often kept me at a distance actually still needed her mama from time to time.

Brittney

"THANKS FOR HELPING, DADDY. AGAIN."

Randall wiped the sweat off his brow with the bottom of his shirt and smiled sardonically. "You're welcome. Just once… one time… if one of you could move in the late fall, even early winter, that would be good."

"Sorry," Brittney said. "I hate when the dirt-cheap rentals become available in May, too."

"I hate it when May is ninety degrees," El chimed in.

"I hate it that you don't know what a forty-five-degree and rainy every day May feels like," Jessie added.

"Uh-oh," Randall told them. "Please do not trigger her winter-in-the-north PTSD. I'll be forced to spend the rest of the weekend at the beach."

Randall put an arm around Jessie, who grimaced for

a moment against the sweat he was covered in but leaned into him just the same. Brittney shook her head. Her parents' PDAs were endless, but their affection was… *Ugh.* She didn't want to think about it, but it was kind of magical. Most of her friends had divorced parents and wished their families were more like Brittney's.

"El, are you coming for supper tomorrow?" Jessie crossed the few feet from kitchen to living room to hug him.

"Maybe," he said. "My mom is supposed to be coming through town, so…"

He didn't have to finish. They all knew El's family was as fragmented as theirs was close. Brittney never really understood why, but she understood enough not to ask him any questions.

Jessie knew no such boundary with her "bonus son."

"Is your stepdad coming, too? Are they staying overnight? They're welcome to join us."

Brittney rolled her eyes in El's direction, but he smiled fully at her mama.

"It's probably just a quick hello. I'm not sure if he's coming or not, but I'll read the room and let you know. Thank you."

He really is perfect, Brittney thought. Life would be a lot easier if they took the *platonic* out of their *soul mate* status, but it just wasn't there.

Mama was still talking about spaghetti and meatballs being in endless supply. Brittney's eyes drifted over to her dad, who was inspecting the lock on her door. She stepped past him, outside, taking in the tiny, paved driveway and the tinier wooden porch. She couldn't believe she was actually going to live here, on her own.

"Whatcha lookin' at, Daddy?"

His analysis had moved to the threshold. "Just making

sure the door is nice and secure."

"In case anyone tries to break into this palace?"

The key lime paint was peeling slightly off the siding. The shutters and trim were bright coral. She'd already spread a striped rug that held every color in the world across the floor of her porch, and Mama was "lending" her two white rocking chairs. She was moving into a total cliché, and she was in love.

"It's a great place, Brit." Daddy finally quit his once-over of the door and grinned at her. "Are you happy?"

She gave her fullest smile in return. "Super happy."

"And El isn't staying here?"

"Dad!" How many times would she have to have this conversation?

"That's not an answer," he said. "But that is a pretty nifty pull-out sofa, and I wasn't born yesterday."

Oh. Maybe he did actually have it right for a change.

"He just… you know… Daddy. He doesn't have what I have."

"What's that, Brit?"

"An emergency landing pad."

Daddy looked inside, where Mama was surely still chatting up El. He sighed.

"I get it. And I appreciate your compassion. It just gets dangerous, Brittney. This is a small space for two people of the opposite sex. *Unless.*"

She muttered a string of cuss words, in her head. She might be an adult and about to live on her own for the first time, but you don't cuss at Daddy.

"He isn't gay, Daddy. Just because he's not my boyfriend doesn't mean he's into guys. A guy could not be attracted to me and still be straight. It is actually possible."

Now Randall rolled his eyes. "I don't see how. I'm a guy, Brittney. I may have been married since the dawn of time, but I know how guys think. Are you really expecting me to believe that Elliot isn't attracted to you?"

I do not *want to talk about this with you.* "I've been saying that for years. I don't expect you to believe me now." She paused thoughtfully. "He just broke up with someone. *A girl.* That's part of the reason he's going to crash here for a minute. He's going to sign a new lease, but most of them don't start in the middle of the month. Think about it, Daddy. He could have taken this place for himself."

El had been hanging out with a few guys at Midnight Sun, a recording studio where, for now, he was just kicking around ideas with a guitarist and a drummer. The guitarist mentioned his rental in front of Brittney, and here she was.

Randall nodded. "He definitely looks out for you."

"He does. So him sleeping on the couch for two weeks isn't even a question."

"Then why didn't you just tell us?"

Brittney pictured her best friend, his tall frame, his lithe beach body, his closely cropped hair with just a bit of perfect tousle in the front, his eyes the color of tree bark that were framed by impossibly long lashes. He always looked put together, whether he was dressed in a shirt and tie for his job at the Myrtle Beach Chamber of Commerce, which didn't require it, or in his jeans and t-shirts for all his "music stuff," (which maybe was starting to become a real thing). He probably was a little metrosexual for the typical Myrtle Beach guy, which led to all the assumptions that he was gay, even though he'd had several serious girlfriends since Brittney had known him. He didn't like to date; he preferred to play for keeps.

"He's just private, Daddy," Brittney said. "This last girl kinda gutted him. He barely talks to me about it."

Randall raised one eyebrow at her, saying nothing. It was his signature Dad move.

She shrugged. "That's it. There's nothing else to tell. He isn't secretly gay. He isn't secretly in love with me. He just needs my couch for a few weeks. And—"

It's my house. She wanted to say it. She wanted to remind him that everything he taught her about being self-sufficient and smart was… well, he was looking at it. But she wouldn't. And she shouldn't have to.

"It's your life, Brit, and your house. I just want you to be careful." He took a step toward her and kissed her forehead. "And I especially want Elliot to be careful."

She just shook her head. If they didn't get her and El by now, they probably never would.

When her mama *finally* left him alone and her daddy took her and her tote bags home, Brittney and El flopped on the sofa that would be his bedroom for a few weeks and stared at the ceiling. They were wrung out from moving day, the humidity, and all the things they hadn't said all day.

"Thanks for letting me crash with you," he finally said.

"Thanks for buying me a couch," she answered.

He laughed. "What do you mean? I'm taking it with me when I go."

She threw a pillow at him. It took all the energy she had left. "I don't think we can get it back out of here without sawing it in half. So good luck."

His voice quieted, not just the volume, but the emotion. "Nah, I want it to stay here. In case I need it again."

Brittney sat up a little so she could look at him. Those doe-eyes of his were weary and bleary. She felt ire rise up in her again; how she'd like to find that little she-devil Jane and—

"Pipe down, Brit. I'm okay."

"How do you know what I'm thinking?" she asked, pretending to be incredulous.

"I know you. Better than you do. And as long as we got us, we're okay, right?"

Brittney looked around the new little mobile home she had already cemented into her heart as hers. She looked at her best friend since high school. She looked at the Rubbermaid containers on the counter, filled with her mama's cooking and waiting to be shared. She looked at the photos of her older siblings and their beautiful, more settled lives that were partially covering her refrigerator door. She looked down at her own sweaty Van Halen tank. She smiled at El.

"Yep. Absolutely! Now let's eat."

Jessie

THERE WAS A VERY BRIEF TIME IN MY 20S, after Randall and I were married, when little Sam was welcomed by my parents for a sleepover most Friday nights, before Maggie or I had our daughters or moved to South Carolina, and during Maggie's stormy beginnings of marriage with my only sibling, Tony, when we followed a few local bands.

By followed, I mean we read every snippet we could about them in *The Star*, our local newspaper, and went to listen to them every possible weekend we could. We fangirl'd before it was a term, especially when Maggie's cousin dated Chip Z'Nuff and when my high school friend Kim Coridino managed to book Urge Overkill for her wedding reception at the Tinley VFW and invited me. (Randall had zero interest, so I brought Maggie as my date.) We even brought Sam sometimes when Dolphins Make Me Cry would play at the bowling alley. They played '70s, '80s, and our favorite, '90s covers, and a few precious acoustic originals that were always sappy ballads. And we loved it all… the music, the vibe, the fun lights, the random run-ins with people we used to know…

And because we were 20-somethings, we also loved the drama.

There was *always* drama.

Usually, there was an obnoxious fan and a jealous girlfriend. Sometimes, because we were all so young (even the band members), there was a drunk parent and a lot of embarrassment. Occasionally, the band and the venue management would have a public feud. But the best drama was between people in the bands, and best when they were in the same band, and bonus when they acted out on stage.

We saw the most of Dolphins Make Me Cry because Maggie, whose marriage to my brother was doomed from the start, had a huge crush on the drummer. And one crazy February night, when we were all literally dying from Seasonal Affective Disorder and cabin fever and sheer twenty-somethingness, Maggie was part of the drama when said drummer's girlfriend found her shooting lemon drops with him between sets, and well, swapping lemon slices in a most inappropriate manner. It continued even after Maggie walked away and sat in a dark corner with me and Randall, who had serendipitously accompanied us that night. He was giving her the disapproving stink eye and giving me the "I can't believe I let you drag me to this nonsense" eye when the lead singer introduced "Cherry Pie" by saying, "This one is for all our groupies. But especially for one in particular. Frankie asked us to go ahead and change the words."

And they proceeded to play it, but replacing "Cherry" with "Lemon," and that same drummer's girlfriend, Missy Mulvihill, who unbeknownst to Maggie, had been one of my coolest and best buddies in high school, ended up onstage, hitting him in the head with her Doc Marten, repeatedly.

At that point, Randall grabbed Maggie's arm and basically dragged her out of Sound Waves, trusting me to trail behind, which I did, while laughing hysterically.

Not long after, we moved to South Carolina, and everything changed. I hadn't thought about *bands* in literal decades, but when I got home from Brittney's, Paul was home from golf and freshly showered (the *best* smell in one's post-freshly-bathed-baby years is Freshly Showered Husband) and ready to *do* something. I was honestly a little exhausted from cooking for Brit and the tearoom all morning and sort-of, kind-of helping her move all afternoon, but his enthusiasm was sweetly contagious.

"Johnny has seen them a few times," he said, referring to both his coffee shop friend and The Salty Lips. "Says they're really good, and they play some real music. Not just your '90s crap."

"How *dare* you?" I said, swatting at him from my station at the kitchen table. I looked at my phone and then outside, in the early-spring bewilderment that it could be after dinnertime and still light outside. "I need to shower or something first."

He leaned down and nuzzled his face right into my neck (*Ew.* I had been so sweaty), planting a few kisses there before standing at attention. "You're so foxy." I giggled. "But go. Get ready. Maybe we can even dance a little."

"Who *are* you?" I said, rising quickly before he changed his mind. We had danced exactly twice in our history – at our wedding and at his daughter Julie's wedding. We danced more at hers than we did at ours. I guess in some ways, it had been a happier and more carefree occasion. She had boycotted ours. By the time hers came around, we were actually friends, and our blended family felt less like oil and water and more like… a protein shake with banana and kale. If you know, you know.

"Mmm. Just a happy man." He kept me from heading upstairs to our bathroom, his hands on my hips and his mouth covering mine. He must have had a really great golf game.

I let him linger for a minute. And then I let him follow me upstairs. The band didn't start until later, and we had absolutely no reason to hurry.

"I wonder if I will ever not feel guilty asking Travis to babysit," Abby said. She had called at just the right time, and Paul didn't seem to mind *too* much that two members of our brood had come along with us. It was pretty typical.

"No," Sam said, just as I said, "Don't. You need it. and they're fine."

"Cali is doing all the work anyway," Sam continued. "Guarantee you Travis is playing Call of Duty while she makes Jacob take a bath."

"And Summer narrates," I added.

Everyone could relate to that, as our eleven-year-old granddaughter was transitioning from precocious moppet to a somewhat unpredictably snippy, ferociously smart pre-pubescent. It was wearing on all of us, though her Mimi would never admit it.

"Don't remind him, Mom," Abby said. "He is butting heads with her every *single* day right now."

"She butts heads with me," Sam replied, clutching his beer. "I'm the dad. And I don't like it."

"Aw, poor guy," Paul teased. "Buy him another one, Jess. Sam, old boy, I had three of those. You better get in shape because it's only just beginning."

I laughed my agreement before walking up to the bar to

refill for Sam. Paul must have been feeling some real unity. A recovered alcoholic, he said he didn't mind when the rest of us drank, but he didn't usually encourage it outright. I felt a nagging sense of guilt in my belly and ordered myself a soda, extra lime, hold the vodka.

Truth was, I was exhausted and didn't need it anyway. Getting older sucks, at least some parts of it.

And some parts didn't. I walked back to the table to see my oldest son and my new-ish husband sharing a pile of sloppy tots *and* cat-who-got-canary facial expressions. It was really unfair how they could eat like frat bros and never gain an ounce.

But I loved that they did anything together.

Maggie had told me earlier in the week that I lived a charmed life. I almost hung up on her, but I laughed it off.

In her eyes, I had everything I could have ever asked for. Sam was the product of a one-night-stand I had when I was eighteen, and before his first birthday, Randall had swept into our lives like Cameron Mathison in a Hallmark movie and rescued us, marrying me, adopting Sam, moving us to the beach, giving me the girls and David.

And I had over thirty-five years of marriage to him. It's not like he was stolen from me on our honeymoon or left me with four kids to raise. We had a whole life together. I could see how Maggie, whom my brother had completely abandoned when her children were quite young, didn't see how I could ever ask for anything more than what I had. And the truth was, I didn't ask for it. It just happened. Paul happened. The great blending happened. Maybe I didn't deserve it, but I sure as hell was going to savor and protect every piece of it.

If it meant my life was charmed because my first-born, formerly illegitimate son was bonding with my new husband, so be it.

"Is Brittney supposed to be here?" Abby asked me.

"She's here," Sam answered. "I just saw her bring Elliot a beer before they started muttering Nirvana lyrics." He rolled his eyes, always more of a country music fan.

"Does she just hang out backstage?"

"You're such an old lady," I laughed. "There isn't a backstage."

Abby sneered. "Then where is she? Surely, she knows we're here."

"Why are you getting so offended? This is her territory. We are probably cramping her style."

"Her territory?" I asked Sam. "We lived here first. Remember that little party we threw here last summer?" I was referring to our awesome, amazing, breakfast-for-dinner, beach-casual, fairy-tale beach wedding reception, right here on this deck.

"Mom. Brittney doesn't want us in her social life." Sam looked at Abby then. "And just because you two are in cahoots with Mikayla all the time doesn't mean she wants to be part of it. Come on."

The silence was awkward for a moment. Sam had just called me out on one of my biggest personality quirks, those same *fluid boundaries* that Paul had mentioned, the desire for approval and harmony and togetherness I always wanted for our family.

"Don't count it out," Paul murmured, with just enough volume to be heard over the driving guitar of "All Apologies." "Let us not forget Julie 'Exhibit A' Jameson-Murray, who texted me and *apologized* that she and Robin couldn't make it tonight."

Wisely, Sam showed concession with a silent nod and a big gulp. The guys were changing songs, and "More than Words" seemed like a good signal for dancing.

"Brit. Brit!" She turned around. "Hey! We're gonna go."

"Oh. You sure? Their second set is, you know, straight fire."

We both rolled our eyes.

"I'm sure. We will catch it another time, though. I gave it my all today." I hugged her loosely, fighting my incessant urge to hang on.

"Mama…"

"Yeah, Baby?" Paul was already outside, and the strains of "Sweet Caroline" on the jukebox were making me twitchy.

"Thank you for today." She hugged me in her fierce way, nearly cracking my spine for the second time that day and hanging on as long as I wanted to.

"Anything for you, Brit." I brushed a strand of hair from her face and left her to the last set.

Brittney

"You want some help with that?"

Brittney had been watching from the bar, in dazed and buzzed amusement and wonder as El and the band broke down their equipment. It was during this phase of the night that all their personalities came out. Mikey, who played the keyboard, was intermittently scarfing down beer and wings and wrapping cords "badly," according to Chris, the bass player, who was trying to both manage and hurry the process. Dave, one of the two guitar players, was sipping the same orange thing he'd been sipping all night and chatting up the bartender, and Geno sporadically joined him at the bar, never walking away without a shot of something and a wink in Brittney's direction. El was being diligent, his best marketing self, talking to random audience members who were hanging around, doing much of the cord-wrapping and speaker-slinging, stealing wings when Mikey wasn't looking, smiling in Brittney's direction. He looked a little bloodshot and over it, which was why she'd hopped down from the stool and tried to engage his drummer by asking, "Can I help with this?"

"If you want," Ringo mumbled back. It might have been a mumble. It may have been a grunt. Brittney studied him as he bent over the disassembled drum kit. The audience had gone bonkers for him on "Give It Away," especially when he took over vocals for one of the verses. And two women were actually in tears during the encore song, "My Hero." They waited for him as soon as it was over. Brittney watched as he nonchalantly flipped his black braids over his bare and muscled shoulder, said approximately two words, and turned back to his kit to start breaking down. He was the human equivalent of a shrug.

So she shrugged back, then started putting the bars into the bag lying next to them. She was sort of afraid to ask if she was doing it right. She was also hoping they could just hurry and finish because she had walked there, and El was her ride, and she was done.

When the pile was piled, Ringo muttered a dismissive "Thanks," but she dutifully followed him as he took a first load to his stickered-up, very rock and roll… Chrysler minivan. Brittney giggled, but he didn't notice.

When she returned to the stage, El was waiting for her.

"I figured since you were my roomie, you might not want to be my roadie anymore," he smiled.

She wiped a little sweat from her neck. May was escorting in all the coastal humidity. "Never. It's my cardio. If I throw some drums around, it's strength work, too."

"Not my drums." They turned around as Ringo was grabbing another load, not looking at them, but nearly grinning.

"I didn't think he smiled," Brittney whispered.

"Like once a week, I think, so be honored."

El took over carrying stuff. Brittney nursed one Tito's and soda at the bar, with Mikey and Geno intermittently keeping her company. It looked like the end of the day was in sight and then—

"Can you get up and help me get this shit put away already?"

Everyone turned and looked as a red-faced Chris slammed his guitar case shut.

"What's the problem, man?" El asked, motioning with his hands to keep the volume low.

"I'm sick of this shit," Chris said, not quietly. "Those two dick around at every practice and every gig and then we wonder why we can't ever get those Nirvana transitions right."

Dave looked up from his conversation and called, "We can't get it right because you're blitzed before we ever start."

Brittney snorted. Mikey and Geno had gotten up to close the circle. There weren't a lot of patrons left and the jukebox was loud enough, but—

"Not the time or place," El said, his voice much more stern than usual.

"Then when is?" Chris snapped. "It's embarrassing what happened tonight."

"This is embarrassing." That was Ringo.

"Let's talk about it tomorrow," Mikey said.

"Nah, we can handle it now," Geno said. "Chris, you weren't even at the last practice, and you skipped out early the one before that. Why do you think you get to have a beef now?"

"We've been playing that medley for a year. One practice didn't ruin it."

"You're right. Bad attitudes can ruin it though," El said.

"My attitude? Look at these two... and Father

Time over there drinking his Kool Aid. Nobody takes this seriously."

"Drama at a venue isn't professional, Chris."

"Missing a whole damn song in a medley we've done eight hundred times isn't professional either. "

"We're done here," El insisted.

Chris still held a handful of chords, and at that moment, he threw them right at El's face.

F-F-S. The Oakley family motto flashed like a neon sign in Brittney's head as she watched. El had a hand to his face but was bucking up to strike back. Mikey was holding him by the shoulders. Ringo and Geno had Chris by his arms. Dave had risen from the bar and went from looking mellow to menacing in a matter of seconds. Brittney couldn't discern all the shouts and cussing as Chris bucked back and freed himself, but it all ended when Ringo's fist connected with Chris' jaw.

"ENOUGH!" Whew. Ringo had gone from being sullen to a little scary. Brittney had not witnessed such an impressive whisper-yell since her mama brought her, Mikayla, David, and Travis to a meeting with her publisher about 20 years before.

Chris must have felt it too because he just stopped struggling. Geno had his arms again. El was seething. Dave had already walked toward Cody, the manager on duty, to try and mitigate the aftermath. Hopefully, there wouldn't be one.

"Go home." El said. "We're done. Not just for tonight. We are *done.*"

"No shit," Chris said. Geno reluctantly released him, and he turned to Ringo. "I see you again, your ass is done. You got me?" He continued with a litany of names, most of them racially charged. At that point, Cody yelled for him to get the eff out or he was calling the cops.

"Take my truck," El said, walking to Brittney and pressing his keys into her hand. "I gotta take care of this mess."

"I can wait…"

"Nah. It's gonna be a while. We're supposed to gig tomorrow. I don't know what we do without a bass."

"Can I help?"

"You already did. Go get some sleep. Make sure you lock my doors, though, and back up toward the cameras. I probably won't unload the equipment tonight."

Brittney waved in the general direction of the band and walked a bit reluctantly to El's Ram. Truth was, it was the most exciting night she'd had in a while.

～～～

The house was so quiet. Brittney was used to it from living alone, but she didn't know where anything was. She contemplated how ridiculous it was that they hadn't hung out at the house more often. It was three blocks from the beach, spacious, basically perfect. It was a family house, bought by his late grandma, passed down to his dad and his aunts, who all lived Away (the official location name for anything that wasn't the beach). El kept saying it would get sold one day, and he'd be living in a van down by the river. She didn't know if that was true or not, but he was definitely blasé about everything except for the fact that he lived at the beach for the cost of utilities, taxes, and (albeit sky-high) insurance.

It took her a good ten minutes to figure out the TV. Why did boys always have such complicated setups? She had a 32" flat screen and a Fire stick and lived happily ever after with her rotating playlist of all the *Criminal Minds* iterations and *New Girl*. Jess was just getting Nick settled into the chair at the gynecologist's office when El returned.

"I'm impressed you figured this out," he said, flinging himself on the loveseat. "Can we eat your mom's food?"

That's when she noticed that Ringo and Geno were behind him. Well, someone had to bring him home.

"It's super late to eat."

No one was impressed with her answer. There was a beeline for the fridge.

She sighed and followed them. There was unceremonious yanking and uncovering and forks going into the containers that hadn't been emptied that afternoon. Damn them if they didn't find the curried chicken salad Mama had hidden behind the milk.

"Geno, if I knew you were going to be here so much, you could have moved in, and I could have stayed where I was."

El widened his eyes at her as his mouth was too full to speak. Ringo made some sort of "ooooh" sound from behind closed lips, and Geno chewed methodically and stared at her before answering.

"Don't be a douchebag, Brittney."

Everyone went quiet for a second. The other guys were looking at her, and she was not going to satisfy them by volleying back an insult, although she had plenty for this middle-aged, beer-bellied guitarist whose wife kicked him out after twenty years of marriage. Brittney wanted her home. That was *her home.*

But she just laughed. And then they all laughed. *Douchebag* was a juvenile term, and, therefore, unexpectedly funny, and no one, not even El, needed to know how alien she felt in this house that was supposed to be... her new *home.*

"C'mon. There's been enough drama for one night," El said.

"Fine. But my mom isn't cooking for the band, okay?

She gets one hint of this, and she'll be catering all your shows and your rehearsals. It's just the sort of ego-love-boost that powers her engines."

"Then why wouldn't you want her to know that I love this chicken salad more than I loved my first two wives?"

Those were the most words she'd ever heard Ringo say.

"First two? How many have you had?"

"Two." He was back to grunting and spreading her mama's masterpiece on a second croissant.

"Whatever. I'm going to bed."

"Brit. Wait—"

"What?"

El looked a bit remorseful.

"Well, we can talk about it tomorrow. But we fired Chris—"

"You didn't fire him. That piece of shit quit!" Geno mocked.

"Shut up. Anyway, I already reached out to a backup bass player."

"Okay…" *Who cares?* Well, she did care a little, but not at two in the morning.

"I just… well… he might need a place to stay."

"Okay…" she repeated, struck dumb as a box of rocks. And then she remembered. There was a spare bedroom, and it was on the other side of her door, and her sense of solitude and even autonomy was growing sparser by the moment.

"I don't…" There was literally nothing she could say. He was asking her for four hundred meager dollars a month to live in a big, beautiful house by the ocean. He could put an escaped convict in there if he wanted to. Or Ace of Base. Or Courtney Friggin' Love.

"Yeah. Tell me about it tomorrow. Good night, you guys. Great gig."

There were muffled goodbyes in between all the chewing, and El slugged her playfully on the arm as she walked past him. She closed the door and stripped down to her bra and threw on a pair of gym shorts, and she could still hear their animated conversation, even with Candlebox whisper-singing in her Beats. El, like her mama, like her siblings, was surrounded by people and plans and his unique brand of drama.

It was not where she used to be, or what she ever thought she wanted. She shut her eyes in her strange new bedroom. The setting reminded her of being little, before David was born when she didn't share a room with Mikayla. Sometimes her parents would have game nights and stay up late and make them go to bed. They never wanted to, of course, so for Brittney's part, she used to creep out to the hallway and sit and listen. Grown-ups talked about a lot of different things when the kids weren't around, like what the pastor was preaching that they didn't like, or what couple from the neighborhood was getting divorced. Mama sometimes said mean things about Aunt Maggie's ex husband; since he was her brother, she usually didn't do that in front of the kids. How could she if she was going to make them be nice to each other?

One time Daddy caught her in the hallway, but instead of her getting in trouble, he scooped her up in his arms and brought her back to bed. She was crying, saying it was unfair that they got to stay up and have fun – Sam even got to play – while all she and Mikayla got to do was sleep.

That's when Daddy told her a secret: he didn't even like game nights. He kept walking to their bedroom to check the score of the Illini basketball game. Mama always made his favorite snack foods to convince him to participate. He told Brittney that as soon as she was old enough, he would go to bed and she could take his place for Catch Phrase,

Skip-O, and Rummikub.

"But only if you keep our secret now, okay, Baby?" He switched off the lamp.

"Why would I tell your secret when you're keeping one for me? Mama would be so mad if she knew I heard that story about Uncle Tony."

Daddy had bit his lip, and only later did Brittney realize he was trying not to laugh. "You're right. All our secrets are safe with each other."

She nodded and let him pull the covers up to her chin how she liked and kiss her forehead. "Good night, Daddy."

"Love you, Firecracker."

She had lain there feeling a little more satisfied, a little excited. Maybe things were boring and unfair now, but Daddy was out in the kitchen with her best interests at heart. Life would get better.

So maybe this wasn't so different. El saw her and knew her, and she was safe with him. It wasn't where she wanted to be, but it didn't have to be where she stayed.

She looked at the picture beside her bed of her and Daddy when she was pretty close to that same age. He was holding her, and she was wearing some pastel frock Mama had made her wear to church, along with his Titans hat, backwards. She was scowling, probably because of said dress, and Daddy was laughing.

"Good night," she said, partly to Daddy, partly to El, partly to herself as a reminder: *Life would get better.*

Brittney

"Brit! You up?"

Someone was knocking on her door, but she'd already told Mama she wasn't going to church. She had to get everything organized before going back to work Monday because –

Oh yeah. She moved. And that was El's voice on the other side of the door.

She sat up and gave her hair a quick tousle and her eyes a quick wipe. He'd seen her in worse condition before.

"Yep. Come in."

He was wearing his band uniform of black jeans and black t-shirt. This one was Foo Fighters. *Hm, aren't those last night's clothes?* He sat at the foot of her bed, and she decided he probably hadn't gone to his own.

"Wow."

"Leave me alone," he said as he relaxed into a recumbent position.

"How can I help? I'm totally, one hundred percent energized."

"Shut up, liar." He sat back up. "Brit, we need to talk."

Her whole body shifted into panic mode. She felt her heart beat faster; she got goosebumps on her arms; and her head thumped. *I don't want to live with Mama and Paul. I don't want to live with Kayla. I can get a second job bartending. I can get a third job writing essays for college kids. Shit!*

"What's up?" she said, smiling wanly, sounding calm.

"You are so completely insane," he said. His brown eyes crinkled into a smile, their familiar sweetness signaling safety. He moved and sat next to her and pressed into her side, an armless hug that was like their secret handshake. "Stop vibrating like a maniac. I'm not asking you to leave. You can stay here forever if you want."

"Okay." She nodded, hating the wavering in her voice. "Thank you. But what's up?"

El sighed. He definitely had a flair for the dramatic, which was part of their eternal bond. Was someone pressing charges over last night? And if so, what did that have to do with her?

"We have a gig at Blitzburgh today..."

"Yeah." She nodded her head to illustrate that she was, in fact, still cognizant of actual life. He had shows on a lot of Sundays. She went to at least half of them. "Do you need a roadie for real? I can skip the gym today." She had zero intention of going to the gym. Or the show. There was supper at Mama's today.

"No. And whatever. I know exactly what you're doing today. Please bring leftovers home."

"For Geno? Not happening"

"Brit." His voice changed to serious. "I called two other bass players last night. And then I called my brother."

"Okay... *Oh.*"

"Yeah."

"And how was that?" She craned her neck to look fully at him. His eyes showed no signs of sleep and plenty of anxiety.

"How you'd expect… But he's coming. He just…"

Brittney eyed the door that led to the extra bedroom. "He needs a place to stay."

She couldn't see him nod, but she felt it. Devoid of words, she blew some raspberries.

"Oh my God." El had erupted in sardonic laughter. "I'm so sorry, Brit. Tell me how I can make this work."

"What are you talking about? It's your house. He's your brother. I mean, I can go—"

"No, no! Brit—"

He jumped off the bed and dashed out of the room.

"Just tell me!" she called after him.

She flung herself out of the bed and went to the bathroom, brushing her teeth as though the harder she scrubbed the clearer her next move would be. There was only one, and that was down the street to her mother's. At thirty-one years old. *Dammit.*

There are worse safety nets.

Now is not the time, Daddy.

She'll always have a place for you. It's only weird if you make it weird.

He was wrong. Living with Mama and Paul at this juncture would be *totally* weird, especially since Julie had just done it last fall, and Katy did it practically once a month, and David was just a matter of time.

"Brit! Come out of there!"

She spit, rinsed, and opened the door.

"Calm down, bruh. I was just making my toilet."

"You're so dumb. Here."

He shoved a mug of coffee at her. "I should have started with this."

"Oh, good Lord, El. What did you put in here?"

"Just a little Baileys."

"Ew. Here—" She handed it back to him. "I don't need a drink, bestie. It's fine. My mom has that whole apartment. It won't even take me the whole day to get all my stuff together."

"Brittney, what are you talking about?"

"I can't stay here with your brother."

"He's staying here with us. I want you here."

She sighed. Reason and kindness coupled were a big trump card. "You can't say no to him if he needs a place. And you need a bass player."

"And I need my best friend. We'll figure it out. Drink the coffee."

"El." She took the mug back from him and inhaled the steam. "Why is this necessary? You know I like my coffee black as my soul." She took a swig. It actually wasn't bad.

"If you're as badass as you want to be, you can handle my stupid brother sleeping in the room next door."

She felt a heavy pit form in her stomach.

"Brit." *Listen to him,* Daddy's voice said. "Brittney!"

"El…"

"You know, right? I would never let anything happen to you. And I won't ask you to do something that freaks you out. He can sleep on the couch. Or in my room. Or you can sleep in my room."

"Or I can just go to my mom's!"

"You are so stubborn! Hey, can *he* stay at your mom's?"

Brittney paused. One of the greatest tricks she learned from her father – and from about a year of karate lessons when she was eight years old and had energy her mama needed her to burn – was the pause. *Stop. I'm too angry to talk. Stop. I need to cool down. Stop. I need you not to talk so that I can listen to my thoughts.*

The problem with pausing was it got too quiet, and quiet made her squirm. El was looking at her like he expected a real answer to his foolish question. He looked as muddled as she felt, and she kind of wanted to reach out and ruffle his dark hair, maybe even cup his chiseled jaw with her hand. But that's not how they rolled. It would be weird.

"El, Jessie would say yes. But I'm not asking her that. If someone's going to stay there, it will be me."

Embarrassment flashed across his face, and without looking back at her, he repeated, "I don't want you to go."

She made her way back to her bed, which at least felt normal with her own perfectly soft old sheets and pile of fleece blankets and the weathered quilt and, possibly, her stuffed Grinch tucked under all of that. She sat criss-cross-applesauce and took a long drink from her mug.

Just like she needed El, he needed her.

They were each other's person.

And maybe El's brother was like him. Maybe they would be fun roommates. Or at least, maybe it wouldn't be so bad. Moving out after a day would be bad. Asking Mama for one more thing would be bad.

There. That felt like a productive pause.

"Let's just give it a try and see what happens."

Relief washed over El's face.

"He's supposed to get here in a few hours. We set up at four. We will make things work. I promise."

Brittney managed a confident-sounding laugh. "You can't promise that. You can only promise to try."

He shrugged.

"I have a few hours," Brittney offered. "Want help getting that room cleared out?"

"I was maybe gonna take a nap."

She shook her head incredulously. "Is he gonna sleep on that horrible futon? Aren't you going to move all the random crap out of there?"

El was starting to turn in other direction. "I'm tired. And anyway, he likes to do things himself."

Brittney paused thoughtfully. She knew this was fragile ground to tread, but she decided to try anyway. "El, are you… happy he's coming? Or at least maybe hopeful? I know you always say you two don't have a brotherly relationship—"

"We don't." Every ounce of playfulness was gone from his voice.

"Then why? I mean, bass players are a dime a dozen in this town."

"Yeah. If they play the same thirty beach-party songs or southern rock anthems. I need STP, not Skynyrd."

Brittney stopped herself from rolling her eyes.

"It just seems like… maybe this will be a good opportunity to work on whatever went wrong. He must care if he's dropping everything to come play… and stay."

El fully rolled his eyes. "Not happening, Brit. Let it go. Your Jessie is showing, and you can't fix this."

The bustle at Mama and Paul's was a little subdued for a change. Paul's oldest daughter and her family weren't there, and Summer, typically Brittney's stalwart sidekick and foil, was at a church thing. The guys were entrenched in some baseball game, except for Altan, who was sitting in the kitchen with her, Mikayla, Abby, and Julie while they watched Jessie swat them away and finish her preparations.

"How's the house, Brit?" Abby asked, pretending to be more absorbed in the spinach artichoke dip than she was on the answer.

Brittney suppressed a laugh. Her family failed at *subtle*. "It's a great location." Let them try harder.

Mikayla chimed in, while seemingly hyper-focused on toddler Josie, who was playing with a pile of Tupperware lids on the floor. "Is your room big enough for all your stuff, or are you like, spilling out into the rest of the house?"

Altan caught Brittney's eye with a twinkle in his own. Mikayla had been teaching yoga during the move, while Josie had stayed with Abby, and clearly, he was basking in the one-upmanship of being the only sibling present to have seen her new place.

Brittney shrugged and took a long sip of her Bubly. "It all fits. I mean, El wouldn't mind if *I spilled out* into the rest of the house, but it's all furnished. And it's not like I'm staying forever. And no, that is not an invitation to ask me what my plans are. Beyond whatever Mama takes out of that oven and a media preview for Gabe the Wacky Tacky Magician, I don't have any. Other than I hate Cristina, and she told me I was toeing the line of casual when I wore a freaking jean skirt on Friday."

"She's the worst. That skirt is *adorable*," Jessie said. "But the band was a lot of fun last night." She was whipping potatoes with the same forced nonchalance on her face.

"Yes, Mama." Brittney nodded emphatically. "They were… What else you got?"

"Oh, come on!" Mikayla finally said to her. "Give us *something*. How is it? How do you feel?"

"Baby Cheesus on a cracker! I feel fine. El is fine. It's weird. He couldn't be more welcoming or accommodating or a better friend. It's just weird. I know you guys don't get it, but I could have stayed where I was forever. I was happy. So I just need a minute to get used to it."

She looked pointedly at Mikayla and Abby, who were

shoulder-to-shoulder across from her. "And I'm not hiding anything. Come over whenever you want. It's just a beach house. It looks like it probably did twenty years ago when El's grandma and aunts decorated everything. And my bedroom is almost the size of the trailer, so it looks like… it looks like my home did. Thanks to Altan." She winked at her brother-in-law. Could this conversation be over now?

"But," Julie's voice chimed in from next to Brittney. "Are you *good*, Brittney?" She leaned in dramatically, staring Brittney in the eyes. "Are you going to be *okay* there? Do you need some freezer meals or a group hug or something?"

Brittney laughed and rolled her eyes. Julie was the newest convert to the family philosophy of oversharing. She had reluctantly joined Sunday suppers with her new husband Robin, and because Paul and Jessie were so excited to have the last holdout of their kids actually blending in, she got away with the abject teasing.

"I *feel* happy, but I would actually *be* happy if Mama's ginormous pan of meat was out of the oven already."

Apparently satisfied for a moment, Abby and Mikayla commenced their own conversation. Julie looked warily in the direction of Jessie and asked more quietly, "Do you know what she's making? I'm starving."

Brittney sniffed the air. "Lamb, maybe? Hell if I know. Hold on."

She made a beeline for the refrigerator, which was right next to the oven. While Mama was whipping away, now with Josie on her hip, she peered inside. Ah. It was a turkey. For good measure, she grabbed another Bubly and walked it over to Julie.

"Leave it to my mama to cook a Thanksgiving dinner in May."

"It's turkey? Also, can I have this?"

Brittney handed her the can. She wasn't used to so much direct attention from Julie. Her twin, Katy, who had always been Brittney's friend, had become a much closer one since… the thing… that ended up making them all family. Julie stayed away for a lot of it, moving to Arizona… *with Brittney's baby brother David.* What a disaster that had been. David hadn't lasted out there long, and when Julie decided to move back home, it had been with her tail tucked between her legs, humiliation, secrets, and plenty of bitterness.

And here she was with a career change, a sunnier outlook, and a hot, if slightly broody, husband. It gave Brittney a bit of hope.

"How's married life?" she asked awkwardly.

Julie finished a long drink. "So weird." *Word du jour.* "I love it. All the togetherness. We're at work together most days." Robin, now *they*, owned a running store in Myrtle Beach. "We even drive together. I just… never get sick of him. And when I do, one of us goes for a run, and it's all better. I don't get it. Also, I really, really like all the money we save on rent."

Brittney nearly spit out her own drink. "I appreciate the honesty!" she laughed. They went on talking about a Chamber of Commerce event they were both attending the next week. *Tra-la-la.*

Then Brittney looked over and caught Mama's eye. In the time it had taken her to agree to train for some 5k with Julie, Mama had taken out the turkey and adorned the counter around it with all the fixings. She was standing there holding Josie, who was getting woozy, and smiling at all of them. Brittney got up and walked to her side.

"You and your cutesy little heart, Mama."

Mama, who was about three inches shorter, lay her head on Brittney's shoulder for just a moment. "Sometimes, babe, I can't even believe my eyes." Brittney filled in all the blanks… the different kitchen, the different combination of people, the fact that their two families were now one, and all the complicated feelings that came with it. Brittney had doubled her number of sisters. And she liked that.

But she would trade all that particular joy to have her daddy back. And she knew Mama loved Paul, and he was good for her, but she wondered sometimes how in the world they could reconcile it all.

Jessie

Nothing makes me feel happier than affection from my children and my own homemade turkey gravy. I was savoring one and inhaling the other. Brittney had her arm around me tightly for a moment. She had been taller than me since middle school, so I finally got used to being the one in our relationship who lays a head on a shoulder. It was strange, like apparently everything else according to Brittney, and also, even though she was a girl on fire and all, sometimes I just wanted to gather her up like a baby and hold her.

I settled for this, Josie sleepily nestled against my shoulder, and Brittney now stroking the back of her littlest niece. Well, Josie was sort of her littlest niece because Paul's oldest, Danielle, had given birth to Lexie just a few months before, and as far as I knew, as far as it concerned all of Paul's and my grandkids, the kids didn't make distinctions between *real* and *step*.

I did. God, I did. It surprised even me. Lexie was Danielle's third baby. Her first was Christian, who was four when *the thing* happened. He'd had a real relationship and memories with his grandma Leah, Paul's first wife. Her second child, Vivi, had only been an infant when Leah died. Danielle had let me in because she was a young mama and overwhelmed and wanted a grandma for her babies. But the birth of Lexie was different and sacred. I didn't camp out at the hospital like I did when Abby and Mikayla had their babies. I tried not to offer too much advice or ask too many questions. When I brought food to the house, I made sure Paul was with me and didn't stay too long. I could vividly remember becoming a mama of three. The transition was tough, so I tried not to take any perceived distance personally, though that was against my very nature.

Josie was falling asleep, and supper was ready, so I handed her to Brit, scooted Dolly into the laundry room for a spell, and commenced the opening ceremonies.

Paul was crammed into our "cousin nook" with Sam, Travis, Jacob, and Robin. It was a room without doors in the center of the house, between the stairs and the laundry room, that housed bunk beds, the biggest TV we could fit, and several gaming consoles. They were standing there almost shoulder-to-shoulder playing something with Mario Brothers, loud as all get out.

Since my husband didn't have a controller in his hand, I was safe to put my hand on his shoulder. He turned at the touch and smiled fully at me.

"Ready, Babe?"

I nodded, basking.

"It smells amazing," he murmured, planting a kiss near my ear. Then, more loudly, he said, "Alright guys. The bird is cooked! Lesseat!"

The perfect chaos then ensued, as it did two or three

Sundays a month. It used to happen every Sunday, but the weeklies fell into the "used to" column after Paul and I got married, and I was promptly diagnosed with stage two endometrial cancer. I tried to act like everything was fine, but Paul's powers of persuasion eventually convinced me I didn't have to pretend, not with him or the kids.

But dang it, when it was my turn to host, I was gonna bring it. I took my regular position at one end of the counter and watched a strong representation of our blended brood pile their platters high with turkey, mashed potatoes, sweet potato soufflé, garlic green beans, deviled eggs, and cranberry-orange relish… and gravy, all the gravy.

"Mama, eat." Sam was next to me, one full plate in his hand while he nudged an empty one into mine. I turned to smile at him but noticed the dark circles under his eyes. We talked every single day, but Sam was definitely my quiet one, and it dawned on me that he'd been quieter than usual of late.

"You wanna eat with me on the porch?" I asked, taking a smaller spoonful of potatoes than I really wanted.

He gave me a smile. "Sure. Just take more now, so you won't have to get up mid-story to come get seconds. You'd never make it back out."

I accepted my defeat by taking another scoop. Paul winked in my direction as my eldest and I headed outside.

The second half of May was steadily escorting in summer weather. The A/C had been running for a week. The end of year school bustle was in full swing for Sam's younger two, Summer and Jacob. His oldest, Travis, had just finished his second semester at the tech college. Soon the streets would be congested with RVs, Slingshots, and northeasterners who weren't sure where to turn to get to their ice cream shop or golf cart rental store of choice. We had also made it through another of Randall's birthdays without him.

Sam and I took appreciative bites in silence. We could hear the chatter from inside the house (the neighbors likely could as well) and the lazy, inconsistent song of the wind chimes. As I wondered how pomegranate would taste in the relish, he broke the silence.

"I'm not trying to hide anything from you, Mama."

He was not prone to drama, so my heart started racing a bit. "Okay…"

"I just…" He put his plate on the ground and sighed.

"Sam, you know you can tell me anything. Anything." *Oh Lord. Please don't let him be sick. Please don't let him be cheating on Abby. Please don't let them be moving away. In that order.*

"It's not any one thing, not really." *Oh, thank God.* "Dad's birthday… well, it was harder this year for some reason." *Great, Jess. So much for getting through it.* "And the fact that it was harder surprised me. Kinda knocked it outta me, to be honest with you."

"Oh, Sam. I'm so sorry. I'm sorry I didn't—"

"Mama. Please. You didn't know because I didn't want you to know. I'm a grown man. I have Abby. You don't have to fix things for me."

I swallowed hard. It was still disarming how well my grown children knew me, anticipated what I would say or how much I wanted more mashed potatoes than what I put on my plate.

"I never want you to think I don't see your grief," I said carefully. "I wasn't the only one who lost him."

When my own father had died, my mom had, understandably, been enveloped in her loss. My parents were a twosome. It wasn't that they didn't love my brother and me, but especially once we had left home, they were perfectly content being just the two of them. There was no busy social life, no need to find hobbies or host or go. And without my dad, she was lost. And when he died, she didn't see that I had lost him, too.

It was one of those things I vowed to do differently. I just never thought the opportunity to do so would have presented itself so soon.

Sam was looking away from me, but I could still see the tears collecting in his eyes. "Mama. Please." He ran his hands over his face. "No one ever doubts you're here for us. I don't. You just can't ever be him. No one can."

He didn't mean anything by that other than exactly what he said. But guilt immediately punched me in the gut. There was never a single moment I wished for my kids to look at Paul like a dad. Even though we celebrated the family blend, that particular role was sacred. Paul would be by my side, and he would be there if any of them needed something, but it was not the same. We all accepted that.

I still wanted to fill the gaping hole I saw.

"Is there…?" I didn't even know how to ask. I understood in that I had also buried a father. We had not been close like Sam and Randall. But a daddy is a daddy, and your daddy being in the world was an anchor, and I hated that his anchor was missing. "Is there a reason why it was harder?" I was quick to add, "There doesn't need to be a reason. I'm just asking."

When he looked back at me, there was a smile in his eyes. "Don't panic. You're allowed to ask." He waited several beats, and I knew he was contemplating whether or not to tell me.

"Sometimes, Mama, I just think about leaving."

What? That was about the last thing I expected him to say. He and Abby were happy. Weren't they? They'd been through their share in the past two years, Sam losing his dad and Abby losing her mom. Both of them had estates of which they were the executors. Abby bought the business with me and completely changed her career and their family rhythm. They had three kids running in different directions. Had the stress been so bad he just didn't want it anymore?

I opened my mouth, but Sam stopped me. "Not Abby, Mama. God bless it, you were writing an entire novel in your head. No. Just *here*. Moving from here. New scenery. Fresh start."

I swallowed. David, my other son, my youngest child, was still living in Tennessee. He had been gone nearly two years, and even though he was finally settled and thriving, I hated him being away. Hated it. How could Sam go, too? And Abby, who might as well be mine? And their babies? Travis was mostly grown, but Summer and Jacob were my sidekicks every Tuesday night and—

"Mama! Stop!"

I dramatically shook my head to clear it and look him in the eyes. "Sorry. Can't help it. Fill in some blanks, then, so I don't have to."

"I don't have any. I need you to believe me on this one. There is nothing specific wrong and nothing to fix. I just *feel* unhappy. I know we are fine. The kids are healthy and happy. Abby loves doing the tearoom. And..." He looked away again. "Parents die. It didn't just happen to Abby and me. I just feel so... heavy... all the time."

Oh, Sam. I didn't say anything. I *could* actually fill in all those blanks, with memories of staring down a fortieth birthday and feeling like something was missing. For me, it had been purpose; it was before I started working with Paul and writing curriculum. I wasn't sure what it was for Sam.

"We will all help you until it feels a little lighter." I squeezed his hand. "Maybe I can keep the kids, so you and Abby can get away for a few days?"

He smiled, but defeatedly so. "If Abby isn't here, how are you gonna keep up with the kids and run the tearoom alone? The point isn't to make things harder on someone else so they're easier for me."

"Oh, for crying out loud, Sam. Are we talking three or four days or a month? I can handle two children. Paul is here."

"Yeah, but the tearoom is a lot, and –"

He stopped short, and I thought he was just not going to argue with me. No way he was going to win. But he was looking up in slight surprise as his Aunt Maggie stormed from her car toward us.

"Mister Sam!" she scolded, taking him in first. "You need a nap." She gave him a small hug and a big kiss on the cheek.

Then she whipped around, her brown eyes blazing at me.

"Are any of your children holing up in the guest suite?"

That could be a trick question. And I wasn't so sure Brittney wasn't going to end up there, but I just shook my head.

"Then take down the shingle, sister," she commanded grandly. "I need a place to stay."

Brittney

Brittney returned home later than she'd intended, not unusual for a Sunday supper. Aunt Maggie's appearance had created a few ripples in the festivities. Normally, a surprise appearance from her would have been like a tidal wave, but today, she'd come in and greeted everyone, grabbed a turkey wing in a napkin, and hightailed it with her suitcase into the guest suite with Mama *and* Paul following her.

Brittney was grateful. Everyone else's smattering of questions was one thing. Aunt Maggie would have expected a dissertation on her living situation, how long she intended to stay, whether she was actually in love with El, because he most certainly was in love or lust with her to make these arrangements, oh, and *who* was this guy moving into a bedroom with a shared door, because surely Brittney would have spilled that tea under the pressure.

Who indeed? She threw a load of laundry into the

washer, conveniently located in the kitchen, because beach houses made that sort of sense, and flopped on the couch. She probably should have been doing something productive to prepare for a busy week, but Mama's leftovers bought her one more night before she had to pretend to think about potentially "meal prepping."

She'd made it through only half an episode of *New Girl* before the door came crashing open.

"Hey Brit!" El's voice was hilariously sunny. She sat up and ruffled her hair, looking warily at him.

"Hey! How was it?"

He ignored her question, setting an armload of equipment on a stool.

"Ew. Summer is clearly here. You stink." She walked over to him, beholding his sweaty head and post-concert-flushed face. "You need anything?"

He grunted, then in walked her new roommate. *Oh, Jesus.* She actually heard Aunt Maggie's voice in her head this time. *Tall, dark, and broody always catches my eye, too, Brit. You get it honest.*

"This is my brother Harry," El mumbled.

"Harrison," the echoing grunt corrected. It came from a truly taller, broader, darker-featured, much less-cheerful looking guy. His brown hair was tied in a ponytail at the nape of his neck with loose, wet waves hanging out, his tan face partially covered in stubble that almost constituted a beard. For a moment, Brittney noticed his gray Sweetwater t-shirt clinging to him, but she shook it off and mustered a smile right at his blank expression.

"Hey Harrison. Good to finally meet you," she said, vocally shrugging. The Mama in her was pressing her to say more, but she knew this type. He wouldn't hear her anyway.

"Nice to meet you," he answered, not looking in her direction but walking through the kitchen toward the hallway. He had two duffels around each shoulder, a guitar case in one hand, an amp in the other. She felt like she was actually on a set of a rock video, and either rain or fire was going to invade the house at any given second.

"Wait for me, Harry," El said, catching up. Brittney giggled. Leave it to a sibling to contradict another person's own name.

The dryer stopped. She needed to put clothes away and probably go to bed because there was an eight o'clock meeting with the mad magician in the morning and even though he would be late, she could not be. Oh no. She was basically in charge of all promotional marketing for Boardwalk Square, which was, in fact, the biggest entertainment complex on the grand strand. That included its live theater, the location of the new magic show. Sigh.

Here it was. She was tiptoeing into her "own" room, not sure what El and Harrison had decided to do.

The shared door was closed, so she dumped out her laundry and hurriedly picked out the pieces she didn't particularly want either of them to see. As she was shoving a handful of panties into a canvas bin on the floor of her closet, the door opened.

Harrison looked fully at her and said, "You can keep the doors locked at night. I'm going to use a ladder and the window if I have to go to bed after you do. Does that work?" The fact that they'd known each other for seventeen seconds did nothing to keep the sarcasm dripping from his voice.

Okay, playa. She shrugged. "Might be kinda hard on you if you need the bathroom in the middle of the night. You got a bucket?"

I see your feeble attempt at intimidation and raise you full stoicism that I can hold all day, every day. I have a hundred siblings, and I will die on this hill.

He surrendered. "I'm not taking my brother's room."

"So don't."

From behind him, El started to chime in, but she cut him off before he could rescue her.

"We've never met. You wanna take one second and see why this arrangement is uncomfortable? I don't want my best friend's brother displaced any more than I want to be. Just chill with the aggression. You literally just made it worse."

El was looking at her with apologies and regret all over his face. Her brain was on rapid-fire, but she didn't have a solution, other than sucking it up and going to sleep in a room she couldn't lock that a stranger could potentially trounce through any time of night.

"I can just sleep on the couch," she finally said.

"Oh, my God," El blurted.

"How is that any different? I still have to *walk past you*." Harrison snapped.

"What difference does it make? You both sleep where you want."

"It makes a difference if I come home at two in the morning with *people*, Brit," El reminded her. "Come on. Just sleep in my bed. I'll crash wherever."

"It's your house!" she insisted.

"No, it's not," Harrison said.

"I'm gonna go for a walk." Brittney almost laughed at her own ridiculous defense mechanism. She didn't walk. Mama did. She stayed and argued, and if not for El, she would have.

"No. *I* am. And I'll sleep on the couch."

Harrison brushed past both of them and glided right out the door.

Brittney looked at El. He looked at his shoes.

"What a long-ass weekend," was all he said.

"I'm sorry..."

"Don't be sorry. If it wasn't for me wanting to fix my stupid band, we wouldn't be having this conversation."

Well, that was true. And she said so. "But your band is your life. And there's probably more to this Harrison stuff anyway, don't you think? You both wouldn't agree to him staying here if it was just for a few gigs a month. That's a pretty dramatic response even for you."

For a second, she thought he was mad, but his mouth turned up from a smile to a full laugh.

"Call him Harry. He's really not a *total* ass." He softened his expression. "I guess I could have found another bass player who didn't need to move in. I just thought maybe, if I saw him, I could..." Brittney had no idea where that sentence was supposed to end. "Anyway, we have to figure out this roommate sitch."

"Don't bat those eyes at me!" Brittney flopped on her bed and felt a familiar sensation come over her. "Just. Whatever. I'm tired. And so are you. I'm not getting into your sibling *ish*. I have enough of my own."

"So, what do you want me to do?"

"Figure it out." She kicked the covers over her feet and pulled them over her legs. "I'm going to sleep."

"Your laundry is all over the bed."

"Very observant," she mumbled. "Tell Harry not to get it dirty when he walks this way."

"I don't get you," El said, turning off the light.

He did though. So, feeling a modicum of peace, Brittney closed her eyes and mumbled, "Good night."

***

Entertainers. Brittney had grown up with a more studious sort. Her dad was a CPA, her mom wrote curriculum. Even though Mama had a hippie-creative side, she was not a performer, and the older Brittney got, the more she figured out that some of her quirkier marching band friends had bigger aspirations, that some of those musicians she dated were intense about everything except her, that often behind a jolly artist or a smoldering one was a depressed human.

Max Wagner ("Magic to the MAX!") was a jolly one until it was time to get serious. Then he was argumentative and impossible. Brittney was spending her first spring as the Assistant Marketing Director for Boardwalk Square, with all its shops, restaurants, kiosks, random kitschy shows. Max had been a sidewalk performer for the past two seasons, and this year, he was being granted a daily matinee at the Boardwalk Theatre.

"You would think he was Criss Angel all of a sudden," Brittney told Mikayla over Marco Polo. "The dude spent the winter heating up cheese sticks at Top Golf, and now he wants catering and laundry service. This is Myrtle Beach, not The Bellagio. Anyway, Cristina holds the budget, so it's her problem now, but I still had to sit and listen to it for a freaking hour and a *half* when my only task was getting a few interviews and pictures scheduled. He's a tool. He won't last the season, and then we're gonna have to scrape the bottom of the barrel to get some lame comedian in there or something."

Uuuuuugh! She tossed the phone onto the seat. Mikayla would be sympathetic, but she didn't get it. She loved her job, teaching yoga part-time at a few different studios and running a water sports rental with Altan. Brittney wished she had the guts to moonlight and be her own business.

Mikayla's response came quickly. She must have been letting Josie watch *Bluey* or something. "Ugh. Doesn't sound like a good match for you at all. You will explode on him any given moment. Um, but Brit, have you talked to Mama since yesterday?"

Sigh. No. What had it been, sixteen hours? Sam and Mikayla were the good children who bugged Mama every morning. She'd been kinda busy figuring out her sleeping arrangements. "What's up?"

"Aunt Maggie is staying."

"Okay. They're kinda overdue for some hijinks, aren't they?"

"No, like she's… *staying.* Indefinitely."

Brittney sighed. She had to get to the office and make sure the press release for Himself's big launch was perfect. And she *really* didn't want to be sucked into anyone else's drama, but if Aunt Maggie was involved, situations were usually irresistible. "What are you talking about? What about Don?"

Less than two years ago, in the great after, their aunt had remarried after many years of being divorced. Mama's brother had unceremoniously abandoned her and their cousins, Nora and Moni, when they were little kids, and only recently had anyone reached some tentative peace with him.

That was a situation only discussed over margaritas.

"She's not sure she wants to be married. That's all Mama would really say."

"That is crazy." She heard the heightened emotion in Mikayla's voice, but she couldn't go there with her. Not today. Actually, she felt immediate kinship with Aunt Maggie. There was a lot to be said for living alone.

Brittney was a wrung-out mess by the time she slogged up El's stairs with a Chipotle bag in one hand and a Sonic Coke (with the best ice) in the other. Mama had given her a full debriefing on the way home, and now she was determined to make this housing situation stick. Her failsafe at Mama's seemed certain to be occupied for a while.

Balancing her dinner, she kicked the door shut behind her. The house was quiet, and it was beautiful – perfectly *May* – outside. Maybe she would change and eat on the porch.

"Wait, what?"

When she walked into her room, all her stuff had been replaced with El's. Everything. Even Altan's meticulously hung shelves were missing from the walls. She walked over to the adjoining room and knocked, and when silence answered, she opened that door. It, too, was transformed, from a catch-all room to a bedroom-office. Everything was gray and masculine and orderly.

"El!" she called, leaving the room, sweating and still packed down like a mule with all of her work stuff and suddenly just wanting to cry in her own shower. "El, what did you do?"

Brittney turned the door of the master bedroom without knocking and he was there, hanging her shelves, a huge, knowing smile across his face.

"I figured forgiveness was easier than permission," he said.

"You didn't have to do this." She blinked back and cursed the tears forming. "This is your *home*."

"It's your home now, too," he answered. "I don't want you to be uncomfortable or afraid. I want you to feel safe."

"I'm just being a baby," she muttered. "He's your brother. If the tables were turned…"

"It doesn't matter. I'm not you. I haven't been through the same things. And he is my brother, but you don't know him, and I barely do anymore. It's all temporary. All of this. Except you and me."

She finally set her stuff on the floor and exhaled. "With all this undying devotion to me, you're never going to find a wife. Or a husband."

"Shut up."

"You want food?"

"You have enough?"

"For a small army," she said. "Of two, anyway."

After Brittney divided her burrito bowl in half, they did sit out on the porch, marveling over entertainers' personalities and how quickly spring was turning into summer.

"We're already booked three weekends a month through September," El said. "I might have to quit my day job soon."

Brittney scoffed. "Right. You can totally live off, what, a hundred bucks a gig? If you're lucky."

"Sometimes it's more," he said, crumpling a napkin and tossing it at her.

"Sometimes it's less. Maybe you should just play the bass yourself and keep the dividend. And actually not be the Chamber's whipping boy anymore."

"You let me know when you want us to start our own thing, and I'm ready. You're the one who keeps doing the same job for different people and expecting it to be different. You're happy for one month, and then you hate it."

"I didn't hate TWL," she muttered. "I would have worked there forever."

"Yeah, well…" What else could he say? Brittney's first real job had been with one of the oldest marketing firms in Myrtle Beach. The hard part about it being old was that she was there for barely two years when the remaining partners, Woody and Lee, decided to retire and shutter the business. "Moving on."

"Maybe you should actually take The Salty Lips full

time, and I could book for you. Do marketing. String the guitars. Bake muffins for the green rooms."

El snorted with laughter. "*Green rooms.* Plastic chairs with green mold, maybe."

"Ew. Anyway. It would be fun."

"Working together would be fun. Look at what your mom and Paul did for all those years."

"Yeah, well. We can't live together and work together. You would be so sick of me."

"Abruptly changing the subject," El muttered. Then he added, "Next time, get two bowls."

"Not three?" she asked. "I thought Harrison worked from home?"

"He goes to the gym afterwards, I think." He shrugged. "I'm sure he doesn't want to be here anymore than he has to."

"What the heck?" Brittney gestured toward the street, where she could see a reasonable sliver of the actual tide and the wet shore reflecting the sunset. "Who wouldn't want to be here? Like I said, just play your own bass."

"He probably should." A deeper, monotone voice came from behind Brittney. She nearly jumped out of her chair. El shook his head, suppressing a laugh.

"Don't worry. I agree with you." Harrison walked right past them into the house.

"Shit," Brittney said.

"No seriously," El replied. "Don't worry. He does agree with you. Also, he doesn't care what anyone thinks."

"Everyone says that to be cool, but most people care a little."

The door opened back up. Harrison passed each of them a can and sat down.

Brittney stared at the label. Tidal Creek. Nice. Local. She hated IPAs, but maybe she'd just take a sip.

"I was just kidding," she said, her tone strangely polite to her own ears.

"I wasn't."

Alrighty then. She took a sip and tried to fix her face. Gross. El was making out with his, though, and she wondered if she should leave the two of them for some brotherly bonding.

He definitely does not care, she decided. *Maybe about anything.* She didn't need another friend, but it would be nice if the air around them wasn't completely hostile.

He just handed you a beer. Good grief. It was a Monday night, not a Sunday morning, but she could hear the slight tone of disapproval in Dad's voice. *If he was hostile, he'd be sitting inside drinking alone.*

Fine. I will try. She stayed seated, but she didn't know what to say. She looked at El. Icebreaking was generally his job.

Harrison claimed it, to her surprise. "Playing bass and singing lead is like being a little manic."

Was he man-splaining her? "Oh," she said, with feigned amazement. "You mean because you're singing melody and playing a harmony? How fascinating!"

He looked at her blankly. "Not everyone gets it."

"She gets it," El cut in. "She used to play. And she's been hanging out with me forever. Helped me name the band."

"I played in *marching* band," she said, shooting El a dirty look.

"Yeah. It's practically the same." Harrison smirked behind his can. "What did you play? The clarinet or the flute?"

"I played the sax," Brittney muttered. "I'm mostly a music *fan*," she man-splained back. "I don't *make* actual suggestions on what El should do with the band, unless he *asks* me for my opinion."

"She's a roadie sometimes, too," El added.

Oh, dear Lord.

Harrison set down his beer and nodded methodically. "So, it's not that you really think El should play and sing? It's just that you don't want to deal with the roommate situation?"

"It's not a situation!" *Ugh. Stop letting him push your buttons.*

"No. Not now that he gave you his room." So much for hostile-free air. "Here's a question. Wouldn't it be easier if you two just shared?"

El's face reddened "I already told you, Harry."

Brittney rolled her eyes. "How unique. Someone assuming we sleep together."

"Yeah. Hate it when people assume things."

"Listen!" El leaned forward in his seat, looking ready to jump. "If you have something to say to me, say it. You don't know Brit, so leave her out of it."

The air went from hostile to heavy. Brittney stood. "Thanks for the beer," she muttered. "El, you already know…"

She walked straight to *her room*, the feeling of displacement she had since Geno gave her the eviction notice still over her like a heavy cloak. El had placed everything in here just right. All she had left was to fill those shelves again, but the piles were going to sit there for a few more days until she knew what to do.

Let them work it out, Daddy admonished. *You have a place. Take your place.*

Yeah, yeah. Soon his voice would remind her, *Remember who you are.* She knew. She just didn't know where she belonged.

Occasionally, that face from Brittney's mid- twenties would visit her dreams. Douchebag Bradley should have been perfect for her. Bradley-and-Brittney. They could have had children with all Br names who would all be some version of blonde. They'd open their own marketing firm and quit shlepping for everyone else. They'd live happily ever after, a Grand Strand power couple.

It was the insecurity that brought it on, she was sure. She locked the door in El's room (she simply could not think of it as hers) every night. But there was still a stranger sleeping in the house. And she should get over it, but it was gonna take a minute.

She made her way through the dark living room to the kitchen, flipping on the dim light above the stove and deciding whether she wanted to eat her feelings or drink them. There was a solitary scone she'd shoved behind the oatmeal in the "breakfast cabinet," which also held bowls, peanut butter, El's disgusting, cheap white bread, a bucket-size canister of protein powder, and at least four different kinds of cereal. She reached for it, set it on a small plate because Mama would judge her if she just used a paper towel, even at two in the morning, and put on the tea kettle. Mama still thought she hated tea, and she mostly did, but sometimes she drank peppermint because it reminded her of Daddy, and no one else needed to know that, not even her tearoom-owning mom and sister-in-law.

She turned it off before it could whistle and settled down at the small table by the window. It only had three chairs, which should have been charming for a home housing three people. But she had not sat there yet and only saw El use it to set down his Polar Pops and the mail. Harrison? She hadn't even seen him linger in the kitchen.

She didn't even know what, or if, he ate.

He probably dines on the heads of rodents, like any dark, murky rocker. The thought made her giggle, which took her mind off the fact that she was still shaking a bit. She didn't think about Bradley a lot anymore. There were even entire days when he didn't cross her mind. Sometimes, though, she would hear that 5 Seconds of Summer song they considered theirs or drive past Drunken Jack's, which was the site of their fancy date nights, and she was transported back to a damp winter parking lot, a Ford Explorer, and the night she discovered she didn't know him at all.

Shake it off already. She took a sip of her tea and felt the temperature and the mint warm her insides. If she closed her eyes, she was fine. She was safe. She was steady. She was, truth be told, at Mama's table instead, and Daddy was there, smelling like peppermint and Polo, and nothing had changed.

And then the light came on.

She blinked upwards, expecting her cleared vision to reveal El. Instead, it was Harrison, blinking at her, wearing a white tank top and gym shorts and an expression that was as bewildered and guarded as she felt.

"Oh. Sorry," he said.

"It's fine," she mumbled. "Do you need the light?"

"Why would I turn it on if I didn't?" He seemed to be asking not her but the atmosphere. Clearly, he thought she was not only an idiot but a completely annoying one at that.

She exhaled loudly, looking back down at her scone, which was much more comforting than his piercing eyes and muscled shoulders, damn him.

"I couldn't sleep either," he continued, as though she had answered him. She didn't watch as he moved past her to the breakfast cabinet. She tried to ignore the rustling and the banging and just focus on her calming tea. And then he had the audacity to sit across from her, his own middle of the night feast consisting of two peanut butter and jelly sandwiches and a bottle of Sprite. "Realized I forgot to eat dinner."

She set down her cup and, sounding more critical than she meant, asked, "How does a grown person forget to eat dinner?"

He grunted, his mouth full. After swallowing, he said, "After the gym, I had a phone call that went on for a while. And then I went to bed. It happens. You know. Life."

"I like to think I have a life," she replied, "but I can't remember ever *forgetting* to eat."

Harrison shrugged. "Just wasn't on the forefront."

"Is your life stressful?" she asked, being careful not to sound more than mildly interested. She *wasn't*, but she could still see Bradley and sometimes her emotions got into a jumbled mess with her words and her voice.

"Are we getting into this, all sleep-deprived and stuff?"

She could. She wanted to. But he didn't need to know that. "Nah. That's okay."

"Is *your* life stressful?"

I guess you didn't hear me. "No more than anyone else's."

"So, what makes it stressful?" He took a big bite and polished off PB&J number one.

"'What makes it stressful?' What makes anyone's life stressful? Money. Jobs. Family. Living in a borrowed bedroom like an idiot homeless teenager."

"A homeless teenager is probably more neglected than idiotic."

"Touché."

He was busy starting his other sandwich while she tried to formulate an intelligent response.

"I make decent money. It's just a bad time to buy

something, and I… was not expecting the need to make a change."

He snorted. "That's golden. Who the hell ever does?"

She felt herself blush. "Yeah, well. Anyway. El's house was the least evil of all my options. Had I known…"

Harrison waved his hand. "The bedroom thing won't be a concern. I don't plan to be here long. I just don't… Well, I guess I'm in a similar boat. I have resources, but I need a minute to regroup, and El needed a bass. Also, he's my only option besides our mother. You probably know enough to fill in those blanks."

"I… guess?" Their mother had moved away shortly after El graduated high school and moved into a dorm. He barely mentioned her, and always did so with hesitation or tension.

"Anyway. At least you had options. What were they, anyway?"

"Well, my mom's house isn't far. And I have siblings with room."

"But…"

He took a swing from his Sprite while she watched him. Did he really want to know? She took her own sip, letting the now lukewarm peppermint linger in her mouth. It was supposed to make her sleepy, but this conversation was making her feel more awake.

"It would be… extremely humbling… to move in with any of them. I am already the shiftless loser of the family. Having to bunk with the siblings or move into my mom's new house with her new husband is just—"

"Wait. Shiftless loser?" He rolled his eyes. "Aren't you like a marketing executive or something?"

People always thought that was more glamorous – and probably a higher pay scale – than it was. So why not break it down for a stranger?

"Well, I'm an *assistant* director, if you can believe such a thing needs to exist. And the rest is like this. My older brother is perfect. My older sister is perfect. My younger brother was born after our other younger brother was stillborn, so he basically hung the moon and stars and sun. And I am… me."

"So not perfect nor celestial?"

"Neither."

"Extreme middle child syndrome. Your mom compares you unfavorably."

Brittney tried not to gape at him. He was pretty keen. Completely wrong, but keen.

"Nah. Mama is the president of my fan club. But then, she basically adores everybody. Ask El."

He shook his head. "I believe you."

Sometimes Brittney was annoyed by or jealous of or even sick of Sam or Kayla or David. But there was something else entirely at play here with her best friend and the brother she somehow had never met.

"Do you and El just never talk? It's so weird to me. I talk to my sister every day. I text with my brothers on the regular. I mean, not judging, but—"

"Not every family is like yours," he said, indicating that was all he would say.

"Of course," she said, her I'm Not Stupid defense shield in place. "But El is a great guy and you seem… I mean, you came all the way here in part to help him, so maybe you have common ground now that you didn't before. It's worth exploring."

"*Worth exploring.*" He wasn't just mocking. There was vitriol in his voice. "Listen, Buttercup, I get that you are the president of Elliot's fan club, and clearly it's a family trait for you to cheerlead people through life. But you don't know me. And maybe you don't know him as well as you think you do if you feel comfortable suggesting he and I should engage in some brotherly bonding. This isn't *The Outsiders*, if you even know what that is."

Harrison pushed himself away from the table. His chair scraped on the floor and made Brittney shudder. She looked up at him and saw only a glower on his face as he exited, leaving the remnants of his meal on the table.

"Well. Good night, Sodapop" she murmured. She dumped their dishes in the sink and stared into the empty living room. Maybe he wasn't a jerk. Maybe he was just another person who was a little lost. But she could not have doubts about El in her head, so when it came to Harrison, she was done trying.

Jessie

"I PUT PAUL TO BED," I SAID, KNOCKING LIGHTLY at the suite door off my kitchen. "And I have wine."

Maggie was standing at the kitchenette counter, looking at the tiled wall. Her hair was up in a signature emerald-green scarf, but nothing else about her looked typical.

"Mags?"

Her head snapped around. "Wine. Yes! In or out?"

"Up to you."

"Eh. Let's just stay here." There were two easy chairs flanking the entertainment armoire, which divided the dining area from the living room. I briefly pictured myself as a musty old woman and knew I could live in this adorable apartment forever if I needed to, likely while one of my offspring ran The Main House. Maybe they would call me Dowager.

I poured two glasses and settled in across from Maggie. She continued looking distant. She hadn't been this quiet since her first night in town more than twenty years ago, not long after her husband, my own brother, had abandoned her and their girls, and Randall had driven to Illinois to rescue them and bring them here, their new home.

"What's up, Mags?"

She'd been in my house for twenty-four hours. After her surprise appearance in the middle of Sunday supper, she hugged all the kids and retreated to my room, hunkering down until they were all gone. Paul cleaned up while I coaxed her out. I managed to get her to eat some warmed-up leftovers but let her uncharacteristic silence stand, even though a quiet Maggie felt completely alien. She had spent the hours since then mostly to herself. Maggie wouldn't let anyone dear to her get away with that in a million years, and I wasn't about to let her get away with it either. She took a long sip and started to speak several times but kept correcting herself.

"Just say it!" I said. Oops. Previously long-suffering, my sixty-ish self believed we were always running out of time.

She gave me a laugh that didn't reach her eyes. "Well, I ain't here because things are so good at home."

I opened my mouth, but she cut me off. "Don't 'Oh, Maggie' me, please. And thank you. It's not him. It's me. I am not so good at home."

"Maggie, what in the world? What does *that* mean?"

She toyed with the knot on her scarf, avoiding my eyes. "Jessie Rose, I lived too long on my own."

Oh, for crying out loud. Maggie had already gone down this road. After her daughters were launched into the world, she'd remained alone in her house until Sheldon came along. She had never planned to remarry. She *liked* her autonomy. And then... Well, I certainly knew how life could come along and change your mind about everything.

"Is that really all?" I asked, trying to keep the accusation out of my voice. "He isn't disappointing in some area? His kids aren't actually hateful? You're not going back to Tony?"

"Too far," she deadpanned, glaring at me. We both took long sips. I hated things being awkward between us.

"Yes. Agree. Sorry, but you *drove* really far to get away from something, and I just want to understand what it is. Do you just not love him?"

"If I didn't love him, this would be easy. I adore him. There is nothing not to love about him."

"Then work it out." I got up to fetch the bottle, feeling like I was talking to one of the kids when they were in high school.

"Yes, Miss Love Conquers All. You lived alone for 17 seconds before you were married again. That's why I haven't said anything."

Ouch. "Bite me, Maggie!" I was going to pour more for her, but I clenched my hand more tightly around the bottle. "We really, really, *really* don't want to compare our lives, do we? Has that ever served us?"

"No. Your thirty-six happy years with your husband before he passed away does not serve alongside my secretly gay husband abandoning us when our babies were small without a word of explanation."

"You're being so stupid that that doesn't even hurt my feelings." I returned to my chair, hoarding the wine and refusing to sulk.

She was in a full pout, though. Her chin was a little quivery, her eyes were glassy, and her whole body was clenched.

"You might not want to hear this right now, but being married wasn't easy, Maggie. Just because we were happy doesn't mean no one ever thought about leaving."

Finally, she looked right at me. "You and Randall would have set yourselves on fire before anyone left."

Oh, how one trigger could take me back. There was only one season in our three dozen years together that had us living on *that* edge. In those manic, exhausting days of homeschooling and caring for babies, my neuroses surely would have been justifiable cause for him to split. Sometimes I think I still have PTSD from it all. Randall would come back from a trip, just as exhausted as I was, and I would want nothing more than to leave. Just for an hour. Just to drink a cup of coffee while it was hot enough to scald me. Just to eat a meal in one sitting. Just to pee without someone calling me or trying to sit on my lap or trying to hand me the toilet paper. And while I appreciated that he was working hard and constantly engaging with people and providing for the lifestyle we enjoyed, I felt like he had freedom – at the very least, autonomy over his own physical body—while I was in a pressure cooker. Sometimes, I said nasty things to him, or sometimes didn't answer the phone because I resented that he was away from all the chaos.

He only took the bait once. He kept calling until I relented, which was after midnight on a Friday morning when he would be spending half the day traveling. He told me in an even voice that was barely holding back his anger that when he arrived, I should leave for the weekend. Go to Maggie's, get a hotel room, he didn't care. But he didn't want my stormy weather raining on the kids, or his weekend at home with them.

"If you don't want my help, fine. But figure out what you need to be happy, Jessie, and do it. You're living in misery of your own making. You have everything you said you ever wanted."

You don't forget words like that. I still hadn't because he was right. I had a dream life. I had resources available that many women did not, most importantly, my attentive husband. My manacles had been locked in place by my own expectations of what motherhood should look like. I was the one who held the key. A few weeks later, he took me to Chicago with him, and we revamped life in our home, sending the kids to school, giving me time to breathe. I didn't even know who I was as an adult before then. Randall gave me space, and it brought us even closer.

"His patience with me was a thing of wonder," I told Maggie. "And you're right. Neither of us ever really wanted to leave. Sometimes, though, I did want to be left alone, by everyone, even the people I loved most in the world. I think that's a natural response to being overwhelmed."

Maggie nodded. "I have never lived in your particular brand of chaos, so I don't think that's it."

"Fair enough," I said. Even when Maggie's girls were young, she made the single-mom life look orderly. I associated many words with her quirks, but never "chaotic."

"But you feel overwhelmed?" I asked, though not really questioning. "You have been solely in charge for most of your adult life. When Moni moved out, you named your house 'The Fortress of Solitude.' It's not that surprising that you're having some difficulties adjusting."

Maggie sighed, got up, and took the bottle from me. After her glass was filled, she straightened her posture and said without any wavering, "I think I ruined myself. I think I became a fortress."

Well. Shit.

She didn't make me respond, which was good, because I had no words. "Sheldon is about as perfect as he seems. He has good people at the firm, so he can take time off. He *likes* to cook dinner a time or two a week. We go out. We've traveled. He makes me laugh. He notices me, compliments me, the color of my nails, when a dress hugs my hips just right. He's like a character in a Harlequin novel."

Oh boy. I knew what was coming.

"Harlequin novels are cheesy and fake," she finished.

"Oh, Maggie." I sighed deeply, but not enough to exhale all the angst building up in me for her. "Yes. Yes, they are. But that doesn't mean he is."

She shook her head at me. "No. That ain't what I'm saying. I'm saying, he was perfectly romantic and sweet and attentive, and it drives me absolutely insane, and I had to get away from it before I turned mean."

"Does he know? Does he know why you're here?"

She shook her head again.

"Maggie!"

"Listen." She held up a hand. "I don't know how to break his heart. I don't know if I have what it takes to look him in those eyes and tell him it's not working."

"Good. I hope you can't ever tell him that because it is literally the *dumbest* thing I have ever heard and the most stupid thing you would ever do. But what did you tell him?"

Silence.

"Maggie!" Now I felt like I was talking to my youngest child, the ever-casual, unfocused, baby of four, when he actually was a baby.

"I told him you were depressed, and I needed to come to you."

I pressed my lips together tightly. We had just passed the second anniversary of The Event, Randall's heart attack behind the wheel. He had picked up Paul's wife Leah. They were going to surprise us at one of our working sessions and celebrate the end of our curriculum-publishing era. Instead, they both died in the resulting crash on what became the worst day of my life. It was also so impossibly complicated and the near beginning of my new life with Paul. Two weeks ago had been Randall's birthday, the third one without him here with us.

The calendar dates served to sharpen what we felt all

the time.

But Maggie had definitely, irreverently, used me as an excuse, and not a totally honest one.

"I kinda can't believe you did that," I said.

"So, you're not depressed?"

I happened to look at her at just the right time and angle, and the way she was staring downward, either at her perfect, tangerine-hued pedicure or my perfect woven bamboo rug, made her look like a child who got caught with her hand in the cookie jar. I laughed.

"You are beyond frustrating."

She shrugged. "I agree."

"You can't leave it like this." I stood, still full of ire but also of fatigue.

Her eyes moved upward to mine. "What do you suggest? I tell my husband, the one I wished for, the one I *moved away* for, that I can't stay with him because I like to unload my own dishwasher and go to bed when I good and damn well feel like it?"

"Yes, Maggie. If that is the truth, if you really wanna go with *that* as your truth, then you need to tell him *to his face*."

She nodded slowly. "Not yet though. Are you kicking my ass to the curb?"

I had more deep sighs in me than I knew. "I would never do that. But I will kick your ass up one side and down the other if you don't get ahold of yourself. Spend a few days *reflecting*, Mags. And then find it in yourself to ask Sheldon for what you want instead of just assuming you can't have it. You *both* deserve that."

I squeezed her shoulder as I walked out of the room and back into The Main House. Everything was locked up, the coffee maker set for the morning, the sink cleared of dishes, the single dim light over the stove lit, Dolly's leash hanging on the little hook by the door that was shaped like a seahorse. Most nights, Paul and I handled all of that together in a delicate, often wordless dance. It had taken us all of approximately two-and-a-half seconds to find our domestic rhythm together. I never understood why it was so seamless, but I didn't question it either. We had our share of hurdles: who did the chores and how to share the space just weren't among them.

At the top of the stairs, I paused just outside our bedroom door and cracked it open. *My* second husband was sitting up in bed in his customary gray t-shirt and his reading glasses on, an impossibly thick hardcover on his lap. I took it all in for only a moment because I actually couldn't wait to talk to him.

He smiled as I popped on top of the bed, fully clothed, and scooched in next to him, nuzzling his neck.

Off came the glasses. He wrapped his arms around me, and I settled against him.

"What's this for?" he asked, like it didn't happen all the time.

"I love you," I answered.

"Aw, I love you, Jess." He exhaled. "What's up with Mad, Mad Maggie?"

"She thinks she's leaving Sheldon," I mumbled into his chest.

He sighed deeply. It was like a love language for us. "I was afraid this was going to happen."

"You were? I wasn't!"

"Of course, you weren't," he said, dangerously edging near his Principal Paul voice. He was steadily teaching a class at Coastal Carolina every semester and working a few shifts at the running store for Julie, and all that interaction with high maintenance people brought it out more.

"You're too close," he continued. "And on paper, it's a

perfect conclusion: a knight in shining Under Amour rescues her, and she lives the rest of her days in a romantic comedy."

"Something like that. Maybe more that the knight joins forces with her. She didn't exactly need rescuing. Just companionship."

"Well, that's kind of the point, Love. She's been on her own for a long time. She doesn't *need* him. And from the little time I've gotten to spend with Don, I'm pretty sure he likes to *feel* needed. He has baggage, too. And he has a lot to offer her, but if Maggie doesn't want it, then…"

"I don't think she's clear on what she wants. She thinks it has to be all or nothing, though."

He nodded silently, rubbing my back.

"I told her she owes him that conversation."

"She does," he answered. "How long is she staying here?"

I shrugged. "As long as she needs to. Or, until she drives one or both of us over a cliff."

He gave a little laugh and kissed my cheek. Then he kissed my neck. Then I turned my head, and we were kissing, slowly at first, then with more intensity. I felt the tension in my body melt into something else, not desperation, but longing for sure. I lifted myself onto him, facing him, took his face into my hands and looked at him, the full attention and affection for me in his eyes. I didn't spend a lot of time wishing things were different, not as much as I used to. What-ifs were maddening. He was peace in the storm. He was my right now and hopefully my entire future. I would spend the last of my energy for the day making sure he understood.

Brittney

Light.

Brittney wasn't sure why there was full sunshine pouring into the room on her Saturday morning. Then she remembered. She wasn't in her own home anymore; she was in El's, sans her beloved blackout curtains.

Sound.

The window itself was purposefully open so she could be lulled by the sound of the ocean, but a series of sustained, electronic booms was drowning it out.

What. The. Actual. Hell?

Running her hands over her eyes then through her hair, she peered out the window to see nothing but the neighbor's siding. She flung open the door, and there was Harrison, the roommate she thankfully had not seen for more than ten seconds since Wednesday night.

Like any proper rocker, he was wearing jeans. Like any proper Southern Man, a Salt Life t-shirt and flip flops. He had his bass on his lap (*Natural wood grain, blackwashed. How cool is that?*), the amp next to him on the floor, his eyes closed as he picked the strings.

She didn't want to notice what he was wearing, or how tanned his sinewy arms were for someone who spent so much time inside. She didn't need to solve the mystery of him.

Why, though, in fifteen years of best friendship, had El not talked more about him?

"It's early!" she shouted.

He didn't notice her tone. He could probably barely hear her, but he finally stopped his noodling. "It's nine o'clock."

"One day to sleep in. Just one."

"What are you, twelve?"

"What are you…" Well, no comeback. That was embarrassing. She finished feebly, "Two? No manners? No sense of day and night?"

"It's day," he mumbled, setting the bass down.

"Where's El?" she called, her back to him as she faced the coffee maker.

"He went to get bagels. I guess neither of you know how to cook."

Knows, she inwardly corrected, but said nothing and began fumbling through El's coffee pods.

"Would you mind getting me one?"

El's Keurig was a pain. One cup took forever, and Brittney reminded herself that her awesome, three-minutes-to-full-scalding-pot Bunn was just feet away in a box on the bedroom floor. But she wasn't ready to unpack it yet.

Instead, she turned around and glared at Harrison.

"So first you wake me up out of a dead sleep, and now you want me to make you coffee?"

He nodded. "I asked nicely. And you're right there."

"Mmm-hmm." She turned her back. "What do you want in it?"

"Just milk, and a bunch of sugar."

"Maybe *you're* twelve," she muttered.

"Pardon me?"

She sighed. The first mug was full. She walked over and handed it to him while saying, "Would you like me to drink it for you, too?"

"Nah. This will do. Thanks."

The fake niceness was too much. She would brew her own and then retreat back to the bedroom. On a Saturday. The whole day stretched before her, but she knew she needed to spend it *out*. Away from here. So much for a relaxing day off and a new home.

"He should be back in a minute. Aren't you hungry?"

Brittney's back stiffened. Was he actually being friendly? *Don't take the bait. Don't.* Especially don't take the bait with all those sexy, black-line tattoos running up his forearms. What did they symbolize? Where else did he have them?

Shut up, Brittney!

Just be friendly back. You like *friends. You are living in the same house.*

She turned around and walked with her mug to the smaller sofa, facing him and his stupid, awesome bass. "One thing about me is that I am always hungry."

"You don't say," he mumbled.

She took a long, fortifying sip and talked herself through it. Her history was no match for a hot musician living in close quarters and teasing her. She had checked every single one of those boxes multiple times through the years, and it never ended well. There'd been Steve the nymphomaniac guitarist who actually had different groupies for different days of the week, which she'd only discovered when she'd surprised him on a Thursday; there'd been Donnie the alcoholic drummer who gave her the only pregnancy scare of her twenties and showed his true, abhorrent nature in the process; there'd been Jason, the lead singer for Faded Spirit, a Nirvana-tribute band who didn't believe in bathing and was so sexy she was okay with it for about two weeks (*Blech, Brittney*).

Bradley hadn't been a musician, but he was the worst of all.

So? Do. Not. Risk. This. Was that her voice? Daddy's? Mikayla's? All of them. Lord, send help. Or at least send El.

"So," she said.

He had picked the bass back up and was cradling it but not playing. *Now, he decides to be quiet.* "So. What did bring you here?"

"Oh, are we going straight for it this morning? Okay, then. Well, I'd been renting a mobile home from one of El's bandmates for literal years, but his wife just caught his cheating ass, so now he needs a different place to live. Hence, so do I."

"Hence. Yeah. I know all about that."

She would take the bait. Just this once. "So, then, what is your hence? You're clearly not happy about being here."

He took his own sustained drink of coffee. Maybe she'd overstepped, but he started it. His eyes were stormy when he looked at her.

"Elliot really didn't tell you anything. I got divorced earlier this year."

She didn't want to tell him that El literally never – not ever – talked about him. She knew he existed, that he was older, that he lived inland a bit. That was all.

"My family is so big and chaotic that they take up a lot of our conversations," Brittney said feebly.

"Yeah. Okay. How long have you guys been BFFs or whatever? It's fine. He doesn't give a shit what's going on with me, and that's mostly my fault. I'm not a great brother."

Maybe it was the coffee kicking in, or maybe the draining effect the week had had on her, but her caution with this stranger who was sleeping thirty feet away from her was melting away.

I have nothing to lose.

"Were you not a great husband either, then?"

Harrison studied her. She sort of found herself wishing she'd brushed her teeth and also felt grateful she slept with a jogging bra on. His stare was unwavering.

"The probable answer is that of course I wasn't. If I was, I'd still be married."

"That's not really an answer. But you don't owe me one anyway."

He shrugged, fingering his strings. "I could have been better. And she could have been, too. But apparently, I was bad enough that she got full custody of the kids, seven hours away, so there's that."

Kids. What was wrong with El? Brittney suddenly felt like a sullen child. This guy was a real grown-up with real problems. She was still mostly existing like a college student, renting until she was evicted, having no idea how to cook, being on "just bring the Cheerwine" duty for family functions. No one ever even asked her to babysit until the kids were out of diapers and halfway reasonable. And he had his own kids? Why was he sleeping here like a fellow hobo?

"I didn't know you have kids," she said softly, pointlessly. Who cared what she knew?

He shrugged. And then with one hand, he unlocked his phone, scrolled to something, and stood up to pass it to her. "Ruthie is ten. Dakota is twelve. And they're in the D.C. area now with their mom. Denise is a lawyer, and she got in with a great firm there."

He said it so matter-of-factly. His tone contradicted the story told in the photo Brittney beheld: It showed a lanky boy with a brown crew cut and his father's intense brown eyes, his expression contrasted by the silly Sponge-Bob shirt he was wearing and how he was leaning into his father's side. On Harrison's other side was a girl with masses of chestnut curls falling well past her shoulders and overpowering her tiny frame. She had wide eyes and a reserved smile, cherubic cheeks that were blushed like a doll's. With one hand she was holding a leash, a little white Yorkie on the end. Her other hand was tightly entwined with Harrison's.

"They're beautiful kids," Brittney said, handing the phone back to him.

He nodded. "Yeah. Thank you."

"How long have you lived this far away from them?" He telecommuted for his job. She was curious why he wasn't where they were.

"About a month," he said. "We sold our house in Winston-Salem and I, um, was crashing at my mom's while I figured out—"

El walked in just then, his arms full with a big, white paper bag and a tray bearing three coffee cups.

"We just *made* coffee," Harrison said.

"*We?*" El let the bag fall to the coffee table and passed out the cups. "Since when are you 'we'?"

"Never mind," Brittney said, tearing the bag open. "Did you get jalapeño?"

El started tearing through the bag with her, and whatever conversation was about to ensue with Harrison was covered over like shmear on a bagel. Brittney was taking her first delicious bite from Benjamin's finest when she saw Harrison out of the corner of her eye. He'd left both of his coffees and was lugging his bass and amp back to his bedroom.

She set down her bagel, feeling childish.

"What was that all about?" El asked.

She sighed. "We were on the cusp of an actual conversation, and I just dismissed it for love of veggie cream cheese."

El shrugged. "He's fine. He never wants to talk anyway."

She thought of the photo he'd somewhat eagerly shown her and wondered if that was true. "El, I know you don't like to talk about your family, and I've always respected that, but he has kids? You've never said you have a niece and nephew. And what is he doing here, so far away from them?"

El sat in the seat Harrison had just left. He stopped and started his words a few times and then let his shoulders slump in defeat.

"We're not that close."

"But you and I *are* close."

"He's actually my half-brother."

"Sam is *my* half-brother. Technically."

"It's different, trust me. I didn't think you would be interested in all the sad story details."

"Complete, utter bullshit."

They marinated in the silence for a minute. Brittney wasn't used to being mad at El or any awkwardness between them, but—

"I feel kind of betrayed, man."

"Because I didn't tell you that my brother, whom I'm not close to, has kids?"

Brittney envisioned the four faces who called her

"Auntie." Travis had always been more like a little brother; she simultaneously adored and wanted to body slam him. Summer was like her mini-me, Jacob a squeezable version of his dad and growing up fast, and now Josie, the quintessential baby princess. She couldn't imagine not being part of their lives, and as complicated as blending a family could be, her new stepsister's kids were unquestionably easy to love.

"You just…" How could she explain? "You've been seeing 'Auntie Brit' in action for a long time. So, it's something we have in common and… this makes me feel like I don't know you as well as I thought I did."

Now El looked angry. "I think this is too much melodrama for a Saturday morning. And it always seems to accompany my brother, so take that into account when you're siding with him."

"Oh, El. Now who's being dramatic? I'm not taking his side. I'm just trying to understand."

"I don't think you can."

"Not if you won't help me."

Another long silence ensued. El methodically finished his bagel, drank his coffee, and softened his face while Brittney waited with, perhaps, a bit too eager curiosity.

"This is one of those times when we are just very, very different, Brit. And I am asking you not to take it personally, and I am asking you to just let it be. If you want to befriend Harry, that's your business. He's not a bad guy or anything like that. We're just not like you and your family."

She nodded slowly and waited in case there was more. There wasn't.

"Do you… do you *want* things to be different?" she finally asked.

El stood, crumpling the now empty white paper bag in his hands. "I don't think I do, Brit. I've tried before. It doesn't work for us."

After a beat, he added, "I'm not mad. I just don't want to talk about it." He walked out of the house.

Brittney sat and listened. The low rumble of the bass fired back up from Harrison's bedroom. She looked around and sighed. It was terrible timing to have tension between her and El. This place was not familiar. Now it didn't even feel friendly. It was not hers.

"It doesn't even feel like home."

A few hours later, Brittney sat forward in her chair and looked out at the ocean. The beach was already packed, and it wasn't even Memorial Day yet. But she didn't care. And neither did her companions.

"Why don't you just buy a house, Auntie Brit? Daddy says you can."

She rolled her eyes behind her sunglasses, where Summer couldn't see.

"Your Daddy forgets sometimes that I'm not in his shoes," Brittney deadpanned.

"He has a point, though," Julie chimed in. "Why not just go for it? Then you don't have to worry about someone else's family drama."

"It's not just someone else. He's my best friend."

"God bless, you are just like your mama." Katy's words were accusatory, but her tone wasn't. "Maybe don't worry so much about what everyone else thinks. You gotta take care of yourself."

"I *do* take care of myself." *No one else takes care of me,* she thought.

Oh really? Daddy's voice whispered.

"I can't believe I'm agreeing with Katy on adulting methods, but paying your own bills isn't the whole story,"

Julie said. "Look out for your feelings and your future, too. Don't let some guy derail it, no matter how long he's been your friend."

They let Julie's words hang there for a second. It wasn't *just* a guy, but Julie had gone her own version of wild after her mom died. The rest of them had been trying to figure out how to be a family and support Jessie and/or Paul while they were grieving themselves, but Julie and Brittney's youngest brother David had moved to Arizona, *together*. Everything about that move had been disastrous. The only redemption was that it led Julie back home, into a surprising new career *and* her new marriage, and as evidenced perfectly by the current scene, into relationships with their weird, blended family.

"It's hard to explain," Brittney said. "El is more than a friend. He's… practically family."

Julie snorted. "You Oakley people say that about the cashiers at Food Lion. Mikayla called us her cousins the first time we all had Cracker Barrel after church together."

Brittney laughed. She didn't remember that, exactly, but it was classic Mikayla and classic Oakley.

"We've been friends since Mr. Schmidt's terrifying Algebra class. I was crying in my seat with my hood fully up, thinking no one saw me. But El did. He always does."

Summer had gotten bored and walked to the water. Julie answered, "You really have that second daughter syndrome, don't you? So does my twin. She should be your twin instead."

"That's offensive," Katy said.

"Whatever. You're both these gorgeous, dynamic unicorns, but you somehow think you're invisible. It's nuts. Get over it, already."

"Hm. I don't know if we are there, yet, Jules," Brittney retorted. "I would throat-punch Mikayla for saying that to me."

Julie shrugged. "I don't pull punches. That's how I do *practically family*."

"That's for damn sure," Katy added.

"Fair enough." Brittney kept her eyes on Summer. It kept her responsible and from looking either Julie or Katy in the eye. "You are probably right. It's a byproduct of having two older siblings who are practically saints. I wasn't like that, so I tried to be the opposite. But I wasn't that either. El lets me be myself."

"Plus, he's hot."

Brittney looked at Katy. "He is," she nodded. "But I don't really notice it anymore. Now, his brother on the other hand…"

"He's hot too?" Katy's interest in the conversation had skyrocketed.

"Unfortunately."

"So, the cranky brother who's newly divorced with secret children in a different city, who has you wondering if you really even want to stay in this living arrangement, is also hot?" Julie repeated. "This has all the makings of something *wonderful*. And *smart*."

Brittney just nodded, unable to argue.

"Don't let her bully you," Katy said. "You're allowed to think he's hot."

"I'm not bullying, Katy! I just don't want her to screw herself over getting distracted by some idiot. I've been there. And you've definitely been there, too." Katy swatted her shoulder. "We are too old for nonsense. You have goals, right, Brittney? That's all I'm saying. Tolerate him. Save your pennies. And get out on your own as soon as you can."

Like you did? Brittney wanted to snap. If she'd been talking to Mikayla or even just Katy, she would have. *Sisterhood* with Julie was new and tenuous, and Julie could probably handle the sass and the truth, but she didn't feel like fighting… even though Julie didn't have to worry about buying her own place. She got married and now co-owned a house *and* a successful business.

There is literally nothing stopping you. Whoa. She was pretty sure that wasn't just Daddy's voice, but Mama's, too.

"I won't let anyone stop me," she said quietly, not sure they'd even hear her over the beach chatter and the wind that was kicking up. "I don't really have a goal, but I guess I need one. I definitely can't do this forever."

"Oh God," Julie said. "Let's work on the goal first. If this dumb guy looks anything like his brother, you need a different fire to run toward, STAT."

It turned out not to be such a bad Saturday after all. After the beach, Brittney dropped Summer off at home and re-joined Katy and Julie for margaritas, which always made a day better. Julie convinced both of them to start her 5K training plan and a twelve-months-to-down-payment savings plan. That way, Julie said, Brittney wouldn't feel like she owed anyone anything and Katy could stop "living in a shack fit for pot-dealing twenty-year-olds."

"She makes it sound so easy," Brittney told Katy, standing in the parking lot of Los Cabos after Julie had gone home to her sexy, successful husband. "Just like Mikayla does. But they're both living fairy tales."

"Yeah. True." Katy cocked her head and looked a bit too closely at Brittney. "But we know it hasn't all just come easy for them, either… right?"

Brittney thought of Julie's upended career and of Mikayla's miscarriage right before their daddy died. "Right. We just need to—"

"Get our shit together," Katy finished.

"Yeah. Yeah, we do. You wanna come see the house?"

Katy looked at her phone, either checking the time or whether a better offer had popped in. She shrugged. "Sure. You got anything going on tonight?"

"I'm sure El's band is playing somewhere, if that interests you." She knew it would.

Another shrug. "Let's see what we can get into. Then we can work on our *goals*."

Katy followed Brittney home. It was just past four o'clock, and El and Harrison were in the driveway, loading speakers into El's Ram.

"It's time already?" she asked.

"Yep," El answered, wiping sweat from his brow and giving a full smile. "We're at the Fishwalk tonight." Brittney felt relieved that the tension from earlier seemed to be gone, but that was typically how it went with them.

"El, you've met my stepsister, Katy. Katy, this is El's brother, Harrison."

Harrison nodded, hefting a square black case into the back of the truck. "Hey." Sweat was glistening around his dark eyes.

Katy looked at Brittney and mouthed, "Wow!" Or maybe it was, "What?!" Either one made sense.

El started telling Katy about their gig that night. Brittney had jumped on to the back of the truck and lodged one speaker next to the other, just how El had shown her.

"You a roadie?" Harrison asked.

"I try to make myself useful," Brittney said. She was still in her bikini with cut-offs and a sleeveless crop over it. Her early-season tan had been solidified by those hours on the beach that day. She knew exactly how she looked, but mostly, she wanted to appear anything but weak in front of this guy who was making her feel so twitchy.

His gaze definitely lingered on her bare arms, not muscular, per se, but toned and strong. She let him. He should be squirming, not her.

"Humph," he said, and handed her the tiny microphone case before he heaved the much heavier mixer case himself.

Brittney turned to roll her eyes at Katy, but she was in a full conversation with El, so Brittney rolled them to herself.

"That's your stepsister?" Harrison's voice asked behind her.

Without turning, she answered, "Yes. One of three."

"That is a big family."

It was the most interested he'd seemed in her so far. She looked at him, sunglasses pulled down over his eyes, his brown ponytail curling from the sweat and humidity.

"I also have a sister and two brothers. And in-laws. A nephew that is almost as old as my youngest brother, and assorted others. So mostly I just say *sibling*. Or family. It's easier than explaining." *Then why are you explaining to him? Who cares?*

"I always thought a big family would be fun. No wonder El likes hanging out with you." And then he actually smiled.

"Yeah, I guess..." she said lamely. Was he trying to be friends?

She looked over at Katy, still chatting up El, and decided that was fine with her.

～～

"You think they'll ever add a chick to this line-up?"

Brittney stirred the lime into her Tito's and soda and shook her head. "No way. El says it brings too much drama." They both snorted.

"Oh, yeah," Katy laughed. "Musician dudes always say

we bring drama. Didn't you say there were punches thrown last weekend? That's why the secret, brooding brother moved to town? Please!"

They were starting up "Dead and Bloated," which always made Brittney revel in that particular mid-tempo feeling. She jumped out of her seat and scurried to the dance floor. Katy followed.

El, who usually paid Brittney little mind when he was in performance mode, seemed to feed off the energy. It was a relatively short song, and instead of breaking, which Brittney was sure was next in the set, El leaned into Harrison and whispered something. Harrison turned around to Ringo and a few beats later, they went right into her favorite STP song, "Unglued." Brittney let out a breathless scream and then continued right on jumping and thrashing her head around, sing-yelling every word. Katy did her best to keep up while a handful of others joined them. The driving guitars seemed to rev up the whole crowd, and when the two-and-a-half-minute song was over, the energy was crackling throughout the patio. El gave a raucous "woo-hoo" before letting everyone know they were taking fifteen. Brittney gaped as he high fived his brother and then accepted an enthusiastic embrace from Katy before walking away with her to take his break.

She would have felt ridiculous standing there if she hadn't been flanked by a hyped-up Geno and Ringo.

"That's Brit's favorite," Ringo said. She was surprised he knew that, much less said it. She smiled at them.

Geno added, "It's so fun to be spontaneous once in a while."

"Yep," Ringo added. "Let's get a shot."

Harrison brushed past her, doing that light grasp of the shoulders thing that was subtle and electrifying all at once. She watched him walk away, forgetting to care if his bandmates noticed.

"Yeah," she finally responded. "Let's."

Ringo liked tequila, and one shot became two before they collectively agreed that was plenty. She half-wobbled to the bathroom, just beyond the pool tables, and there was El and Katy, lodged in the corner, kissing.

"Oh, for fuck's sake." She spat the Oakley-Jameson family-mash-up-motto before she could help herself and hurried away.

She waited outside the one-holer, tapping her foot. She couldn't go to her car yet, and she really didn't want to sit close to the stage anymore. What was wrong with El? What was wrong with *Katy*? Wasn't this stupid living arrangement precarious enough without adding a fling on top?

"It's practically incestuous," she muttered out loud, just as Harrison came out of the bathroom. He stopped and raised an eyebrow at her.

"Nothing!" she snapped. She practically fell on the toilet and started counting down her options, again.

Bite the bullet and move in with Mama.

Bite the bullet and move in with Mikayla.

Bite the bullet and use all her inheritance on a down payment, housing market and future be damned.

Move to upstate or to Charlotte, near her cousins. Maybe Moni wanted a roommate.

I hate *needing roommates.*

Burn it all down. Cut her hair. Relocate some place where no one knows her. Maybe it would work better for her than it had for Julie.

Someone knocked on the door. *Dammit.*

She didn't waste energy answering. She got herself up

and out as quickly as she could, avoiding eye contact with the woman coming in after her.

The opening strains of "Better Man" were calling to her from outside. It was another of her favorites. It was one of the songs El kinda sang for her, for the idiot she was in her twenties and the choices she made to tolerate what was beneath her.

Was she doing that now? No. El would never let her. He would never intentionally hurt her.

El deserves to be happy.

Katy deserves to be happy.

And then Daddy chimed in. *You deserve to be happy.*

None of these things are mutually exclusive, he added.

She made her way back to her table. Katy was sitting there, a fresh drink in front of her and one at Brittney's place. She smiled brightly at Brittney but didn't stop singing along.

Brittney chimed in on one of her favorite choruses of any song, ever.

She looked at El. He winked at her.

She looked at Katy. She was looking everywhere, oblivious that Brittney saw anything, entranced by the music and the musicians.

She looked at Harrison. When the song picked up during the second verse, he came alive, and he stared back at her, even while he was doing that adorable jumping thing that guitar players do.

This isn't complicated. She wasn't sure whose voice that was, but it sounded mostly like her own. *You're all still young and relatively free.*

Harrison wasn't free. But holding that blackwashed bass and mouthing the words, occasionally smiling at her and even at El, he looked it.

"I freaking love them," Katy shouted across the table to her.

Brittney kept watching, her best friend and safe place, and his increasingly intriguing older brother. Without looking back at Katy, she just said, "Me too."

Brittney

Ninety minutes and just one more teeny-tiny little drink later, Brittney was still sitting at the table. She could have helped carry some stuff, but they were in a zone that she hadn't observed frequently: post-gig euphoria. Even Harrison was smiling, trading barbs over this song and that riff, that table of crazy women and that one overly drunk guy with the dancing black dog who showed up at every gig. Dave was standing in the center of it all holding his Fanta and eating a cupcake, saying something about the absolute ridiculousness of all Stone Temple Pilots lyrics.

"I never even hear the lyrics," Ringo said, walking past her with two armfuls of cymbal cases.

"You're lucky then," Dave retorted.

Brittney giggled and looked over to where Katy was wrapping cords, standing next to El and talking non-stop. She shook her head and walked inside to settle her tab. On paper, Katy was possibly a great catch: She looked like a beach girl pinup, she'd built a sort-of lucrative business teaching music, and she was the kind of free spirit most music guys preferred in a woman.

But El wasn't just a music guy. And she didn't want to see either of them – or honestly, herself – get hurt. More likely, El would need space first. No one knew how to properly put away his cords.

El was ringing her up himself, jovial and talkative as usual. She answered while tapping her foot in time to CCR on the jukebox, scanning the room. It was still pretty busy in there for so late at night, and she noticed yet another couple crammed into the corner, making out. Was everybody hooking up tonight except for her?

She thanked him and took her receipt, and when she turned back around, the couple had broken apart and Mikey was sheepishly wiping his mouth. The woman walking away from him was stout, dark-skinned, taller than he was, incredibly stunning with purple hair and sparkly eye shadow to match, and absolutely *not* his wife.

"Brittney." She was going to just walk away and ignore it, but he clearly wasn't going to let her.

"Mikey…"

"I just want to explain."

"You don't have to explain to me. It's not my business."

"Yeah, but…"

Brittney stopped short at the threshold to outside and turned around, looking at the redhead in his blushing face.

"This is *the deal*. I get it. I'm not going to say anything." His wife – *Alison?* – was rarely around, at least when Brittney was. What was she gonna do? Look up her socials and tell her?

"Ali and I are—"

"I don't care, Mikey!" If he was really worried, he shouldn't have been shoving his tongue down another woman's mouth in the first place. Musicians ran such a fine line between larger-than-life arrogance and crippling insecurity, and she'd had enough for one night. "Leave me alone!"

She stomped outside, not even sure why she was so mad. He could do whatever he wanted. They all could.

"Katy, I'm gonna wait in the car, unless…"

Katy wasn't paying attention. She was walking with El, each with one arm full of gear, one arm around each other.

Why did she feel like she was suffocating?

They were less than three miles from the house. Maybe she could walk.

She probably shouldn't. Stupid tequila.

"What's up?"

Harrison was standing in front of her, his dark gray Linkin Park t-shirt blackened with sweat and sticking to him, his bass case slung over his shoulder, a half-eaten cheeseburger in his free hand.

"Nothing. Finish eating. I gotta—"

He nodded in the direction of his brother and her sister. "You gotta not worry about that."

"I'm not."

He nodded in the direction of Mikey, wheeling his keyboard toward his car. "Or that."

"You have no idea what you're—"

"Yeah. I actually do. C'mon. Why don't you just ride home with me?"

"I barely know you."

He took a big bite and waited a beat.

"I heard it," she muttered.

"Good." He swallowed. "Let me try again. Can the stranger who sleeps down the hall from you give you a ride home, or are you actually sober enough to drive your car?"

All the voices in her head shouted that if she had to

include the word *enough*, then she was definitely *not* "sober enough."

"Can you give Katy my keys? In case she needs them?"

"Keep your keys. She doesn't need them."

"Harrison…"

He turned around to one of the servers who was bussing outside. "Sarah, we will get this one's car tomorrow."

"K!"

It felt like a walk of shame, across the patio, across the lot, to the side of Harrison's silver Tacoma while he threw his stuff in the back and then came to her side and opened the door for her.

"It's okay," he murmured, like he knew her.

Did anyone see her leave with him? Did anyone care? Did it matter?

Probably not. Definitely not.

And of course, it did.

<div align="center">~~~</div>

"My brother is smart. Booking everything so close to home. I'll give him that."

The drive took the eleven longest minutes of Brittney's recent memory. The tequila fog was lifting, and instead of feeling blurry and stupid, she already felt clearheaded and embarrassed.

"Come on, Brit. We're home."

Brit. Home. The unexpected familiarity of his words felt like a gut punch, just a little one, like there was something empty inside her, previously filled with something indescribable, everything she missed.

"Come on," he repeated.

Harrison held the door open, and she wordlessly climbed out of her seat. She missed the tequila fog. Without it, she could smell the cologne underneath the sweat, mingled with a little beer, ketchup, pickles. Wouldn't her mama love to cook for these men after a show? She tried not to notice, and when that failed, she tried to *pretend* she didn't notice. All her attempts just added to the electricity coursing through her. She murmured a "Thanks" and *tried* not to hope he was watching her walk away.

"Brit."

There it was again, like all of a sudden he was her friend.

She ignored him and walked to the kitchen, suddenly ravenous. She rummaged through the cabinet that was sort of hers, found her Peanut Butter Captain Crunch, and ate a handful.

"You're kind of a mess," his voice said from the doorway. "Or kind of a child. I can't figure it out."

The cereal's crunch was the most obnoxious sound she'd ever heard. It took literally forever before she could swallow and answer.

"Why are you trying? Honestly. I thought you couldn't stand your own brother, much less his other roommate."

"Well, from the looks of tonight, we might have another roommate soon, so it's high time I make an ally here."

She shook her head and took out a bowl. "No way. Katy, you mean? That isn't happening."

"Okay."

"Don't do that."

He shrugged, slinging his case down to lean against the counter. "Do what?"

"Don't say *okay* with all the innuendo. The three dots at the end."

"I'm sorry, the *three dots?*"

"The ellipses!" She sighed loudly. "Just say what you want to say."

"You, Princess Buttercup, don't want to hear it."

"You're maddening. I'm going to bed."

"I just know him better than you do..." he said to her back.

She whipped around. "What is this, a contest? Who knows El better? Look, you may have known him longer, but I *know* him. And he's not moving Katy in here. That's just –"

"What? Inconsiderate? He moved me in."

"Dumb. It's dumb."

"This conversation is dumb."

"You're dumb!" She practically screamed it. And then she slammed the bedroom door.

Angry tears slipped down her cheeks. *Dammit. Damn him.*

Why are you crying? Why are you even mad?

This is what happens, she told herself. You don't feel safe, so you react like a fool. Everything is fine here. El can like Katy. He can date Katy. He can fall in love with Katy. It is no threat to you. And neither is Harrison. He's just being nice.

She heard a noise. Was he outside her door? Because that was pushing it.

She flung it open. He was still in the middle of the living room, and he was laughing. Like, cackling.

"Why are you laughing?" she exclaimed. She realized she was jealous. She wanted to be able to laugh at all of it.

He composed himself, stood straighter, looked at her.

"Oh Jesus. Are you crying? Don't cry."

Brittney swiped furiously at her eyes. "I'm fine. Are you just out here laughing at me?"

He still was. "I mean... Brit...you called me *dumb*. And *slammed the door*. It's pretty funny."

"Great. Good. I'm glad I amuse you. Look around us. Everything is dumb. We are in our thirties... you have kids, apparently… and we are living like a bunch of idiot college couch surfers. And I hate it. I hate feeling insecure. I hate feeling like I don't know what's going to happen next. I hate that El didn't talk about you and I thought I knew him and now I feel like I don't know anything. So *haha*. It's hilarious. You *are* dumb, and so is your stupid brother. And I… *ellipses*… am the dumbest of all for thinking this would work out!"

She should have stormed off, closed her door again, and started packing. But instead, she stood there with her tears drying on her cheeks and her chest heaving with frustration, and she didn't move when he crossed the room and put his strong, reassuring arms around her.

She didn't shrink away. No one had held her in months and all she did was deny how much she wanted it. So, she wouldn't right now. She let him, even when he started laughing again.

"Why?" she managed, a giggle behind her voice.

"Don't you write for a living? Your use of words is not so good after a couple drinks, Buttercup."

"Why are you calling me that?" She let her lips vibrate off the soft cotton of his shirt. How did he smell so good?

He ran his fingers through the ends of her hair. "It's the blonde. And the attitude. You just remind me of her."

"Is that why you're laughing?"

"No." She felt his lips now, vibrating off the top of her head. "It's because you said I 'apparently' have kids. Who would make that up?"

"I didn't think you lied about it," she pouted. "I just… still can't believe El didn't tell me. And I feel like, when someone has kids, it's just… I don't know. Obvious."

He pulled away to look at her, not quite letting go. "So what? I don't have a Dr. Huxtable sweater on, and it's that shocking to you?"

She shook her head. "None of my friends have kids. I don't mean anything by it. We're a bunch of aunties and uncles and… dumb-dumbs… Well, except El, I guess."

"Why does this bother you? We aren't close. You know that."

"It's unlike him," she insisted. "He's always been wonderful to me. I don't get it."

Harrison let her step out of the embrace. The regret was immediate.

"I haven't made it easy," he said. "But I don't think we should talk about it. It's between him and me, and if he didn't share it with his bestie, there is probably a good reason."

"I just can't imagine one," she said, shrugging. "My nieces and nephews are my whole heart. He knows that. He knows *them*."

Harrison reached up and gently, briefly, touched her cheek. "You're sweet. Even if you try not to be. Now listen. Don't worry about all this. You don't have to leave. No one is usurping you or replacing you or whatever it is you have a tick about. And if you want to, we can even be friends."

Friends. She touched her cheek in the same place he had.

"You don't make things easy," she said softly. "I thought you hated me."

He sighed. "Yeah, well. I just needed a minute. Sometimes *things* actually *aren't* easy."

His brown eyes were looking at her so intensely she wanted to shrink. But she also still felt the power of his arms around her, and she wanted it back. So, she stepped forward and put her own arms around his neck, her lips against it, and after pressing them briefly to his skin, said, "I don't really need another friend."

Her words opened a gate. Harrison's arms tightened

around her waist, pulling her against him. Her lips moved to his, and he kissed back with an intensity that matched his stare. She moved her hands to the side of face, caressing his strong jaw, his cheekbones, and finally, the brown tendrils that had come loose from his ponytail. She wanted to tell him how sexy he was, so instead she pressed her hips forward to show him.

"Mmmm," he whispered in between kisses. "Oh Brit."

"Mmm-hmm," she said back, not wanting to stop. Knowing they had to decide, now, before El and Katy walked through the door.

"Brittney…" He kissed her again, deeply, lingering, running his fingers through her hair, falling in messy waves abused by the humidity.

Then he stopped.

"We have to take it slow," he said. "I…"

She stifled a giggle. "Three dots?"

His face morphed from worry to a smile. "Yeah. Yes. Something like that."

"Okay. I understand." At least, she wanted to, but she wanted him more.

He reached up and touched her face again, "Go to sleep, Buttercup. Maybe tomorrow we can, you know, walk on the beach or have lunch or something."

"Lunch," she repeated, bewildered.

"Or something." He winked.

"Something." She put her hand over his, hugging it between her cheek and her shoulder. Mournfully, she let go and walked away, and hoped he was watching, and even hoped he'd follow.

He didn't. *He's a gentleman.*

But what the hell was that?

The thoughts flashed on a ticker: Harrison's scowl the day they met, El reassuring her, El kissing Katy, the mobile home she missed so much, her Mama's old front porch, her Daddy's memorial service, Mama and Paul's house, and something like a neon sign flashing one word: *Failure*.

She looked at her shelves hanging on the wall. She focused on the warmth in his eyes when he said her name, or her new nickname.

Maybe not. Maybe not this time.

Jessie

"Oh no. She better be. I haven't seen that child's face since last Sunday, and that was—"

I crossed my arms, waiting for Maggie to finish. She didn't.

"That was when you rode in like a bat out of hell and barely greeted anyone," I reminded her, spreading shreds of Parmesan on my Caesar salad. "She didn't text me anything, but she's usually the first one here."

"Katy texted. They're on the way." Paul strolled into my prep space and did what only he was allowed to do: he picked an olive from my charcuterie board and popped it into his mouth.

"Oh." It was unusual not to hear from Brit at all. Also, I almost forgot the mango habanero jam. I turned to the refrigerator. "Did Katy just get to town?" She didn't come every Sunday; Wilmington was a far drive, even for someone who took home a week's worth of lunches with her.

"Not sure," Paul answered, grabbing for the mini salami. I had turned back around and swatted his hand. "Dude. This is the main course today. Back off."

"We're having a giant Lunchable for Sunday supper?"

"It's *charcuterie!*" I yelled a little bit.

"And there's salad," Maggie added, a twinkle in her eye.

"You're both evil," he said, walking away. "And the lasagna smells great, Jess!"

I blew a kiss to his back and caught Maggie gaping at me.

"What?"

"Y'all," she said, shaking her head. "You set the bar really high for this second-time-around thing."

It was my instinct to feel a little judged, except I remembered that Mags was probably a little jealous, maybe?

"Well," I began carefully, "That isn't exactly our *goal*, but… thank you?"

"Oh hush," she said. "I know it ain't easy, sister. It just looks easy… when you're swatting each other's booties in the hallway or making doe eyes across the supper table. It even looks attainable."

I sighed. "Mags, you—"

She held up a hand. "Nope. Don't. I know what you're gonna say, because you've said it fifteen-thousand times this week. It sounds like the marriage equivalent of 'no one cares, work harder.' But we aren't football players, or cross-fitters, or special forces. And we aren't *you*."

I had no response.

She picked up the salad bowl and headed to the dining room. "And it's okay, Jess. It doesn't mean I'm not happy for you, because I'm not sure I could be happier for anyone else in the world."

As soon as she was out of the kitchen, because my life

still didn't include much solitude, ever, Brittney and Katy burst through the side door, each with arms full of two-liter bottles.

"Well, hello there." I simultaneously grabbed two bottles from Brittney's hands and hugged her. She smelled mildly of a distillery.

"Hmmm," I said into her ear. "Let's talk later."

I heard the sigh but didn't care. I greeted Katy similarly and then shooed them out of the room to where everyone else was. We were a smaller crowd again that day... Sam and Abby and kids were visiting Abby's dad; there was no Danielle and Matt and their kids because Lexie didn't let them sleep the night before and they *just cannot today*, so the house was quieter than usual, with Josie being the sole grandbaby and Mikayla dozing on the porch swing while everyone else took turns fawning over her child.

Maggie returned to the kitchen. It was good to have a wingman, and more specifically, to have my best friend-sister-by-choice-ride-or-die at my side, but it was also weird. In all our years together, we had never been roommates (save for a few weeks when she and her girls moved to town and stayed with us, but that had been so chaotic, I barely saw her face). The fun, extended slumber party feel was overshadowed by the fact that she was convinced her marriage was over, and nothing I said seemed to persuade her that a different outcome was possible.

"I guess we're ready," I announced.

"You're gonna have a lot left over," she said. "You should book something to cater tonight."

"Hmmm..." I agreed. "I'll probably have Paul drop a load off for Danielle. She's on the struggle bus, I think."

"A lot of babies," Maggie murmured.

"We know how that goes."

"You do," she said. "I had my quiet little life of three

ladies. And then two. And then one. Yours just keeps getting bigger."

"I guess." I could vividly remember a time that I had to wake up at 5:30 in the morning in the hopes of stealing maybe thirty minutes of quiet before David would wake up. He was my last baby, my clingiest – and truth was, after having a stillborn son the year before he was born, I was clingiest with him, too. I also remember the first morning he got up for school and walked *past* where I was waiting for him in our usual spot, on my reading chair, near the entrance to the kitchen. Before that moment, we would watch TV and cuddle for a few minutes every day before breakfast. The year of third grade changed everything, and without warning, he was quickly shoving a muffin or banana in his mouth, so he had a few minutes to ride his scooter or play Guitar Hero before school. Randall came home from a trip that week to find his wife in a full state of mourning. He didn't get it. I had what I wanted: physical autonomy, four kids who were all somewhat self-sufficient. It was the strangest bittersweetness I'd ever experienced, and it was still happening thirteen years later.

But Maggie was right. There was still almost always a crowd.

"I like it loud, Mags," I said, balancing a few platters in my hands. "I think it used to be because I didn't want to deal with the voices in my head, you know? But now it's just because it's life. The signs of my life, of family, of who we gather. I like my quiet, too, and I like that Paul knows when I need him to be quiet, which is rare. But this…" I gestured with my chin toward the chatter in the next room. "This is where I thrive. Where I feel most alive."

"Bless it." She laughed at my rhyme, and we headed to the dining room.

The "small" crowd was kept entertained by two stories. The first was Paul's tale of a student's elaborate ruse to get an extension on his semester final essay. It included the near-death of the student's girlfriend, the arrest of his father, and the family dog being diagnosed with leukemia. Paul looked equal parts amused and nauseated recounting it. The second story came from Katy, talking quite nonchalantly about an interview she had scheduled for the next morning, at a kind of famous music store inside the mall.

Julie stiffened, receiving a look from Robin that signaled something like, *your sister is an adult. Don't say a word.* Brittney raised an eyebrow (hereditary, and Randall's signature move for years). "Like a real interview, or like, you're going in there, showing them some reels of your kids playing their recital at the Market Street Chick-fil-A?"

Paul choked on his Pellegrino, likely because it rang true.

Only because it rang true, Katy was unphased. "A real one. Their guitar teacher is leaving. There'd be some sales, too. So not a total loser job, and El knows someone at the Chamber starting this new Myrtle Beach karaoke thing—"

"Karaoke?" Paul had less chill than Brittney did. I looked at Maggie to signal that drama might be coming.

"Yes. Like a host, a DJ, and a camera person going to events around the city and getting people to sing."

"For pay?" Brittney asked, at the same time Julie said, "Who's gonna pay for that?"

"He doesn't have all the details yet." Katy picked her fork back up and jabbed it with fervor into her lasagna. "I'm just exploring what's here. Because let's face it: nothing is in Wilmington. Not for me."

"I'm just saying that artists rarely get paid much, if at all, for performing around here, much less for conducting karaoke." Brittney's face was a little flushed. Something was up with those two.

"I'm just *exploring*," Katy repeated, and shoved a forkful in her mouth.

Between that and Paul's unblinking glance toward Julie, the conversation was definitely over. Mags gave me one of her knowing smiles and the chatter picked back up around Julie and Robin's plans to watch Danielle's kids for an overnight.

"Do you want to, um, watch them here?" I said, only half joking.

"Yes!" Robin replied, while Julie blinked and seemed to be considering whether I was serious. Of course, I was. Unless they were using the experience as some kind of extrinsic birth control, they needed all the help they could get. She started to answer me when the doorbell rang.

"I got it!" Katy yelped, sprinting from her chair.

"Aunt Maggie, will you pass the salad?" Altan asked. "So I can keep pretending today doesn't seem bizarre."

Robin nodded and Paul snickered again. I admired how those guys could just shrug off any sign of tension or anxiety and eat more lasagna and also not gain a pound. Grrr.

Brittney's back was to the door, but she had her head cocked in that direction. I wasn't sure who might be stopping by. Most people we knew wouldn't bother to ring the doorbell, especially on a Sunday when there were already half a dozen cars in front.

Julie told her, "Imagine if you just go see who's there" at the same time Maggie admonished, "Well, go see who it is!" Brit scowled at each of them in turn before she got up and tried to be nonchalant as she walked that way.

"So really, is there a full moon?" Mikayla said, while Josie fed herself a piece of pepperoni in her lap. "Mercury in retrograde already?"

"Like that's necessary for this crowd," Paul chimed in.

I shrugged. The concept of the cosmos affecting our

behavior was lost on me. For years, at least one person close to me (and of course, sometimes I) had been crazy at *any* given time.

"We are talking about the two unicorns here," Maggie said, with a nod toward the door. I could admit, I was starting to feel a little curious myself. I pretended to be caught up in Josie's pepperoni fascination until Brit returned to her chair, her shoulders back and a look of completely fake nonchalance on her face.

"Where's Katy?" The unison between Maggie and Julie was another sure sign of the apocalypse.

"Outside."

Paul was first. "Well, who was at the door?"

"El."

Oh.

"He gonna eat?" Maggie asked, eyeing me instead of Brittney.

"I don't know."

"Well, is he still here?" Julie followed up.

"Why don't you ask your sister?" Brittney snapped.

So, there it was. Before anyone could answer, Brittney left the table and stomped off, through the kitchen, out the back door.

The table was momentarily silent save for the clinking of forks and jabber of Josie. I had silent conversations with Maggie, Paul, Mikayla, and Julie before I pushed my chair away and followed my youngest daughter.

She was sitting on the swing, her eyes closed, and her face turned toward the sun. In that moment, I wanted to sit next to her, wrap my arms around her, run my fingers through her blonde locks, and pretend she was six again and that would actually make her feel better. But my Brittney... she had to call the shots, even when it came to how to love her.

"I wondered which one of you was coming," she said.

"I won." I sat next to her. "What's up, babe?"

"That." She gestured vaguely toward the street. "El and Katy are make-out buddies now."

"Now? Since when?"

"Since last night at El's show."

I nodded slowly. Singles. Musicians. Drinks. It all added up.

"Is that why he came over?"

Her face got flushed and her volume rose. "He came, supposedly, to talk to me. But she opened the door, and now they're talking, so…"

"Brit."

"*What?!*" Dear God. There she was, sixteen, or maybe six, again.

"Katy is not a threat to your relationship with El. No one is."

She glared at me. "You don't know that."

I nodded slowly. It had been a while since I diffused this bomb, but I still remembered how. "He just met Katy."

"No. He met her before. Fourth of July when we all went to Daniel Island. Your wedding. Daddy's funeral."

Such memories. "I stand corrected. But you all spent time together, what, yesterday?"

She shrugged. "Not a lot of quality time at a gig. Unless you're kissing outside the bathroom door."

I felt so relieved to be an old crone who only kissed near my own bathroom, if any bathrooms at all.

"Brittney."

"Mama! I know what you're trying to do. I don't care. I don't care if he kisses Katy. I don't care if he moves her into his room or *my* room or the couch. I'm just sick of this."

"Sick of what, Brit?"

"All of it!" she yelled. And then the tears started. "Nothing is mine. Nothing lasts. Everything is changing all the time. I just thought that El was… for keeps."

I wanted to hug her. Instead, I asked, "Brit, have your feelings about El changed?"

"*Noooo*, Mama! Jesus!"

I nodded. "You knew at some point it might be that you'd have to share him with someone. Like, I get that sharing him with your stepsister, if that is actually what's happening, would be complicated, but having a platonic soul mate of the opposite sex was always going to get tricky. I'm sure he'd feel the same way if he saw you snogging his brother."

"Whatever," she mumbled.

"Okay, Brit. I'll say no more."

She said no more either. I started to walk away when El came around the corner.

"Mama Jess! Hey!"

We hugged. Brittney glared some more.

"Come inside and get some food when you're… done." I didn't look at Brittney again. I just walked inside.

And there was Maggie, standing in my kitchen, *yelling* into her phone.

"I already *told* you!"

What the heck now?

Paul came in from the other doorway and put his hands on Maggie's shoulders. She started to shrug him off as she kept barking into the phone. "Mags." He said it in the Principal Paul voice. She stopped yelling and walked through the third doorway, into the guest suite.

"Who is she talking to?"

He looked pointedly at me. "Don. He called right around the time you chased Brittney outside, and she's been working toward the yell ever since. Kayla and Altan are gonna take the baby home. It's too nuts here today."

"Lightweights," I muttered, starting to walk toward the dining room.

"Jess." He grabbed my elbow.

"I just want to say goodbye—"

"Jess, I know she's our sister, but she can't disturb the peace in *our* home, okay?"

I felt my heart sink.

"She's not a kid. She's being unreasonable and she's running away, and we can only enable that for so long."

He covered every possible caveat. And he called her "ours." There was no arguing with Principal Paul.

"Okay." It was all I could say.

"Maybe she and Brit can find a place together," he added wryly.

Maybe we should give them this place and run away together, I thought. But I didn't say it out loud, because he would probably agree immediately.

Brittney

HARRISON HAD SENT BRITTNEY A TEXT BEFORE she even woke up that morning. It said,

> SOUNDS LIKE RUTHIE BROKE HER ARM AT A ROLLER-
> SKATING PARTY. HEADING UP. HOPE YOU SLEPT
> WELL AND WILL BE IN TOUCH LATER. – H

She didn't even know how he had her number. Did he ask El? Was that awkward? And she had no idea how to answer. So, after previewing it on her lock screen, she just left it unread. Maybe he would assume she was hungover and being a lazy sack of trash all day.

So, she was on the swing at Mama's, not knowing what to say, sort of looking up at El. The sun was in her eyes, and she didn't really want to see his face anyway. He was probably feeling sorry for her, which was the last thing she wanted.

"Brit, I am sorry you saw Katy and me. It wasn't a big thing, but it was probably a bit inappropriate. We're adults. She's your sister now. And I'm sorry."

"She's not *really* my sister," she muttered.

"I know that's not how you actually feel."

She shrugged.

"Brit, I came here to see you. I came here to say I am sorry this whole rooming thing hasn't been nearly as easy and fun as I expected. You're the closest person in the world to me, but Harry is my brother, and I was asking him for a favor, so, I couldn't say no—"

"You shouldn't have to," she said. "I'm sorry. I'm sorry that I'm thirty-one years old and without a place to live. And I'm sorry I got—whatever I am – about Katy. Who wouldn't want to make out with her? She's all gorgeous and sparkly and fun. But I still don't understand about you and Harrison. You always mentioned him like you weren't connected to him at all, and there's obviously a lot more to it than that if he came to live with you. And his kids—"

"Brit, that's his story. Not mine. I just want you and me to be okay."

"We are."

"Promise?"

She stood up so she could see his eyes without the sun burning hers. "I promise, doof. What did you tell Katy?"

"I told her no one else can crash with us."

Brittney sighed. "You don't know her very well yet. If that's what she wants, it will happen."

He didn't answer.

"You better come eat," she said. "Otherwise, Mama will never forgive herself."

He sighed. "We don't deserve her."

Brittney gave him a quick hug "She's making me learn how to cook, so maybe we do."

El paused before they reached the door. "Listen, about Katy."

Oh geez. Here it comes. "Yeah?"

"She's, uh…" *Was he actually blushing?* "She's staying in town for a few days, but not with us. She's staying here." He paused. "Yeah, this is weird. But anyway, I do want to see her some. I hope it's not a big deal."

It's a big deal that I have adolescent anxiety at my age. It's a big deal that I'm jealous because Katy does whatever she wants while I feel frozen. It's a big deal that you're going to fall in love with her and forget all about me. Both of you.

Another voice chimed in. *Is it a big deal that you were kissing his brother?*

She couldn't tell her own dad to shut up, even if he was just the voice in her head. But she really wished he would.

"It's fine." She shrugged and smiled. "Katy's awesome."

"At least one of us has an awesome sibling-type-person to hang around."

She winced. "El, maybe Harrison isn't… I mean, maybe things could be better, you know. Give it a chance. You guys were having fun last night!"

He didn't answer.

"I know it isn't easy," she added.

"I know you like him." El paused thoughtfully, sighed, then put his arm around her. She tried not to stiffen; he would know something else is up.

"I feel like everything is about to get complicated."

Maybe he did know. But Brittney thought of her blended family inside and shrugged. "I'm good at that."

"Are they actually yelling?"

Brittney raised an eyebrow at Mikayla, who passed her

the clean lasagna pan to dry.

"Well, if they were whispering, I don't think we could hear *every word they're saying!*"

Mikayla heaved a sigh. "Obviously. I just can't believe they are carrying on with all of us here."

Altan had taken the baby home, while Julie and Robin read the signs and avoided the aftermath of dinner. Katy and El were supposed to be helping with the cleanup, but they were eating the rest of the cheesecake out of the tin and singing along to Paul's "Red, White, and Booze" station on the satellite radio.

"I can," Brittney answered, setting the last big dish on the counter for Mama to put away in a place only she could find. She wiped her brow and threw the balled-up towel into the sink, where Mikayla immediately picked it up and folded it over the edge so it could dry. "Case in point," she continued. "Someday I will absolutely lose my shit over you always correcting everything I do, and when I start yelling at you, I will not care who can hear."

Mikayla rolled her eyes. "I don't correct you. You just don't like it when I show enough of a backbone to do things my own way instead of falling on the ground for everyone to walk all over me."

"Whoa, whoa! Calm down. I'm just saying... sisters yell."

"Yeah, but Daddy is up there," Katy added, pausing between bites. "He doesn't do the yelling thing, unless I'm being an idiot."

Brittney stared at her. "I'll refrain. It's too easy."

"Neither of you needs to keep referring to your younger selves," El chimed in. "You're adults. No one cares what you did ten or fifteen years ago."

Mikayla cleared her throat. "We do a little..."

"Shut up!"

El stood up. "I think that's my cue."

"Oh, toughen up," Brittney snapped. "We aren't really arguing."

"I forget," he said. "My family only has three settings… formal, fighting, or silence."

"We are never silent," Mikayla said.

"Unimaginable," Katy agreed.

"You're so silent you don't even mention actual people in your family," Brittney added. Oops. She hadn't meant to start anything, but she was still smarting from those little faces on Harrison's phone.

"Are you serious right now?" El said, just as Katy said, "Oh. Marshall."

Marshall?

Brittney watched for a moment. El glared at Katy while making a slashing motion. Katy's eyes got wide as she looked sideways at Brittney.

She swallowed. "Who's Marshall?"

"Oh, my God." Katy said.

"This isn't the time or place," El answered.

"Time or place for what? Who the hell is Marshall?" She turned to Katy. "Who is Marshall?"

"Brit, calm down," Mikayla said softly.

Brittney felt the heat rising from her core to her face. She didn't know why, exactly. Maybe because everything around her that afternoon already felt unsettled and chaotic. Maybe it was because *Marshall* was douchebag Bradley's last name. But it was definitely because El had kept something else from her, *and* Katy knew what it was. She felt herself unraveling.

She looked at Mikayla and Mikayla only, because hot tears had collected in her eyes.

"I'm gonna walk home. Katy will still give you a ride."

"Brit—"

She was already out the door. She started to jog, but her flip flops weren't cutting it. She walked quickly, but she was only a block away when Katy caught up with her.

"Just wait a minute!" she huffed. "I'm sorry!"

"Oh my God, just let me go. I'm not mad at you!"

"But El—"

"Katy!" She stopped walking, faced her, and put her hands on her shoulders. "I'm *not* mad at *you*. Okay? Please don't make me say it out loud. You know how I feel. We are practically the same person."

Katy looked at her like she'd grown another head. "What are you talking about?"

"I'm jealous, okay?"

She rolled her eyes. "Duh. Okay. But we are not the same person. You have no reason to be threatened by anything that has to do with me. I'm just your loser stepsister."

Brittney rolled her eyes right back. "Loser stepsister? Who looks like Miranda Lambert copied all her sexy from you? Who breezes in and out of every room with every eye on you? Who plays guitar for a living? Who—"

"Who is the butt of every family joke. Who lives in a shanty. Who barely makes enough money *teaching* guitar to drive here most weekends. You're the one who has an actual college degree and career and —"

Brittney waited, because suddenly her anger was subsiding, and Katy looked like she was going to cry. *Don't say it,* she willed silently.

"Your mama adores you and *you still have her.*"

Sigh. "Katy—"

"I know."

"What do you know?"

"We can't use our dead parents as an eternal trump card for our stupid shit."

Brittney didn't even try to suppress her giggle, and

Katy joined in.

"We really can't," Brittney finally said. "But you – your mama adored you, too. And Katy, so does my mama. We are just –"

"Stupid. I already said it."

Brittney looked away, nodding.

"I'm not trying to steal your bestie. That would be stupid."

She nodded again.

"And I am not trying to move in the house where you already live in crowded quarters."

Still looking away, Brittney said, "The whole living situation is stupid."

"Is it that bad? They both seem really nice. And the place isn't exactly small."

"No. There's just not—"

"A place to hide?"

This sisterhood is absurd sometimes. "Mama always says your dad sees right through her," Brittney said. "Sometimes I feel like you do the same thing."

"We're alike."

"That's what everyone says, but I think it's just because we are both the flighty ones."

Katy looked incredulous. "You think you're the flighty one? What about that moppet brother of yours in Tennessee? Are you kidding?"

"The baby of the family can mostly do no wrong." She raised one eyebrow at the younger of the twins.

"Absolute, unadulterated B.S."

They both sighed.

"I'm gonna walk home," Brittney said. "I'm not mad at you. I'm not convinced I shouldn't be mad at El, but that's our deal. And your deal with him is… your deal?"

Katy nodded.

Likely, they were both unconvinced. But Brittney told herself they were too old for drama, and she kept walking.

Paul was sitting on our bed, his face flushed, shaking his head.

Maggie was standing in the doorway to the bathroom, her arms crossed, tapping her foot.

And I was about to run screaming from the room, maybe the house.

"You had *no* right," Maggie seethed.

And my normally pure-of-language husband answered, "Bullshit. Since when does this family have boundaries? You brought Don into all our lives, and he's my friend. He's completely confused and *gutted*, Maggie. You really want me to just ignore him?"

She glared at Paul, then at me.

"Don't look at me!" I snapped. "This is ridiculous!"

"Says the one—"

"No!" This time, I was shouting. Normally, Maggie was the bolder of us, but—

"This isn't about *me*," I continued. "I'm not perfect, but you're being a petulant child. If you don't want to be married, answer your damn phone and *tell him*."

"I answered the phone, and *your* husband almost threw me out of the house."

"Because you were screaming into it ten feet away from our grandbaby!"

In the absurdity of the three of us arguing in the bedroom like middle schoolers, my insides warmed again at his use of "our grandbaby."

"Just tell me," Maggie continued, looking directly at me. "Are you kicking me out?"

"Maggie…" Paul and I had talked about it, about timelines and *boundaries*, his favorite new word. I couldn't say no to my sister; she was closer than a sister. But there had to be guidelines, and she didn't play well with those.

I wasn't looking at Paul, but I could feel him staring at me. This was one of *those* moments for us. His instinct had always been to protect himself and shut people down; mine had always been to prove myself and give way too much. We were helping each other, here in our third act or whatever it was called, but whatever common ground we found, Maggie felt like an earthquake in the center of it.

"We want you to stay," I said carefully. "But we will not lie for you, and we will not disrespect Sheldon." I knew she was hating this, and I was trying really hard not to use my mom voice. "And you have to have a plan. It's not a condition…" Her eyes were flashing. "That part is just a sister thing. This isn't *good* for you, walking around with steam coming out of your ears and adding more bricks to the wall. I have literally *never* seen you like this before." I would not say Tony's name, but we both knew what I meant. "Not ever."

"I am sorry I yelled in your kitchen," she said. Nothing softened in her tone or expression changed. "Are we done here?"

"Maggie—" I started as Paul answered, "Yep."

"I will be out of your hair tomorrow. Good night." She turned somewhat dramatically on her heel and left the room.

"That went well," he deadpanned.

"Of course, it didn't." I tried to keep protest and aggravation out of my voice, but both of us talking to her was never going to work. I would have hated it in her shoes, and I knew her better than to have tried it if he hadn't insisted.

"Jessie, she's not one of the kids. If she wants to leave her husband for whatever absurd reasons, she can. And she can also find a new place to live. The kids aren't even kids. We don't have to be a boarding house for everyone who comes undone for a season."

Don't, I told myself. *Do. Not.* But the only person in the world I'd grown up *and* was growing old with was downstairs thinking I'd dressed her down and kicked her out, and I did not stop myself.

"No. Just for your daughter. Everyone else can fend for themselves."

I don't know what I was expecting, a snap, a crackle, a pop, or at least an angry response.

Instead, Paul rose to his feet, walked to me, put his hands on either side of my face, and said, "Just once in a while, I want to be enough for you."

Then he also left the room.

The two people I counted on for external wisdom had both just stormed away, and I was left marinating in my own inadequacy.

I took my phone from the back pocket of my jean shorts, deftly unlocking and pulling up Abby's name at once. No. She had enough to think about. Morgan? She'd become my best friend by proxy in Maggie's absence and kept plenty busy co-pastoring our church with her husband and keeping up with her own burgeoning family. She didn't seem to mind not hearing from me beyond a church-hallway catchup, sometimes for weeks at a time. No... bothering her with my current state of complications didn't seem right either.

Calm down, Jessie.

The voices in my head were typically a mix of Randall, Maggie, and Paul. Every once in a while, my mom would pop up, and like Maggie, she was almost always telling me what I was doing wrong.

I didn't need that now. I already knew.

Randall and Paul's voices were more affirming, sometimes pointing me in the direction of using my strengths to find a solution.

Did I really need them to tell me?

Paul was right. And so was Maggie.

And so was I.

Now to take that knowledge and actually do something. But first, I stopped and prayed.

I found Paul first. He was in the laundry room, which was bigger than some bedrooms I'd had in my life, pulling on running shorts straight from the dryer. This was sign number one that he was mad; he never ran in the late afternoon when the sun was still blazing hot.

"I guess you must really want to get away from me."

He fished for a shirt instead of looking at me. "I never want to get away from you."

God, he made my heart flutter. "But you walked away."

"I walked away because you said something stupid, and I don't want to fight. If Brittney was staying here right now, the conversation would be different." He sat on the bench and started pulling on his ever-present ankle brace.

I watched him, thinking about his resiliency. Most six-ty-five-year-old men with recurring injuries and orthopedic surgeries behind them would not bother running. Most retired principals and part-time professors didn't go to work in a running store for fun. Most widowed, empty-nest men who'd had a quiet, calm marriage the first time around would not marry a bundle of chaos who was always inviting more. But there he was. *And* he loved me.

"I love you so much," I said.

"But."

"There's no 'but', Paul. You *are* enough. That has nothing to do with this. It's me, always wanting to make everything okay. Right now, I am standing here wishing you didn't have to wear that brace, wondering if there's a different therapy or something that would let you enjoy running a little more—"

"I enjoy it plenty, Jess."

"You know what I mean."

He had moved on to his shoes, white with purple, blue, and neon pink along the soles. There was a time I'd have never believed it, but he swore by his Hokas, saying he could run for miles and never feel a thing. They looked a little like moon boots to me, but he grew up in the south and never had to wear those.

Finally, he was done getting dressed. He sat leaning forward with his elbows on his knees, looking equal parts exasperated and amused.

"I do know what you mean. I know that you know you cannot fix my loose ligaments, Maggie's marriage, Brittney's insecurity, Katy's immaturity, Sam's melancholy, Abby's overwhelm, or your own guilt over not being able to fix any of those things. That's why I don't often get upset with you, Jess." His thoughtful pause made me nervous. "But I do get tired of watching you spin your wheels."

I started to respond. I wanted to. But he was, well, obviously right. And he wasn't the first husband of mine to notice my idiosyncrasy.

"I thought I was getting better at staying in my lane," I muttered. "But when other people veer, I get twitchy."

Paul laughed, just a little. "Is that what you call it? Come on, Jess. Could it possibly be a need to control? To fill up every minute with noise? Whatever it is, you play it on repeat, and it must be exhausting."

He was no longer laughing or smiling. I could see why, not on his face but in my mind. There were all the times I had done the things that seemed momentous and maybe brave but could definitely be classified as impetuous. Moving him into my house too soon. Selling my house when we broke up. Buying the tearoom with Abby when I was still recovering from uterine cancer.

Moving my intense and unfiltered sister-friend into a home that had barely been free of chaos since we moved in... on the heels of Paul's daughter staying there, with her own share of drama. No wonder he felt like—

"Paul." I walked to him and, ever mindful of my own creaky joints, knelt on the floor in front of him. "It's not you. It's me."

He looked at me solemnly for a moment, but then he laughed again.

"Oh darlin'." His arms reached out and pulled me into him. "I know."

I laughed along and swatted his back. "I don't know what to do, Paul."

He nudged me away so he could look at me. "Jess, I would not ask you to do anything to hurt Maggie, no more than I would ask you to hurt one of your kids…"

"And everything that goes with that," I finished.

He nodded a little mournfully. After Julie moved out, which thankfully coincided with her and me beginning a cordial-bordering-on-warm relationship, we agreed on No New Things in our second year of marriage, which, technically, wouldn't be starting for a few more weeks.

"None of it means that I'm unhappy being *just us*," I insisted. "It's just timing, Paul."

Running his hand from my temple through my typically messy hair, he said, "It's always going to be timing. It's *always* going to be something. And we haven't been *just us* yet. Come on, Jess. Between the band of wayward daughters and the tearoom and Taco Tuesdays and Sunday Suppers and Hurricane Maggie and weddings and grand-babies… is it ever going to be *just us?*"

I bit my lip, felt my face scrunching up. I was thinking really hard about it, and I only saw one answer. "I mean… probably not…?"

"Oh my God," he answered, shaking with new laughter and now pressing my hand to his lips.

"Am I wrong?" I asked, not finding it funny.

"I hope you are," he said, trying to catch his breath. "Are we not allowed to be just the two of us? Just sometimes? Have we not earned it?"

I thought about Maggie, all those years raising her daughters alone, while I had a husband who not only took care of our kids and me, but even adopted my son and made him his own – made him *ours* – and made all of us feel like the center of the universe. I thought of dozens of ladies who came into the tearoom who were widowed with no obvious prospects, some with no hope, some with no desire to find love again. I thought of Abby's father, who lost her mother and himself in one fell swoop, who seemed to give up any zest he'd had for life.

And here we were, both of us losing spouses after years and years and *years* of marriage and daring to be fabulously happy together. "Do we deserve it?" I echoed. "I don't know if that is even possible to gauge. Who deserves what we have? Look around us, Paul. We have literally everything."

"It's not our fault that some people don't," he said, rising to his feet, holding on to my hand. "And I'm not going to feel bad about it.

"I'm only going for thirty minutes," he continued, heading for the door. As he opened it, he turned around and added, "I won't feel bad about this either, Jess; to me, having you *is* literally everything."

Brittney

GABE THE GREAT DEBUTED TO SOLD OUT SHOWS his entire first week. He was covered on three local stations; his opening day highlight reel got over 500,000 views on Instagram (this had to be the science of hashtags, not him making a surfboard disappear and then reappear with a hot surfer girl standing on it), and the governor was bringing his grandchildren to the show following Friday. Brittney had help from her old boss Woody scoring that particular connection, but it didn't matter. As far as anyone could tell, it was all her doing.

She'd sat through the show twice, and that was enough. It was Friday again, and The Salty Lips would be playing Saturday. She'd finally given Harrison a thumbs-up tapback to his text, but he hadn't sent or said another word to her, and El hadn't con-firmed whether he would be back to play their gig the following night. So Katy called in a friend to be on standby.

At least she'd been busy, which distracted her, somewhat, from Harrison's silence. Freed, for now, at least, from a week's worth of dealing with high maintenance Gabe and his equally high maintenance entourage, she'd come home to El's and decided to busy. She made a quick list from the three recipes she'd chosen for the brunch she was *cooking the next day, dear God.*

Then she kicked off her shoes, wiggled out of her skirt, blouse, and bra, and threw on a black tank and a pair of cut-offs. *So much for busy.* A night alone on the porch listening to the waves and remnants of music from down the street sounded perfect.

With a Bold Rock in one hand and a bag of Takis in the other, she made her way outside. Scroll, scroll, scroll to the Summer of '69 station she'd created on Pandora. Ah. She sat back, her bare feet on the chair next to her, her phone face down, the tart sweetness of the apple ale all combining to make her exhale the week away a bit.

She had seen earlier that Julio and the Saltines were playing at Neal and Pam's that night, and Offshore Chaos was at The Pier. Maybe El and Katy would want to go out.

They probably wouldn't go without each other.

I miss my best friend.

But I am happy for them.

Katy was the belle of the beach ball now that she had scored the job at Rogneby's Music School. She'd spent a day emptying out her apartment, scored storage space in her sister's garage (because post-partum Danielle was too delirious chasing three kids to care), and was bouncing back and forth between El's couch and El's bed, pretending like Brittney didn't notice.

Her bottle was empty by the time El's truck pulled in the driveway.

"Hey!" he called, heading up the stairs with his hands

full of empty drink containers and a bouquet of daisies.

"Hey yourself. You shouldn't have," she teased.

Was El blushing? "It was Katy's first day at the shop. She was nervous. I just thought—"

"You don't have to explain. She really wants this to work. She really wants to be here."

"Yeah…"

"We will all have you to thank for that. You want anything? I need a refill."

Brittney stepped inside without waiting for his answer. She grabbed herself another Bold Rock and a Corona for El.

"She's not here because of me." He took the bottle and sat across from her, all his end-of-day stuff littering the table between them.

"Okay."

"Brit, she missed her family. I think she's over the living away and setting herself apart thing."

You can live two miles away and still be an outsider. "Yeah. It doesn't seem like it's working for her."

"I know you think this is about me, but you're an influence on her. You don't even see it."

"Me? Please. Everyone looks at her and me like we're the same. We could be the twins and Julie the unrelated one."

"You're all related," he said with a smile.

She nodded. "Yeah. Well, you're part of the family, too."

They sat in their historically comfortable silence then, and Brittney sighed, letting her shoulders relax and feeling peaceful for the first time in weeks. She could hear the waves and smell the salt in the air, her work week had been successful; her best friend was still her best friend; and the weekend stretched before her with possibilities.

Katy's Mustang was the next in the driveway. She

bounded up the stairs in her sky-blue Converse high-tops, with her backpack on, her hair in long blonde braids, looking like a teenager, not only for her fashion sense but for her countenance. Brittney couldn't even wish she liked her less. Katy was magnetic.

"How was it?" she asked as El said, "Good day?"

"It was *awesome*!" Katy sat and reached over for El's beer. "I met a million people. I have three students already. And I am not being paid on commission. They pay me to be there. I can play all of the guitars. After thirty days, I get a sic discount. It's awesome!"

They exchanged all the questions and pleasantries, and Brittney noted that Katy's joy seemed genuine. Katy, who was virtually homeless, had no health insurance, and whose father was still a trustee on her inheritance, didn't seem nearly as unnerved by life as Brittney often was. Brittney had nothing but soft places to land, yet she kept walking around with her tail tucked and her head down.

She needed to be more like Katy.

Maybe you just need to freely be yourself. Finally. Daddy's voice was far away, but his message never changed.

"I'm really happy for you," Brittney told her.

When she snapped her eyes from her own daze to her stepsister, El was holding her hand, and they both were beaming.

Brittney shook her head. "Wow."

El looked sheepish while Katy just kept radiating. Brittney took a deep breath, careful that they couldn't tell.

"You wanna grab dinner?" Katy asked. El was making an apology with his eyes, one that Brittney wanted but didn't want to want.

So, she smiled at them. "You guys go. I'm gonna enjoy relaxing. I'm fixing brunch tomorrow, for Mama, Mikayla, and Altan. Should be interesting."

"I can't believe you kept it down to three people."

Brittney couldn't either. "Your dad is working at Julie's store, and I didn't invite anyone else. So, if you guys want to eat, you can help me cook. They're gonna be here at noon."

"Uuuuuuumm…" was Katy's response. She cooked less than Brittney did.

"Gotta rest up before the gig," El said. They both rolled their eyes at that.

"Let us know how it goes, though!" Katy said, rising, gathering, looking hyped to go.

"You'll do great, bud. Keep it simple." El was already heading for the door.

She nodded and smiled as they headed inside, presumably to get ready for something in which they really didn't want to include her. It was fine. She sipped her second bottle more slowly, scrolling through her #myrtlebeachsc and #localmb feeds to see what else she should know, either for her weekend plans or for work come Monday. Grandiose Gabe hadn't seemed to register with the locals yet; she'd have to work on that next.

Somewhere in there, El and Katy dashed off, hugging her from behind but practically skipping to the Mustang. It made her smile. And it made her hair stand on end when less than two minutes later, Harrison's truck pulled in the driveway.

He slung a messenger bag over one shoulder and grabbed a larger rucksack from the backseat. His gait was a little sluggish and his eyes a bit bloodshot, but he smiled when he saw her sitting there.

"Welcome back," she said, butterflies fluttering.

"Hey, Buttercup."

"I missed you," she said, before she could stop herself. She couldn't help the full and likely goofy smile that filled her face upon seeing his.

She was rewarded with a smile in return. He dropped his bags on the deck and sat down right next to her, reaching over for her bottle and taking a swallow, which somehow seemed more intimate than him kissing her almost a week ago.

"How is Ruthie?" she asked. *Everything* was fluttering.

He sighed, sitting back and handing his phone over to Brittney. Again, touched by the familiarity, she looked at the screen. The little waif with poofy hair was smiling into an impressive ice cream cone covered with sprinkles. She held it with the same hand that was partially encased in purple plaster. "She's fine."

"Oh, that's good. I'm sure she was happy to see you."

Harrison shrugged. "She was honestly pretty unfazed by the whole thing. She was mostly just pissed she had to leave her friend's skating party early on Saturday. We took her to the orthopedist first thing on Monday. It barely required the doctor to set anything. Four weeks in the cast, and he'll check it again."

"That's good…" Brittney could recall at least three times one of her brothers had broken something. The scenarios ranged from the one he just described to surgeries and their mama going a little extra insane for four to six weeks. "It's nice that you could be there."

He gave her a solemn look, eyebrows raised. "In case you're too shy to ask, I didn't need to be there. Denise is usually pretty levelheaded about things, but neither of the kids has ever gotten hurt before, and she's new in the city and didn't have a doctor. It was a whole thing."

Brittney just looked wide-eyed at him. "You don't owe me an explanation." For that matter, El hadn't even known where Harrison had gone or how long he was going to stay.

"I wanted to talk to you," he continued, as though she hadn't said anything at all. "I nabbed your phone number from the band's website—" Wow. That had taken a little digging. She had forgotten her number was there, listed as the booking contact, though El did ninety percent of it himself. "And even though you answered me, well, sort of, I felt like that was an invasion of your privacy. I'm sorry about that. I just wanted you to know..."

Calm down, Brittney, she told herself again. Was this for real? He went from broody and sullen and smoldering to... kind and thoughtful and smoldering.

Jesus, take the wheel.

"I'm glad Ruthie is okay," she said. "And," with just a small amount of flirtatiousness she added, "I'm really glad you're back."

"How glad?" He reached over and took her beer back again.

"Mmm. So glad, I'll let you keep that while I get another."

"Bring two," he said.

Less than a week ago, she was steaming over his assumption she would make him a cup of coffee. Now she was trying not to run to the fridge and back so she could have a drink with him.

She set the bottles on the table and tried to maintain an appearance of calm as he held his arms open to her. He looked so inviting, a little vulnerable, but she hesitated.

So, he stood. And he wrapped those arms around her, at first just embracing her tightly, his face pressed against her bare shoulder. Then his hands found her face and tilted her toward him, and he was kissing her with longing. She accepted and returned it, stepping forward, closer to him, until she couldn't get any closer. He was almost impossibly tall, so she was on her toes. Once he noticed, he slid back into the chair and pulled her onto his lap, the denim of his jeans a rugged contrast against her bare legs. His lips, his breath, his hands all over her, his hair coming loose around his shoulders, his murmured, "I missed you," made her lose her senses.

"What is on these sheets?"

"Who cares? We're in them."

Brittney's legs were entangled with Harrison's. His arm was around her, and her head was against his bare chest. She pictured an after scene in a Scarlett Johansson movie, though she knew she probably looked more like a drowned creek rat.

They'd gotten really sweaty.

"They're Care Bears," she said, refusing to be embarrassed.

"Care Bears?"

"Look, they're old, but feel them. Flannel is the best, the softest. And they were a gift... a long time ago. A *looooooong* time ago."

"Clearly. Like from 1985."

She elbowed him lightly. "I wasn't born in 1985!"

"Yeah, me either Brit. I also don't have Star Wars sheets on my bed."

They giggled. And then, after a short debate with herself, she told him, "My parents bought these for me after I got my first real marketing job. I had a difficult client the very first week. She wanted some things changed in her press release, and her ideas weren't really professional; she demanded a lot of superfluous editorializing. My boss took over and helped her, um, *see* that, but she gave me ten kinds of hell for it. And I took it, even though it went against my nature, which is to immediately fight back with everything I have. Daddy was so proud of me for keeping my mouth shut, and Mama told me I'd perfected my Care Bear stare."

Brittney pictured those little multi-colored bears shooting rainbow beams at whatever the world threw at them.

She felt Harrison nod, his chin brushing the top of her head. "Makes sense. Ruthie has watched them a few times. I don't think she has the stare yet, though."

"Yeah, well. Tell her she doesn't have to. Most people need to hear the truth without rays of light before they finally get it."

There was silence as they thought that over, until Brittney's stomach rumbled, loudly.

"You okay?" he said with a laugh.

"No!" she replied. "I'm actually starving."

He kissed the top of her head. "You're always starving. You should really learn to cook."

Brittney sat upright. "Oh my *God*! I am *cooking brunch* tomorrow! For my *mother*! I haven't even shopped yet. What am I doing?"

He put his hands on her hips and pulled her back to him. "Me."

"Ugh. I knew you were trouble when you walked in." She sang the words, smiling. "I pinned three recipes on Monday and have thought about it for seven seconds since then. I have to go. I have to get to the store!"

"Not yet." He was kissing her shoulder, then her arm, and then he was moving to the rest of her. She sighed. Food Lion was open until eleven. Her stomach was still rumbling, but she was hungrier for him.

Getting groceries at ten o'clock on a Friday night by

the beach was less harrowing in May than it would be in a few weeks. Brittney ping-ponged between the list of ingredients on her phone and the man pushing the cart next to her. She felt whiplashed. After more time in the Care Bear sheets, she and Harrison had quickly gathered themselves, stopped at Chimichanga Llama to share a giant trough of brisket con carne nachos, and then instead of parting ways, he drove her right to the store to *help her shop.*

"Do your quiche with no crust. Call it a frittata. It's easier than an omelet and you can throw in whatever you want."

"Who actually are you?" she said, studying the eggs. "Do I need more than a dozen, you think?"

"Is your whole family coming?"

"God, no." She picked up the ones that said "cage-free" and "organic" because those were the kind Mama always bought. "Just Mama, my sister, and maybe her husband."

"What about my brother?"

"*They* are sleeping in, I'm sure."

Harrison sighed and started pushing the cart forward. "We're probably all a little stupid, don't you think?"

"Stupid is my M.O.," Brittney said, without missing a beat.

"Listen." He stopped again and looked piercingly at her. "You're not stupid. I don't know what the deal is, who told you that you were dumb or less than or whatever, but you're successful and smart and just fine. But I think you should make a salad tomorrow instead of soup. It's too hot and too complicated."

He kept walking in front of her, presumably to the produce. She looked at her phone and scratched "soup stuff" off her list. Then she looked up at his muscled back, outlined by his black t-shirt and military posture. If she was stupid for following him, she sure felt smart at the moment.

After carrying the two sacks of groceries inside, Harrison kissed her goodnight and went to his room. She wanted him back with her, making fun of her sheets, but the voice inside her that was not Daddy's and non-descript was repeating, *Whoa, girl.* She knew he was tired, and she knew her own history of moving too quickly. She would calm down in hopes he would turn out to be for real.

Mama, et al. planned to come over at 11:35. This was Brittney's quirky compromise when she'd suggested eleven. Even though sleeping in didn't mean what it used to (*Ugh. Was this already a symptom of "getting older"?*), she still liked to have one day when she wasn't in a hurry to do something or be somewhere.

Thanks to Harrison's advice, everything she prepped was easy. The frittata was basically a version of dump cake, which she used to make with Mikayla and David every year for Mama and Daddy's anniversary. They would dump a cake mix and a can of cherries together and somehow it became a cake. This time, she started by dumping half a bag of frozen fajita veggies into a skillet of melting butter. She dumped her dozen eggs into a big bowl and whisked them with a little milk. Then she dumped the veggies into that along with shredded pepperjack cheese and pre-cooked bacon that she had chopped into pieces. She added the spices suggested by the recipe: salt, pepper, dill, garlic powder. She dumped the mix into a pie plate and set it in the oven. *Bam!*

Harrison had shown her the packages of pre-sliced fruit in the cooler. "It would get expensive if you were cooking for a crowd, but to save time and effort, this is the way to go." Apparently, contrary to any evidence since they'd become roommates, he was a meal-prepper. She sliced up the mango into bite sized pieces, added her strawberries and blueberries, and dumped the vanilla Greek yogurt into a cute little bowl. She sprinkled cinnamon and drizzled a little of the local honey on top that Mama had brought her from the local beekeeper, Alex, who, of course, was a friend of Mama's. There. The pretty fruit salad and the smell from the oven almost made her feel in command of the meal, and Harrison had been right. It wasn't that hard.

She set the table and waited, singing with the Foo Fighters on the Bluetooth speaker that sat on top of the refrigerator. El and Katy had not shown their faces. Harrison had just gotten back from the gym and, after kissing her slowly and nearly making her knees buckle, had retreated to his room, carrying a protein shake and a banana. She wasn't sure if he was ready for a meal with part of her family, so she awkwardly ignored the whole thing.

"Knock-knock." The only person who would say *knock-knock* besides her mama was her sister. And of course, they already had cracked the door open.

So, Brittney didn't bother to say "Come in." Instead, she accepted Altan's combination of a hug and the passing of Josie to her.

"Hey sugar britches!" she called in her best southern-auntie voice. "I'm so happy you're here to see me! Are you hungry?"

"Cheese!" Josie answered. Everyone had been so proud of her third word, and now it was one only thing she said.

"Auntie Brit has a whole bowl of cheese, just for you!" She carried her to the counter and showed her another item procured at Food Lion the night before: a Princess Elsa bowl, filled with tiny cheese cubes, Goldfish crackers, and a few grapes cut in half.

"Nice job, Auntie," Mikayla said, eyeing the baby charcuterie. "If this is the menu, I am totally in!"

"Shut up!" Brittney retorted, though she knew that baby charcuterie would be just fine with her sister. Heck, it would be fine with her, too.

"Paul is sorry he couldn't come," Mama said, kissing her cheek and handing her a bottle of champagne. "I didn't bother with the juice," she added with a knowing smile.

"Good!" Brittney said, setting it on the counter where the glasses were waiting. "We can garnish with strawberries instead. Here, I cut them myself. With my own hands." Handing Mama the first glass, she proclaimed the spontaneous cocktail "Fancy."

"Perfect," Mama said. She started in on how good the room smelled and how neat everything looked, the whole while looking around, as was Mikayla.

"She only has four places set, you two." Altan kept Josie from prying the fridge open and smirked at Brittney. "Quit being so nosey."

"Where are your roommates?" Mikayla asked. "I figured El would at least want to see us."

"El has a gig tonight and will probably stay in bed until noon. And Harrison..." Sigh. What was she doing? "He just got home Core and Cardio Day at I.S.I. I don't know if he'll want to join us, so I—"

"Oh, Brittney, please do not say you cooked a meal and didn't ask the people you live with to *eat* anything."

"Mama, for God's sake. None of them are starving. Or... or, *handless*. If they're hungry, they'll come eat. This isn't a B and B."

Altan was laughing. "Handless?"

"Shut up."

"Who's 'none' of them?" Mikayla asked, narrowing her eyes. "Who's here besides El and his brother?"

"What?" *She is so annoying sometimes.* "None. El and

Harrison. None of them."

"That is not how you talk. You would say neither. *Neither of them* is eating with us. Spill it, Brittney."

Katy's damn car was in the driveway. It was flanked by the brothers' big ole trucks, but did they really not see it?

"I think the frittata is ready," she said, restraining the urge to snap. "Mama, you want to 'mix' the 'mimosas?' Kayla, your child is heading outside. This place is not babyproof."

Mikayla turned to scoop Josie up from the doorway while Altan turned around and laughed into Brittney's shoulder. "It's not Katy-proof either," he murmured. At least someone wasn't completely blind. She wasn't sure if Katy wanted her presence to be a secret, but Brittney sure didn't feel like talking about it, much less lying about it.

"Brit, this smells really good," Mama murmured from over her other shoulder. "And the Mustang is about as invisible as the cast of Charlie Brown with sheets over their heads."

Brittney murmured the family motto back and broke away from her mom-and-sister bookends, walking to the oven to grandly produce her main course.

Mikayla led everyone in a few oohs and ahhs. Brittney rolled her eyes but felt herself blush a little. She'd always maintained that she didn't care whether she could cook like Mama, or even Abby or Mikayla. She had other things to excel at, is what she said. Every woman in the family didn't need to be a domestic goddess.

But feeding this little portion of her family – not to mention getting help from Harrison – felt really good.

She had moved the table away from the wall and brought in two random chairs from the dining room. She motioned for them to sit, including Josie, for whom they'd brought a booster seat that strapped on to the chair next to "A-tee Brit."

Altan sprinkled a little hot sauce on his frittata, took a bite, and gave her a huge smile. "This is great, Sissy. Especially the real bacon."

"We don't believe in turkey bacon," Brittney and Mikayla chorused together, and then laughed.

Ah, it feels good to laugh. That particular family line stung a little because it was reminiscent of one time when the sisters were in middle school when Jessie had dabbled with turkey bacon during one of her many trendy-weight-loss attempts, and Randall, having returned from a stressful trip that kept him away over a weekend, uncharacteristically hit the roof, dumping a full breakfast-for-dinner plate in the sink and declaring dramatically, "I don't believe in turkey bacon!"

The next morning, they all woke to a bouquet of roses for Mama on the counter and him cooking up three pounds of thick, applewood Carolina Pride.

Mama was taking a sip of her champagne with a sad smile on her lips. Brittney resisted the urge to apologize because they all had an agreement that they could talk about Daddy whenever they wanted, no matter who got sad about it. Being sad was allowed. Being awkward about the memory of the most important man in their lives was not.

Altan picked up the banter and they continued eating. Brittney did not roll her eyes once, even though Mama's compliments on the *cut-up fruit, for crying out loud,* were over the top. They were stacking the dishes and contemplating a quick stroll on the beach when Harrison appeared in the doorway.

He was showered. Brittney could smell the musky, mineral scent of his charcoal body wash. His ponytail was damp. He was wearing a signature black tee (this time, it was a Smashing Pumpkins "Zero" shirt), but instead of jeans, gray swim trunks with a white Hawaiian flower print. Bare feet. All hotness.

"Hey," she said, a little too much in her voice. Mama and Kayla would immediately know... everything.

"Hi," he said, smiling formally. "Sorry—"

"Oh, don't apologize," Mama cut in, being quintessentially Mama. She stepped forward and took his hand in both of hers, a signature compromise when she wanted to hug someone who might not be ready for her. "You must be Harrison. I'm Jessie. We're so happy to meet you."

At least she didn't add, *Are you hungry?* Brittney rolled her eyes at him, but he was fixated on her mother.

"I've heard all great things about you," he said warmly. "I was just going to grab a sandwich and head to the beach for a few hours. I haven't made it there yet, which seems a little ludicrous."

"Oh, it happens," Mikayla gushed, picking Josie up from her Tupperware kingdom in the middle of the floor. "When you live here, it's easy to take for granted."

"Yeah..." Brittney could tell he was thinking of his kids as he added, "I haven't been here long, so it doesn't feel like I'm living here just yet."

Awkward silence, broken again by Mikayla.

"Oh, you didn't grow up here?"

"My older brother and I stayed with my dad in North Carolina when El and our mom moved here, so... no salt life for me until now."

He had turned to the refrigerator while Brittney gaped at him. Mama elbowed her and she just shook her head. *Older brother. What the hell?* So that was the missing link of who Marshall was, which she had been trying to forget about all week.

"Oh, sure," a clueless Mikayla continued. "Otherwise,

you guys would have been camping out with El at our house during high school. It was where everyone always was. Mama cooked for it."

Brittney glared at her. Mikayla shrugged. Jessie ran the next play.

"Hey Kayla, if we're going to take Josie to the beach, we should go before naptime falls upon her."

"Yeah. She gets hangry, except with sleepiness," Mikayla explained.

"I'll be over in a minute," Brittney said, accepting Mama's hug and willing them to hurry. Her heartbeat was accelerating, and she didn't really know why.

They left with a chorus of "Thank you," "Good job," "Next chef in the family," and blah, blah, blah. Harrison was nonchalantly piling ham and turkey onto a hoagie bun and practically humming.

"So, um… that was part of my family at least," she stammered.

"They seem really nice." He had moved on to his Dijon. "Pretty much what I expected."

"Yeah. Mikayla is more like our mama every day. They'll get all up in your business."

"Mmm-hmm." He added lettuce and Havarti, and Brittney was afraid her stomach was going to growl again.

"So, um—"

"What do you want to ask me, Buttercup? You want a sandwich? We can both go to the beach. I would like that."

God, he smelled good.

"Harrison, I—" Why did this make her so nervous?

Because of El. Because you thought you knew him.

"I didn't know you guys have another brother."

He stopped short, put down the butter knife, and turned to her, snapping, "What?"

"Your older brother. I thought *you* were *the* older brother." Something was starting to make sense.

"El never talked about Marshall? Since high school, you never knew about Marshall?"

"No." Her voice got small as she felt herself shrink away. "Where does he live? Why wouldn't El—"

"He's dead."

Her rapidly beating heart sank. She tried to swallow back the million questions she had, and just reached for him with her voice.

"Harris—"

"Listen." He paused, gathering words. "This is the most I want to say right now. Marshall died in a… tragedy. You can Google it. It wasn't long after Elliot and Mom moved here. I have no idea why he wouldn't ever tell you about it, but it sucked for him just as much as it did for everyone else, so I'm sure he has his reasons. I have mine."

That was on the list of her least favorite phrases. *I have my reasons.* It sounded so selfish and faux-mysterious and passive aggressive. She wanted to argue, but how could anyone argue with someone who lost what he had?

After a beat, he asked, "Are you coming to the beach? Your family is already there."

She didn't want to. She wanted to forsake the dirty dishes, go back to bed, and wallow in the shadow covering her that suggested she didn't really know the truth about anything and didn't really have anyone. But she smiled at him instead.

"I doubt they stayed long with the baby, but sure. I'll come. Just let me –"

"I'll help you clean up so we can get there faster." He planted a kiss on her forehead. "But first, I'll make another sandwich because I can tell you're about to pounce on this one, and I can't let you have it. You didn't even share your breakfast. How was it by the way?"

She felt herself slowly unclench as she told him about total frittata success, that it tasted good, that her family seemed to like it, that she actually enjoyed the cooking process. But she didn't tell him that she was missing him through the whole thing because now that another of El's family secrets was revealed, she wasn't sure she could give him any more than she already had.

The first hour at the beach was fake. They'd packed a cooler with their sandwiches, leftover fruit, a bunch of water. They took a frisbee, their towels, their chairs. Brittney felt like one of those Insta-couples as they crossed Ocean Boulevard with all their gear, shades on, bathing suits showing off their tans and fit frames and tattoos. Since it was her profession to make *salt life* look cool and inviting, she knew that's how they looked, like two attractive young people who were chill AF, spending their allotted leisure time from their fruitful and exciting careers on the expansive and beautiful shore because, where else?

The reality was that her stomach was in knots; her hands were almost twitching with the desire to text El and ask him what in the actual hell; her head was a mess from Harrison's intoxicating smell and the sweet way he was talking to her, looking at her, touching her arm or her back as they gathered their stuff and headed to what was, in fact, the jewel of Grand Strand, right there in their backyard. It was a good thing that Mama was gone because she might have hidden behind her like a child.

As soon as they set up their stuff, Harrison headed for the water, which was frigid for her native bones. She sat in her chair with her towel over her torso and arms, sunglasses in place so she could unashamedly watch him. Now that they'd crossed *that* line, she had no problem admiring how gorgeous he was. But he had baggage and secrets and was most likely absolutely no good for her.

Everyone has baggage.

Nope. That couldn't be Daddy's voice. There was no way he would encourage this.

"Wanna throw the frisbee around?"

Harrison dripped cold saltwater precariously close to her as she shook her head.

"You will find me to be completely unambitious when I'm here. I want to snack and nap and tan and make fun of people who are actually doing stuff. I actually have a t-shirt somewhere that even says all that."

"I'm not surprised." He sighed and sat down in the sand next to her, rather than on his chair two feet away. She snuggled deeper into her towel. "Want me to peel some grapes for you, Princess Buttercup?"

"I wouldn't refuse," she murmured, engaging in a momentary fantasy about life being simple, about being as happy and together with Harrison as Mikayla was with Altan, as Julie was with Robin.

They sat there for the rest of that first hour, with him silently passing her *unpeeled* grapes and chunks of mango. Every time her fingers touched his, currents she hadn't felt in forever coursed through her body.

She'd been ignoring her dinging phone, but after a series of four or five in a row, she finally looked. Every text was from El, wondering how brunch went, wondering where she was, wondering if she was coming to the show, blah, blah, blah. She threw the phone back in her bag, the signature sign of her exasperation that did not go unnoticed by Harrison.

"Who needs you so urgently?" he asked, casually.

She didn't want to feel weird about having a close, half-a-lifetime relationship with the brother of a guy she'd just slept with. But there they were, and she definitely was.

"Your brother," she muttered, her voice betraying how mad she was at El.

"Your *bestie*," Harrison teased.

"Some bestie."

She said it before she meant to. He didn't need to be dragged into what she was feeling. They weren't close enough for that, regardless of what had happened the night before.

But with that utterance, the sparkly filter fell away from their beach excursion, and Real Brittney was exposed.

She threw her towel off for emphasis, gearing up, answering questions without acknowledging that Harrison hadn't asked them.

"I just don't get it. I've known El since high school. He's been around my family. We *talk* about family. Why didn't he tell me about your older brother?" Saying his name felt too sacred, too soon.

Harrison scratched his beard. He looked past Brittney, formulating his answer.

"You'd have to ask him. He doesn't talk to me about Marshall, either. Ever."

"And you don't know why?"

He shook his head. "I never asked him. The last time we talked about... it... it got ugly. I don't do ugly, and I don't do drama. So, I left it. Some people just don't like to talk about painful stuff. I leave it at that."

Brittney let the silence sit for what felt like several minutes. She knew it was probably only seconds, but, whatever.

"When my daddy died—"

He was staring at her in a way that made her stop. She felt her face redden under his study.

"I'm sorry. But... it's not the same."

She scrunched up her face. "Of course, it's not the same. Why would you even say that?"

"Because you were looking for common ground where there isn't any."

"That's not necessarily what I was trying to do, but, *what*? There's no common ground between losing a father and losing a brother?"

"No. Your dad is supposed to die before you. If we live long enough, all of us will bury our parents. You're supposed to grow old with your brothers. Your siblings. And I'm old without him. It's not the same."

"You're not old," she muttered.

He scoffed. "You missed the point."

"Do you think everyone but you is stupid?" she snapped. "I *get* your point. I just don't think grief is worth comparing. I never even met my brother Jamie. That doesn't mean I don't mourn him. And *that* doesn't mean it's the same as what you feel for your brother, or what I feel for my dad, or whatever the hell El feels, and none of that even matters. It's not a contest!"

Harrison jumped to his feet. He kicked at the sand and made Brittney shudder. She looked up at him and saw only a glower on his face. He walked back toward the water, signaling the conversation was over.

Brittney sat and cursed the tears pouring from her eyes. Regret was also pouring all over her. She had sworn to herself she would never again be with a guy who made her feel stupid, and here she was, an apparent idiot for assuming grief united people.

And she had no one to talk to about it.

Your mom.

She almost giggled through her tears. "Your mom" jokes were one of Daddy's lasting quirks. Mama always pretended to hate them, but they were funny ninety percent of the time.

He might have been right, but she wasn't ready to talk to Mama. She was a fool for moving too fast, for making her complicated home situation decidedly more complicated, for losing focus on what mattered, and that was being able to take care of herself and not depend on anyone.

She watched Harrison body surfing like a kid. The action was such a contrast with the heaviness of him. A divorced man with two kids in a different state, a less-than-happy home life with his family of origin that no one would talk about, *and* a brother gone too soon? Even in the unlikely event that he could and would open his heart to her, she knew she wasn't equipped to hold everything he had inside. She wouldn't settle for fake. Not again. And thinking of losing her dad reminded her about how she let Bradley cause her to lose herself.

TWO YEARS EARLIER

Brittney sat next to Mama in the front row of the church. One of Daddy's blue and white plaid handkerchiefs was in her pocket. A girl should always have a dress with pockets, preferably black, for formal occasions during which function was more important than fuss. She wanted to hold the hankie, but she saw Mikayla clutching one, and she didn't want to look like she was copying. She didn't want anyone to look at her at all.

Pastor Carter had told a fun story about Daddy taking her and David to the Hot Air Balloon festival, but then he started droning a little bit, and to be honest, Brittney was having a hard time staying alert. She'd been sleeping at Mama and Daddy's, in bed with Mama the first night, on the couch the next few because Mama seemed to want the space. Brittney usually wanted to be alone, too, but this was the worst alone she had ever felt in her life, and she couldn't sleep no matter how hard she tried.

MS. LEAH AND I ARE GONNA SURPRISE MAMA AND PAUL. WHERE DO YOU THINK SHE'D BEST LIKE A CELEBRATION DINNER?

When his text came through, Brittney had been conducting some light internet stalking of El's new girlfriend. She had been mildly annoyed at having to stop, and she zipped off three suggestions of restaurants she knew Mama liked and probably wouldn't have a long wait in the early spring.

THANKS! {FIRECRACKER EMOJI} LOVE YOU.

Almost like an autoreply, she answered, I LOVE YOU, TOO! And that had been that, her last exchange of words with her daddy, ever. The next night had been the dinner plan, the heart attack behind the wheel, the immediately fatal accident for Daddy and Ms. Leah.

He had been the solid rock of her entire existence, and as lost as she'd felt the last few years since the illusion of Bradley ended, whenever she saw Daddy, he gave her this secret smile, reminding her of all the uplifting words he'd said when the bottom fell out of her world.

El sat on the other side of her, playing the role of boyfriend. She squeezed his hand instead of the hankie. He didn't have a dad, and she felt selfish next to him, mourning a dad who was the absolute best and whom she'd gotten to keep for twenty-nine years. And she still had her mom, and her siblings, and El, who was practically family.

It was all good. All except for the gaping hole. She would pretend to be alright because she had no right not to be. But she wasn't sure Daddy's Firecracker, her father's joy, was going to exist anymore.

Case in point, in the here and now of the aftermath of what should have been a lovely afternoon with a hot guy who liked her, she was swallowing every fiery word she wanted to say as they commenced on an almost unbearably awkward but mercifully short walk home from the beach. Harrison left her with a grunt and went off to get ready for the show. Brittney dumped the contents of her hamper into the washing machine and retreated to her bed, pulling the shades, trying to nap, smelling him on her sheets. She was almost relieved when there was a knock on her door.

Almost.

"Hey, are we riding together tonight?"

The stepsister known as Hurricane Katy entered the room, turned on a lamp, and pounced on the bed. She had energy that Brittney had often tried to drag out of Mikayla, the boundless, spontaneous kind. But now there was a wall, one that Brittney had built and named *Don't take El from me.*

She sat up and stretched, biting her lip thoughtfully.

"I wasn't necessarily going to go."

"What?" Katy launched a throw pillow, the silly one she had bought for Brittney that had Danny DeVito's face on it, in her direction. "Of course, you're coming. They're playing Dead Dog. Isn't that, like, your favorite place?"

It had been. It was a weird place for her now because Dead Dog Saloon was traditionally a family favorite. She'd only been there a few times since Daddy died, and two of those had been on Christmas Eve Eve, a night that now held an Oakley family celebration, one without Paul or his kids or their kids. She didn't know if Katy knew that. She didn't think Katy would care. She wasn't sure such traditions would hold for long because the family was blending just fine, but that meant the blurring was happening, too. Daddy's memory was getting a little blurry, and it hadn't even been that long.

She shrugged. "I like it there fine. I just… There's been a lot of family togetherness already this weekend."

Katy raised her eyebrows and stood up.

"Really? I think I missed my invite to your brunch."

"Katy—" She stopped short, having no simple defense. "I'm sorry," she finally continued. "I love you. You're my sister. Sometimes this all just gets a little weird."

"Even for the magical unicorns who go along with everything."

It could have been posed as a question, but Katy stating it the way she did was more proof of what Brittney already knew, if she just calmed down long enough to admit it.

"Just like I'm not stealing your mama, I'm not stealing your bestie either."

Brittney felt her face redden. "There's always room at the table," she muttered. It was the sign hanging in Mama's dining room - in both houses, a permanent Oakley sentiment and an open invitation. Mama made sure it was written in their hearts, too. Was she really so insecure that she couldn't share two wonderful people she was blessed enough to have?

"Why do I feel like there is more to this story?" Katy asked.

Because you and I are practically the same person. Making the same impulsive decisions.

She took a deep breath, looked at her practically-a-twin, and told her the short story entitled "Harrison."

Brittney

If Brittney was going to get treated like a punk, she was going to make Harrison regret it.

That's what she told herself as she burned her hair into submission, the long, stick-straight, highlighted strands dramatically framing her face, which she'd given a little extra attention to with smoky eyes and matte, pale pink lips.

"That will show him," Katy said from behind her.

"Dammit, Katy! If you're going to live here, you have to start knocking. I like to be naked, okay?" Luckily, she wasn't at the moment. Instead, she was wearing a faux-leather corset with cut-off jean shorts. She was out for revenge.

"Hello, hottie!" Katy responded. "Looking like that, I imagine *someone* will be seeing you naked before the night is over."

Brittney sighed loudly, turning away from the mirror and glancing at Katy appraisingly. It was equal parts amusing and annoying how much they resembled each other. Katy's long, blonde hair was falling in beach waves down her back. Her sun kissed face was mostly free of makeup, save for a little glitter and mascara that might actually have been magnetic lashes. She was wearing a red halter top and black shorts and was going to make it hard for El to remember all his lyrics. The thought almost made Brittney giggle.

"Shush," she told her, deciding she was done getting ready.

"I'm glad you decided to go."

"Mmm." Brittney still wasn't sure it was a good idea, but normally she wouldn't miss a "big show," and Dead Dog was right there under House of Blues for a local cover band, and just because everyone else was acting like jerks didn't mean she would.

Strategy was employed. She and Katy arrived minutes before the start. El had a small table near the stage in reserve for them, informally covered with an iPad case and a jacket over one of the chairs in hopes no one would take it because the bar crowd didn't have much regard for saved seats or those "with the band."

Katy walked right over to El for pre-show affirmations, and Brittney scanned the drink menu, as though she didn't know it by heart, trying her hardest to ignore Harrison and everyone else for that matter. Seconds later, Geno occupied the seat next to her and pushed a half-empty cider her way.

"Here Brit. I can't finish it before we start."

Just what she wanted, the dregs of a dude's drink, especially the dude whose idiotic antics had been the catalyst for her ridiculous living situation.

Don't be a victim.

She willed Daddy's voice to just be quiet and smiled

wanly at Geno.

"Thanks. I think."

"How's it going with your roommates?"

"It's pretty weird and mostly not fun. How's everything at my dream house?"

He laughed. "I haven't changed anything pink yet," he said. "You really did love the place. I didn't realize…"

Would it have mattered? She told her heart not to dwell on that question.

"Well, I hope you find it cozy. I miss it. It was perfect for me."

"It's a soft place to land that I probably don't deserve," he said. Brittney knew he had cheated on his wife, that upon finding out, she'd kicked him out and declared her intentions to divorce him ASAP, that he couch-surfed for nearly a month in the hope that she would reconsider and take him back. Perhaps her bitterness about him moving into a house he owned was misdirected.

"You probably don't," she said with some gentleness. "But it is your house. And I am sorry things didn't work out how you hoped."

"Ha. It wasn't that things didn't work out. It's that I ruined them. I know that."

She had no response for that.

"I know you're not asking for advice from a middle-aged cheater," he continued, eyeing the stage as some of his bandmates started to gather. "But don't look a gift horse in the mouth. Look that up if you need to. I had more than I knew I had and didn't appreciate it. I know it sucks to be bunking with your high school buddy and now his brother, but at least you have friends. And family. And a soft place to land."

Brittney nodded, following Geno's glance to Dave strapping on his guitar and making his signature wide-eyed "Let's get this show on the road" face at both of them. She then looked over at Harrison, clad in black, his hair pulled back and highlighting his deeper tan from their time at the beach, his black bass reflecting the lights, his face reflecting its typical stoicism.

"You're right," she murmured. "And hey. We all make mistakes. Doesn't mean we don't deserve those things."

"Thanks Brit." He stood and smiled at her before joining the rest of them. El was grinning from ear to ear as Katy walked away from him. Mikey was in his own world, fixing a newsboy hat atop his red hair. Ringo appeared to be scowling out at the audience but caught Brittney's eye and broke out in a grin. It made her feel victorious.

As the opening of "Breath" began, Brittney took a sip of Geno's drink, closed her eyes, and felt immediately warmer. The familiar patio, with the smell of the marsh mingling with fried seafood, beer, Katy's perfume, and El's voice, washed over her with the deep sense of home. It was not the usual song they started with, but she could feel the room coming alive to the drive of the drums even while the lyrics stirred something in her. "You take the breath right out of me; you left a hole where my heart should be." It wasn't Harrison's fault. It was just where she was.

So, she looked at him as he played. He wasn't mic'd, but he was singing. She wished she could hear him. He didn't look at her, so she looked away, and when her eyes moved to El, he was staring straight at her. Or was it Katy? No. It was her. She needed a drink.

Katy didn't even glance her way as she left the table for the bar. She stood there through the rest of the set, drinking her starter drink – Diet Coke with Tito's and grenadine, then nursing a Tito's and soda until the break. As much as she felt familiar for the first seventeen seconds of the night, she felt untethered now. Katy was already flanking El. Maybe one of the guys would come chat with her. They weren't exactly her people, though. She thought of them as recess friends, like the kids she'd see only at lunchtime. They'd run on the playground and trade snacks, and when they got older, share secrets and gossip and even try to make plans outside of school. And then they would forget all about it until recess the next day, and if they didn't have lunch together the next semester, they'd forget forever.

No. It wasn't one of those guys who would make her feel less alone.

There's only one you want here anyway.

Hot damn. Was *Katy* a voice in her head now?

Ringo appeared next to her, his sleeveless Alice in Chains shirt already soaked with sweat. Brittney wrinkled her nose.

"Mas tequila." He was looking at her, but she wasn't sure if it was a question or a statement, and whether he was talking to her or the bartender. So, she just smiled and nodded.

When his hand materialized in front of her face with a shot glass in it, she was clear.

"To recess friends," she said aloud. Whether he heard or understood, he clinked his little plastic cup to hers and nodded at her as he walked away.

And *then*, El was there.

"Hey," she muttered. Was the tension real or imagined?

"Thanks for coming," he said.

"Are you mad at me about something?"

He motioned to the bartender. "Why do you ask?"

"You started off with a pretty angry song, which is unusual, and then you glared at me during a whole bunch of it."

"Did you sleep with my brother?"

Her mouth dropped wide open. It wasn't that she was hiding it, but she thought it was less obvious than that.

She stiffened. "Apparently you already know the answer to that, so I will respond by reminding you that you're sleeping with my sister."

"I didn't keep that a secret. And I love her."

"You *what* her? You've known her for an hour, El."

"I've known her almost as long as I've known you."

"Saying hi at some random Fourth of July parties doesn't mean you know her." She tore her eyes away from him and looked around the room. Katy was talking to Geno and Mikey. Harrison was nowhere to be seen.

"You don't know Harry. So, I am saying this for your protection, and you can do what you want with it. He doesn't stick around. His kids are in a different state, in case you forgot."

"El—"

"No." He held up his hand. "Brit, this is what you do. You see the best. You lie to yourself. He's lonely, you're lonely. So do whatever you want, but do it with your eyes wide open."

Whatever formality, politeness, quest for peace had kept her calm fell away. "Eyes wide open? Are you sure?" She struggled to keep her voice low, and the room was so loud it convinced her not to care. "I've known you half our lives, and I didn't even know about Marshall. So maybe I don't know you either."

A storm washed over El's face. She wondered if she had gone too far, but it was too late to change any of it now.

"Brittney." The seriousness in his voice unarmed her. "If I wanted to talk about my brother, I would have. All I have ever done is protect you and stay loyal to you. Trust that. Respect *that*. If you can't, because Harrison shared something with you that is private to me, then we need to reevaluate who we are going forward." He ordered his drink and stood there, not looking at her anymore.

"I'm just surprised," she said, as softly as she could to still be heard. "I thought I knew everything about you. You sure know everything about me." And she hated that fact in that moment.

"You do. I just didn't need you to know my brothers, too. You're the family I chose. And I chose to leave them in the past."

"Until you needed a bass player?"

Well, shit. That's when Harrison showed up. Of course.

"I wasn't talking to you, Harry."

"Well maybe you should, instead of talking to her. Say what you wanna say and quit stomping around like a ten-year-old."

Instead of talking to her? Every alarm in Brittney was sounding off and flashing. She felt like she was caught between two strangers.

"You're the best bass player I know, and I don't want to see anyone sleeping on Mom's couch. Ever."

"And that's it?"

"That's all."

"Then I will get out of your way after tonight. Bass players are all over this town, and I don't need your pity."

Brittney gaped at him. He didn't look back.

"Fine." El slammed his bottle on the bar and walked away.

"So, you're just gonna leave?" Damn her racing heart. She didn't want to care.

"I bet that's what my brother told you I would do."

"Harrison, I'm flying blind here. You and El have a thing that's only yours, and I'm in the middle, and I don't want –"

"We don't have anything, so there is no middle. I'm sorry I let things get more complicated than they need to be."

"Yeah? More complicated?" Her tension turned to anger. "That's it. A complication. You used me. Dammit." She shook her head vehemently. "I'm so stupid."

He stepped forward and put his mouth over hers. She started to verbalize an objection, but her protest was lost in her own desire.

"What are you doing to me?" he said as he broke the kiss.

"You? You're doing this to me. You act like you hate me and then you throw yourself at me and take me grocery shopping."

"I take you shopping, and you don't even ask me to eat with you."

"Like you wanted to hang out with my family. You don't even like *me*."

"Brittney, for God's sake. Grow up. Do I seem like a man who *likes* anything? I live 400 miles from my kids, and I'm bunking in my grandmother's beach house. With my brother. Who *hates* me."

She stared at him, his eyes dark with their chocolate-brown hue and their intensity. He was just lonely and lost. That had to be all it was, and she couldn't be his soft place to land, especially if he was just going to leave.

"I'm sorry about brunch," she finally said. "It was really, really good."

He snickered. "I forgive you. I'm sorry I'm a brooding ass. I just can't... I kind of can't believe this is what my life is."

The sadness dripped off of him like his drops of sweat. She was catching it, longing to dry him with empathy and hugs and if she was super honest, some time back in her

Care Bear sheets.

"Maybe your time here, however long it is, doesn't have to be awful. I like spending time with you. Can we just start there?"

She saw his shoulders slump with an exhale. He was looking at the stage, and the vibration of the room denoted that intermission was almost over. Dave was walking past them with his orange drink in his hand. He stuck his tongue out at them and said, "Safe to say you guys started somewhere else and something else already."

Harrison looked at her, and they both laughed. She gave him the briefest of hugs before he headed back to the stage.

Do I stay here? Do I sit? Do I leave?

Do I stop debating ridiculously small issues like a child and just be in this moment?

Katy, who had been around El and the band for exactly one week was sitting at the front table hootin' and hollerin' like the number one fan of the century as they launched into "Mr. Brightside." Brittney had been by their sides since they started.

Take your damn place and stop shrinking.

It wasn't anyone's voice but hers.

Drinkless and head high, she sat in the seat next to Katy, scream-shouting the words as her eyes went from El to Harrison.

The song said it was only a kiss. No way.

"El wants to go home. Are you staying for a while?"

She knew Katy just wanted to ride with him. "Give me your keys." She pretended to be a little put out.

"I can drive. It's not like it's far."

"I know, but you'd rather go with him, and I want to

keep my options open."

"Brittney?" When Katy looked at her or anyone else like that, there was no resisting her.

"Yeah?"

Katy took a step forward and wrapped her arms around Brittney. She didn't let go. And then she swayed a little. And just when Brittney thought it might be starting to get a little obnoxious, Katy actually wrapped a leg around hers.

The laughter was immediate. "You're an idiot!" she told her, breaking the embrace. "And the best. Go home. Have fun. Make good choices."

Katy turned to leave. Brittney wasn't sure where El was and was glad she wasn't watching them walk away together. It wasn't lost on her that she'd used the word "home" with Katy. It was very likely true, or about to be. And it was up to Brittney alone to either get comfortable with it or change her own situation.

"You staying?"

There he was, his voice gravelly. Brittney had noticed Harrison singing to most of the songs tonight. He hadn't done that before.

"Maybe," she answered. "You lost your voice."

"Long time ago." He delivered the sad words in a matter-of-fact voice. "You want anything?"

"Nah. I'm back to hydration," she said, holding up her ironic half-empty glass of tea. "Why don't you sing with him? Do you actually suck?"

He motioned to the bartender for his tab and shook his head with a little laugh. "No. I don't. But it sucks between me and my brother. I don't know how to fix it."

"Civil discourse?"

He shook his head. "It must be some family you have, if you think sixteen years of hostility and resentment and regret can be cured in a conversation."

She stiffened.

"Hey." He put a hand on her shoulder. "I'm not being critical, Brit. Jeez, do you always default to that? I'm just saying that ability seems rare. My family is barely a family, so I'm not even counting us when I say that *most* families have something nobody can talk about without starting a fight."

"We have stuff," she said. "I think we just make peace with it so we can move forward."

She felt her posture change, how she raised her shoulders and her chin and spread her feet apart, hands clenched like a battle stance. He noticed.

"You wanna go talk about it?"

"Where?"

He shrugged. "We're the smartest couch crashers in the world. Let's go to our beach."

She couldn't have ordered a more perfect night, or morning. It was almost one when they got there. With only a crescent moon in the sky, they momentarily had to use a phone flashlight to find a place to sit, careful to point it toward the water in case any sea turtles were nearby. The tide was going out, and they sat in the sand while she told him the story of Mama, Daddy, and Paul.

"It's not fake," she said, remembering Mama's face while wearing her bohemian wedding dress, not even a year ago, right there on that beach. "We want her to be happy. We love how he takes care of her. And we love him. If you meet him, he's… I mean, Paul is just amazing. He has overcome a bunch of his own stuff that he never talks about and he's smart and accomplished but like… he's just mellow. He works at the running store for fun. He coaches his grandson's t-ball. And he puts her so at ease."

"But he's not your dad."

She shook her head vehemently. "He's not. He doesn't

try to be, which makes him even more likeable. He doesn't force a thing, but I know if I needed something, he wouldn't treat me any differently than he treats Katy or her sisters."

"So, you're grateful. You know what you have. It's okay not to view him as a dad."

"It's not just that." She looked at where the water was, listening to the waves and wishing she could see them in the dark. He waited for her.

"I think Mama is a little happier now than she used to be."

To Brittney, the words were deafening there in their private outdoor space. She'd never really even said them to herself before.

Harrison scooted a little closer to her, and she could sense his nodding head. "I sort of get it. I haven't experienced that, but I understand. Denise is happier now than she was when we were married. I don't think that's all my fault, and I know it's not the same. But my mom? I don't know if she's been happy a single day in her life. She's always restless, searching for something to fill a hole. When Marshall died, she was devastated, of course, but I don't know if it changed her like that kind of thing usually changes mothers. She was melancholy and lost for as long as I can remember. After Marshall, she stayed melancholy and lost. She is on her second husband since then, and she had two before then. This one seems to give her some peace, and since no one or nothing else has been able to, I'm just relieved."

"I think El should know that," Brittney said in a quieter voice, not sure she should say anything. "He... you know, he kinda seems to hate her. It might help him to know."

"It *would* help him to know," Harrison said emphatically. "But he would have to be willing to listen, and he would have to admit that he actually has compassion for all of it. El was screwed over the most because he was the youngest. The soft side he shows to you and the charming side I assume he shows as 'Director of Marketing' for the whole city, or whatever he is, that's not who he is to me. He's hard and resentful and has every right to be."

"Jesus." It was the only response she had.

"Thank you for not asking me what happened." He put his arm around her then and pulled her closer, his chin resting on her shoulder. "Today caught me off guard, and I just didn't feel comfortable talking about it. I'm sorry I got so edgy with you, and it's fine now, but I think you should talk to El first."

The loyalty and respect in that said more about his feelings toward El than anything else he could have added.

If you learn to trust yourself, you won't have to worry so much about whether you can trust other people.

That wasn't Daddy being Jiminy Cricket. That was a memory of something else he said after Bradley broke her.

"El is the only man outside my dad and brothers that I have trusted since Bradley," she murmured. "And out of all of them, I guess I trust El the most. Or I did. I'm not trying to overdramatize things, I just—"

"Talk to him," Harrison said, and then shushed her with a kiss. "You'll feel better. And maybe if it works out for you, I'll try to talk to him, too."

"Hmmm." She sighed and snuggled into his side. Everything felt perfect, even if a little blurry from a long day and the early morning hour.

They sat quietly until both of them were nodding off.

"We should maybe go home, Brit."

"I love how we keep saying we're homeless and calling it home."

"Yeah." He scooted himself up and held a hand out

to her.

Inside her room, she kept the lights off and pressed her cheek against his chest.

"Thanks for listening tonight."

He caressed her hair, falling in tangled waves down her back.

"Thanks for talking. Almost like you trust me."

She sighed. "I almost do. And I want to."

"Scary, though." His lips brushed the top of her head. "For you, too?"

"Brit." He pulled away, his hands going to the sides of her face, and though it was dark, he looked into her eyes. "I already do. I don't have any fear about trusting you. But my future is unknown, and I want you to have more than that. The one thing everything about you shouts is that you want stability in your life. That's one of the things I don't have."

"You're not wrong," she said. "But we don't have to figure everything out right this second, do we? That's a good lesson for me to learn, to wait."

He pulled her tighter. "So, we learn something together? That sounds very mature and wise."

"Let's try it anyway."

Jessie 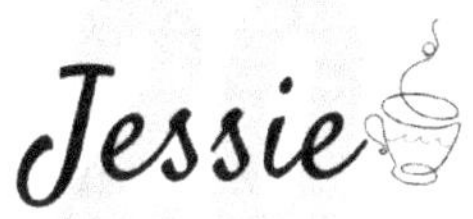

"I'M READY."

Maggie stood in the doorway between the kitchen and the guest suite. It was her first appearance in over a week.

Paul agreed with me that we would ignore her until she came out of her cave, even if said cave was in our house. She couldn't stay there forever, and now that she knew how we felt, our goal was to preserve our relationship with her.

Her response had been to stay within feet of us but out of our sight, until this moment. The whole thing had felt like a bloodletting.

"Your tenacity knows no end," I said.

"Well." She sighed, slipping into one of the chairs. "It's Tuesday, I want pie, and of all things, I can't handle the Farmer's Market without you."

I refused to laugh. My market-friendly canvas totes were sitting right there on a different chair, with my wallet and keys and sunglasses. I rarely missed the Surfside

Farmer's Market. Abby and I were even considering being vendors there if we could grow extra hands and a few more hours in the week.

"You want some coffee first?"

"Jessie Rose, I have been in your house for a week without your coffee. What do you think I do every morning?"

"Maggie Moo, I have no fricken idea. I was just staying out of your way and hoping you weren't destroying the place in your unadulterated ire."

She rolled her eyes dramatically. "Sometimes I detest having a writer for a sister."

I sat across from her and studied her face. Her eyes were tired, but she seemed less prone to explosion than she had since her arrival.

"I'm still your sister, then?"

"Don't be stupid. We've been through a lot more than this."

"Yeah, but—"

"Jessie." She reached out and patted my hand. The gentle reassurance of it almost brought me to tears. "I put you in a bad spot. And no matter how I feel about my current state of affairs, I never want to make yours difficult."

"I knew that."

"And I definitely don't want to stress out that beautiful saint of a husband you've managed to land yourself."

We both cackled then. Maggie's crush on Paul was one of our ridiculous and long-accepted running jokes. She idealized him, and he adored her, and I was so relieved their last conversation had not jeopardized that.

"You don't have to tell me anything," I started carefully. "But you certainly seem to be in a better frame of mind."

She stared out the window above the sink. "I don't have anything to tell yet. But I'm going back tomorrow."

"You are?" I left the unasked questions in the air.

"Yes. And I gave Sheldon a heads up. We haven't talked all week either. And I don't know what's going to happen, but I know two things."

I waited nervously.

Ever one to command a room, she stood, poofed her up-do, straightened the scarf around it, and declared, "I want to stay married. And I want to move home."

As if "home" was a simple concept of late with some of the women in my life... I had to clarify and ask, "Back to Greenville?"

She lifted her chin higher. "Home is here, not there," she answered. "And I want to be married *here*!"

The tearoom was at its late afternoon lull when Maggie and I arrived, fresh from the market with an overflowing bag of strawberries, a tomato pie from Jupiter, dinner rolls from Benjamin's for our supper, Caleb Wygal's latest Myrtle Beach mystery (I needed that guy on our marketing team; he was everywhere), and a little shell necklace from Creations by the Sea that I got when Maggie wasn't looking, so I could sneak it into her luggage before she left.

She was coming home.

I was so excited at the prospect of having her back that I didn't press her too much on how exactly she was going to pull it off. Sheldon was a partner in his law firm and leaving had been out of the question, but that was before the possibility of Maggie leaving altogether.

Ultimatum? Fair compromise? The price of love? That was theirs to decide. Randall and Paul were telling me firmly and practically in unison to stay in my lane.

There was one table for two occupied in the dining area. I dropped Maggie off at another table and walked to the kitchen to put my pie in the fridge. I expected to see Abby in there "brewing and stewing." The after-school hours were usually the most stressful for her, getting the kids off the bus, ensuring all the homework was done and the papers signed and Summer to dance and Jacob to karate or soccer or Lego Club or whatever was his seasonal passion. I tried to handle those for the most part, but I had Tuesdays and Fridays off, so she handled them while hosting the tearoom and… well, trying not to explode sometimes. This time, though, she was standing next to the stove, leaning on the counter, crying into Sam's chest.

"Oh."

I didn't mean to say it out loud, but it came out anyway. And of course, they both heard me. Abby just stood motionless, but Sam looked up and just shook his head. He pointed to the order pad sitting on the counter. I cast a glance and nodded. He held up a finger, and I set my wares quietly in the fridge.

"Your order is taking just a few extra minutes," I told the two seated ladies. They were already sipping their tea. "Your dessert today will be on the house."

They nodded politely, and I returned to Maggie, catching her up in a hushed voice. Less than five minutes later, Sam escorted Abby hurriedly out the door. I headed to the kitchen and finished the tea tray she had only just started. Once the mini sandwiches, scones, and berry tarts were placed, I carried everything to the table with more graciousness and apologies. Moments after I returned to Maggie, Sam materialized.

"Sit down, Sam," his Auntie Maggie said, reading my mind. He tended to loom.

He obeyed. We both let him have his minute.

"Mama, we need to find a way for Abby to get out of this."

Oh, my God. Was she crying over the tearoom? That

was all? In the ten minutes since I'd arrived, I thought a child was sick, Sam had lost his job, her daddy had sunk further into depression, and a few things that were worse. The tearoom was mostly for her. I could walk away at any minute.

Only, if she wasn't there, it was fixin' to be all mine.

"Oh, Sam. Is she okay? I mean, like, besides not wanting this anymore, is she healthy? The kids are okay? Are you... ?"

He sighed, loudly. That was my cue to stop it. Maggie stifled a laugh.

"She's fine. The kids are fine. We're fine, everything's fine. This year has just been hard on her, like it has for everyone else. I think... she thought having her own place would make it easier, but, as you know..."

As I knew, owning a business was hard. Owning a niche business with a very slim profit margin surely took a toll on their household income. I paid myself minimum wage and didn't take any tips. It drove Paul crazy. We kept additional employee hours to a minimum as well, which meant I did most of the food ordering and prepping—second nature to me—and Abby did most of everything else, which included some learning curves for her.

Summer and Jacob were getting older, and Travis was grown, but the weight of raising kids and losing parents was heavy, and it was visibly taking its toll on Abby.

That didn't mean I knew what to do.

You cannot fix it, Paul's voice said.

Just wait, Randall added.

"Well, bud, we'll figure it out," I finally said. "If she just needs a break, I can swing more time here right now." Sam frowned. Paul's voice in my head protested. "If it needs to be more permanent, we will cross that bridge—"

"I'll do it," Maggie said.

Sam's eye roll was immediate, as was his, "Oh, for crying out loud."

"No," Maggie said. "No crying. You can be the second one to know, son. I am moving back home, and I'm gonna need a job."

"What is she talking about, Mama?"

I threw my hands in the air as Maggie snapped, "I'm not actually losing my faculties, boy, so don't be asking her."

"Sorry, Aunt Maggie, but it's not like… getting a new bank job. I think Abby wants to sell her half of the business, not just have someone come work in her place."

Now Maggie gaped at me. "Can you please tell your child that I am not an idiot? Just because I've had two weeks of well-earned lunacy doesn't mean I can't comprehend his words."

"I'm telling both of you to cool it," I said. "I still have customers in here."

With that, I stood up and began the business of finishing up. The two ladies asked for their strawberry shortcakes to go (no doubt due to the fact that our family chaos was spilling over into our normally peaceful haven), and I locked the door with gusto behind them. We didn't need one more person to experience our specific brand of crazy.

By the time I set the dishes in the sink full of water and put on coffee to brew, my two people seemed to have moved from conflict to cahoots.

"Well, Mama, if you were going to partner with anyone else, this is the best-case scenario."

Maggie beamed, gesturing grandly as if to say, "Look how perfectly all the pieces of life are coming together."

Well, didn't they just have it all figured out for two actual hot messes?

"I think we are forgetting a few central points here." I did not sit down. "One, this is *my and Abby's* business, and nothing is transpiring until she and I have a conversation about it. Two, Maggie, you haven't yet had a conversation with your husband, and you also don't have a place to live, and there ain't enough room in this kitchen to cook, much less crash. And three, I don't know what I want to do. Maybe this is the end of this road *for me*. So, you two can flap your jaws all night long if you want, but it isn't up to you."

I marched back to the kitchen for my coffee, suddenly feeling like I could also use a good cry. I wished Abby had talked to me, though I certainly didn't blame her for talking to her husband first. I was ready to go home to mine, and as excited as I was to have the only person who'd known me my entire adult life back in town, I was ready for Maggie to go back to hers.

Brittney

"I don't want to go."

Brittney was nestled in her bed, trying to remember a rainy Thursday morning on which she had felt so happy. Harrison was nestled into her back, his arms around her, his face burrowed in her neck. The drops on the tin roof made a hypnotic drumbeat that had lulled them back to sleep for almost an hour after her alarm.

She couldn't remember a better Wednesday in her life. After work, they ran on the beach; well, he mostly ran in circles around her as she walked. Then he talked her into cooking for him. Without too much stress, she'd made quesadillas, filling them with scrambled eggs, cheese, and green chilies from a can. It was the fanciest dinner she'd ever made, which was sort of embarrassing, but he rewarded her by washing all the dishes and then washing her hair.

They had been up late.

"I don't want you to go either." He peppered her neck

with small kisses leading to her ear. "But you gotta."

"Mmm. Give me one good reason."

He turned over to seemingly search for answers on the ceiling. "Hm. Well, for one, my child support came out of this paycheck, so dinner is on you tonight."

She made a pouting face as he gave a sardonic little laugh. "You don't play fair," she said. "I want to have dinner with you, but I still want to stay."

"You don't have to pay, silly Buttercup." Now he was caressing her arms, sending a shiver over her. "But you should probably go to work."

She had questions about his child support, his custody arrangement, his divorce, but instead, she uttered, "Five more minutes" and snuggled deeper between her pillows and him.

When the snooze sounded again, she mustered all her willpower to jump from the bed and *not* look at his muscled frame contrasting with her pastel bedding. She grabbed her phone and started reading through the morning's first messages.

"You want to go to the gym with me first? Like right after work?"

She paused halfway through gathering her clothes. "Ew. Probably not."

"I thought you liked it?"

"I liked it the one time I went with you, but I'm better over with the other neophytes at Planet Fitness. Barbells scare me."

"We don't always use barbells."

She examined a pair of pants and decided they were unwrinkled enough. Then she looked at him and sighed. "But you'll be there, pumping and jumping with all your sweaty muscles. How am I supposed to focus on anything with that going on?"

He smiled, and then made matters worse by getting out of bed and walking to her, putting his hands on her hips. "I believe in you."

Maybe he meant it tongue and cheek, but she took it straight to her heart and decided she would be late for work.

He smiled, and then made matters worse by getting out of bed and walking to her, putting his hands on her hips. "I believe in you."

Maybe he meant it tongue and cheek, but she took it straight to her heart and decided she would be late for work.

"Brittney. Let's talk."

She rose from her desk as soon as Cristina said her name. It rarely happened and was typically not a good sign.

"Yes, Cristina. How can I help you?"

It was such a fake phrase, but the only benign thing she could think of to say.

"Come on in my office. It's been a while since we had a chat."

Sweet baby Jesus. It had been a while mostly because she couldn't stand talking to her, not least of all because of her antics the night The Salty Lips had played at the Boardwalk Square Italian Festival in March, when they opened for Jeremy's Ten, a well-known Pearl Jam tribute band. It could have been a nice boost for them, but a drunken Cristina had made a scene trying to sit on Ringo's lap and play his tambourine. She'd ruined the set and the vibe of the whole night for Brittney, El, and anyone else who had to deal with her.

Brittney grabbed her planner and sat stoically across from the desk.

"So, we have a few gaps in the schedule for Hall-o-beach. I need two bands, at least, and not that gloomy '90s grungy goth crap." Brittney willed herself not to visibly cringe. "We already have the name sponsors, but we need some secondary ones from the complex. Some new things. Get that crazy, gargantuan shake place involved. That pirate makeover place. And maybe your magician."

Her *magician. Ew.*

"Yes ma'am. I'll get right on it." She started to stand.

"Brittney, I'm actually not finished."

"Oh, sorry. I was just ready to run with it." Fake tiny laugh. Fake smile.

"A couple of things are changing with the new VP in place. There will be more official communication, but I knew you'd want to know, so you can plan your time better. Work from home days will be extremely limited for special circumstances, and there will be no more comp time for event days. Roland feels strongly that as a marketing team, events are simply part of the job, and since the atmosphere and vibe is the brand, we need to be on-site when we work."

"I can understand that," Brittney answered. "So, what is being offered to replace those benefits?"

Cristina tilted her head and scrunched up her face. "Replace?"

"Yes. Since comp time was given instead of overtime, does that mean we will get paid more for being on-site outside of regular office hours?"

She shook her head, the condescension evident. "Those were really more informal perks than benefits. I would not expect anything to 'replace' them off the bat. Maybe in time, when evaluations roll around, there will be some tangible rewards for the hard work."

"Performance reviews notwithstanding, this is kind of a blow, Cristina."

Cristina shrugged. "I obviously don't have any say at this level. Upper management sets the benefits."

"I thought they weren't benefits?"

She gave a tight, forced smile.

"Brittney, this is a corporate job, not a mom-and-pop

business. You can't negotiate special one-offs for yourself. You have to work in the office. You have to be here on time. If you're looking for something with a looser structure, maybe something smaller and slower paced is a better fit for you."

Maybe you should kiss my— "I appreciate your candor, Cristina. Is there anything else?"

"Not at this time. Let's get a few sponsorships cemented by the end of the week."

She went quietly fuming from the room and slumped in her chair. Hall-o-beach was in the middle of a wild festival season, so hopefully getting their tenants on board wouldn't be too difficult. The four-day event would draw thousands of locals and vacationers alike. If it was anything like last year, Brittney would be there for every minute of it, now with no time off to compensate once it was over.

You free for happy hour?

She and El had managed to avoid each other beyond *hello* and *goodbye* since the past weekend, but now his text came through like its own magical perk. She would love nothing more, except—

I am supposed to work out with H at 6, but—

His reply was immediate.

I really need to talk to you. Can you skip out early and come for a meeting at 4?

Occasionally, their jobs allowed them to work together enough to pretend to need meetings. Did anyone ever really *need* meetings? Based on the one she just had, she wasn't sure she could get away with it that day.

And she wasn't sure her relationship with El could take another hit just then, either.

TT is being extra. Let me adjust some things.

5:15? Tidal Creek?

He agreed, and then Brittney's task was telling Harrison, without withholding the truth, apologizing without feeling guilty for making a choice she felt was right. *Yes, yes. This is right in your wheelhouse.* She rolled her eyes at herself.

Her instinct to was to go out to the hallway, get near a window, and send him a really cute selfie and a thoughtfully written text to change their plans. Something told her that would not do this time around. She took a deep breath and called his number instead.

"Hey Brit." His voice was so casual and familiar it sent a fresh wave of butterflies to her stomach. Was this real? Was she… becoming his?

Shut up. Too soon. "Hey Harrison. How's your day?"

"It's fine." She could hear the smirk in his voice. "I feel like it's about to go down a notch, though. What's up?"

One more deep breath. *He's a grown man. He can handle a small change of plans.* Mikayla's voice. What did she know?

Yeah. No biggie that you're breaking plans to hang out with his frenemy brother. Katy's voice was just as unwelcome but likely more accurate.

"I know you'll think I just don't want to work out," she started lightly. "But I got a message from El asking to meet up after work, and I think I should, and I don't know if I'll be done in time. I was thinking maybe we can run later if you want." She did *not* want, but it seemed like a reasonable offer. "Or we can grab a late dinner." That sounded better.

There was a seemingly weighted pause at the other end. She braced herself.

"Let's not plan anything specific, that way you have more time without worrying about getting to the next thing."

She exhaled deeply. She had already been feeling the

pressure of time, and it was as though he knew and had relieved her of it.

"Okay," she said. "I'm really sorry. I—"

"Brit, it's no big deal. You should talk to him. You don't want to do Cardio Core day, anyway."

Heck no, she didn't. She smiled, hoping he could hear the gratefulness in her voice.

"I'll see you at home, then." There was that word again.

"Yep. And thanks for the call, Babe."

What was it about him that made her feel grounded? When they met, he'd undone her, and now she was almost willing to believe he was something steady.

She glanced at her watch. Hopefully, in just a few hours, she would be armed with some truth.

There was, as usual, an eclectic mix of folks filling Tidal Creek Brewery, where she met El. It looked like the brewhouse was being set up for some kind of function, which could have been trivia, a bonsai tree workshop, a chess meetup, maybe a book launch. It was too nice to sit inside anyway.

El was waiting out in the beer garden, a half-empty pint of something in front of him as he focused on his phone.

"Still working?"

He put it down and smiled at her. "Always. I think we're losing another social media coordinator." Brittney's eyes widened. That had been her exact, soul-sucking job not too long ago. "Don't worry, I wouldn't let you, much less recruit you. You're way overqualified anyway."

"Ha." She slumped in her seat. "Not according to Tambourine Tina. Apparently, I need more direct supervision these days. No more working from home. No more comp time."

El shook his head and lifted his glass. She perused the menu, feeling the events of the day and maybe the week and maybe the last two years putting pressure right behind her eyes. She mentally organized and reinforced her defenses.

"It's on me today," El said.

"You don't have to do that. I kicked you out of your bedroom and everything."

"Brittney."

"Elliot."

They'd called the meeting to order.

His hand had gone to the back of his head, running his fingers through his hair as he looked over at the dog corral where a few pups were running around together while their owners watched their phones. When he turned back to her, his eyes were glistening.

"I chose you first," he said.

Her heartbeat immediately accelerated, wondering which of the loose ends entangling them he was referring to.

"I chose you before Katy. I chose you before I called Harrison. I chose being around you and your family over being with my mom and dealing with mine. In effect, you are the only family I have. I know that's not the case with you. Your family is overflowing with people you actually like. You don't need me, but I have needed you. So, I'm sorry for the missteps lately. I don't mean any of them as disrespect to you. I don't want to lose you, ever."

Hand to heart, she asked, "Why would you lose me?"

His smile was sad, and those were definitely tears. "Because I kept things from you. I broke your trust. And I know you don't trust easily. You just have to believe me that my past with Harry and especially Marshall is a subject I can barely stand to talk about. It's my problem. I'm an adult, and I should deal with it better, but avoidance is so much easier, you know?"

"El." She leaned forward and took his hand; it was shaking, and his being shaken was something she definitely wasn't used to. He'd always been the Forrest to her Jenny, his hurt hidden under his quips and kindness and also, secondary to his protection of her. "You don't have to talk about anything you don't want to. I just… it sounds so stupid when I say it out loud."

"Katy knew."

She nodded. "Katy knew."

He squirmed in his seat a little. "We always knew there would come a time…"

"Yeah, yeah." The server had appeared, and Brittney ordered an Off Main cider and pierogis. "We knew. And yet, I am blindsided."

"Well, it was fast, and it is your stepsister."

Brittney shook her head with a smile. "You can't really slow down a whirlwind. And I'm happy for you both. I can see what it's doing for you, and you deserve it. You both do."

"But Harrison."

"Harrison," she repeated. "And Marshall."

"How much did he tell you?"

She looked away because what she'd discovered had been brutal. "He told me to Google it. So, I did."

El was silent and still. She took a sip of her drink as soon as it was set before her. She couldn't think of a single word to say in condolence to her best friend, or to the little boy he had been when his big brother had been senselessly killed.

Just say what you mean, Mama's voice reminded her. It was a struggle they shared, trying to be polite or profound or able to fix something when all they really had to offer was empathy.

"I don't even know how to say how sorry I am."

He nodded without looking back at her.

And then he answered the question she wasn't sure how to ask.

"I was here with Mom, and Harry was old enough to make his own choices about where to live. I thought for sure he would come here, since, you know, his father's competence as a human being was in question after what happened. But he didn't. So, I was left alone with Mom, who was more of a train wreck than usual. *He didn't come.*"

El almost choked on the words, and Brittney saw his countenance turn almost to one of a little kid. Without knowing the context of all he was presenting, she could surmise well enough. It was a case of one kid letting another down. Harrison had only been a teenager at the time, his older brother killed, his father partly to blame, his mother historically unreliable. What else could he have done? Would he have been any good to a nine-year-old boy suffering from the same fallout?

He knows all of this, Daddy told her.

"Is this the first time you've seen him since then?" she asked quietly, but incredulously.

"We were both at the funeral. And then after he made it to college, he came to visit a few times. When he heard about the band, he reached out because he and his wife were looking to relocate. I ignored him."

El turned his eyes to her then. He shrugged. "So, this is as much my doing as his. He tried to make some kind of amends through the years, and all I wanted was to be resentful."

Brittney traced circles around the rim of her glass. She'd fought her own battles with bitterness. There was never a winner.

"So, what now?" she finally asked.

"Now I have to try to make amends, and it feels a little like I'm going to have to surgically reopen an old wound. So, I'm not excited."

She reached over and steadied his hand with hers once more. "I'll be with you, if you want."

He smiled the closed lip smile that had first charmed her in ninth grade. "I know you would, but no. This needs to be between just Harry and me."

She nodded, pushing her plate toward him. "Pierogi?"

He hated them.

"No, but fried pickles on me?"

"Wait. I thought this whole thing was 'on' you?" she recalled.

"You're right. It is." He swiped at his eyes with his napkin, super quickly as though that would make his tears less real. "So on to the next battle. What are we going to do about Tambourine Tina?"

"Ugh!" She finished her drink. "I need a new job!"

"I'm not hiring you!" he laughed. Then, they launched into one of their oldest adult daydreams: working together, probably with their own marketing firm, starting small with social media management and branching out slowly until El could quit his job and they would be the go-to advertising gurus on the Grand Strand.

Brittney wasn't sure it could ever happen, or even if it was what they really wanted. But in that moment, seeing his face brighten was enough.

Happy hour turned into happy two-and-a-half hours, as they realized how much of their typical conversations they'd missed since becoming roommates and subsequently sleeping with each other's siblings.

Brittney encouraged him to open up completely to Katy, to do the opposite of what seemed safe and smart. Maybe it would be good for both of them.

El encouraged her to shop around for a better job, even if it wasn't marketing. She could stay at the house as long as she wanted; what he wanted was for her to quit miserably schlepping in a place where she felt devalued.

He paid the bill and put his arm around her as they left. For the first time in forever, she felt a little awkward with the posture. She had enjoyed every second of their conversation, but afterwards, she realized she was missing Harrison.

"You going home?" he said at the door of her car.

"Yeah. You?"

She swore he was blushing.

"Where are you meeting Katy?"

"She gets off work at eight. I'm meeting her at Abuelo's."

Brittney shook her head and teased, "You keep taking us girls out like this, you'll need to double your gym time."

He patted his flat stomach in return, holding her car door open. She waved and found herself smiling the whole way home.

She gathered her bag, her lunch tote, her ginormous water bottle, and trudged up the stairs. Harrison was sitting on the porch, his gym clothes still damp and ripe, a big, half-empty cup of something green sitting in front of him.

"Aw. You got all cleaned up just for *me!*" She laughed and planted a kiss on his sweaty face.

"I got a little tired sitting here, and then I kinda figured you weren't coming any time soon, so I made myself dinner." He toasted her with his shake.

"Looks yummy," she said, trying to mask her disappointment. She didn't want to seem too invested in the alternative plans they'd never really made.

"You hungry? I can make another one."

"I think I'm good." She slid into the chair across from him and finally kicked her shoes off. "Doesn't a man of your impressive stature need more than processed protein powder after a fifty-minute lifting class?"

He shrugged. "You would think, wouldn't you? But my superpower is that stress makes me lose my appetite."

"God bless, that is absolutely not a thing for me." She studied him in the dimness of the porch light and the twilight. "Why are you stressed? Too many jump squats?"

"Ha. Partly. Also, Dakota called as I was leaving, wanting me to come get him for the weekend."

"Come get him? Does he know that's like a seven-hour drive?" She said it before she thought about how much it wasn't her business.

"Yeah. He doesn't care about that." Harrison finished off his shake. "Denise is going to see her sister this weekend in Virginia Beach, and she's leaving them with her parents in Alexandria, and he doesn't want to go. He actually asked if I could come to Virginia Beach and get him since it's closer."

"Oh, wow." Something was nagging at her. She wished she could swat it away like a gnat. "He doesn't like his grandparents much, then?"

"Eh. They're fine. They just aren't very exciting to a twelve-year-old boy who's just made his first friends in a new town. He probably wanted to eat pizza rolls and play Roblox all weekend, and now he'll be forced to go to a museum or a play. Don't feel too sorry for him."

That was it, though. She did.

"I'm no expert," she said, "But I bet part of it is he just

misses his dad."

Harrison stared at his empty glass and nodded.

"You know, you can take the weekend and—"

"Thanks, Brit." Something in his voice told her that he was really saying *no thanks*. "We have a gig Saturday, and honestly, I can't do the drive again so soon, gas plus a hotel, and all three of us eating out for the weekend." He sighed. "School will be out in less than a month. Then I'll have them for two weeks."

Where was he going to stay with them for two weeks? She knew it was not the time to ask.

"You sure you don't want anything to eat? I think I'm going to make a grilled cheese."

He smiled up at her as she rose from the chair. "Look at you. Ever the chef now."

"Uh-huh," she answered, bending to kiss his cheek. "Wait a second. You smell like—"

"Sweat? Iron? Hard work?"

"A cheeseburger!" she said. "You did eat dinner, you big doofus!"

He laughed and held up his hands. "It's still just processed protein."

She kissed his lips then, lingering for a second. "I'm going to go cook now. See you later."

"Mmm," he said, then added, "Brit, I'm gonna sleep in my room tonight, okay? Nothing is wrong, I just… need the head space, I think. I need to try to figure out this visitation stuff. It's not—"

"Sure, of course," she said, cursing the tiny waver in her voice and hoping he didn't notice it. "Sleep tight."

She could tell he was starting to say something, but she didn't want it. She had done it again, overplaying her claim, assuming she meant more to him than she did, that her perspective made any sort of difference in the things he was dealing with. *So, so, so, stupid*, her own voice repeated to her. *He has an actual life, and he does not need you.*

Changing her dinner plans, she grabbed a bag of pretzels and jar of peanut butter and closed the door to her room, locking it for good measure and an extra side of ridiculousness. She put her Echo on blast, with Papa Roach singing to her about tearing her own heart open and sewing herself shut. Once again, she felt stupid and weak for caring too much.

The drive of the guitar drowned out her urge to cry. The lyrics were persuading her to maybe just stop trying to make her life better.

The night everything came crashing down with Bradley had been her secret at first. She stayed away from her family, even skipped a few Sunday suppers. She made excuses with El, but it was winter, and they were all prone to depression and hibernation, so he didn't notice anything was wrong.

Bradley kept trying to call. And text. He even stopped by the Chamber office one afternoon, but when the receptionist called for her, she hid in the bathroom for forty-five minutes. He sent flowers the next day, and she started to wonder if he would ever leave her alone, if he was crazy or dangerous. At her worst moments, she'd wondered if he was really sorry, and she had it all wrong. She felt crazy for never really knowing him, and with a quest to protect herself, she finally asked El to come over, that it was important. Ever the person who seemed to know her best and know best what to do, he came with three things in tow: vodka, chocolate, and her sister.

She made El and Mikayla swear up and down and all around that they would never tell a soul, and then she spilled everything. By then, the bruises had faded, but her description was enough. Both of them were hollering, threatening, telling her Bradley had assaulted her and she should make a police report. Mikayla cried. El said he would kill Bradley himself. And Brittney had just sat there, trying to feel the love around her instead of the humiliation.

Of course, she never filed anything. El went to Bradley's office and told him to stay the fuck away, or next time he would make sure the whole place, the whole town, knew what kind of guy he was.

Brittney got one last message. It just said, "I'm sorry." She responded back, "I hope so, but never as sorry as I am." Then she had blocked Bradley from everything except her memory. Through the Myrtle Beach grapevine, she'd heard a few months later that he moved to Atlanta. Sometimes she would still creep his social media, but it was locked down, his profile pictures generic and mostly unchanging. So, that was that. Except for her barely being able to trust anyone since then, especially herself.

～～～

"Brit, what is up? Will you open the door?"

The knock startled her awake. The voice accelerated her heartbeat.

At first, she couldn't tell which of her male roommates it was. The brothers sounded just a little bit alike, especially in her groggy state. She wrapped a throw blanket around her bra and shorts and opened the door.

Harrison.

Not even three weeks ago, she was a little afraid of him but also too afraid of being impolite to lock the door. Now she had barred it to keep her own feelings at bay, and they all rose to the surface at the sight of him.

Don't cry. Don't cry. Don't cry. But there were the tears, betraying her.

"Oh, my God, what's wrong?" His hands flew up to her, caressing her shoulders, his face full of such concern that embarrassment now joined everything else she was feeling.

She shook her head, not trusting herself to say anything.

"Brit, what happened? You just disappeared. I came in right after you, and then I gave you time, and then I fell asleep, and now… you're barricaded in here. Did I misunderstand something?"

No. I did. If she wanted to keep things simple and honest, that's what she would have said.

"You said you were sleeping alone anyway, and today was… just a lot," she said, trying to keep the quaver out of her voice. Her mental list read something like *My career is going nowhere. I am treated like a child. I might as well be a child based on my living situation. (No, I'm still not over it.) El is in love with Katy, and who are we kidding? He will not need me anymore. No one needs me. Everyone else is happy and has someone. Harrison might like me, but he has his kids, and he's going to leave, and I actually think he should leave, and why can't I fall in love with someone who actually has the capacity to love me back?*

"You can talk to me."

How could she possibly bother him with her list when his concerns ran so much deeper?

Why do you always belittle yourself?

Not now, Daddy.

She started to say words over and over, but nothing felt right. His hands slipped down to her wrists. He used them to pull her closer, and then he wrapped her tightly in his arms. She let herself melt, sink, and fade into him.

"We don't have to figure out everything right this second," he said, reading at least a little of her mind.

She laughed sardonically. "We couldn't. You have no idea the war that is actually being waged in my head right now."

"I might have some ideas," he said, his lips vibrating off her hair.

"I think the only thing scarier than not knowing what I want is knowing what I do want."

His only response was to hold her a little tighter. The vibration between them was rising.

"I don't want to love you—" she finally said, "—but here we are."

It was the age-old trick, saying the words without saying them. Her heart pounded at the question of whether he would take the bait and what his response would be.

"Here we are," he repeated, and then he pulled her face to his and started kissing her.

There they were.

Brittney

THE ALARM WENT OFF WAY TOO EARLY ON Saturday morning. Brittney hurriedly pushed "Stop" instead of "Snooze" so as not to wake Harrison. He'd been on the phone half of the night before with Dakota and went to bed right after, his eyes bleary from emotional exhaustion, his arms wrapped around Brittney in a way that made her feel like a lifeline.

As quietly as she could, she grabbed her clothes, headed for the bathroom, and within minutes, was driving down the street toward Johnny D's. The only way to get a table big enough for all of them on a Saturday morning was to go as early as she would agree. None of the rest of them cared much – or had much ability – to sleep in.

Haley greeted her at the door. "They're in the corner," she said, nodding toward the brood. Brittney sauntered over, happy to see a mug of coffee waiting in her place. Of course, she was the last one there.

"Where's Josie?" she asked Mikayla. Her niece had been a standing guest at their monthly sibling soiree since she was born.

"I let her spend the night with Mama."

"What? The blessed child had her first overnight?" Sam exclaimed.

"Shush," Mikayla answered. "It was actually the second time. She stayed when Altan and I had the stomach flu in January."

"January 22," Altan added, a knowing smile across his face.

"You're supposed to be on my side!"

"Always," he replied, kissing her cheek.

"'Morning, Abs."

Abby smiled tiredly at Brittney. "Hey Brit. Drink that coffee before I snatch it right out of your hands."

"Yikes. Good day already?"

"She hasn't been sleeping well," Sam interjected, frowning slightly. "And there is a big party at the tearoom this afternoon.

"You don't have to talk for me. I'm not made of glass."

Brittney widened her eyes at Abby. "Did you order yet?"

Mikayla chimed in. "Just the starter. We picked the banana bread French toast."

"What? It's supposed to be a waffle."

"Just order a waffle if you want one, Brittney."

"Don't say my name, *Sam*!"

"Oy! Ve! Can we not let the coffee kick in first before we start?"

Altan's admonishment seemed to settle them.

"Need a mimosa, Brit?"

"Shut up, Sam! I know you're the only one ever allowed to be edgy about anything. All I want is a damn waffle."

"Sweet Lord." Sam got up from the table then. Brittney shook her head as he stormed away.

"We are starting right in at Defcon 1, I see," Mikayla muttered.

"Whatever." Brittney took a fortifying sip of her coffee. Refills were going to be needed soon.

"He's in a bad mood because of me," Abby said. "I've been crazed and snappy lately. That's one of the things we want to talk to you guys about, but I'll wait for him."

"For what?" Sam asked, sliding back into his chair. "I ordered a red velvet," he said to Brittney. "Now can we move on with our lives?"

"You're exasperating," she said in response, and smiled at him to show her gratitude.

"So I hear."

"So, what's up, Abs?" Altan asked, steering them back on track.

"We just… I just… hit a rut, I guess? Maaaaaybe it's an early midlife thing, although we're a little young for that. Sam and I are just restless. Well, he's restless. I am exhausted. Like, I cannot get a grip on how tired I am. Nothing helps. Sleep, a spa day, a weekend away, all the little coping mechanisms. All the freaking herbal teas. My energy is just down. I am down. I miss my mom. I didn't know that without her, the world would look so gray so much of the time."

Mikayla was already wiping her eyes. Sam put a protective arm around his wife.

Brittney couldn't find words. Grief over Daddy came in unexpected waves, and sometimes they did drown her inside herself. She couldn't imagine if it were Mama who was gone because if Daddy was the outline that made up their lives, Mama colored it.

"I feel like a bad mom," Abby continued. "I'm distracted, impatient, moody. And tired. They deserve better than what I have to offer lately."

"So do you," Brittney said.

"So, what are we going to do about it?" Mikayla asked.

Abby looked at Sam, and then back around the table, forcing a smile through her tears.

"We're looking at a move."

"Oh, wow. Are you gonna do the farm in Aynor thing? Are we gonna have some baby goats in the family? Ooh! Fresh eggs!"

Mikayla shot Brittney a look. "Maybe they don't mean *houses*. Are you thinking of getting out of the tearoom, Abs?"

Abby looked at Sam again. He squeezed her hand and started talking. "You know, now that Abby's dad lives in Blue Ridge area, we've explored it quite a bit. There's an adjunct position open at University of Northern Georgia. I'd be teaching biology at this beautiful campus in the mountains, and it's an easy drive from where Abby wants to stay. She has an old friend in a little town nearby."

"We're thinking of trying it for a year. Summer will be in high school before we know it, and then it gets more complicated. It's quieter up there, slower, so pretty. There are plenty of little shops where I could work during the day and then be there for the kids—"

"And rest," Sam added.

"And that for sure. I really need to calm down a little," Abby added.

Silence permeated the table. Brittney couldn't separate the different feelings she had. She finally looked at Altan and said, "You ready to be the man of the family around here?"

Mikayla winced. Sam said, "Um... Paul will still be here."

"Yeah, but… Altan has seen us at our best and our worst. We still try to behave for Paul." *It's not the same,* she told herself. *Everyone is leaving.*

"I know it's weird," Sam said. "But think of it this way… it gives y'all a nice place to visit that isn't too far away."

"Because we travel so much," Brittney muttered.

Abby was eyeing her. "I'm sorry, Brit. I know it's more change."

"I'm fine!" She hadn't meant to snap, but why did everyone assume she couldn't handle it?

"We've got her," Mikayla said, putting her own protective arm around Brittney, which she in turn shrugged off.

"I'm not a baby, you guys. Move. You have every right to live your lives. And Kayla? You're a *year* older than me. Just because you're married with a kid doesn't make you so much more mature."

Cue the awkward silence, but only for a moment.

Sam cleared his throat. "Brit, we thought you might want to rent the house from us."

That was not what she expected.

"I…" She tried to picture it, moving into their family-filled neighborhood in "fake" Murrells Inlet, in a perfect HOA community with man-made retention ponds where little kids learned to fish and "Don't Feed the Alligators" signs, a heavily populated and senior-citizen-policed pool, lots of bus stops and dog walkers. They had three or four bedrooms and a big extra room over the garage that housed a gigantic TV and sometimes a wayward family member or one of Travis' friends.

"It's the sweetest offer ever," she told Sam, and meant it. "What's your timeline?"

He launched into a few logistics, citing the academic calendars and whether Travis was going to come with them. It was at that point she started to feel tears prick her eyes and interrupted him: "Does Mama know yet?"

She watched the face of her older brother morph into something between panic and sorrow.

"No! And no one can tell her until I do."

"She's going to freak out," Altan said.

"No shit," Brittney said.

"Do you think we should all tell her together?" Mikayla asked.

"I think," Abby interrupted, "that y'all seriously underestimate her. She's not made of glass either." She looked at Sam as she emphasized "either."

"But David, and now Sam and you and the grandkids and her Taco Tuesdays…"

"Mikayla, before you know it, Josie is going to be eating tacos with her. And any other kids that come along. It's the circle of life. If anything, Jessie has taught me how important it is to make changes when we need to. She moved here from Illinois. She stopped homeschooling when it wasn't working anymore. And there's the obvious swerve she is living now. Will she be sad and maybe heartbroken? Yes. But it's not going to take her down. Give her a chance, Sam. And give yourself a chance to look at her like a grownup, not just your mama."

Sam's eyes got wide, and then he broke into a smile.

"That's the most you've sounded like yourself in weeks."

"Good. Then maybe you don't have to go after all," Mikayla said. They allowed themselves the laughter, and then they paused to order their meals.

"Brit, you got any news? How's it going over at Club MTV?"

"You sound like an old man, Sam. And it's fine."

"Fine like 'everything's fine' or fine for real?"

Altan and Mikayla were smiling behind their coffee mugs.

"What?!" Abby asked.

"Brittney has a boyfriend. Bona fide!"

"What?" Abby repeated.

Brittney grimaced, but her face wrestled against a smile.

"I'm not using that label. We aren't fifteen. And I'm not sure he'd be into it."

"According to Katy, he's into *you*, though," Mikayla said.

"God bless it. No one tells you that this whole 'blended family' thing means you have twice the number of siblings to tattle on your every move."

"So does that mean she's right?" Abby asked.

Brittney clapped as the server chose that moment to unload their fare. In seconds, the table was filled with bountiful platters and luscious little side plates. Hers was the chicken and waffles, with a side of cheesy grits and a grilled blueberry muffin because, as Aunt Maggie would say, "God said live." She would hit the gym later. Or the beach. Whatever.

Everyone fussed with the hot sauce and salt and their first bites, and then the spotlight shined right back on her.

"Go ahead and spill it, Brit," Altan said. "They're all going to find out one way or another."

"They always do," she murmured. "I don't know what to say, you guys. I really… Harrison is great. I wasn't sure about him at first because he's El's brother, and like… I barely even knew he existed. I'm just glad he does. I mean, I'm glad he's here. He's surprisingly sweet and refreshingly honest and so, so hot. But there are complications…"

"I mean, of course," Abby said.

Brittney smiled at the solidarity. "Two of them are his children, who live near D.C. with his ex-wife."

"Wow," Sam said.

"Can't imagine," Mikayla added.

"Exactly," Brittney said. "We don't talk much about it, but the distance is new, and he and the kids are naturally having a hard time with it. And then there is stuff with El. I don't know all the details. They're half-brothers… different dads… same mom who drives them crazy, and…" She filled them in on the vague story of Marshall, her conversation with El, and her conclusion as of that very morning.

"I think I'm in love with him," she said with a small voice and a tiny shrug.

The four people around the table looked at each other before looking back at her. Her elder siblings and their respective spouses had been together for years.

"It's okay if you are," Abby finally said. "Even with complications. Complications make the payoff even better sometimes." She gave Sam's hand a squeeze.

"It just scares me. I don't know if I have ever felt this way, or at least not since…" Mikayla was the only one of them who knew the whole story about Bradley. The others only knew he was a douchebag, and she was going to keep it that way.

"Brit, I've been playing this safe for a long time. All it gets you is *safe*. Look at Dad. He was still working when he died, even though he didn't need to. Maybe that's why Mama's choices since then don't bother me as much. Why shouldn't she have some adventure and excitement? What is the point in waiting? What is the use in *not* taking chances? You might get hurt either way. "

Everyone stared at Sam. Those were not words he would normally say, but for the first time since Daddy had died, he seemed confident and enthusiastic again.

Mikayla had tears in her eyes. "Is it okay if I tell you guys something now?"

Brittney looked sharply at her. "If you tell me you're

moving, too, we are going to fight."

"No, no." Mikayla shook her head, looking to Altan who responded with a fortifying nod.

"We're trying to have another baby!"

"What?"

"Oh my God!"

"That's *not* sad news."

"You should have told us sooner! We're just prattling on…"

The exclamations layered on top of each other. Mikayla smiled as her tears fell. Altan was beaming.

"This is not complicated," Abby said. "Silly girl."

"No, but it's super early. And we are not telling anyone else yet, just this little circle of trust."

Mikayla didn't have to add to that thought. Her first pregnancy had ended in a miscarriage, which made her entire pregnancy with Josie, during which their father had died, especially tumultuous.

"Yes, but maybe this time can be happier," Brittney said.

Mikayla nodded. "I would like that. I want that."

"Let's toast!" Sam added. And they did… with coffee, forks, or whatever they wanted. "To la dolce vita!"

The sweet life was an old family toast, one that had begun at Mama and Daddy's wedding. Brittney looked at her siblings, missing David, watching the care-worn but hopeful expressions around her. Her own news of being in love felt a little insignificant, except that if she was ever going to have what they had, not just sweetness in life, but fullness in it, she was going to have to take some risks.

Jessie

"YOU ARE MAGICAL."

After handing him a stack of three freshly baked snickerdoodles, I blushed under the adoration of my husband.

I sat in the chair next to him on our porch. "Just doing what I do, Baby." I took a sip of my own magic, a margarita made with fresh lime juice, Surfside Alex's honey, and just, like, a half shot of Patron. Who said mimosas were the only socially acceptable breakfast cocktail?

"Well, thanks for saving me some. What time do you need to go in?"

"Abby wants to meet before we open, so I need to leave in about ten minutes."

He eyed my juice glass. "Do I need to drive you?"

I rolled my eyes. "No, Love. It's a sip. Abby has been so tense lately it's been bleeding on me. I'm just getting relaxed. It's easier than getting a Prozac script."

He rolled his eyes back at me. "So people say. Just…

you know…"

I knew. A recovered alcoholic, Paul was tolerant of my enjoyment of libations, in moderation, of course, until he wasn't. I walked the line between indulgent and respectful.

And with that, I put my glass down. I was easy, and a sip or two created the chill I was craving.

"Do you think she's ready to talk about the next steps?"

I shrugged. Nothing had been said since the episode with Sam, nor did I say anything about what he had told me and what Maggie had proposed. She'd only been home for a few days, but she assured me that talks with Sheldon were going well. *Progressing.* That was the word she had used. He was "warming up to all her ideas." The combined dramatics of my sister and my kids was driving me bonkers.

"Even if she is, I don't know what to say. And I don't know what to do, either."

Paul reached across the little table that sat between us and took my hand, immediately comforting me with his knowingness. "You don't have to know. Just listen to her, take your time, and come home to me. I'll listen to you, and I'll help you if you want me to."

"You always help me," I said, already entertaining a little daydream about more mornings like this, except when I baked it would be because I wanted to, not because I had to, and I wouldn't have to go anywhere.

～～

Thirty minutes later, I could hear Abby on the phone. I could tell she was talking to Paul. But I was still sitting at the table in our empty little tearoom, and I couldn't speak. I had no words. I didn't want to be there and yet I couldn't seem to muster the strength to move.

Don't let this one be your undoing, kid. What a time for Randall's voice. If he was still here, none of this would be happening. David would not be gone. And Sam would not be leaving. Sam and Abby… and the kids. Jesus. The kids.

ELEVEN-ISH YEARS EARLIER

"I'm not going to be *that* kind of grandmother. How can I be? Travis has been like one of ours, part of the mix. This one has to feel the same way. Not like the world revolves around her. More like a special new part of the big picture."

"Okay," Randall had said, with complete and utter phony acquiescence. "So, we're gonna walk in there, and you're going to take one look at the first grandbaby born in eight years, the first one born to an established, married couple and not to two scared kids trying to finish college, and you're gonna be cool. So cool."

"Yes. I am." I raised my chin defiantly and walked in the room without waiting for Randall or letting him lead me. I went directly to the bed, where Abby was holding an impossibly tiny figure in a blue and pink striped blanket. They hadn't told us anything, not that she'd gone into labor, not the sex of the baby, nothing. Just, "Get here."

"Hi," Abby said, an exhausted smile filling her face. Sam stood at her side. He was also beaming. "Okay, baby. Time to meet your Mimi and Grampy."

"Oh, my goodness," I said, and waited as patiently as I could while Sam scooped the baby from Abby's arms and placed him… her?… into mine.

"Are you going to introduce us?" Randall had said, taking one for the team. I was surprised all the questions hadn't yet burst forth from my brain.

"Dad, Mama, this is your new granddaughter."

"Oh," I said, one hand going to my mouth. It had come out like a sob. There was no coolness to be found.

"Hello, sweet girl," Randall greeted, putting one finger to her cheek. She was perfection. It's so easy to forget how small and how miraculous a newborn life is.

"W—what… oh, you guys, she's beautiful!" I exclaimed, tears falling on the little blanket. "Did everything go okay?"

Sam nodded, casting his eyes sideways to Abby. She gave me a wan thumbs up and just said, "Lots of stitches. So many stitches. But yes. We're fine."

I made a sympathetic face. We would talk more about that later. I looked at the baby in my arms, with Abby's milky skin and soft jaw, Sam's cheekbones and hairline and lips, and quite possibly, my very own nose. I was in awe. Travis had looked completely like Abby; the only thing about him that was Sam's was the color of his hair. This child resembled my first born quite a bit, which only added to her wonder.

"Did you tell Mommy you're sorry for giving her such a hard time?" I asked. Little Miss Perfection did not respond. It was fine. I was going to hold her forever.

Randall could most certainly read my face and my vibration and was barely suppressing a laugh. I would hit him later. I couldn't do anything to jeopardize a perfect moment with this baby girl. Baby Girl…

"Have you named her yet?" I finally asked. I couldn't believe what a stupor I was in.

"Well, I know you think themed names are sort of silly, but given the time of year and all…"

Oh God. Did they name her June? Or Pearl, for her birthstone? Such old lady names for a little sprite.

"Oh, you're killing your mother right now." Randall was pretty much guffawing. He thought he was so cool.

"Just tell them," Abby said. "So someone can go get me a milkshake."

Sam grew suddenly serious and looked straight into my

eyes. "Mama, this is Summer Rose."

A namesake. I was blown away.

"Well, I knew she was perfect," I said, tears falling more rapidly onto her poor little blankie. "But this is the icing on the cake." And then I sobbed, holding her closer as Randall put his arm around me.

There are many things no one can tell another person about having a grandchild. When Travis was born, David had been two. I became his nanny, and my life was such chaos, it was all a blur. Seeing Summer, and holding her, and knowing her, made my love for each of them just deeper and sharper, like the whole world was suddenly in focus.

It was Tuesday as I sat in the tearoom with Sam and Abby's news of leaving. Moving. Taking Summer and her baby brother Jacob, now eleven and eight, and moving six hours away from me. For nearly every Tuesday since Summer was maybe two months old, she had been with me. It was our night. We ushered in the Taco Tuesday era together. We danced together in my kitchen the night her baby brother Jacob was born, and again the day after her baby cousin Josie was born. We had movie nights with her aunties, I went to every dance recital and many practices, and just a few weeks ago, I had thrown her an impromptu, cheer-up pancake party when she got her first period.

Everything I'd done wrong with my own daughters had been redeemed with my Sunshine Girl. Every moment I had spent stressing over feeding four or five kids on a daily basis was relieved every time Jacob sat at my counter and had some ridiculous Lunchable for dinner because he'd grinned at me with his irresistible charm.

"Mama, Paul is coming to pick you up."

I snapped out of my blurry flashback. Sam was looking

down at me like I was a mental patient, and maybe I should have been.

"That isn't necessary," I said, wholly embarrassed.

"He wants to."

"Sam, I'm fine. I am a grown-ass woman, and you are also grown and allowed to make your own decisions." *Even if they suck,* I added to myself.

"Mama, you've been sitting here still and silent for almost an *hour.* I already have a wife on the verge of a nervous breakdown; I really don't want you joining her there."

"Sam!"

The last thing – oh, the very last—I wanted was for my son, or any of my kids, to feel responsible for me. I was fine. I was taken care of. I had more good in my life than I had any right to have. I knew dozens of widows, and indeed had heard from many more since publishing my books, who had all but given up on ever being happy again. Some of them had checked out on their kids, some of them even resented their kids being happy. It was heartbreaking to imagine. It was not who or what I ever wanted to be.

"I promise you," I said, with more resolve in my voice than I felt, "I am fine. I'm just a little shell-shocked. You and Abby are like my… I don't even have a word for it."

"Your little besties? Because I thought that was Summer and Jacob."

I put my hand up to his face and let my tears fall. Sam couldn't know. He'd had a baby when he was young and unmarried just like I did, but Abby had been there, and they'd taken all the next steps together. For the first part of Sam's life, it was just him and me. There was no Daddy. There was no certainty. I tiptoed through my parents' house and my hometown trying to keep our existence small, until I met a man who convinced me that we were worthy of more and allowed to dream. Sam was my anchor and sidekick and true love through every era of my life since I was nineteen years old, and forty years later, I could not imagine a week going by when I wouldn't see his face. And then there was Abby, who was also a hybrid daughter, little sister, fellow mama in the trenches, *my business partner*. The hole was just gaping. My kids were going to try to convince me I was just emotional, and my instincts would equate that to weakness, but it wasn't true. Just like when Randall died, just like when David left, just like when Maggie moved away, someone who was a part of me would no longer be near, and I felt it deeply, and I was not ashamed.

"Something like that."

I stood then, to show I was sane. I walked to the kitchen where Abby was busying herself with the counters, a classic move of mine. They were already clean, and since we'd only technically been open for six minutes, the place was silent. Our reservations were an hour away.

"Don't avoid me," I said lightly.

She looked up, squeezing her sponge.

"I feel so bad about this."

"Abby—" I started to tell her she shouldn't, but she already knew that, and I understood. I would feel the same way. But guilt was almost always a wasted emotion. "I, of all people, am still a safe place to you. We said when we started this that we would do it as long as it makes sense. I wish you could find your 'sense' here, instead of four hundred miles away, but we do what needs to be done. That's how we roll."

Her chin was quivering a bit, and I was trying hard to avoid more tears.

"You are my safe place," she said, so quietly I almost couldn't hear her. "And this decision is possible because I have watched you for the last two years, making hard choices to take your life to a different place. You haven't settled for what was going to make everything easier for everyone else. You haven't stepped down when someone challenged you. And you've never once been insensitive about it."

"Oh, come on!" I laughed.

"Well." She shrugged. "Not most of the time. And never to me." It was a running joke to my daughters that Abby was my favorite. She was certainly the easiest. "I want to try new things now. I don't want to be afraid to change. I can't tell you why Sam and I have been struggling. We're not unhappy. We're not disappointed. We're just… restless. Losing Randall and Mama and handling the fallout has just worn on us. And I'm not so deluded I think a move like this isn't daunting. But I hope – I believe – it will be worth it."

With more confidence, she added, "And if not, we'll move back. Because nothing is forever."

I nodded my head. I couldn't help the smile that formed on my face. Abby was right about my trajectory the last two years, how I had to find my own way after Randall died. My whole process of navigating life had stopped resting on his guidance or everyone's approval and started being intentional, driven by me, making peace with God about it and plowing ahead when I saw fit. And watching Brittney lately, floundering over where she was going to live and who she was going to love and how much she hated her job, intensified my prayer for my kids: *Get there faster.* Not to any specific destination, but rather, to a place where they felt equipped to make their lives better, comfortable doing what was right for them.

"Have you told the kids?"

At that, for a moment so fast I'm sure she didn't think I saw it, all the resolve crumbled from Abby's face. I would not speak of it. She needed to be confident in the path she and Sam had chosen, in the flexibility of it, in herself.

I felt like I was reeling backwards, the opposite of sure or brave, but I wouldn't let her see, and I hoped *my* moment of crumbling was invisible to her.

When Paul came to collect me, I had already done the job. I took to the bathroom, with its sweet Edwardian mirror, splashed cold water on my face, dabbed under my eyes with concealer, and reapplied my mascara. When he saw me, he saw right through me, but I was determined to handle our three high teas that day with Abby. Sam had left to go to work, looking at me like a ticking bomb as he said goodbye.

"Don't make me cry," I whispered to Paul. Then I went to Rosie's table. She was one of our favorite suppliers; her cupcakes were out of this world, and occasionally she came in with her three daughters and her adorable granddaughter Natalie, who lived back in the northeast, where Rosie was from. I was so relieved to see someone I considered a friend. I lifted a strand of her long, magical, silver hair in greeting.

"You look amazing as always," I told her. She leaned in for a hug. Her daughters were chatting amongst themselves, and Natalie was busy with one of our coloring pages. "How long do you have them here?" I asked.

She stood so she could answer me quietly. "They got here Friday and leave tomorrow. And it's never long enough." She laughed in her signature style, which sounded equal parts nervous and in on a secret. Rosie was a bit younger than me, but she had lived a lot of life. Her book club sometimes met at the tearoom, and once they invited me as a guest when they read my book, *Grace and the New Normal.*

Seeing her reminded me that I had barely written a word since publishing that one, and that I really needed to get together with friends, cupcakes, wine, books, and laughter more often than I was.

"I just found out my son and his family are moving away," I murmured. "Is there a support group?"

She widened her eyes in empathy. "There should be."

I nodded, feeling embarrassed and inspired all at once.

"Why don't you get a hold of me after they leave, and we'll have brunch? Or happy hour. Your choice."

I smiled. "That sounds perfect." And I squeezed the hand at the end of her tatted arm. She was one of the coolest people I knew, and I loved how she showed bravery without pretending to have it all together. None of us did. "Thank you so much. I'll be back with your tea in just a few."

When I walked by Paul, he just nodded at me with his knowing smile. He didn't always realize how well I knew him, too. He was worried about me; that was plain to see. But I saw something else there, too. He and Sam had bonded. He and Jacob had bonded. It had only taken a few months for him to morph from Mr. Paul to Poppy Paul to *Poppy*.

Poppy stayed in the corner with his laptop and sweet tea for three hours while Abby and I handled the first two high teas. The last one wasn't until four, and it was only for three people, so Summer would be there to serve. She was adept at it, and the customers found her charming.

Of course, they did. Summer was delightful and efficient and basically perfect.

Blairsville, Georgia was going to be lucky to have her.

With that thought, I couldn't leave the room quickly enough. I gestured to Paul, bit my lip as I waved goodbye to Abby, and darted out to my car. All his running was turning him into a gazelle because he materialized at my side around the time I threw my bags into the backseat. He set his on the ground and wordlessly wrapped his arms around me.

Then I was safe.

Then I didn't have to be strong.
Then I could start to grieve, again.

Brittney

Brittney stared at the screen. She felt the familiar racing of her heart. Her neck got hot. Her stomach turned. How and why in God's name was this happening *now?*

> *Brittney,*
>
> *I obviously hate to do this over email, but we have a date requirement and as you know, I am out of town.*
>
> *Due to budget cuts, this email serves as your notice of release. Your last day at Boardwalk Square will be this coming Friday, though you will receive an additional week of pay equaling a two-week notice.*
>
> *Thank you for your dedication to the Boardwalk Square family over the last nine months. Attached, please find*

A LETTER OF REFERENCE FROM OUR GENERAL MANAGER. LET IAN KNOW IF YOU HAVE ANY QUESTIONS DURING YOUR REMAINING DAYS.
RESPECTFULLY,
CRISTINA JOHNSON

Brittney told herself not to do it. She picked up her phone and put it down. She picked it up again, started to send a text to El, slammed it back down. She hit "reply" on the email, closed it. Then, with the flush reaching her ears and her face, she stormed down the hall to the corner office, where Ian was sitting at his desk, laughing, probably at reels of people falling down.

"Sorry to interrupt," she snapped.

He almost seemed nonplussed. He cleared his throat and straightened his tie. Who wore a tie in the Myrtle Beach tourism industry on a random Tuesday in the office? Puffed up asshats. That's who.

"Good morning, Brit."

Brit?

"Ian, I'm here to tell you it's not a good morning, as I am sure you are aware. You're copied on Cristina's email. Email? What kind of unprofessional way is that to drop a bomb on someone?"

"Well, we had a deadline, and Cristina's vacation—"

"Yes. I read it. You didn't even have the professional courtesy to tell me yourself. Have I been that horrid of an employee? I don't even get the minimum amount of respect to be dismissed in person? And what budget cuts, anyway? You just hired a group sales assistant. You just posted for a second social media coordinator. I am *baffled* here. Flummoxed, even." She might as well use a few big college words before she started looking for bartending jobs.

"Brittney, you're not new to this industry."

He looked as though he was saying everything that needed to be said. She tried to breathe deeply before she answered. *Put the matches down. It's a small town. You don't burn bridges.*

"I'm *not* new to this industry, Ian. Thank you for noticing. I'm not new to this marketplace, either. To be honest, at this stage, I am expecting promotions. Not the opposite."

He shifted uncomfortably in his chair. "While your work here has been appreciated—"

"No, it hasn't. You've never noticed a thing I've accomplished, and all Cristina has done is criticize me while offering no professional development whatsoever. So please start over."

"I don't think that matters now that the decision has been made." He cleared his throat and sat back, straighter.

"But it does. Did you even know that the '12 Days of Winter' promotion in February was my idea *and* my execution? Fifteen of our stores doubled their business from last year for that period. Did you know that I got our four anchor restaurants to agree to the Lucky Living Giveaway in March? It raised our Facebook engagement by *fifty-one* percent."

She already knew nothing was going to change, but the surprise that flashed across his face was all the vindication she needed at the moment.

"I appreciate those efforts." *Grrrrrr.* "Sometimes things need to be shaken up and taken in different directions..." he started. She waited for him to finish. He didn't.

She nodded. "We both know the budget thing is crap. We both know this is because Cristina doesn't like me, never has, views me as competition, and is forcing me out of her way. I know you won't acknowledge the truth. I know South Carolina is at-will employment. So, I will say thank you for the form letter, and I hope you choke on every lie you two spew about me."

She started to turn and then stopped. "Oh, and shall I assume you don't need me to work out my 'notice?' You probably don't want me here the next four days telling everyone I see that you have no idea who's doing the work in your department. You probably just want to pay me my two weeks and be done with me?"

He stared at her blankly before nodding his concession.

"Great. I'll pack up. It's been nice not knowing you, Ian."

Her insides were quavering as she hurried back to the mail room to fetch a box. She blinked back tears as she threw her pictures and tchotchkes and half a dozen souvenir cups into it. She flung her tote over her shoulder and left an office she never liked and a job she'd been certain was a perfect opportunity for her.

⌒⌒⌒

"There is no shame in bartending. Actually, maybe I'll do it, too."

Brittney glared at Katy. "Can you at least wait until I find a job before you land your second one?"

Katy rolled her eyes. "We'll both get hired immediately, and you know it. And you'll get hired first because all the good bars already know you."

"Yeah. As a customer and a Salty Lips groupie. Most of those people think I have some great executive job. Oh, my God. What am I going to say to my mother? Katy, this is the worst. The worst."

I am effectively homeless and now unemployed. My prospects are zero. Zero!

"Don't tell her anything yet," Katy said. "I know news travels fast in the blender, but I manage to keep some secrets, still. She doesn't have to know."

Yes, she does. Daddy's voice was loud and clear.

"The truth is," she told Katy, "As much as I don't want to tell her, she will probably be super helpful. "

"You sound very grown up."

"We are adults, Katy. I don't feel like one, but alas."

"Yeah." She looked down at her phone as a message from Julie popped up.

"Don't tell her either," Brittney said.

"Fine. But she would understand. Why are douchebags always named Ian, anyway?"

Brittney giggled. Julie had moved back to the beach after a job and a fling with an Ian went all wrong for her. *Why, indeed?*

They sat in unprecedented silence at the foot of Brittney's bed. Katy was off on Tuesdays. Brittney had no idea what she did all day in a house that wasn't hers. It wasn't even really El's. All the furnishings in the living room, dining room, and kitchen were set up for beach vacations, not a thirtysomething man living his life there, and certainly not one living with three makeshift roommates. No wonder it had only taken him a few hours to switch bedrooms. What did he have here that was actually his? What was personal?

Why were they living like people who had no roots and no ties?

"Sam is moving away," Brittney finally said.

"What? What *happened?*"

"*No.* Not just him. The family. Well, maybe not Travis. They're moving six hours away. To the north Georgia mountains."

"Wow."

Brittney was so relieved that Katy got it without her explaining.

"Does your mom know yet?"

The question sent a little alarm off inside of Brittney.

She picked up her phone to check. "If she does, she hasn't said anything, which would be weird."

"She'll be devastated, though."

"Yep." Brittney wasn't ready to admit that she was also, so she just said, "I want to call him right now and ask him what to do. But I already feel like I should give him some space. He's kinda been Mama's… co-parent… a lot through life, like when Daddy was traveling and stuff. This isn't his problem. I just… don't know what to do."

"But you do know," Katy said. "Serve some drinks or wait some tables this summer. You will make bank. Go to the beach during the day and work all night. And make your plan. There's no rule that says you're a loser if you take a service job in a service town, especially if you've hated the last two jobs you had on your *career path*, Brit. Come *on*. Stop apologizing for yourself."

She was positioned to argue, but stopped because Katy was right, and because there was a noise from outside the bedroom door.

No. It was a crash.

"I'm so sick of this!"

The brothers' voices were a little indistinguishable through the door.

"Sick of what? Freeloading off me?"

Definitely El.

"Freeloading? You don't *own* this house. You pay taxes on something that isn't yours. Just like you resent me for things that aren't my fault. Grow up already, Elliot. Everything isn't about you."

Brittney looked at Katy to convey just how bad the situation was.

"Nothing has ever been about me, you selfish son of a bitch."

Katy looked back. It was clear she got the message.

"Shit. Should we...?"

Brittney shook her head vehemently. "Absolutely not. I don't know what Harrison is like when he's angry, but this level of emotion from El is unheard-of. We need to stay out of the way."

Harrison's voice got quieter but was still teeming. "Elliot, maybe we should actually talk about how things were back then, and how things went down after Marshall—"

"I don't want to talk to you!" El yelled. "And especially not about him. I don't want to talk to you about anything!"

"I thought when you asked me to come here—"

"You thought wrong!"

"El—"

"No!"

Brittney cringed. She knew she wasn't meant to be hearing this, but clearly, the guys knew she and Katy were home. She wanted to go to them, to calm El down and be there for Harrison and try to get them to be reasonable with each other, but it didn't feel like her place.

Nothing feels *like your place, Firecracker.* Take *your place already.*

Not now, Daddy.

"I think you need to go." *Oh no.*

"Are you serious right now? Elliot—"

"Harry, we knew this was going to be a disaster. I just didn't know how big of one—"

"You think? Can you at least give me time to—"

"No. I need you to get your stuff and get the hell out."

"What about Brittney?"

"What about your kids? Don't give me *Brittney. I* will take care of Brittney."

Brittney cringed again as Katy stiffened.

"Don't you mean *Katy*? Are they interchangeable to you, or do you need to be everyone's little helper? Except mine, of course."

Brittney let out a long, slow exhale. Katy murmured, "This is so effed up."

"I think—"

There was another crash.

"Okay. Enough."

Brittney flung the door open. The source of the most recent crash was a beer bottle that had been thrown toward the door, thankfully empty, but right in her pathway. She walked across all of it in her bare feet before she noticed.

Katy was shouting from behind her. El was shouting, too. Brittney walked toward Harrison, his eyes following her, and she put her hands on his forearms, noticing that his hands were shaking.

"You can get your stuff now or later," she said softly. "I know where to take you."

"Brit, please," he said.

"Brittney, no!" El shouted.

She turned around and looked at her best friend. "El, I'm trying to stay out of it. I love you. But everyone deserves a second chance. Everyone deserves a safe place. It feels crazy in here. Is that what you want?"

"You don't understand." He was still seething, but at a normal volume.

"No, I don't." She let herself take Harrison's hand. He grasped hers tightly. "This is a part of you that you've always kept from me, and you're allowed. But all of this—" she gestured around the room with her free hand, "—has happened. Harrison and me. You and Katy. And you and I let it happen without talking to each other first, so…"

El was staring at her incredulously. Maybe she wasn't saying it the best way, but she knew he understood.

"I'm taking care of him right now," she said with a confidence she didn't feel. "And I am asking you, as my best friend, as practically family, no—*family*, to please take a day and calm down and then work this all out. Because the past will keep you from enjoying the future if you let it, and that is just stupid, El."

"Brit, your feet are bleeding," Katy said, in the smallest voice Brittney had ever heard her use.

She looked down and shrugged. "I have trailer park feet, sis. It's fine." She turned to Harrison. "Meet me outside."

She marched to her room, ignoring El's piercing gaze and Katy's protestations. There wasn't a lot of blood, nothing seemed very deep, so she put on some black socks and stuffed her feet into her running shoes, grabbing her keys and phone.

Katy watched her from the doorway, looking scared.

"Hey!" Brittney said. She walked to her until they were almost nose-to-nose. "You're my family, too. What is happening here—" She pointed to the living room, where El was sweeping up glass, "—I don't ever want this for us, for our family. You can come with me if you want. You know where I'm taking him. But you can also stay here and try to talk some sense into El. He trusts you. And you're strong enough, Katy. We have to stop acting like we can't handle being adults. We *are* handling it."

Katy hugged her fiercely. There was no comic relief, no leg wrapped around her, just an embrace that was tight and sisterly. Brittney let out a deep sigh and maybe understood in that moment what Mama called a *holy exhale*.

"Okay. We got this. I'll text you later."

El ignored her as she walked past him, out the door, down the stairs, to Harrison, waiting by his truck door looking embarrassed and exhausted. She put her arms around his neck and pulled him close to her. Her left heel started to sting.

"C'mon," she said. "We're going to my mama's."

Jessie 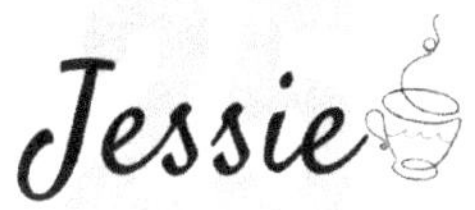

"It doesn't kill me to miss a meal," I protested. Paul had made grilled ham, cheese, and tomato and delivered it to the porch, where I was serving as host and guest of honor at a very elaborate pity-party.

"You're in training," he reminded me. I had agreed to run the 4th of July 5K in Market Common like I was "being chased." This meant I had to start running with him three days a week instead of one. He had no idea the depths of my dread over this. I turned to him as he planted a kiss on my cheek. "And also, I am fully and completely trying to cheer you up using your own arsenal."

"Mmmm." He got points for that. He didn't need them, as he was practically perfect most of the time. "Thank you."

"Um, do we know this truck?"

"What?" I looked up at our driveway. Brittney's car had materialized, and behind it, a vaguely familiar blue Tacoma had pulled in.

"That's not El's?"

"No," I shook my head. "His is red. Um, that might be…"

I hated how everyone had their dang windows tinted. It could have been Kevin Costner for all I knew, which would be a shame because I would get in the passenger seat and have to leave Paul momentarily. John Dutton was on my list.

Thankfully for all of us, it was Harrison.

"Baby cheesus on a cracker," I said, shaking my head. "She barely let me see this man when I was at the house, and now they're here."

"Whatever it is, the answer is no," Paul started.

"Paul, we don't–"

"And if she's pregnant, they're definitely not staying here," Paul said.

I hadn't even thought of that yet. "Shut your face."

Brittney strolled gingerly up the driveway. Harrison had not yet exited the truck. I watched her blondish top-knot glisten in the remains of the sunlight and vaguely wondered if she would want to get married before or after the baby came.

Stop it, Jess, Randall warned me.

"Hey Mama. Hey Paul." Brittney kissed my cheek and then slumped into the swing.

"You're walking funny," Paul said. His newfound expertise as a gait-analyst followed him everywhere.

She shrugged. "I'm fine." I knew that was a fake *fine*. "I have something important to ask you, and it feels big, and I'm not excited about it, so I'm just gonna let it rip, okay?"

Paul nodded, his very best Stoic Retired Principal look on his face. My stomach immediately turned to knots, but I nodded, too. Did my kids actually plan their crises to happen at the same time?

"Harrison and El had a big fight, and Harrison really needs a place to stay for a minute until he finds his own place. I was wondering if the suite—"

"Jesus H. Christ," I exhaled. Paul started to shake with laughter.

"What?" Brittney cried. "*What*?!"

"Oh, nothing," Paul said, trying to catch his breath. "This is just a normal question, Brit. *Of course*, the strange man you just met a few weeks ago that your best friend barely mentioned for fifteen years can bunk with us. Why would you even ask? I think your mama had it deep cleaned from Aunt Maggie's stay in anticipation. Everything is set."

Brittney gaped at him. There was a time I would have been set on edge by his sarcasm, but this time, in my attempt to hold in my own laughter, I snorted.

"Mama!"

"Oh, God, Brit. I'm sorry." I was also shaking with laughter at that point. "Just give us a second."

"Why is this funny?" she asked in earnest.

"Brittney, come on," Paul said, serious in the very next beat. "Take one step back and tell us it isn't, just a little bit. We could install a revolving door on that apartment."

She shrugged.

"And I've never even met this guy."

I cringed. Paul went with so many Oakley flows. My half of the family was chronically so much more chaotic than his, and he was almost always down for it, but this was—

"I know," Brittney said, with patience and apology in her voice. "I am so sorry to be asking this. I don't want to be asking this." She looked at me and gave a small smile, but she already knew what my answer would be, so she addressed Paul. "He's waiting in the truck feeling like a class A idiot. He and El had a huge fight, and El told him to leave, immediately. Harrison didn't ask me for anything, but I do feel like maybe you would understand him. He… they… there is a lot of history in their family that they don't want to talk about. I just feel like… maybe there will be a breakthrough soon. Maybe not. But this is the safest place I know, and I love him, and I want him to feel how I feel when I'm here."

Well. I didn't look at Paul because one of us might have started laughing again, not in the face of Brittney's solemnity and compassion and gratitude, but because there was no way either of us was going to say no to that plea, and we knew it.

He cleared his throat. "Brit, your mama has had quite a day."

"What happened?" She looked at me expectantly, ready to panic.

"Sam," I answered.

"Jesus…" she answered. Obviously, news had been shared with the siblings before creaky ol' Mama.

"Yeah," Paul said. "So, I appreciate everything you're saying. Emotions are high all over the place. And you know it's my job to protect her, right?"

"Yes, sir," she answered. I stiffened. I really had no idea where this was going.

"But it's also my job to trust her. So, while I want to say, no, this isn't the best time, I also know that her heart is already saying yes. And I also know what it means to both of us that you feel like *we* are a safe place, that *our* home together is a safe place. And Brit, it means a lot to me that you trust me with… someone you love. So why don't we go inside and have some food and get to know each other a little, and then we will see how everyone feels, and what your mama says after she's had caffeine. Okay?"

Brittney's chin was quivering, and I had to look away. He

was being a daddy to my girl in the gentlest, most needed way, and I just couldn't handle it.

Paul stood, so we followed. Brit and I didn't look at each other. I only looked up after she stepped forward into Paul's waiting arms, and I didn't bother holding in my tears. Instead, taking a cue from the patriarch of our blended/gathered/chosen family, I walked to the door of that pickup and knocked on the tinted window. When Harrison rolled it down, I looked into his guarded, weary eyes and said, "You want some coffee?"

He nodded wordlessly. I tried not to think of his mother, who'd let El down so many times since I met him, and I tried not to think of Sam or David, for whom I would do absolutely anything, who would soon both be so far from me. Instead, as he followed me inside, I pondered how, sometimes, God gives us people to fill our gaps. So, if Brittney loved Harrison, I would be more than ready to love him, too.

I cleared the dishes. Harrison was reluctant to eat at first, but Paul was a quiet master of atmosphere, and my grilled sandwiches were even better than his (I used the panini press, which he refused to do over his disdain for "small specialty kitchen appliances created as marketing scams"). They were still mostly making small talk as I brewed coffee and put some snickerdoodles on a plate.

"Harrison, when we bought this house – well, when I found this house and took a big risk assuming Jessie would want it – I knew that little apartment would be put to use and probably often."

Ignoring the ironic notifications from Maggie popping up on my phone, I sat down, my interest peaked.

"Jessie and I had broken up, and there were no signs

of us getting back together. I needed a place to live. I had crashed at one of the vacation rentals I used to own, and then with my oldest daughter, and life was just getting ridiculous. Directionless. When I found this place, all I could picture was our kids and our grandkids and Jessie's sister Maggie rotating through it. And it's happened."

Brittney shot me a look across the table, and I shrugged, having no idea where he was going.

"My adult life was always quiet until then. Even with three daughters, my first wife and I kept things orderly and neat and predictable most of the time. If you know Katy at all, then you know it had its moments. But since I started life with Jessie, I've made room for the unexpected and loud and messy circumstances that having a big family and a big heart will bring."

Harrison nodded, and I felt a little sorry for him. He seemed to have enough of his own problems without Paul's second act coming-of-age adding to them.

"You're a different kind of messy, sir." Ah. "Not only do I not know you, but neither does my wife, and from what I understand, Brittney doesn't know you that well, either. But her heart is big like her mama's, so I am going to try to understand here. I know life gets stupid for all of us sometimes, so I just want a few simple answers from you."

I tensed up, looking at Brittney. She was pinching one hand with the other. The air felt heavy. Harrison just nodded again.

"Why do you live away from your kids, and how long do you plan to stay away from them?"

The man across from me and next to my daughter shifted in his seat. He looked down at his lap, looked at his hands around his coffee cup, and then looked at Paul in the eye.

"I appreciate you being straight with me," he started.

"And while I don't believe this is anyone's business, and I haven't even shared it with Brittney yet, she's asking you to let me in your home, and it's your right to ask me whatever you want. Peculiar questions, I think."

Paul nodded. Brittney's eyes kept getting wider, but the conversation was growing increasingly familiar to me. Men just speak in a different language sometimes.

"I let pride make my decisions over this past year." Harrison let that linger. Paul nodded and waited. "My ex-wife took the job of a lifetime in D.C. Had we still been married, I would have looked at it like an adventure. Move the kids somewhere new. Explore. Live near a big city, which I've never done. I can work anywhere with my job. It's I.T., project management stuff, software implementation. It pays well. She knows my location is flexible. My kids don't."

I watched Brittney watching him. If she didn't know the gravity of loving a man with kids, she was about to.

"My son raised no questions. He wanted to go with his mom. That hurt my pride. My daughter was worried about me. She assumed I couldn't move. Her ten-year-old understanding was fuzzy enough for me to hide behind, so I let it all happen. I told myself they'd be better off. I stayed in Winston-Salem and licked my wounds and sold our house. I even crashed with my mom for a few weeks until Elliot called. And I answered that call out of pride, too. I thought my little brother who has resented me for years finally needed me, at least someone needed me... and as you can plainly see, it all turned to shit. Pardon me, Ms. Jessie."

"Ms. Jessie has heard much worse," Paul murmured. "So that's the first question answered."

Harrison cleared his throat. His demeanor changed as he glanced at Brittney, who had scooted closer to him and rested her hand on his forearm.

"This is difficult for me, Paul. Logically, after some time to get clarity, I know my kids are young, and they need what I never had. I know I can't afford to stay away much longer and still be the kind of dad they deserve. But it *is* complicated because even with all the messiness here, I have, in fact, fallen in love with your stepdaughter."

Brittney's head snapped to attention. She sat straight up and took her hand from him. My sweet girl, always at the ready for a fight or flight situation that maybe didn't exist.

I couldn't blame her, though. Harrison made two big statements in one.

And I was trying not to think about the fact that it could mean one more of my children moving away from me.

"I appreciate your honesty," Paul said. "I don't know Elliot very well either. That's on me. You're welcome to stay here while you get your ducks in a row, and I will talk to you more about that in private, but maybe. Well—" Paul looked at Brittney, then at me, and gave a small, knowing smile that melted my heart. "If you find that you need more than just a bed, I'd be happy to help you think through some things. I haven't been exactly where you are, but I had a brother, too. And I also had a rough spot with my kids when I was around your age. Being old has to have some perks, so I try to dole out the wisdom it's brought me once in a while."

Harrison nodded solemnly as he stood up. I watched him bring his coffee mug to the sink and turn around with some resolve and possibly hope on his face. Brittney was looking at me, and I nodded my reassurance. I wasn't exactly certain what was taking place, but I knew for certain it was one of those mystical-manly things that defied my female understanding even while it peaked my intrigue.

And if Paul was involved, I knew it would be good.

"We can talk some more," Harrison said.

Brittney let out a breath. Harrison smiled at her, and I got up from the table in the hope that she would follow. Taking Paul's hand in mine briefly as I passed, I led her back outside to the porch.

"I should go get his stuff," Brittney said, jiggling her car key in her hand.

"Why don't you wait until they're done, just in case?"

"In case what? Paul already said it was okay, which by the way, was weird since he didn't ask you first."

I smiled. "He already knew it was fine with me."

She shook her head. "So, you were having a whole wordless conversation while everything else was going on. How, Mama? How did you find that *twice* in your lifetime? I am hoping to find it once, and maybe I just did, but you heard him. He's going to move away."

"Brit..." What could I say to her? I was lucky. I was blessed, twice. I believed she would find it, too, but not by holding out and being afraid. I told her that.

"I don't want to move away," she said, with a resolve that surprised and frankly, relieved me. "Not that he is asking. It's too soon for that anyway. But he said *in love*. Did you hear him?"

Of course, I had. "Just wait a minute, Brit. Nothing is getting decided tonight. Well, except whatever Paul is asking of him in there, and that doesn't concern us." My phone buzzed in my pocket again. I took it out and saw Maggie's name, again.

"Maybe when Maggie gets here tomorrow, she can join this conversation, too."

Brittney shook her head. "Has she found a place to live?"

I rolled my eyes. "Maybe she can move into El's."

"Mama, would you come there with me to get everything? If it's okay, I'll pack an overnight bag and sleep in the cousin nook tonight."

I put my arm around my girl and took a quick mental assessment of all our sleeping spaces. We already knew what my answer was.

"Finally."

Paul was reclined bleary-eyed against his pillows as I plopped gracelessly beside him. I rested my head on his shoulder as we silently gathered our thoughts.

"Yeah, I got nothin'," he finally said.

I giggled. "That's clearly a lie. How is your new friend?"

I felt him shake his head. "He's fine. He's a dude. He's gonna handle his stuff. He's embarrassed. And I think he's pretty alone, so Brittney is good for him. For now."

"Did he say what his plans are?"

"He only said he needs to make them. I didn't pry. He was comfortable signing a little rental agreement for the next two weeks. He let me have Tom run a background on him. Then I gave him a key and told him we could talk more if he wanted. I think he does."

"Well, I have more news."

"Good night," Paul answered. He reached to the nightstand with his free hand and turned the light off.

"Paul!" I laughed. I couldn't blame him.

"Like seriously, what now? This day has been about sixty-seven hours long."

I filled him in on the three bullet points that had ended my day: Brittney losing her job. Maggie returning to town to find a house. Katy doubling down with El and "officially" moving in.

"Sweet Jesus," he said after I listed them in rapid succession. "Jess, seriously, as long as you're okay, I think I just want to go to sleep."

"You're not mad?" I asked. I figured each of those things would set him off.

"Brittney will figure it out. Maggie doesn't want to stay here anymore than we want her to. She'll find a house by Friday. And I already heard from Don; I just haven't had a chance to tell you. And Katy? That's the one I'm choosing not to think about right now."

I nodded and waited.

"Remember when thirtysomething meant married with a couple young babies and mortgage angst?" There it was. "Now they're acting like they're freshmen in college. They walk around with their energy drinks and communicate over Snapchat, and they job-hop and couch-surf. That beautiful beach house is wasted on them. They should just live in a bunk house."

I murmured my agreement. I didn't understand it either, other than the world was different than it had been in the '80s.

"Brittney will be fine," he reiterated. "Katy? I'll let you know my thoughts if she ever talks to me about anything."

His other arm encircled the rest of me, and I burrowed a little deeper into him, stirring.

"I wish I wasn't so sleepy," I murmured.

"Even if you weren't, I'm about twenty seconds away from a coma."

I sighed. "We used to be fun and sexy."

"Babe, I stopped being fun and sexy decades before I ever met you. That is the conundrum of us."

I planted a quick kiss along his collarbone. "There are many," I said, and repeated the gesture. "My body is completely done and also completely wants you right now. You are an amazing man, and I love how you love."

He exhaled deeply. His hands started to wander.

"Dammit, Jess."

There were many times in my life I expended energy I didn't have to accomplish something that seemed necessary. I lifted my mouth to his with every intention of repeating that feat. He was worth it, and so were we.

Brittney

She waited until the house had been quiet for over an hour.

She might have been thirty-one, but she wasn't going to be disrespectful. Only sneaky.

So, Brittney left her lower bunk, tiptoed to the doorway in the kitchen that led to the increasingly popular guest suite, and knocked lightly.

Harrison appeared almost immediately.

"I didn't wake you?"

He smiled. "Not even close. Would it matter anyway?"

"No." She walked through the door and as close to him as she could be. Everything about him received her. Everything he might have been holding back was released. The declaration he'd made seemed to have freed him.

When they had collapsed on the bed, exhilaration just starting to escape them, arms and legs wrapped around each other, she asked, "Was me staying out of here one of

Paul's stipulations? Because if so, I don't want to linger."

His first answer was to linger near her ear with his mouth. She sighed deeply and then giggled as his tongue tickled her neck.

His second answer was, "No. His stipulation was to let his friend at some leasing office do a background check on me and that I pay two-fifty a week."

"Seems like overkill. Were you offended?"

"Offended? Brit, I never met the dude, and he's letting me stay in his house. They could probably Airbnb this thing for that much a night in the summertime."

"Yeah, just… Eh. Never mind. I'm always gonna be the one to question authority." She briefly thought of Cristina and Ian, and then of Daddy. Her instinct to rebel used to drive him crazy, until she was mature enough to take some direction, and then he encouraged her.

"You got daddy issues?" Harrison asked.

"Paul's not my dad." The words came like a breath, without her thinking about them.

"I know. I didn't say that. Just…"

"Satan himself had daddy issues. *Everyone* has daddy issues." she answered. "The easy answer is yes, but not because I didn't have a great one. I just always felt second fiddle. It wasn't anything he did or didn't do. I refuse to blame him for my inability to get myself together."

"You're plenty together." Now wasn't the time to tell him about her day.

"Do *you* have daddy issues?" she asked, knowing it was delicate ground she treaded.

"I *am* a daddy issue!" They both giggled while his hand caressed her back. "My dad did his best, I think. Maybe what happened to Marshall would have happened even if he had been… better."

Brittney lifted her chin so she could see his eyes. "What

about what happened to you?"

He gave another sardonic little laugh. "That's a whole combination of things, but the fault is all mine, Buttercup."

"Harrison…" She didn't know how to ask what she wanted to know.

"I don't know what to do, Brit," he answered. "But I know I need to fix it. I can't change the last few years, what I did to Denise, what I let her do to me. Maybe I can't change things with Elliot. But I can change the future for Dakota and Ruthie. I have to. That's the whole point."

She nodded. Tears sprang to her eyes, not out of sadness that he was going to leave, but that someone so mature and passionate loved her, and that she couldn't fix anything for him.

Mama was right. Love could conquer all. But it wasn't always the love between a woman and a man. Sometimes it was the love of a daddy for his kids.

"There is a little more to my story" she said quietly. "Maybe why I am the way I am or whatever. I don't talk about it to anyone. Most of my family thinks I had this serious boyfriend for a couple years and that after we broke up, I lost my mind a little. They don't know why, though. Only El and Kayla know. And Daddy kind of knew, too."

She told him the whole Bradley saga. In the dark, she could envision him rolling his eyes at her naivete, she could feel him stiffen when she got to the pathological lying part, and she could feel him squeeze his hands into fists when she got to the assault in the parking lot part.

"You should have let El kill him," he said when she was finally done. He sat up and turned on the light, and she suddenly felt more undressed with him looking at her, knowing her most guarded truth.

She shrugged. "Probably. I could have run him over with my car, at least crippled him for awhile if nothing else. But I was just as mad at myself as I was at him."

"That doesn't surprise me, Brit. You sell yourself short on every level. And whatever happens with us, I hope you start to see how strong and wonderful you are. Quit putzing around and believe in yourself."

A man who agreed with her mama. She sighed. "I know. I'm trying. And look, I am letting my family know you! I mean for a long time I purposely dated losers. No one for more than a few weeks at a time. Only a few I brought home to my family. One had possibilities, but then his brother knocked up my cousin at a one night stand the night of my aunt's wedding. And they actually decided to get married and make a go of it. So that got awkward." She heard it all out loud and almost laughed.

"Your family is so weird," he said. "Hey, Buttercup?"

"Yeah..." He melted her with that stupid nickname.

"You know that it wasn't your fault, right?"

Her stomach knots tightened.

"Brittney!"

"What?"

"It was *not* your fault."

She didn't pull the covers over her face like she wanted, but she did look away.

"Please tell me you know that," he prodded.

Brittney sighed. "El and Kayla said the same thing. And so does NOW, Ashley Judd, about 500 million Instagram accounts, and every 'Me Too' PSA. But the fact is, I punched him in the face. Maybe if I just walked away--"

"*Brittney!*"

"Maybe if I just walked away, he would have left me alone. He would not have forced anything. But I was humiliated and angry and what my dad called a firecracker just ignited inside of me, and I wanted to make Bradley pay. If I had walked away, he might not have–"

"Tried to *rape* you, Brit? Do you think a guy like that needs provoking? Do you think one angry punch invited him to force himself on you, to attack you, to try to take what wasn't his?"

One tear escaped. She swiped at it angrily. She didn't want Bradley to have any effect on her again. And she wasn't quite ready for Harrison to see her so clearly.

"I guess... I *know*... that is correct. It's not the easiest thing in the world to reconcile. I just thought, after what happened, that maybe I just needed to be quieter about things, about everything, maybe not be so *fiery* or whatever. You know... 'sit still, look pretty.'"

He nodded, waiting for her to finish, and she felt completely disarmed.

"So, I just stopped looking for anything exciting, for a storybook romance, for an amazing job, for fireworks and explosions. It's safer that way." She paused. "It's also why I've been bored and probably boring for the past five years."

She stopped, because the truth of it hit her cold. Harrison must have sensed it, and he reached over to hold her face in his hands, staring at her in a way that made the fire burn quite a bit.

"You didn't make him do anything. You are not boring. And you do not have to be afraid."

"I don't feel afraid with you," she said. She didn't add *but you're probably leaving so what difference does it make?*

"It's not me that makes you brave. It's the fire. I hope you can grasp that."

She nodded. "Maybe. But you are helping me... I haven't talked about this in years. You're making me believe you a little bit."

"I'm honored. Really. And Brit?"

She shrugged and waited.

"I promise you, you know everything important about

me now, too. I don't trust easily either. I don't know why it's been easier with you. But I hope it's also easier *for* you."

They lay there silently, some music channel playing in the background on the TV. Brittney heard the opening guitar chords of a sacred song. Her instinct was to turn it off, but she felt Harrison stir. His hold on her tightened.

"You like this song?" she murmured.

He nodded. They were still through the quiet first verse and chorus, the buildup of the second verse, and then Harrison was singing the words, about angels, lightning crashing, the circle of life.

The lines ended before an instrumental break. His voice astounded her, gravelly, emotional, strong. He drummed on her back, and when the lyrics resumed, he sang again. She wondered if he even knew she was still there.

El had sung that song to her two years before. There was a horrible, lonely stretch of three days between Daddy's death and the memorial service. She'd spent all her time collecting pictures with her sister, keeping Mikayla's pregnancy her main concern and biggest secret from Mama, comforting Mama and Summer, feeling simultaneously wrecked and numb. She hadn't been alone for one second, and she and David almost got into a fight over what he was going to wear to the service. Mama told her to take a break, and she left for El's. She found him on the porch with his guitar and several empty beer bottles. He loved her Daddy, too. They didn't say much, but he played her "Lightning Crashes," and they both cried.

When the song ended this time, Harrison said, "We played this at Marshall's funeral."

Brittney nodded, letting her tears fall again. It all made sense.

"You and El need to find peace," she said quietly. "You have the same grief, you lost the same person, you lived the same tragedy. Not just Marshall but your mom and your childhood and what you didn't have."

She raised herself up so she could really look at him. "All my life, I've watched my mom do this thing. This redemption thing. Sometimes it was excessive, how she tried to give us the security and the love she didn't feel growing up. I get it. We can't change history. But part of the reason we have kids and families is to redeem it."

Harrison nodded. He was looking away from her, his eyes glistening.

"You're going to do fine by your kids," she added. "El wants the same thing from you. Just to know you love him, that you want something better for the future."

She lowered her head to his chest and let him hold her.

There was work to do the next day. She brought Harrison coffee, blueberry muffins, and a plate of maple sausage from The Kitchen of Mama and Paul, and then gave him space to start his workday and figure out his next moves.

She had a lunch date with Mama at the tearoom. In the meantime, she drove to El's to assess the aftermath of the previous evening. He and Katy had been locked away when she returned the night before. She expected Katy to be there and El to be at work. She found the opposite. He was in the driveway, his sound equipment spread out, wrapping cords.

She snickered. The guys always helped El put everything away after gigs. She did, too, but she knew better than to deal with the cords, which outnumbered the snakes on Medusa's head. No one did it "right" except for El, so this was not an unusual sight.

"When do you play next?" she said in greeting. She already knew.

"Fishwalk on Friday," he murmured, not looking at her. "Katy is working on the bass parts."

That answered two of her questions and put a hole in her fortitude to ask the others. She waited him out, but he staunchly avoided looking at her. So many cords…

"El—"

"Brit. You chose. It's okay. You don't have to explain."

She nodded, having expected him to say that. "What I chose was to help my boyfriend last night. Please don't make me choose between him and my best friend."

He kept working. "Boyfriend is a pretty ridiculous word, don't you think? I mean, we aren't boys. And Harrison isn't anybody's friend. I know you think you see something in him, but—"

She considered her words much more carefully than she usually did. Words were easy for her; they were her job and art form and defense. But El didn't need something polished and marketable. He needed her sincerity, though he wouldn't like it.

"You don't actually know him, El. And I get how that sounds, like *Oh my God. I've been seeing him for two weeks. No one knows him like I do.* I just mean that you have this figure in your head of a big brother who was so much older and far away and could have come to rescue you and didn't. But that isn't how he experienced it. Those years that separate us from our older siblings mean so much to us when we're little. Sam used to seem that way to me, too. Now he's just a guy with a few years on me, dealing with the same ridiculous anxiety everyone else in my family suffers with. And Harrison deals with the same grief you have. The exact same. You wanted someone to save you, and he wanted someone to save him. And you know what? You *both* saved yourselves. You are *both* strong, wonderful men who overcame the shitty hand that was dealt to you."

El grunted, but he had stopped moving around. He was looking at his shoes.

"I can't fix it. Katy can't fix it. You can choose to make it alright for yourself, somehow, and move on without changing anything. Or you and Harrison can fix it together. But El? Forget about me in the equation. He is being honest with me, and I have to figure out my own future. You deal with yours. But *deal* with it. Because I love you, and I don't want to see you how I did last night. That isn't you."

"What if it is?" he asked, so quietly she almost didn't hear him.

"What if you're actually unforgiving and aggressive and childish? Nah. Everyone has their moments."

El shook his head. "Even I know he didn't deserve my reaction. He was making a freaking bowl of cereal, and I started on him about his kids. I'm just mad, Brit. I have like, rage inside me that I guess has been dormant for a long time. Seeing him has reminded me it's there, but it's not toward him. He's just this… figure… that reminds me of what it was like when Mom moved us away, when he and Marshall didn't come with us, and then when Marshall died. You're right. I made him some mythical figure that could have fixed things for me and chose not to."

Hadn't she done the same? Sometimes she caught herself thinking that *if Daddy hadn't died…* Then what? She wouldn't have hated her job and gotten fired? Sam and Abby and David wouldn't all be going away or gone? Mama wouldn't have gotten cancer? She would be married and settled and not feeling like a floundering swimmer caught in a riptide? No. All of that was life. No one person was meant to fix it.

"El, tell him what you just told me. I think… it's not my place, not my area of expertise for sure, but you are both suffering the same, and you can help each other be a little free from it. You don't have to be BFFs if that isn't what you want, but I know from experience that your siblings get it in a way no one else can."

He nodded. "Yeah. I believe you. Even the fake ones?"

She smiled. "Even the ones you choose. Yes. Those are good ones. But Harrison might be a good one, too. Just try. You deserve not to feel this way."

"Katy said something like that, too. Only she didn't use as many words, and she also told me I was being a pigheaded dumb-dumb."

Brittney giggled. "Sounds like she got the point across."

"We're going to be okay." He looked at Brittney, finally, to indicate which "we" he meant.

"They could never tear us apart," she promised.

"God bless, that's a good song. Rest in peace, Michael Hutchence."

"You should sing it sometime."

"Eh." He rarely took Brittney's song suggestions. "Not alt enough."

She shook her head, pondering. "I didn't know Harrison can sing."

El looked at her, a moment of resurfacing anger flashing on his face before he shut it away. "Yeah. Probably better than I do."

"Just different."

She watched El pack his cords in his road case. They fit perfectly, and he looked satisfied, so she waited a moment.

"He's probably not going to be in town much longer."

"Yeah?" He went back to avoiding her eyes. "Are you going to D.C. with him?"

El was the first person to articulate the question. She hadn't even been able to ask herself directly.

With a head shake, she answered, "He hasn't asked. So, I honestly have no idea. If he does want me to… I don't know. I think I'll pray for a sign."

"You gonna stay at your mom's in the meantime?"

Now she looked at her shoes. It was all so stupid, the couch-surfing, the impermanence. She just shrugged.

El laughed. "Probably the only reasonable answer." He sighed. "Brit. I can't imagine life without you being here. If not in the house, at least in town. Just promise me you'll think it through. Don't *only* rely on the signs, okay?"

"Are you saying I can't trust myself?" she asked.

"I would never say that." He finally walked away from his project to her side. She let him hug her, feeling peace about this one thing, this one person.

"You probably should," she said when they broke apart. "I have to go look for a job now."

Jessie

I ONCE HAD A FITNESS COACH TELL ME TO BREAK my day down into hours and write down everything I did. He said once I saw how much time I was wasting, I would be able to clearly visualize how I could exercise at least thirty minutes every day. Once I had all the hours filled in, he had me work on fifteen-minute increments.

It was the period when Sam was going to Coastal, the other kids were all in school but none old enough to drive, Randall traveled seventy-five percent of the time, I was working with Paul creating textbooks, and I had even fewer boundaries, which meant I did PTA, church groups, a book club, and Lord knows what else.

I filled those grids out with total indignation. The coach's only response was that if I didn't quit some of those activities and rid myself of mom guilt, I was destined to stress eat and heap on belly fat forever. So, I fired him.

With time, I had learned how to say no to things gracefully (sometimes), about the effects of cortisol on weight loss, and most recently, thanks to my surprise and practically perfect second husband, that exercise didn't have to feel like torture. I wrote Coach Chuck (I called him Chuckles) a Facebook message after my cancer treatments, when I was suddenly at my lowest weight since giving birth to the girls and not constantly fighting with my schedule. I conceded that he was probably right. He wrote me back two words: "F---. Yeah."

So, after the day we had, with all the Sam and Abby and Maggie and especially the Harrison and Brittney goings-on, my old self would have slept in a bit. Would have drunk extra coffee. Would have had a consolation bagel or whole brunch. But the me that was growing older with Paul was accountable to him as a fitness coach of sorts. After my scary and thankfully resolved bout with endometrial cancer, he insisted that we both eat less sugar (I used fricken monk fruit in his cookies), balanced our diets, and worked out on the regular, especially when we were stressed.

He usually wasn't stressed. I wasn't usually as stressed as I *used* to be. But he could have knocked me over with a feather when *running* started helping me deal with stress. And I was especially confused after we finished two miles that morning, walking for two minutes, running for one, and so on, that I actually felt better when we were done. I even walked my customary mile on the beach afterwards, sans fancy running shoes, letting Dolly play in the surf and the salty air cleanse my head.

If I were still writing down those fifteen-minute increments, *almost* two of them would have been filled with "RUN!" A few would have said "COFFEE," "READ BIBLE/ PRAY," and so on. But I was banking that the rest of the day was going to read something like "DUCK FROM THE POOP HITTING THE FAN."

So, I arrived prepared for my lunch date with Brittney. If things worked predictably, Maggie would arrive while she was still there. With a lick and a prayer, my idea might work.

We didn't have any reservations that day, so Abby was covering our first few hours, and then I would take over. We hadn't discussed the timeline for her exit, but that was another bullet point on my Supermom Agenda for the day. God, help me.

"Are you and Brit eating?" Abby asked.

"I got it," I said, brushing her cheek with a kiss. "Hopefully, we will have a few walk-ins to keep you busy. You don't need to wait on us."

"But I—"

"We aren't starting that, Abs. I'm making grilled cheese, for crying out loud. You're not putting me out. In fact, do you want one?"

She smiled. "No. I gather you two have things to talk about, and if the text chain I read this morning was accurate, you won't be alone for long."

The number of iterations of the family text chain in existence was infinite. I didn't bother clarifying who reported what to whom; I was just thankful on that day that the task didn't fall to me.

By the time Brittney arrived in her flourish of messy hair and big sunglasses and ginormous tote bag and even bigger energy, our comfort food was waiting on the table, including her requested dang Cheerwine Zero, and I was ready.

"Thanks, Mama." Her eyes showed a lack of sleep, but her energy was crackling. Maybe she already had her own plan.

"Have a good morning?" I asked. I hadn't seen her since she had taken Harrison some provisions from the kitchen.

"Yes," she said breathlessly. "Harrison was okay. I stopped at the house and talked to El. We're okay. I don't know about them, but I have to let that be on them." Whew. I knew that was hard. "Then I went and applied at a few places." Looking like *that*? Good Lord. My youngest daughter was gorgeous, but she was dressed like she just got out of bed or off the beach. "I start at Fishwalk tomorrow."

"That's… great, Brit. Doing what?"

She looked at me like I was an amnesiac on *General Hospital*. "Bartending. Well, they're gonna train me for a little while during lunch, but I should be able to handle the nighttime crowd by Fourth of July."

I closed my mouth, nodding slowly.

"The people are great there, Mama, and the tips will be, too. I can stash a bunch of cash during summer and find something more permanent after the season."

"I thought there wasn't a true tourist *season* anymore, Ms. Marketing?"

"Well, there isn't an off season, but summer is still the height of tourism. And don't call me that. I might be done with marketing."

"Might?" I shook my head, trying to clear it. "Brit, I thought this was the opposite of what you wanted. I thought you were tired of things feeling temporary."

She took a bite of her sandwich, in my mind, relishing the mix of Havarti, sharp cheddar, and Pecorino Romano, but likely she was just avoiding my question as long as possible.

"I am," she finally said. "I'm so tired of it. I talked to Katy and El and then to Fishwalk Eddie. He already knows me from the band, and he predicts if I'm as fast at pouring beer as I am 'the charm,' I can pocket a thousand dollars a night on the weekends."

I had read about Ed Einhaus, the owner of Fishwalk

tavern. He was one of thousands who'd moved to the beach from New Jersey and opened up a combo sports bar/live music venue near the water with distinctive flair of some kind. His was that he ran it with his daughters and didn't act like a rude, pompous transplant trying to change the southern, coastal vibe. He also hosted a jazz festival in the spring and the fall, which both Randall *and* Paul loved attending. The place just celebrated its sixth anniversary; it was legit.

I took a big swallow of my soup and another of my pride. "That's a great plan, then, Brit. Make the money. Have work you can leave at work for a while."

"Exactly." If she was surprised at my reaction, she hid it well.

"Where will you be sleeping?" I asked.

She dropped her spoon.

"Well, Mama, that's the question of the day, isn't it?" It sure was. "It would be weird for me to stay at El's when Harrison is at your place." It sure would. "But I know you won't approve of me staying with Harrison…"

Approve was a strange word to wield at a thirtysomething woman who had likely spent the previous night with him anyway.

"Brit, I'm not naïve and neither is Paul, but come on. That would be a lot, don'tcha think?"

"Yeah," she mumbled. "But if he's leaving soon, I want to spend as much time…"

"Brittney, if he is leaving soon, maybe you should be detaching instead of growing closer."

My Mother of the Year Award was losing its shine by the second. She stared at her plate, biting her lip, and then exhaled loudly before answering me.

"Mama, I have no idea what is going to happen yet. But I do know that I have this window of time with a man who loves me, a man I love, and I want to enjoy the dregs life is momentarily giving us. But don't worry. We will enjoy them out to dinner or at the beach or the gym or something. No problem."

I will not *feel guilty about this. Get a room.*

"I had another thought before Aunt Maggie gets here." I might as well go in for the kill.

At least her countenance brightened at the thought of Maggie, no doubt since her energy would fill the room with distraction.

"Maggie is going to take over the tearoom." I was fixing to say aloud things I hadn't even told Paul yet. "She had already said she would fill in for Abby, whatever that means. But she and I talked, and we are going to sell the business to her. Well, more like a transfer, really. I'll still work some, baking, helping with events here and there. But it's served its purpose, and now, we move forward."

She was gaping at me.

"You're saying these words like you're telling me *I'm going to Charleston for the day*. Mama, isn't this a big deal? Wasn't this like, your new dream?"

Was that how I'd made it appear? I shrugged. "Brit… no. It's been fun, and it will still be fun, but it's been more like… a happy distraction."

With a scrunched-up face, she asked, "From what?"

Oh, Brit. I sighed. "From death. From getting older. From losing your dad and everything changing."

"But Mama, you're so happy. And you're so happy *here*."

Did she really not see? She was just like me, whether she wanted to be or not.

"I am so happy, Brit. So happy to be alive, to be loved, to have people to love, to cook and host and live. But it's not tied to a place anymore, for one. And for two… you have to know: I am still grieving. I am still devastatingly, eternally sad. Just over two years ago, our little family was whole and mostly together, and I was getting ready to enjoy some real time with Daddy. Time we dreamt about for literal *years*. When that changed, it changed everything. It changed *me*. So, I am happy. I am happier than I ever thought I would be again and certainly happier than I deserve, but I'll never be *just* happy, and I'll forever distrust happiness. It gets a big fat side-eye from me."

"Mama, that's terrible," she exclaimed, having the exact opposite reaction from what I wanted. "That's about the worst thing I've ever heard."

"Oh, Baby," I said, reaching across the table for her. "It's not terrible. Not really. It's *life*. Look at the choice you're potentially facing. You're in love. Maybe for the first time, I gather?" She blushed. "And it's so wonderful that he loves you. But it's complicated. You understand complicated. I hope you feel *equipped* to deal with complicated."

She nodded solemnly. "You're right. I do understand."

"Okay then." I took a bite to give myself time. She had thrown a wrench in my plans. "Now listen, Fishwalk sounds intriguing, but just consider. As a potential *additional* gig, if you want it: Work here."

The giggle-snort was my answer. Thankfully, the Cheerwine did not spray in my face.

"You're kidding, right?"

"I wasn't," I insisted, already defeated.

"Mama, what would I do here? Make grilled cheese? Come on. She needs to hire a few fourteen-year-olds. Or seventy-four-year-olds. I need to make money."

I hid behind my mug because, of course, she was right. In my head, she and Maggie maybe could have been partners like Abby and I were, but once again, I couldn't fix everything, even by force.

"But" Brittney added, "maybe I can help in another

way. That was the other part of my conversation with El this morning."

"What's that?"

"Social media marketing. There is a huge market for it here that is still a bit untapped."

I waited, the ellipses hanging in the air.

"El can't leave his job or anything yet, but he's willing to side-gig with me if I decide to try going on my own."

"So, what would you do?" At that point, Abby seemed to have declared the area safe and sat in the chair between us.

"I would peddle my wares to small and medium sized businesses. Independent stores. Real estate offices. Bars and restaurants and even bands. People who have good stuff but don't have the time or big budget to market."

"Like Altan and Kayla's?" I suggested. "Or here?" Brittney nodded.

Abby sat up straighter. "My friend in Blairsville, the one whose mom runs a tearoom? That is literally her job. She supports herself as a single mother doing just that."

"Isn't that a teeny-tiny-little town?" I asked.

Abby shrugged. "Super tiny. But it's a lot of virtual work, so she has clients all through the county and state, and even some from where she grew up in the Midwest. If you're a good communicator and apply strategy, you can do a good job for anyone, anywhere. It's perfect for you, Brit."

Brittney sat up straighter under the encouragement. This was one of those times when having a bunch of kids paid off; Abby was able to give to the moment in a way I hadn't been. The pressure was lifted.

"Everything will work out," I said, and mostly meant it. "Oh, boy," I added, looking outside. An unfamiliar, shiny Bronco had just pulled up into one of the front spaces, with a U-Haul trailer attached. A very familiar brown goddess with bronze locks piled atop her head exited the driver side, mission march fully engaged. "Looks like Aunt Maggie has arrived."

"Well, Mags, it looks perfect."

Paul had one arm slung around my shoulder as we stood in the middle of a great room, in the real estate *and* the practical sense. Our bunkhouse was getting a small reprieve.

"I still can't believe you bought it sight-unseen," I said. "I know that's all the rage these days, but seriously. It's a *house*. It's scary."

"Well, look at it. I think Akemi and I did just fine, thank you very much." Maggie had known her realtor for years when she worked at the bank. "She knows what I like, and she made absolute magic happen with this deal. We close in two weeks, and I'll rent it until then. And Sheldon can't wait to get here."

I felt a little tremor go through Paul, though whether it was annoyance or amusement, I don't know. The word via the husband network was that Sheldon had mixed feelings about the couple's new arrangement, which was long weekends together a few times a month until he was ready to retire from his practice and move to the beach. Maggie, however, painted a much more glowing picture. We knew better than to question her; time would tell.

The gleaming chestnut floors and ivory walls seemed to be waiting with their own bated breath for whatever Maggie would bestow on them. She led us through the pristine space, a model home from a new construction site about three miles west of us, modestly sized and holding all the trappings of suburban-beach bliss: a small outdoor kitchen, a big deck, a southern hostess-approved entryway, and a

Carolina room, which would be called a sunroom in any other state.

"I can't wait to see what you'll make of this canvas," I said. "Are you sure you're going to start sleeping here tonight?" It was already late afternoon, and there wasn't a stick of furniture in sight.

She waved her hand. "Sheldon is tracking the movers. They'll have the truck unloaded before dinner. It's just the basics." Uh-huh. "And your favorite take-out is on me if y'all want to help me get the bathroom, the coffee pot, and the bed all set."

Paul was fully vibrating now, and it was definitely with annoyance. No one said no to Maggie when she was in high octane mode, and I never said no to Los Gordibuenos' empanadas for dinner.

Her words had trailed off in one of the back bedrooms. I turned to him and stroked his arm.

"Don't pet me," he said, half-smiling. "I did not sign up to be her handyman tonight."

"We can call Sam and Altan," I said. "Or maybe we can ask Harrison."

Paul rolled his eyes. "Maybe we can have everyone stop moving around for a minute. I found four dilapidated cardboard boxes in the garage earlier, marked 'K.J.' Did she think I wouldn't notice? I told that girl I wasn't storing her crap."

He was working himself up, and I couldn't blame him. If I stood still long enough, I would realize how tired I was and that would not bode well for Maggie's plans.

"Sam already sent me a text thanking me," Paul continued. "I gather we will be making the moving trip to Georgia with them?"

Oops. "I never committed you," I said. "I know you have obligations at the store." Julie and Robin likely would let him schedule time off whenever he wanted, but I knew he didn't like to ask.

"It's not that." He took my hands. "I assumed we would go. And it's beautiful up that way. We… Leah loved Dahlonega, and I wouldn't mind showing you that on the way home. Jess—"

It typically wasn't difficult for him to tell me anything, but he was hesitant with his next words. I squeezed his hands to prod him.

"I know we are still young and vivacious and all, but I seriously wouldn't mind clearing the calendar more often and doing things we want to do. Do you know how blessed we are to be our age and be… whatever this is called? Semi-retired. But how often do we have the same day off? How often have we traveled together since you got better? I'm not frustrated with any specific person or circumstance. I'm glad to help. I just want…" He moved his hands to my waist and pulled me closer. "I want our life together to be more about us. We know how short life is."

I nodded silently, steeling myself against my instinctive propensity to feel torn in half. I didn't actually mind being at the beck and call of my adult kids. There was freedom and satisfaction in it. But everything Paul said was true and was something I wanted as well. So, I hugged him and murmured my agreement.

"Let's do it," I said. "Dahlonega or bust."

Five hours later, Paul had gone home to walk Dolly. Maggie and I were in her kitchen, deciding on the best cabinet for those pesky marketing scams. She had kept wine flowing since the moving truck had left, and I was starting to feel flushed.

"So, spill it," I finally said. "How are things really with

Sheldon? How does he feel about this arrangement?"

She took a long sip before answering. "He isn't thrilled," she admitted. "But he isn't mad, and he understands. Who knew I wouldn't be a city girl, sister? I really expected to love it upstate with more culture, closer to my girls, an accessible highway, The Cheesecake Factory. But my *soul* is here. This is where I was meant to be. And I think he appreciates that. It's mostly leaving Kendall and Quinn for him, which I get. I'm *leaving* my girls and that sweet baby boy. But isn't that what happens? Kids grow? We don't live on top of each other anymore?"

"I guess." I was hardly the person to comment on that. For the longest time, I was practically smug that all my brood stayed in the same place, and now…

"Anyway, I think they may trickle down here eventually. Well, maybe not Nora in her actual career job." Maggie's oldest was a marketing director at the Charlotte Ballet. Then again, nothing was permanent.

"Listen, as long as you and Sheldon have peace with what you're doing, that's enough. Everyone else has to be in charge of themselves. They're adults."

"Well, don't you sound like a woman who knows?"

I sighed and picked up my glass. I hadn't been drinking much wine since my *training* started, but being with my sister unleashed all the worries I tried to keep under wraps in front of everyone else, including Paul.

"I don't think I actually know anything," I said. "I woke up this morning with grand plans. I thought Brittney could come and run the tearoom with you while she looked for another job and tra-la-la. But I'll be shocked if she doesn't move away, too. Wait until you see this guy. He looks like if Eddie Vedder had a more chiseled younger brother with longer hair. She never stood a chance."

Maggie shook her head. "These dang guys." Eyeing me

in a familiar upsizing, she added, "So you gonna move to the mountains, too? Because that would be just like us. I make it back here, and you leave."

"I'm not moving anywhere," I answered vehemently. "I am a beach girl, and I cannot imagine summoning the energy to move again, especially without being fueled by humiliation and rage." I had sold mine and Randall's home less than two years ago in that state of mind. "But—"

"There it is," Maggie interrupted.

"Hush. I just mean, Abby makes it sound so charming there. And Paul wants to travel more. Maybe we will spend a month that way sometimes. Like in the summer when the tourists overrun us like ants with no traffic laws."

"Jesus God," she whispered. "I don't know if I'm ready to face that again."

"Well..." I topped off both of our glasses with the rest of the bottle. "It's too late now. Welcome back to the beach, Babe. Welcome back to the madness."

Brittney

She had never felt more sisterly toward Katy than when Katy answered the beach house door and threw her arms around *Harrison*.

"I'm so happy you guys came," Katy said. "El's in the bathroom. Um… Brit, you wanna go to the beach for a few?"

Though it had all been decided in advance, Brittney looked at Harrison. He nodded, expressionless.

"Um… text me…" she murmured, brushing his lips with hers, not wanting to go.

He grabbed her hand and held it, saying nothing, then let go to signal he was ready.

The short walk to the beach was silent. Brittney kicked her shoes off at the dune line and walked directly into the water, stopping when she was knee-deep.

Katy had followed. Brittney felt her right at her side, and as all the nerve endings churned in her stomach, she couldn't help but smile.

"I know we're supposed to be stepsisters," she said, looking into the waves. "But I do feel like for the first time since middle school, I have a girl best friend."

"Ha. What an honor," Katy answered. "El will be jealous though."

"Yeah, well… everyone has to share."

"We should be used to it by now," Katy continued. "Haven't the past two years been lessons in sharing?"

Brittney nodded. "And swerving."

"The hell of it is, I always wanted a bigger family. I always wanted brothers." She gave a sharp laugh. "Now both will live away from here, not that they consider me a sister. But you know what I mean."

Brittney considered how often all of them had some versions of this conversation, with disclaimers. No one could be too happy over anything in their blended family. It felt weird and a little disloyal, even if it was reality.

"I'm sure Sam and David have no idea you see them that way," she answered. "The thing about brothers is that they are boys. They don't notice things like we do. I would bet Sam doesn't think you give him a second thought. You should tell him sometime. He deserves to hear nice things."

"I bet you're sad he's leaving."

She nodded.

"Do you think El and Harrison will… still be brothers after this conversation?"

It would have been a silly question if they weren't in the middle of a family made by choices rather than bloodlines. And if Brittney hadn't been raised by a mother who called her ex-sister-in-law her *sister* while having virtually no relationship with her actual brother, the douchebag in Aunt Maggie's story. It had all weighed on her heart as she subtly helped convince Harrison to take the meeting

El had called for.

"I hope so," she said. "I think they just learn how to be after all this time. They both lost a big brother, and they both wanted that back. But now they're adults, and they need something different."

"You're so smart," Katy said. "You're gonna make a great bartender."

Brittney shrugged, unconvinced. And then her phone began to buzz.

"They're done," she told Katy.

"What? That was like, seventeen seconds."

"Boys," she emphasized, though she agreed it had been awfully fast.

"Do we go?"

Brittney looked back at the water, her instinct being to stay there and wait for Harrison or even El to come to her, or even to them. And then, suddenly, she could not stand her own inertia one moment longer.

Then go! she heard her father's voice telling her.

"C'mon, Katy!" She broke into a run, only stopping for her shoes, across the road, up the stairs, through the door. El was sitting on a stool at the breakfast bar, Harrison was standing in the middle of the living room. She ran to him and gave him a Katy-level, full-body hug. After a moment of surprise, he was hugging her back.

She heard El clear his throat. She heard Katy giggle. She heard Daddy's voice further instruct, *Okay, but calm down a little.*

"I love you," she said into Harrison's ear.

He squeezed her tighter and said, directly to her for the first time, "I love you, Buttercup."

Brittney closed her eyes and soaked it in for a moment. She had no desire to let go, save for one more act that needed to occur.

Breaking away, she looked across the room at El, thinking of how Katy had wanted brothers and how lucky she was to have an extra one all these years, who saw her and knew her and kept her safe. She walked to him, and he peered at her from under his ridiculously long lashes. They shared a look that could have said everything by itself, but he answered all her questions with a nod. She threw her arms around him, then, and said, "I'm so proud of you. And I'm so, so happy for you."

He hugged her back, and a moment later, she felt Katy behind her. "Brittney sandwich!" she called out. Laughing, shedding a few tears, Brittney sent a silent thank you to Daddy.

The firecracker had sat in the box for too long.

Fishwalk was filled with people on Friday night, and Brittney sat at the bar before the first set began. After two lunch shifts and a three-hour course to obtain her license, she discovered a newfound appreciation for the art— and complexity – of mixing drinks. Looking around at the crowded counter, she was happy to stick to afternoons for the moment, even if the money wasn't as good.

Katy had gone to the bathroom, leaving her stool empty when Geno and Ringo sauntered over after soundcheck.

"What's up, Brit?" Geno asked. Ringo pantomimed a shot glass, wordlessly asking if she wanted one. She did.

"Well, I spend so much time here, they gave me a job." She gave him the animated, angstless version of her *career change*. She wasn't sure if Ringo was listening. He just handed her a glass, tapped it, and was gone before she could say "Gracias."

"Hm." Geno focused on his sweet tea for a moment. "I had something to run by you. I don't know if this changes your feelings on it."

"I'm super intrigued." There went her stomach. What could it possibly be?

"The missus and I have come to a new understanding," he said. *Oh my God. Oh my God!* "And by 'understanding,' I mean she is going to forgive me, and I am going to stop being an idiot. So, I will be vacating the premises formerly known as Brittney's Pink Cabana. For good."

For good. She could not afford to misinterpret him. "What does that mean? Are you renting it out again? I get dibs?"

"Nah." With the shake of his head, her hopes sank as quickly as they had risen. "I don't want a failsafe anymore. Or an excuse. And truth is, I'm not a beach person. Too much traffic over here. Too many ice cream shops. I'm much happier in Conway with some grass and space and more Horry County natives than vacationers. I want to sell it. So, if you want it, there's your dibs."

He's selling my house. He's selling my house!
The market still sucks!
I am functionally unemployed.
I have a down payment in the bank.
It's a freaking mobile home.
It's mine! It's my dream home.
Oh, my God. I don't know what to do.

Brittney quelled her inner panic, reminding herself that she wasn't stuck. She had at least one great option in front of her. She undoubtedly had employment opportunities to supplement the glamorous life she was about to lead there at the Fishwalk. She had a down payment *in the bank.*

I left you that for a reason. I trust you with the reason.

Was that Daddy? Was that her? Could she trust that voice? Mama taught her that if she was quiet for a minute, if she remembered who she was and that God loved her, she would hear *His* voice. That's what she wanted. She wanted an answer so right that it must be sovereign.

Geno was staring at her pleasantly if a bit quizzically. She glanced at her phone. The show was still thirty minutes from starting.

"So, because of the job situation and… other… situations… could I have, like, the weekend? Are you in a big hurry?" She felt like she was asking the world.

He shook his head and took a big drink. "Brittney, girl, have I ever seemed like I'm in a rush? And do ya think I don't feel bad about making you move out and now here we are a month later? And maybe it's my fault you got all tangled up in that…" She waited for the rest of that sentence, but he just nodded toward the stage, where Harrison was in conversation with El and Ringo. She smiled.

"If you're the reason *that* happened, then thank you. And thank you for the opportunity and the time. I just need to consider some… things. And I can't wait to hear you guys play tonight." She bounced off the seat and up toward the stage. She wanted to be with Harrison, close to El, near the music.

By the end of the first set, Brittney noticed that El was a little hoarse. She started to say something to Katy, but Katy was already mixing some concoction of whiskey and lemon – which looked positively revolting. She brought it to him while Mikey was finishing up his Spacehog piano solo, and El gratefully drank up while Mikey dragged it out and then talked to the audience.

El had turned to Harrison and Brittney found herself clenching. Neither of them had shared much about their Come-To-Jesus conversation. El's summary had been "I said what I needed to say. And I asked him for what I needed from him. And things will be different now." Harrison had non-specifically thanked her and told her it was all okay, and he didn't seem closed to questions, but she also didn't feel free to ask.

But their conversation on the stage was way deeper than what usually took place during a set, and she couldn't begin to think what was going on. And then, Katy's elbow dug into her side as Harrison took his bass off and handed it over to his brother.

"Baby Bro is having a moment tonight," he said, and Brittney had to stop herself from a full-on swoon hearing his voice over the speakers, throaty and confident and dearer to her than she'd realized. "Sometimes we forget how potent the spring can be down here." He winked in Brittney's direction. She'd just been complaining that morning about people who complained about the pollen. "So, I'm gonna give him a minute here and do a song for you."

As soon as Dave started the opening chords, Brittney reached over and took Katy's hand. Harrison's voice in its fullness was just as gorgeous and a thousand times stronger than it had been while he was lying next to her those few mornings before, but this time he sang "Lightning Crashes" to a good hundred people who were entranced.

Katy let her squeeze away until the second chorus, when everyone started collectively losing it. Brittney couldn't remember them ever playing this together, but they were so together, and El hadn't played the bass at a show in years, and at the end, he was harmonizing with Harrison and everyone in the beer garden was singing along. Katy jumped to her feet, and Brittney followed suit.

Whatever had happened when the brothers talked, Brittney and her sister knew they were watching the healing right here.

It also happened to be epic.

When the song was over, Harrison turned around to take his bass back from El, but before he lifted it off, El threw his arms around him. Brittney didn't bother to swipe at her tears. She saw Geno smiling over at her.

"I feel so damn hopeful," she told Katy.

"About the guys?"

"About *everything*."

"We're gonna eek out a few more for you all tonight," El said. The driving opening of "Unglued" started, and as much as she loved hearing it, she almost couldn't wait for the show to be over.

El delivered a subdued version. They followed with "Breakfast at Tiffany's" and ended with one she hadn't heard them do in a long time. Not all the guys loved it; it made Dave full on roll his eyes and question his allegiance to these Gen-X music playing fools, and while Brittney enjoyed it, Katy looked like she was about to rush the stage.

The moody ballad "Fade Into You" sure ended the night on a solemn note, but it was the perfect vehicle for El's failing voice, and the crowd again went a little nuts for the different turn the show had taken.

She waited the requisite few minutes, letting the guys talk to audience members and each other, and as soon as she saw the first cord being unplugged, she started walking toward the stage. Katy hadn't waited; she was at El's side with another tonic and her unbridled adoration. Brittney tried not to stare, only smiled at her sister, who seemed to be changing the very essence of her best friend.

Ringo was still sitting behind the drums sipping a beer. Mikey had catapulted off the stage, toward someone or something. Dave was talking animatedly to Geno and Harrison, and Brittney willed herself to wait patiently. She stood next to Harrison and tried to calm her heartbeat as he smoothly put his arm around her shoulders. She leaned in with her head and probably with her whole essence, too.

Dave went on about Mazzy Star being a stretch and "most lyrics are total crap" before he went to fetch his Fanta. Geno smiled at them and left as well. Brittney tried to refrain from what she wanted, but Harrison knew. He pulled her in close and she faded into him, the sweat running from his hair and on his neck and the unmistakable longing coming from him that matched hers.

Ringo interrupted them as he walked past. "You should sing more." He kept walking, but Harrison smiled sadly at the back of his head. She read his mind.

"Wanna sit for a second?" she asked.

"Yeah. I could use some water."

"I'll get it. I'll find you."

She found him at one of the only open picnic tables – the afterparty was in full swing and The Doobie Brothers were singing to them now from the speakers over the bar.

"I loved the song," she said, hoping it encompassed the rising adoration she wanted him to feel.

He nodded. "It was something. A moment for sure."

"I guess you and El really did fix things up. It takes a lot for him to shake up a set list, even if the stupid pollen is getting him."

Harrison gulped from his glass before he answered. "Yeah. That was a show of trust from him. The forgiveness came yesterday. It was..." He searched for the right words. "Freeing."

She nodded her understanding. "I guess you have some family too, solving those sixteen years in one conversation after all."

He just smiled.

"So, what now? Do you still want to stay at Paul and

Mama's until…?"

He put his hand over hers, and her whole body tensed.

"It's been a full day," he started. "So, I didn't get to tell you. I found a place in Fairfax. Denise actually… she's going to look at it tomorrow to make sure the pictures and the listing are accurate. But, if it works out, it's about… thirty, maybe forty-five days."

She felt herself go cold and wondered if he could tell. Was her hand freezing like the rest of her? Still, she managed to dig up a smile.

"That's great. You have pictures?"

"Brit—"

"No, really, Harrison, I wanna see."

"Brittney."

Hot tears started rolling down her cheeks, and her skin felt cold. Was steam going to rise? How many times was she going to cry in front of this guy who had waltzed in her life without warning and was about to waltz right back out?

"I want you to come with me," he said.

The Doobie Brothers had given way to The Allman Brothers. Normally she would be air-guitaring to "Whipping Post." Under the stars, with him staring intently at her, the buildup seemed cartoonish. There should be violin music swelling about them, she should be wearing a long, billowing dress. The whole thing should fade to black with the words To be continued crossing the screen. Because—

"Oh my God, Harrison. Wow. I—how does life go this fast from nothing to everything?"

He didn't prod her. He already knew her, which made it harder.

"Geno just offered to sell me his house. *The* house, the one I lived in before this… unfortunate homeless era. I also got a call today from Downtown Alive. El told them

I was available, and they want to take their social media to, you know, a 'whole new exciting level.' It's a contract position, which is what I want, so I can spin things into my own business, but… I don't think an organization like that will be okay with a remote person. Not that I have to take it on, I just…"

You're prattling. Was that Daddy or the Dowager Countess? Either way, it was accurate.

"Hey. Buttercup? You don't have to. It was just…" He looked embarrassed, which she could barely stand.

"Harrison—" She wished she had a nickname for him. She loved his name, so distinctive. Harrison Brooks sounded like a bank president, and he could have been, but here he was, looking like he walked off the set off a Van Halen video.

"You asking me is everything. You…" *Just say it, Brittney!* "You *loving* me is everything. The best surprise. You *knowing* me… No guy I've been with has ever really known me. It's probably my fault. But it's the best gift. So, I feel ridiculous sitting here with my insides torn to pieces telling you… I just need a minute. Not a long time. Just a minute. Because *I don't know what to do.*"

He leaned across the rough planks of wood like he was going to gather her up right there across the table. But he just held onto her hands and said, "I've taken so long just to figure out I'm supposed to be near my own *kids*. I'm not gonna judge you. I just want you. I want you to know I want you. And I love you, Brit. It's the biggest surprise of all of this, even more than Elliot forgiving me. So, I have to believe it's for a reason, even if… "

She nodded. *Even if.* Even if he left her behind. Even if going with him turned out not to be the right thing. Even if this was just a few weeks of the kind of passion she used to dream about. Even if it took her forever to detach herself from him.

"I believe too," she said. "Let's get your stuff and go, okay?"

He nodded, finishing his water, and holding his arm out again as they stood. She thought of that *thing* that Mama had found twice, the puzzle pieces of a relationship fitting together so seamlessly. She knew it was work, but the ease of an arm around her, a person fully inviting her, that was the thing she thought would elude her forever.

"Let's go back to El's and sleep in my bed tonight," she said. "I don't want to be anywhere but by you."

He nodded, the air between them thick with emotion. She put her arm around his back, and they walked together like partners.

Jessie

As a Mimi, I usually loved the end of the school year. Largely unscheduled days for Summer and Jacob meant lots of extra time together. Since Travis had gotten older, Sam and Abby started taking an almost immediate weekend away by themselves right as summer break started, and Summer and Jacob were all mine. I relished the fort-building, constant popsicles, getting new beach toys from Dollar General, and at least one of my precious grandbabies inevitably falling asleep on the couch. In time, Taco Tuesdays morphed into weekly slumber parties. As Summer got older, she started inviting friends sometimes, and Jacob had taken to video games in the bunk room with Paul. They usually Facetimed with Uncle David, too.

I treasured the unhurried, much-more-mellow-than-Momming pace of my grandkids. Josie was still a baby and couldn't be part of it yet. Now suddenly, the two who were *the two* were spending their first days of summer… packing while Abby was giving Maggie a crash course in tearoom operations. It was just another day in the life of a woman with many kids going in many directions.

"I want to give this to Josie," Summer said, her voice businesslike as she held up a yellow Belle costume.

"It won't fit her for a few years." I tread lightly, injecting a bit of logic but not so much as to turn a fun time into a dramatic one.

"She'll love it, though," I added. "Your Aunt Kayla used to have one just like it."

"She did? How about Aunt Brit?"

I smiled at the memory. "She preferred Merida, but mostly just her bow and arrow." Somewhere there was a picture of Brittney in the height of her princess-rebellion, dressed like a ninja, accessorized with some Disney crown, Cowgirl Jessie's red boots, and holding the preferred princess accessory from *Brave*.

"Mimi, can you fix this?" Jacob came into the room holding a frame that had come apart in one corner. The photo inside was him with his Daddy and his Grampy. I swallowed my feelings.

"Of course. Let me see if your mama has some glue. Did you finish your boxes?" He nodded and followed me. It was almost lunchtime, but he was still wearing Spider-Man pajama bottoms that were about six inches too short, as all little boys do and should do. Clearly, he was doing more playing than packing anyway because he was also wearing a pirate patch, Chicago Bulls wristbands, and his brother's old Pokémon t-shirt.

I dug through the junk drawer until I found the right tools and set to fixing his frame. Jacob didn't wait. He grabbed a Capri Sun from the pantry and bounded off. I looked around the kitchen, almost as familiar as my own. When I sold the beach house where Randall and I had ha planned to spend our empty nest years, Sam and Abby's became the gathering place, at least until everyone's comfort level with Paul and me and our magnet of a house had settled. Their scrubbed kitchen table had been mine and Randall's before our big move, the one Sam had grown up around. I wondered if they would take it with them.

The move was in two weeks.

My phone rang. I expected Paul, likely on a break at the store. But the screen read YOUR FAVORITE DAUGH-TER, which Brittney had, of course, programmed in herself. Why call when you can text? Mildly irritated and almost panicked, I answered immediately.

"Mama, where the heck are you? I thought you weren't working today?"

She had been sleeping either in the bunk room or at El's for the last week with no notices given, just frolicking to and fro, but oh, the indignation in her voice over me not being where she'd assumed I was.

"Where are *you*?" I answered.

"Duh. At the house. Where I thought you were."

"Brit, I'm with the kids, cleaning out their closets. How can I help *you*?"

If she registered the sarcasm, she didn't let on.

"Can I come over? I just need to get something hashed out once and for all. I can bring the kids lunch. I can bring you unlimited mimosas. I will even help, but I feel like my skin is peeling off, and I need to *talk* to you about all this!"

Brittney's anxiety was nothing new, but the level she expressed was possibly more intense than the daily. I had noticed she was positively clingy with Harrison, but also, on the sporadic occasions I saw him, he seemed the same. Paul said that he was planning a move near the end of the month, too. I hadn't asked Brittney. It took all my resolve, but I knew she would come to me.

"Bring it all," I said. "And remember Summer is a vegetarian this month."

"I'll be right over."

I walked back to Summer's room, determined to distract her with something. The effort was likely folly, but my big crazy family had taught me resilience.

"It all comes down to what you want to *do*, Brit. And to accept that nothing about this has to be permanent. I know buying a home is a big step, but you can also sell it. Don't listen to Sam. Mobile homes sell just fine around here."

I had repeated the same mantras and key facts no less than eighty-thousand times. Summer even got bored and left us in her room amongst her discarded stamper collection and a pile of 6x clothing we'd unearthed on the closet shelf.

"Who just moves to a different *state* because they're in love? Look how that worked out for David."

"Well, Uncle David was being a very specific kind of idiot," Summer called from the doorway.

"Summer, go check on your brother. Make sure he puts his stuff in the dishwasher."

Brittney was smiling. "She has a point, Mama."

"She does," I agreed, thought I felt the need to defend my David a bit, too. "And you have made several very specific idiot moves yourself. There is nothing new I can say to you. Give yourself a deadline. Harrison might be willing to wait forever, but Geno isn't going to. When you wake up tomorrow, whatever your prevailing thought is, go with that."

"That sounds really bohemian, Mama."

"Have you just met me?"

She shook her head impatiently. "I know *you* view you

as a Zen-Jesus-hippie-mashup, but we don't buy it. Where do you think your children's anxiety comes from? You were not always like you are now."

Didn't I know it? "Well, Brit, learn from me, then. Just because something is big doesn't mean you can't overthink it. And you are. You're going to gain *and* lose no matter what decision you make. And either way, *you can change what doesn't work.*"

That was the key. Nothing except death was forever in this world. And since I believed in Jesus and Heaven, even that had an expiration date.

"I'm gonna go," she said abruptly. She kissed the top of my head and hurried toward the bedroom door.

FFS. "Text me later!"

I walked to the kitchen and checked Jacob's frame on the counter. Randall was looking up at me, immortalized in a happy moment of his grandson's first tee-ball game. Jacob's eyes were covered by his red and blue baseball cap, Sam's by his sunglasses, but Randall's were jovial and alive.

I was a different person than the woman who took the photo, than the woman who raised the man on the left and married the one on the right and even the one who'd welcomed and doted on the little one in the middle. She tried so hard to make everything storybook perfect. Now, I just wanted to make every moment count, even if it sucked.

⌒⌒⌒

"Sheldon is coming Thursday night!" Maggie told us enthusiastically. We had another take-out feast, this time from Fishwalk because #eatlocal, spread out over a stripped-down table in the tearoom. Paul was eating fried pickles like potato chips, and I was snarfing down a crab cake platter. Running, and not knowing the future, made me hungry.

"You guys want to come over for dinner?" I said, and Paul laughed. It was pretty much always about the food.

"Let's plan Friday," she said. "I want his first night to be at the house, so I can show him how splendid it is."

"Good strategy," Paul said, shaking his head at me. "And Jess, you made plans for Friday."

I peered at him as though he had two heads, and then I remembered we were going to Julie and Robin's. "How about Saturday?" I bargained, and he rolled his eyes.

"Sure. Let me know what to bring." It came out so casually and naturally, my heart swelled with gratefulness to have her back down the street from me again, even if it was *complicated*.

What the hell wasn't?

Paul picked up his phone. "Harrison just pulled up at the house. Looks like Brittney is getting out of the truck with him."

This signaled several things. One was that my husband was addicted to the cameras installed outside our home and all the notifications that I had promptly turned off. The second was that Brittney was not planning on spending the night there. No telling if Harrison was.

"Does she look like she's sad?" I asked. "Shut up," I told Maggie. "I know it's spying. We're all deluding ourselves if we think it's not."

Paul did not entertain me with an answer. I walked to the kitchen to refill my glass. I paused to look around. Maggie was already coloring the place with Maggie-ness. Our subtle, pastel dish cloths were replaced by a bolder set that was red and turquoise and emerald green. It would take more time and effort to change the palette of the whole place, but I was certain she planned to, and she didn't even know my plans yet.

Paul followed me. I was leaning against the counter, a

prime target for his affection. He walked over and leaned into me, kissing my neck. Then he whispered in my ear, "I'm going home so you can tell her."

"What?" I pushed him away. "You're not going to tell her with me?"

He shook his head like I'd just asked him the obvious question of whether he liked golf or snickerdoodles. "This is all you, babe. I gotta break my own news to Julie. One hurricane a week for this guy."

"If Ed Piotrowski had that attitude, we'd all be dead. Or living inland for half the year," I murmured. Our local celebrity meteorologist had saved me from evacuation-panic more times than I cared to count.

"He's a better man than I am," Paul said. "With much more energy. I'm going home. I'm walking Dolly. And I am going to bed. Don't make any more plans for the weekend, okay? And we're gonna like, grill hot dogs on Saturday, so keep yourself and your soul-foodie sister calm. Got it?"

I had it. I kissed his neck in solidarity and waited until I heard the door chime and Maggie locking it. Then I returned to the dining room to share my big news.

"Why do I feel like I see you more on this porch, in that chair, than in any other place?"

Paul looked up from his newspaper. Yes, newspaper. He was the only living being under the age of eighty who still read *The Wall Street Journal* in print, and for this, I loved him even more. "Because we see each other coming and going. Which is why I am delighted to tell you that as of the end of this month, I will no longer be a part-time running retail associate."

"Whew!" I said, dropping into the chair adjacent to him. "How did that go? How do you feel?"

"It was fine, probably even expected, and I'll tell you after you tell me about *your* conversation."

I sighed and looked heavenward. "In a nutshell, it's also fine. But it took Maggie a hundred minutes of rapid-fire questions to get there."

"Questions or comments?"

How well he knew her. "Well, a mixture of both, I'd say."

"Hot dogs, Jess." I grimaced at him. "That's our dinner for Saturday, and that's our new code word for simplifying."

I nodded. "I like simplifying. Exactly what else are we simplifying?"

"Conversations with Maggie."

"That sounds like a very tedious Hallmark movie."

He raised his eyebrows and spread his hands apart. Point received.

"Anyway, I am 'delighted' to tell you that at the end of this month, I will officially be a *consulting* partner at Whitney's Tearoom."

"That doesn't sound like *silent* partner." He mumbled a very specific string of cuss words before saying that. "It sounds like the opposite, Jess. What the heck is that?"

"I told her she gets one phone call a day for the first three months."

The cussing was not mumbled that time. "Jessie Rose. That's not freedom. That is *ridiculous*. How will you track that? Are you going to block her number every day after her first call? And what about when she wants to Marco Polo about something stupid Sheldon said? Or something amazing the Little Prince did? How can you possibly quantify this? And I want a real answer. Don't start quoting '90s lyrics."

I knew he was only half-serious, only half-aggravated. So, I waited a beat before I said, "But I *do* pray every single day for revolution."

An ice cube went flying toward my face. I reached out and caught it before it landed on the ground, plucking it into my mouth.

"Don't underestimate my abilities," I said. I sucked on that ice cube until I could talk again. "Don't underestimate how much a southern woman wants ice. All the time. And especially don't underestimate my newfound superpower."

Paul was shaking his head. "I never underestimate you, but you always forget that. How are we gonna try writing together again if you're on Maggie's leash? Eh. Nevermind. You always figure it out. Now tell me our new superpower."

I stretched out in my chair, feeling, even in the face of ninety days of Maggie-business phone calls, lighter and freer. "Boundaries," I said. "And sixty years is faster than some people get them. But someone already wrote that book, so we need to think of another one." I felt sure the possibilities were vast.

Brittney

IT ONLY TAKES TWO HOURS TO PACK AN ADULT'S bedroom. Brittney learned that when she moved from her parents' house the second time, the summer of post-collegiate grunt work. And here she was again.

Harrison had packed the rest of his things the day before. Most of it had already been transported to Mama's and was boxed up there. A few totes were still at El's, in that silly attached bedroom that had been the bane of her existence for a few uncomfortable days that inevitably ushered in…

Him. She was watching him from the doorway, in the kitchen, making his requisite post-gym PB&J times two. El had gone to work out with him, and they had one more show together that night.

Brittney's stomach hurt when she thought about it. There was a nagging pressure behind her eyes all day. It was Saturday and The Salty Lips were playing at Fishwalk.

Harrison was leaving the next day. Sam and Abby were leaving Monday morning.

And she was staying.

Not still, though. She'd been counting on Daddy's voice more the past few weeks. It helped her to drown out the questions and filter out the unnecessary voices, because in this case, only two opinions had mattered: his and hers.

He had been perfect about it, lying in her bed the morning after the Fishwalk show, entangled in the Care Bear sheets for what she'd hoped would not be the last time.

"Geno told me he was moving out of the house. He didn't tell me he was offering it to you. I didn't know."

Brittney propped herself up on one arm. "I didn't even think about that. I didn't think you band guys talked about anything of substance, especially on a show night."

Harrison shrugged, caressing her wherever his hands rested. "I doubt he thought it was of substance to me. Those guys don't know… I mean, they might know about me leaving, but they never thought I was staying."

She traced hearts on his chest with her finger. "Maybe they're like me, and they hoped you were staying."

"Ugh," he said. "I'd rather not think of you and a bunch of weirdo rockers as anything alike."

"Oooh," she said, faking a sad face. "It's okay. Those are my people."

"You really mean it, don't you?"

"They've been together for years, and I've barely missed a show. It's just what I do."

"I can see that," he answered. "So, did you hear about the new bass player?

"No. But I assume it's Katy."

"Yeah." She rested her head back on his chest. "It's Katy. I don't know if all those boys can handle it."

"I think they're cooler than you've gotten a chance to know," she said. Then she sighed. "I know it's stupid and moot, but I wish you could stay. I'm happy you're going to be with your kids, and I know it's right. I wish we had a portal or something, and you could do both."

"You love it here, don't you?" he asked.

She swallowed against the lump in her throat. She hadn't meant to give him a preface to her decision, but he sensed one anyway.

"I do," she answered. "It's simple, and nothing special, but it's home. I haven't had the itch to travel far and wide or transplant myself since college. Even though my life isn't… buttoned up, and definitely not exciting, I just can't imagine…" She stopped then. Maybe finishing the sentence wasn't necessary.

"I knew it was a lot to ask," he said. "And I knew your answer was probably no. Everything is new for us. Hasn't been more than a few weeks since you thought I was a class A jerk, and with good reason. And your brother is moving away; I know you want to be here for your mom. If I had a family like yours, I wouldn't want to move away either."

"You have El," she said. "And you'd have us, too."

He smiled, but the pain in his eyes betrayed him. "I would have liked that," he said. "But it's too late for me to have it all. Whatever gaps were in my family of origin, I can only redeem them by making sure my kids have better. *You* told me that, Buttercup. And you were right. Ruthie and Dakota are how I make it better. They're how I make *me* better."

Damn the timing and damn the new tears falling from her eyes and soaking his skin. She picked a fine time to have exhibited any kind of wisdom.

"I'm sorry," she said. "I thought all I wanted was to fall in love with someone who loved me back."

"I could have told you life isn't that simple, Buttercup."

"The good news is," she said, trying to convince herself, "my schedule will have some flexibility. Once I know what I'm doing at Fishwalk, I can string some days off together, handle my accounts remotely or off hours, and come see you. Often. I mean…"

She couldn't expect him to wait for some random visits.

"As long as it makes sense," she added.

"I'm not looking to love anyone else, Baby." He kissed the top of her head so tenderly, her tears renewed themselves. Trying to resist the love or the sadness was futile.

So, the question of a long-distance romance was left hanging in the air. They would play it by ear. Maybe at some point she would be sick of living where she'd always lived. Maybe Denise would decide she wanted to live in a coastal South Carolina town that she'd never even visited. Maybe they would blink, and Dakota and Ruthie would be going off to college. Maybe Harrison would get there, join a gym and another band, and find another woman who was more mature, more together, and absolutely not four hundred miles away.

She watched him eat his sandwiches, facing the counter and not even realizing she was there. El walked in from the bathroom, his fresh t-shirt sticking to him and his hair still damp. He looked at Brittney, obviously watching his brother, and shook his head, smiling.

"I've never seen her like this, Harry. You could probably scoop her up and carry her away if you just try a little harder."

"Shut up, El," she answered, but she wasn't entirely sure of her own answer to his supposition.

"Be nice," El answered. "Or we won't give you your surprise tonight."

"The two of you have something for me?" she asked.

The brothers exchanged a look, and Brittney felt her heart swell at how differently they'd treated each other in recent weeks. There was teasing and inside jokes and an infinite lessening of the tension. They behaved like brothers.

"I'm going to get ready," she said, beckoning Harrison with her eyes.

"I'm coming," he said.

"Ew," El said. But she was already starting the shower and waiting for Harrison to join her one more time.

The surprise was a song, one Brittney wasn't sure she'd ever heard before. They ended the show with Van Halen. It was another brand-new cover, pulled from seemingly nowhere. Katy came up on stage for it, and Harrison handed her his bass. The crowd went wild for that. Harrison took a few steps forward to share El's microphone. They traded lyrics back and forth. Brittney went wild for that:

"You can change your friends, your place in life, you can change your mind. We can change the things we say and do anytime. Oh no, but I think you'll find that when you look inside your heart, oh baby, I'll be there."

Her best friend and his brother, the greatest, most unexpected, truest love of her life, were both looking at her as they sang the words. Katy was locked in with Ringo, enjoying her new place in the rhythm section. Dave and Geno were doing their typical trading back and forth, playing their guitars side-by-side like a secret language. Mikey had his sunglasses on in the dark, flashing his big, beaming smile like he didn't have a care in the world except those keys on that piano on that stage. Brittney didn't know how it was all going to work out, but she knew she had gathered the best people to be her family, and they would find their way.

EPILOGUE

JESSIE

"Hello, the house!" I called, channeling my terrible Gaelic accent after binge-watching *Outlander* for half the previous night. Harrison and Brittney were moving that morning, and Sam, Abby, and the kids two days later.

The freezer reserve of snickerdoodle dough was gone, absolutely gone. I was going to have to replenish it before Paul noticed, but my energy reserves were also depleted. Some of the cookies were right there in a tote bag, along with dishes to fill my youngest daughter's new fridge, the first one she had ever owned.

"Did he already leave?" I asked. I walked through the door to find her sitting on the counter of the small kitchen. Looking around, I could see that nothing about the house had really changed since she moved out. Only her sparkle was missing, and we were about to start putting it back.

"We said goodbye at El's this morning," she said. Her hair was pulled through the back of a Pelicans cap, and her face was free of makeup, making her red, puffy eyes stand out. "Look what he gave me."

She gestured to the couch where a bundle of sheets was folded inside a factory satin bow. The label still attached told me they were bamboo. They were a light shade of sky blue and covered with rainbows.

"He said they aren't to replace my Care Bears. Just so I can have an extra set that I love and maybe have clean bedding more often." She laughed while swiping at her tears. "Mama, what am I doing? He loves me! He *knows* me, and he loves me. What if no one ever loves me again? And I am letting him go for what? A house?"

I let my bags drop to the floor and crossed the few feet between us, wrapping up my firecracker with every intention of letting her explode.

"No, Brit. You know that isn't it." She stiffened at the implied admonishment, getting ready to toss me off, but I held on tighter. "He loves you because you are worthy of love, and he isn't automatically stopping, and if he ever does, there *will* be another. Anyone you open your heart to is going to love it so much."

I heard myself, sounding like a greeting card. It wasn't my kids' fault they had a cheesy writer for a mother, or that my sincere pep talks sounded that way, too. Luckily for Brittney, my phone started ringing.

"I'll take it on the porch," I called behind me. "Paul."

"Hey Babe. Harrison was just back here."

"What? Why?"

"He was looking for Brit. I didn't realize he hadn't seen

her house. I gave him the address. Just a heads up. Don't get involved. I love you."

I hung up, insulted and smiling. *Don't get involved.* How dare he?

At that moment, the big, metallic blue truck pulled in front of the house. It would never have fit in the driveway, which could have meant nothing or could have been a sign. Who knew these days? Smarting from the sight of my daughter's broken heart, I looked sideways at Harrison as he walked toward me.

"What are you doing?" I asked.

"Ma'am," he said, nodding. "I'll be respectful. I'm just not done."

He went in without a moment's hesitation. I sat myself on the steps, where I would wait, at least for a while.

BRITTNEY

She was staring out the picture window at his truck, so though it was no surprise to her when he walked in, she didn't turn her back. She waited, telling herself it wasn't a dream, until he put his arms around her waist, nuzzling her neck. Their intense goodbye had been less than two hours ago, and she'd thought it would be weeks before she felt him again.

"What are you doing?" she cried. She knew he wasn't staying. She knew nothing had changed.

"Look at me," he said. When she turned around, he put his hands to her face and looked unblinkingly at her. "Wait for me. Will you try? I'm going to wait for you."

She shook her head, not to say no, but in an attempt to clear it. "Wait for what? How will we know?"

"I don't know," he said, and the hint of desperation in his voice almost put her on the floor. "But what if I come here for a weekend every other month, and you come to me on the others when you can? And we talk a lot. And we keep an open mind. And maybe we'll just… know… when it's the time we're waiting for."

She put her hands to his face, brushing his hair away, stroking his cheek, memorizing the feel of his skin on hers. Nothing she'd felt before him compared, and she was in no hurry to try to duplicate it with someone else.

"I don't mind waiting," she said, breathlessly. "All I needed you to do was ask."

He kissed her fully, and aware her mother could burst in the door at any second, she kissed him back. She couldn't imagine what she looked like, her care-worn face still splotchy from a morning of tears. They would continue through the day as she put the pieces of her home – all hers now – back together. And she wouldn't curse them, or her big heart, or her timing being so different from that of her older siblings. Her timing had brought her Harrison, and she had to believe it would bring him to her again.

BRITTNEY – TWO MONTHS LATER

"Gosh, it's cute in here, Brit." Mikayla took a handful of pretzels from the tray and sat back on the couch. "I always loved your pop culture decor, but this took it up a notch."

Brittney followed her sister's gaze to the biggest wall in the mobile home. It was basically wallpapered in music posters, ones she already had, ones she'd scoured for on the internet, some she'd picked up from a guy at Hudson's Flea Market. Some of the not-as-special ones had been cut to make them fit along the edges of the walls and outline of the windows, but the effect was glorious. When insomnia struck, and it had more often in the past few weeks, she would sit on the couch and recall a song or a memory connected to every single artist represented on her wall.

"Robin would love it," Julie agreed. "We hardly have any pictures up yet. I guess we're the boring ones."

Brittney could picture Julie's white textiles/bamboo furniture/green plants motif and just smiled. She could hardly just agree without seeming mean.

"Did you order the food?" Katy asked. She was stretched out on the floor, having just told them that playing with The Salty Lips was the most exhausting and exhilarating job she'd ever had.

"How are you so skinny?" Danielle called. She was in the little chair in the corner, nursing Lexie.

"Don't body shame," Julie said.

"Be quiet, Gen Z. That is not body shaming!"

"I am not ashamed of my washboard abs," Katy called, rubbing her belly.

Mikayla threw a pillow at her but kept one in her lap. Her own tummy was starting to blossom.

"The food should be here in thirty-five minutes," Brittney said. "Do we want to start the movie now or wait?"

"Let's wait and catch up first," Mikayla said. "Are we calling Abby?"

"She and Sam were invited to the 'Union County Educators Supper Club' tonight," Brittney answered. "So that's a 'no' from her."

Mikayla shook her head. "They're in a whole different world up there."

"They're either going to become rural mountain people or get sick of the whole thing inside a year," Katy said.

"Yes, brainless," Danielle told her. "That's usually how it

goes. People adapt or they don't."

"I hope they do," Mikayla said at the same time Brittney said, "I hope they don't."

There was nervous laughter. Brittney had been in her emotions lately, stressed about her new business while working Fishwalk and the tearoom a few days a week, missing Harrison, and having to replace her air conditioning the third week she lived in her house. Everyone agreed that Jessie was handling Sam's move to Georgia better than she was.

"Sorry," Brit said. "I'm a bit of a mess."

That was an oversimplification. On the contrary, her life circumstances had lined up just fine, save for the man of her dreams moving away. It was complicated. But she was used to complicated. Her current situation was –

"Well, while we're waiting," Julie said, "I wanted to tell y'all first. We just found out, so Daddy doesn't know yet either. But… I'm pregnant!"

The squeals and hugs filled the room.

After the requisite questions, Mikayla gave a sly smile from her seat on the couch before she announced what Brittney already knew. "So am I."

"What?" Julie cried *"Oh my gosh!"*

Brittney watched the celebration, listened to more squeals and the sharing of due dates and the call for some mocktails. She felt her heart warm a little. Her sister and stepsister, and the step was becoming increasingly easy to leave off, were due just weeks apart, in the spring.

"Excuse me a minute." She got up from the couch and walked to her bedroom for a moment of quiet. Sitting on the bed, she held her phone in one hand, looking at her home screen. It was Harrison's face, smiling at her from a Facetime call they'd had last week, when he told her he was bringing the kids to Surfside Beach for Thanksgiving, and he hoped she loved them as much as he loved her.

She put her other hand on her stomach as she texted him.

"Do you have time to talk later? I'm having dinner with the sisters, but I have something really important to tell you."

THE STORY GOES ON...

More Surfside Beach series is coming soon!

Catch up:

THE TENTATIVE KNOCK - Book 1

ANOTHER AT THE TABLE - A Christmas Novella

THE SECOND DATE - Short Story (Online Only)

RUN THIS WAY - Book 2

KEEP READING FOR
BONUS MATERIAL.

THE SALTY LIPS

#SURFSIDEROCKS

SET LIST · FISHWALK · SAT. MAY 20

Mr. Brightside

One Week

Last Tattoo

Hole Hearted

In the Meantime   *Let Mikey Go!*

All Apologies   */or Nirvana Medley*

Give It Away   *-Ritmo - Last 2 ✓*

Cumbersome

Comedown

Run

Jealous Again

The Act We Act   *- Gene Vocals*

Dead and Bloated

Unglued

Learn to Fly

One   *- Creed - NOT U2*

Sugar, We're Goin' Down   *- Gene*

Ana's Song (or More than Words)

Wishlist

Breath
   - pick me up off the ground

INTERMISSION

All the Small Things

Spinning Around Over You

Better Man

Come Out and Play   *- Gene*

You

After All

Best of You

Vaseline

Numb

Lightning Crashes   *- Harrison*

Scars

Show Me How to Live

Breakfast at Tiffany's

Fade Into You *- Even though*
   Dave Hates H! ☺

The Middle

Dog Days are Over   *- Gene*

I Can't Stop Loving You
   ↳ for Brit! ☺

maybe "Knockin' on Heaven's Door" because I want it! - Katy! ☆

ENCORE: My Hero
   - or - Read the room
   No Rain!

LISTEN AT **THESALTYLIPS.COM**

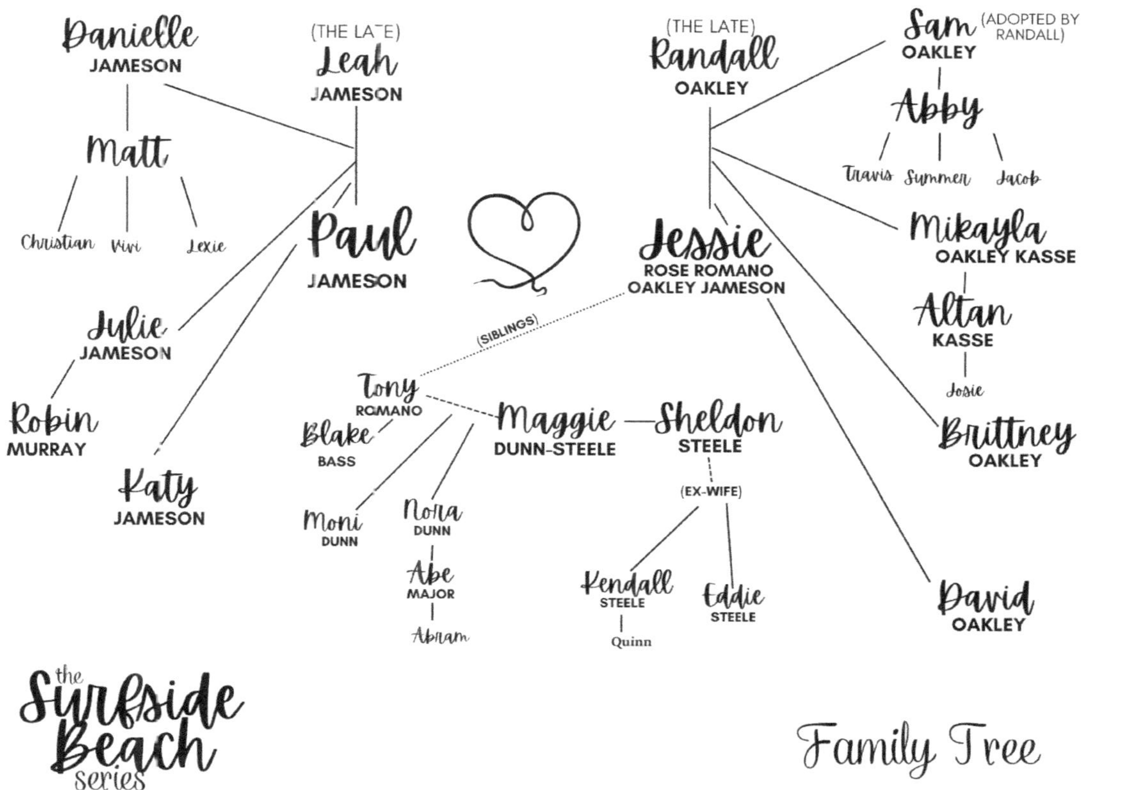

Danielle JAMESON
(THE LATE) Leah JAMESON
(THE LATE) Randall OAKLEY
Sam OAKLEY (ADOPTED BY RANDALL)
Abby
Travis Summer Jacob
Matt
Christian Vivi Lexie
Paul JAMESON
Jessie ROSE ROMANO OAKLEY JAMESON
Mikayla OAKLEY KASSE
Altan KASSE
Josie
Julie JAMESON
(SIBLINGS)
Robin MURRAY
Tony ROMANO
Blake BASS
Maggie DUNN-STEELE
Sheldon STEELE
Brittney OAKLEY
Katy JAMESON
Moni DUNN
Nora DUNN
Abe MAJOR
Abram
(EX-WIFE)
Kendall STEELE
Quinn
Eddie STEELE
David OAKLEY
the Surfside Beach series
Family Tree

LOCAL COLOR

A few of the places mentioned in this book either no longer exist
(Whitney's Tearoom) or are fictional so far
(Ed's Fishwalk Tavern). But these are for real local places,
and you should check them out when you are in the
Surfside Beach/Murrells Inlet/Myrtle Beach area.

Benjamin's Bakery
Blitzburgh
Brookgreen Gardens
Bruiser's Burgers
Chimichanga Llama
Creations By the Sea
Dead Dog Saloon
Drunken Jack's
Garden City Pier
Huntington Beach State Park

Johnny D's Waffles
Jupiter Pies
Los Cabos
Los Gordibuenos
Neal & Pam's
Ocean Lakes Campground
Surfside Beach Farmer's Market
(Tuesdays, April - October)
Tidal Creek Brewhouse

Meanwhile, Ed Piotrowski is a real person, an actual celebrity
meteorologist with our local ABC affiliate and the nicest guy
around. And Jeremy's Ten is a real and totally stellar Pearl Jam
tribute band that I had the pleasure of catching live at the
House of Blues in North Myrtle Beach. Julio and the Saltines are
another favorite local band, and author Caleb Wygal is as real
as they get and a friend of mine to boot.

A native of South Chicago Heights, Illinois, Kelly Capriotti Burton is a professional running enthusiast, a licensed minister, and a marathoner, who resides in Surfside Beach, South Carolina. She does life with her husband Rod, their five kids, two granddaughters, parents, two dogs, a Harley, a rock band, and lots of gathered family. It is the perfect setting to explore for her writing mantra: happily ever-afters for complicated relationships.

Kelly is the author of the Surfside Beach series and the inspirational collection, *Swerve: When Life Throws Curves, But God Said Live*, an Amazon #1 New Release.

Stay in touch:
kellofastory.com

ACKNOWLEDGMENTS

There are people out there who accomplish their goals alone.
I am not one of them. The support of my best friend, lifelong
love, and partner in all things is the one who runs the kids and
folds the laundry and listens without laughing too much when
I am in the throws of creating, editing, and finalizing. So first
and always, thank you to my Rod, for *literally everything*.

Every story is a journey – the one the characters take and the
one the author takes. During the writing of this novel, I became somewhat of a student of a real rock band, the one that
my husband leads. Through the generosity and friendship of
those musicians, I have learned so much about what it takes
for a bunch of working folks to get themselves on stage during
the weekends – and in them, I see the same passion for music
that I feel about writing. Because of them, I listen to music, including songs I have heard my entire life, in a whole new way.
So thank you to the guys of Rod's band, Southern Comfort
Myrtle Beach, past and present:
• Robert Blair (it's his bass on the cover)
• David Panzer (drinker of orange Mio and great storyteller)
• Rick "Ringo" Richey (co-creator of The Salty Lips playlist)
• Brandon Causey (also my baby brother)
• Jack Grezel (who always asks me how the writing is going)
• Larry Stevens (my second favorite Uncle Larry).
...and to their collective wives and girlfriends and the great
places that host us!

And from the wholeness of my heart, I also thank:

Shannon and Diane – the sisters who chose me. I choose you
every day, you strong, hilarious, amazing, crazy women.

The sisters whose relationship I idolize – Paige, Miranda, & Kaity. How blessed I am to call you my girls.

My sunshine boy, Jack Burton. I don't know if I would have had the drive to write these books without you.

Josh, Kirsten, Nora, & Rhea... what a joy to see the beautiful, vibrant family you are growing.

Mom & Dad – As this book is released, you are celebrating 50 years of marriage. Thank you for the legacy and showing what it means to stay.

Whitney, thank you for being the big sister I always wanted and a much easier critic of my work than of your husband's!

My editors Mike and Carla Hopkins. I cannot believe the time and dedication they have given to these books. As Carla said, "Between the three of us, we will get it perfect." Anything you read that isn't is my fault.

Caleb Wygal – I am so grateful for the journey from following your breadcrumbs to having you as a friend.

Rosie Miller and Ed Einhaus – both wonderful people in real life that I was all too happy to feature in the story. We all have Rosie to thank for The Salty Lips and Ed for "his" Fishwalk Tavern. I hope both of those ideas become real one day, too!

This book cover was a team effort, so my very heartfelt thanks (again) to Rod and Robert, and also to Andrew & Crystal Costa, Sarah Sweeney, & my own sweet "baby" cousin Jade Alexa Guttman.

Special friends through all the ups and downs, sacred and silly in life: Tracy, Alex, Tai, Liz, Deanna, Martha, Maureen, Jen, April, Tana, Shelley & Brandon, Sav, Annie, Laura, Obea, Heather. So much love, always.

Kelsey and Aaron – thank you for the beautiful space you bring to Myrtle Beach with Back Again Bookshop, for your kind and fun friendship, and for the opportunities you have given me! Thanks to Holly at Barnes & Noble Myrtle Beach: for being a dream-giver, to Horry County libraries for all you do for readers and writers, Cortney at Bookworm for your encouragement, and all the bookstores you'll see me in soon!

The new writer friends I have made in the past year, especially Shari, Tonya, Maegwen, and Susan. It means so much to have not only your witty and lasting words to read, but your lovely souls in my life!

Thank you, Amy (Amy Jane Photography), for sharing your time and gift with me!

Thank you Missy Mulvihill Dotson for your cameo appearance. When I think of being a teenage writer and music fan, you are right there in every memory!

My cousin Pat, thank you for offering unexpected peace.

"You need it. And they're fine." – Amy Paris. Thank you for this quote on parents of big, chaotic, blended families taking breaks. It was the best advice and has followed me for years!

My heart will always be grateful for Black Dog Running Company, the Black Dog Pack, and the extended community of runners that I live and work in daily. My own little family in this realm grows and changes, but eternal thanks remain to the ones who travel this road with me by running, walking, rucking, coaching, training, and making up words for everything else, especially Diane, Daniel, Bill, Tracy, Akemi, Sarah, Brent, Joe, along with Surfside Jim, George, Tucker, Kelsey, Janet, Mylena & Brian, Nancy, Bridget, Pat, Gypsy, and so many more!

Mort Castle, who will always be a voice in my head and the one who said, "You can." I did!

To Jan Narvel, who is resting in paradise as of August 2023. We shared many deep conversations through the years, and something she told me about boundaries was so profound I wrote it on a card and have kept it. Now I cherish it. I am so happy you published your book, loved your husband Jack and others so well, and called your shots until the end. See you soon, my friend.

I am thankful for the circle of support I get from friends who are also readers and readers who became friends! It's tempting but dangerous to try to name them all. Please know that if you read, share, like, follow, review, subscribe, purchase, invite me to your book club (my favorite!) ... you have an impact on my life and are the reason I keep writing!

'IF THERE EVER WAS A BOOK
HIGHLIGHTING THE
GINORMOUS NEED FOR GOD'S
GRACE TOWARD US,
THIS IS THE ONE.'
Deanna Mason

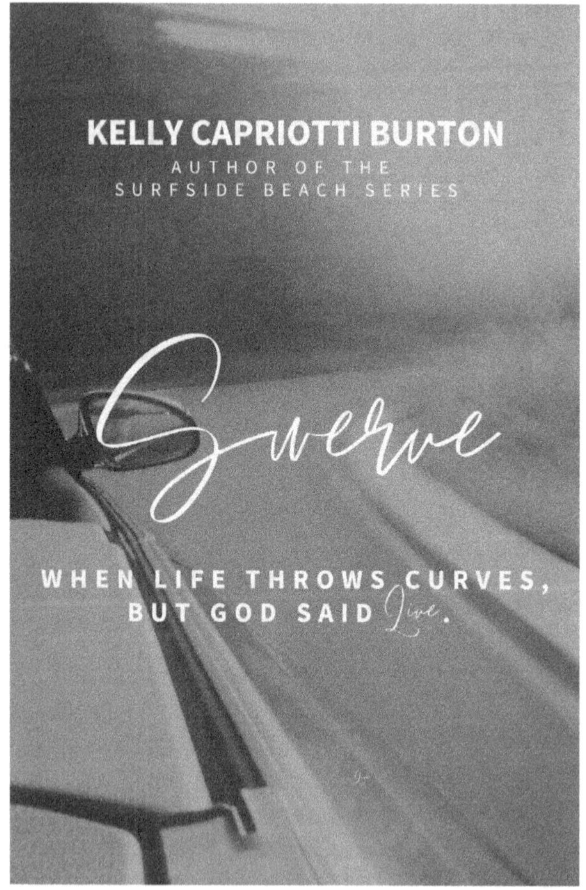
KELLY CAPRIOTTI BURTON
AUTHOR OF THE
SURFSIDE BEACH SERIES
Swerve
WHEN LIFE THROWS CURVES,
BUT GOD SAID Live.

21 STORIES OF MESSY LIVES &
AMAZING GRACE.

www.ingramcontent.com/pod-product-compliance
Lightning Source LLC
Chambersburg PA
CBHW071402200726
48294CB00002B/277